USA TODAY bestselling author **Rita Herron** wrote her first book when she was twelve but didn't think real people grew up to be writers. Now she writes so she doesn't have to get a real job. A former primary school teacher and workshop leader, she traded storytelling to kids for writing romance, and now she writes romantic comedies and romantic suspense. Rita lives in Georgia with her family. She loves to hear from readers, so please visit her website, ritaherron.com

USA TODAY bestselling and RITA® Award–winning author **Marie Ferrarella** has written over three hundred books for Mills & Boon, some under the name Marie Nicole. Her romances are beloved by fans worldwide. Visit her website, marieferrarella.com

Discover more at millsandboon.co.uk

THE BODY IN THE WALL

RITA HERRON

CAVANAUGH JUSTICE: SERIAL AFFAIR

MARIE FERRARELLA

MILLS & BOON

First Published in Great Britain 2022
by Mills & Boon, an imprint of HarperCollins*Publishers* Ltd
1 London Bridge Street, London, SE1 9GF

www.harpercollins.co.uk

HarperCollins*Publishers*
1st Floor, Watermarque Building,
Ringsend Road, Dublin 4, Ireland

The Body in the Wall © 2022 Rita B. Herron
Cavanaugh Justice: Serial Affair © 2022 Marie Rydzynski-Ferrarella

ISBN: 978-0-263-30340-7

0422

MIX
Paper from
responsible sources
FSC® C007454

This book is produced from independently certified FSC™ paper to ensure responsible forest management.

For more information visit: www.harpercollins.co.uk/green

Printed and Bound in Spain using 100% Renewable electricity at CPI Black Print, Barcelona

THE BODY IN THE WALL

RITA HERRON

To my fabulous and very patient editor, Allison Lyons!
Thanks for always supporting me!

Chapter One

Sheriff Stone Lawson sank into his desk chair and stared at the letter marked "To My Older Self." Yesterday at the reunion, he'd opened the time capsule and found the notes his classmates had written themselves, predicting where they thought they'd be years after graduation.

In his, he'd vowed to follow in his father's footsteps and work in law enforcement. He thought he'd probably get married and have a bunch of boys, his own football team in the making.

But that had all changed the day of the shooting. The day his little brother, Mickey, had been partially blinded by a bullet.

Stone's hands bunched into fists. He was the older brother. He should have protected him.

Guilt thundered through his chest every time he saw or talked to Mickey. They'd grown up roughhousing, diving off the ridges into the river in the mountains, pranking each other. Playing football. Hiking and fishing.

Then Mickey's future had been interrupted.

He closed his eyes, the image of his injured brother fighting for his life fifteen years ago taunting him. He swallowed back the pain, then opened his eyes and called Mickey's number. When he didn't answer, worry nagged at him. He hoped to hell his brother wasn't already three sheets to the wind. Mickey had been drinking way too much lately.

His deputy poked his head in. "Sheriff, Hazel LeCroy just called. Said someone just broke into the pawnshop. Stole a gun."

Someone stealing guns couldn't be good.

He found his deputy Murphy Bridges in the break room and told him where he was going, then headed outside to his police-issued SUV. His gut burned with a bad feeling.

There had been protestors against the new school Kate McKendrick had lobbied for. People in town blaming each other for what had happened. Although the new school was under way and a memorial had been built for the students lost that fateful day. And he and Special Agent Macy Stark, another former student, had finally discovered the reason behind the shooting and who had given Ned Hodgkins the gun—Macy's ex.

What if the recent publicity surrounding the shooting had triggered enough anger and emotion to cause someone to retaliate? Or another student to want the attention Ned had received?

Special Agent Macy Stark had dreaded this moment for years. Had vowed never to return to her childhood home in Briar Ridge, North Carolina.

The night of graduation she'd packed her bags and run away the next morning. Her mother had still been in bed, so doped up on meds that she probably hadn't realized her daughter was gone for days.

Guilt for leaving her had nagged at Macy as she'd boarded the bus out of town, but her mother had abandoned her so many times, even the night of the shooting when Macy had been traumatized, that she'd had to go or she'd literally drown in depression.

With her mother in a long-term treatment facility, she

was only here to clean out the house now and get it on the market. Then she'd go back to her life and try to put the past behind her.

But her phone buzzed and her ex-husband's number appeared on the screen. She'd arrested Trey a few days ago for supplying Ned Hodgkins with the gun he'd used to slaughter the students at Briar Ridge High fifteen years ago. But the DA had thrown out the charges, saying they had no proof that Trey knew Ned's intentions.

She let the call go to voice mail, knowing it was probably another irate message from Trey threatening to get back at her for humiliating him in front of the town. All she wanted to do was be done with him, just as she wanted to do with her childhood home.

The old house had been run-down when she'd lived here, but it was nothing compared to the state it was in now. Dust motes hung heavy in the musty air. The once-white walls had faded to yellow, the paint was chipped and battered, and the wood floor was scratched. The linoleum in the tiny kitchen that her mother had never used was lifting in places and was a nasty pea-green shade scarred with cigarette burns where her mother had dropped lit cigarettes when she was stumbling around, incapacitated.

Macy had had to stomp them out several times. Her senior year on Thanksgiving, she'd woken up and smelled smoke. When she'd tiptoed into the den, she'd found her mother passed out on the couch. Smoke was seeping from the vinyl couch cushions. She'd dragged her mother off the couch, then dumped water on the sofa until she doused the fire starting to shoot from the bottom.

That orange vinyl monstrosity still sat against the wall, tattered, soot-stained and reeking of smoke. Swallowing against the emotions churning through her, she flipped on a lamp and noted the place was piled high with clutter. Old magazines were stacked waist-deep by the woodburning fireplace, along with boxes of junk items that must have come from the thrift store, a fire hazard in the making. The rocking chair in the corner needed re-caning, and one of the legs on the old maple table in the kitchen was broken, making the table slant sideways. The scent of dirt, cigarette smoke and mildew permeated the walls, and the kitchen counter and stove were scarred and stained, sticky clumps of something smeared on the surfaces. Ants congregated along the edge of the rotting windowsill, and dead fruit flies dotted the counter.

Bile rose to her throat. How had her mother lived like this?

A rotten odor wafted toward her as she neared the refrigerator, and she held her breath as she eased open the door and looked inside. Except for condiments she was sure were outdated, it was bare, a sign her mother had been gone for months. In the freezer, Macy found a butcher-wrapped package of some kind of meat that was covered in frost it was so old.

Closing the door, she decided to tackle cleaning it out later. First, she had to assess the gravity of the job. Maybe she should hire someone to clean out the place so she wouldn't have to spend more time in this disaster.

The sound of her mother's shrill voice echoed in Macy's ears as she walked down the hall to the bedrooms. Everything looked older and dusty, but her mother had not changed anything, as if she'd expected Macy to one day return and for them to be a happy, smiling family.

They never had been, though. She'd given up that fantasy a long time ago.

The faded yellow bedspread remained; her childhood teddy bear sat on the bookshelf along with a rag doll and the river rocks she'd collected when she'd bypassed the doll stage. She gasped, though, as she surveyed the walls. She'd never hung posters of rock bands or movie stars. Instead, she'd idolized track stars and had taped posters of the high school team on the wall above the knotty pine desk.

Those posters were gone now, scattered on the floor in shreds as if her mother had ripped them apart in a fit of rage.

Maybe at that point she'd given up on Macy coming home.

A clap of thunder burst outside, and through the window, lightning zigzagged across the darkening sky, catapulting Macy back in time to that night when she was five.

It was storming outside. Macy hated storms. The loud booming frightened her, and the lightning flashes lit up the dark woods where the monsters hid. Except sometimes at night when her mother locked her in her room, Macy thought those monsters sneaked inside.

Tonight, she heard one of them. Boots pounding. The floor creaking. Cold air wafting through the eaves of the thin walls. Thunder mingling with other noises. Furniture being knocked over. Her mother's shrill cry. The basement door squeaking open...

The basement...it was off-limits. Scary dark. Her mother told her the monsters would get her if she went down there.

Macy believed her.

So why was her mother opening the door? Why was she going down there tonight?

Terrified, Macy crept to the door and listened. Another scream. Some grunting sound. More thunder. She covered her ears with her hands and pressed down hard to drown out the sound.

She pushed her bedroom door open slightly and peeked through the crack. Suddenly her mother jerked the door open. Her hair was a tangled mess, her eyes wide, her breath puffing out. She looked wild and scary.

"I told you to stay in your room!" she shouted as she dragged Macy from the room.

*Something red on the wall caught Macy's eyes...blood...
The room swirled. Everything went black.*

*Then suddenly she was outside. Her mother scream-
ing at her to sleep in the doghouse where she belonged.
The rain was coming down hard, big pellets that stung her
cheeks and soaked through her pajamas. Her feet were
soaked, and a chill cut through her.*

"Please don't leave me, Mama," Macy cried.

*But her mother slammed the door shut and Macy heard
the lock click.*

*Thunder boomed again, the lightning shattering the
dark sky and dancing across the tops of the trees. A noise
from the woods made her startle, and she started to cry.
Terrified, she ran around the back of the house. The porch
and doghouse were too rotten to hide under. Water was
pouring through the holes like a river flooding.*

*The house next door had a nice porch. It was covered
and safe from the rain. Her bare feet slipped as she slogged
through the mud and wove through the bushes. When she
reached the porch, she crawled beneath the cover, then
sank onto the dry ground. She hugged her knees, cold
and shivering.*

Macy jerked herself from the memory. She'd forgotten
some of the details of that night. What had happened in
her house? She'd blanked out for a minute. Had tidbits of
different memories over the years that didn't make sense.

Had there been blood on the wall?

STONE SCANNED THE area surrounding the pawnshop as he
pulled into a parking spot. He cut the engine, searching
for signs the thief might still be here. But the parking lot
was empty, and he didn't see anyone lurking around. The
front window had been shattered, and glass had sprayed
all over the ground.

Still, he pulled his gun as he climbed from the vehicle

and walked up to the door. With each step, he searched the woods beyond. The older concrete building was free-standing and sat on a corner where the road forked. One direction led to mountain cabins popular for vacationers while the other led to camping and hunting grounds. An outfitter store sat catercorner across the way.

The owner, sixty-six-year-old Hazel LeCroy, met him at the door, looking frazzled and angry. Her long wiry gray hair was frizzy with the humidity, her usual outfit of a flannel shirt and jeans rumpled. "Hey, Sheriff," Hazel said with a wave. "Thanks for coming. I can't believe I've been robbed."

"Were you here when the store was broken into?" Stone asked.

Hazel rubbed at the back of her head. "Sure was. In the back. I heard a loud noise, the window shattering, and grabbed my shotgun and came running. But someone jumped me from behind and hit me over the damn head."

Anger at the person who'd hit Hazel surged through Stone. The older woman might be tough as nails and knew how to shoot, but still she was a grandmother.

"Did you see who hit you?"

"No, like I said they jumped me from behind. I reckon I ought to be glad they didn't shoot me, but they got away with two of my guns."

"We'll get to that," Stone said. "Tell me what happened before the break-in. Have you been busy today? Any customers come in who seemed suspicious?"

"You mean casing the place?" Hazel pulled her frizzy hair back into a ponytail, snapping the rubber band with her thin fingers.

"Yes," Stone said. "Maybe even a couple or a pair working together. Someone who asked about what you had in your case but left without buying anything?"

Hazel shook her head. "Only folks been in were a couple of hunters stocking up on ammo."

"No kids?" Stone asked, holding his breath.

Hazel gestured across the street. "Saw a couple of teens over at the outfitter's store, but they didn't come here."

They could have been watching to see if any customers showed up, left, then parked up the road and sneaked in on foot.

Stone gestured toward the light post where a security camera had been placed. "Let me take a look at the footage."

"Camera don't work," she muttered.

Stone silently cursed. "Call someone and get it fixed. I'll get my forensic kit and look around. If we're dealing with amateurs or teens, maybe they left some prints."

FURIOUS WITH HERSELF for letting the memories get to her, Macy straightened and banished them from her mind. She had a job to do, and she might as well get to it.

Her phone buzzed, and she checked the number. When she saw it was her boss at the Bureau, Special Advisory Director Abraham Holland, she connected. "Hello, Chief."

"How are things going?"

Macy wiped a hand over her face and pulled herself together. "Fine. I'm planning to clean out and put my mother's house on the market ASAP. Hopefully I'll be back at work next week."

"That fast?"

Stone's face flashed in her mind, but that reunion dance last night meant nothing.

No use getting any more involved. Work was her coping mechanism, and she would be leaving soon. "Yes. There's nothing for me here." Nothing but painful reminders of the miserable childhood and the fact that her mother hadn't loved her.

Stone had his own life.

She hung up, yanked her long dark hair into a pony tail, and hurried back outside to her Ford Escape. Now that she had a definite timeline, she opened the trunk and pulled out the giant box of garbage bags she'd bought. She'd probably toss out most everything, but she might donate some items to Goodwill. Although judging from the state of the house and furniture, she doubted much would be salvageable.

Outside, the rain had fizzled out, leaving a cloying humid air. Sweat beaded on her forehead. A sudden feeling that someone was watching her from the shadows of the woods again swept over her, and she surveyed the property.

Brush shifted and crackled. Leaves fluttered to the ground. A deer scampered through the forest.

Another reason she had to leave this place. Old ghosts haunted her, resurrecting her childhood fears and insecurities. Sure, she chased real live monsters on the job, but they were tangible and impersonal. Saving victims helped her forget the fact that she hadn't saved Kate's mother or any other students the day of the infamous school massacre.

Anxious to be finished, she hurried inside to tackle the kitchen. Pushing up her sleeves, she yanked on rubber gloves and started with the pantry. A few canned goods, tuna, peanut butter, all outdated, along with a bag of bug-infested sugar and flour. A box of cereal that was nearly empty, and a canister of rice also full of insects. Old cooking oil and spices that hadn't been used in at least a decade.

Her mother had never been a cook. Obviously, that hadn't changed after Macy left.

The refrigerator came next. The stench nearly knocked her over. She tossed the condiments and the rotting meat into the bag, tied it, then carried it outside to the dumpster.

The next few hours she spent going through the cabinets. None of the rusted pans, cracked dishes or plasticware warranted donating, so she pitched them into the trash. The drawers held junk and old bills that needed paying and her mother's work calendars so she left those for now until she could go through each one.

A set of kitchen knives on the counter made her pause and sweat beaded her neck as a snippet of a memory flashed through her mind. Her mother...a knife in hand... blood trickling down her arm.

Macy stiffened. Had she cut herself?

Jerking back to the present, she noticed one of the knives was missing from the set. She looked around but didn't find it anywhere in the kitchen. Deciding it didn't matter, she left the others on the counter in case she needed a knife for some reason.

The bathroom came next. Nothing salvageable there. Toiletries, a toothbrush, half-empty toothpaste tube, hair spray and cheap makeup. Bottles of painkillers and over-the-counter drugs filled the medicine cabinet, so she raked those into the bag.

Next, she jerked down the faded shower curtain and liner and tossed those. She tackled the den next, piling the magazines and knickknacks into the trash.

Her childhood bedroom came next.

For a moment, she couldn't breathe as she stepped inside the room. But the sight of her track posters ripped and shredded hardened her, and she tore through the room, swiping the few dolls and toys she'd once had from the shelves, then emptying the drawers of high school notebooks she'd used for assignments.

No sentimental attachments. When she'd left home, she'd never looked back.

She cleaned out the closet, filling another bag with the clothing items she'd left behind. Jeans, T-shirts, tennis shoes...nothing was worth keeping or giving away.

Most had been secondhand when she'd gotten them and were so out of style no kid would want them now. Her hand raked over the top shelf where she'd kept the shoebox of photos and ribbons from her track meets, and pictures of her, Kate and Brynn.

A couple of pictures of them were the only things she'd taken with her.

When her room was cleaned out, she started on her mother's. Adrenaline churning, she quickly scooped up her clothing, shoes and the bedding and filled another bag. She didn't pause to reminisce although an image of her mother sprawled in a drug-induced state on the bed taunted her. How many times had she helped her mother to bed?

How many times had Macy locked herself in her room to keep her mother from coming in and taking her wrath out on her?

Pulse pounding, she spent the next hour hauling the smaller pieces of furniture to the dumpster, then grabbed a bottle of water and phoned a service to pick up the sofa, kitchen table and beds.

Covered in dust and grime, and sweating, she sipped her water, but stopping gave her time to think, and she turned to face the basement door.

Her head swam with the sound of her mother's voice. *"Never go down there, Macy." Her mother jerked her arm, shook her and forced her to look into her eyes. "Never. Do you understand me?"*

Macy's heart pounded at the memory. Then the night of the terrible storm and the noises and the screams. The red splattered on the walls…

Her lungs strained for air. She had never been down there.

But she couldn't sell the place without cleaning it out. Hands shaking, she found the key to the basement door on top of the refrigerator where her mother had kept it, then inserted it into the lock.

Her mother had made the basement off-limits for a reason.

Did she have the courage to find out why?

Chapter Two

Stone finished searching the pawnshop for forensics, but according to Hazel, several people had been in the store over the last twenty-four hours. It was going to be difficult to sort out what was what. He'd taken special care to dust the glass case where the guns had been kept, but most likely the thief had worn gloves. He found a rock outside that had probably been used to smash the window and bagged it.

"A .38 Special was taken," Hazel said. "And a .22."

He jotted down the contact information for the original owners to follow up in case one of them decided they wanted their weapon back and didn't have the money.

"You got someone coming to fix those cameras?"

Hazel nodded. "In the morning. I also called about having the glass window and gun case replaced."

"I'll board up the window for you for tonight and have my deputy do a drive-by this evening." If word leaked the pawnshop was compromised, looters might come. The last thing he needed was more guns on the street.

MACY'S PULSE CLAMORED as she opened the door to the basement. The steps were pitch-black, the air musty, dust coating the stair rail. She reached for an overhead light and flicked it, but nothing happened.

Suffocating as the darkness engulfed her, she flipped the switch again, but the light was burned out. Pulling her phone from her pocket, she aimed the flashlight at the stairs. Cobwebs dangled from the rail and ceiling, and she pushed them away with her gloved hands and tiptoed down the steps. The boards creaked and moaned, buckling beneath her feet as if they might give way any second.

Her pulse jumped with every step she took, dread curling in her belly. One step, two, three, slowly she descended, aiming the light around the concrete floor and dingy walls. Shadows seemed to jump out of nowhere, the sound of water pinging onto the floor and trickling down the wall echoing in the tense silence.

Her mother's voice taunted her again. *Never go down there, Macy. Never.*

Ignoring the voice, she moved on, determined to break this hold her mother had on her. She was no longer a child. Her mother couldn't hurt her anymore. She'd see what was down here once and for all, quiet her imagination from the horrors of what she'd feared, and then her nightmares would cease.

A few boxes sat in one corner, along with a broken rocking chair and an ancient armoire. Shelves on one wall held cleaning chemicals her mother had used when she worked as a housekeeper. The sound of the water pinged, a stench assaulting her. She aimed her flashlight around the room and spotted the source. The far wall. The ceiling was leaking, water trickling down the wall and onto the floor. The rain or one of the toilets?

Mold grew along the baseboard and up the wall fanning out in a spiderweb-like pattern. The acrid odor grew stronger as she walked toward the source; the walls were pocked with holes where the drywall had literally rotted away.

Her heart hammered as she shone the light along the space. What had her mother not wanted her to see down here?

The armoire. Holding her breath, she crossed the room to it, then reached for the door. Her fingers clasped the metal latch, and she pulled it open, bracing herself.

But her breath whooshed out when she realized it was empty.

Stumbling sideways to take a breath, she bumped the damp wall, then felt the drywall give way in one section. Hurling herself away from it, she gasped in horror.

Bones protruded through the opening, the skeleton of a hand curled as if clawing to escape.

STONE'S PHONE BUZZED just as he was leaving the pawnshop. A quick check of the number, and he saw it was Macy.

He quickly connected and said hello.

"Stone…" Her voice cracked. "Y-you need to come out here."

Her voice was raw, pained. Something was wrong. "Come where?"

"My mother's old house," she said, her voice shaky. "I f-found a body in the basement."

Stone stood, tension coiling inside him. He heard the fear in her voice, could see her big brown eyes filled with terror. "I'll be right there."

MACY STAGGERED BACKWARD, her phone nearly slipping through her fingers. Unable to drag her gaze away from the skeletal hand, she visually scanned the hole and noticed a larger hole above it.

Bile rose to her throat as she spotted the skull, eyes mere hollow sockets staring back at her.

Her first instinct was to start ripping away the rest of the wall and expose the body inside, but her detective instincts kicked in, and she reminded herself not to touch anything.

Mental images of what might have happened here flooded her.

Had her mother known the body was down here? Had she found it?

Or had she put it in the wall?

Trembling at the thought that her mother might be a killer, she covered her mouth with her hand, then turned, crossed to the stairs and climbed them. The squeaky steps sounded even more eerie now, her erratic breathing louder. She fought images of her mother in one of her out-of-control states unleashing her rage in such a violent manner. Panic-stricken when she realized what she'd done. Stuffing the body in the wall, then covering it with new drywall and leaving it to decompose while she lived upstairs and went on about her life. While her own child slept in a bedroom above the hellhole where she'd disposed of a body.

She pushed through the door to the hall, breathing out raggedly, desperate to blot the images from her mind. But they bombarded her, tearing at her control, and she stumbled toward the living room, then opened the front door and stepped outside. The rain had ceased, the scent of damp grass lingering, rainwater still dripping from the gutters, a reminder of the leak in the basement.

Dizzy, she gripped the porch rail, leaned over and dragged in several deep breaths, a chill invading her that had nothing to do with the rain. She rocked back and forth, her body shaking, as she looked at the gloomy sky. Seconds bled into minutes, tension thrumming through her.

The sound of a siren shattered the silence, and relief poured through her as the sheriff's SUV careened into the driveway. She lifted her chin and pulled herself together. She was an FBI agent. This wasn't the first body she'd seen.

Except none had been in her own house. None had been personal.

Stone cut the siren and lights, then stepped from his vehicle and strode toward her. A faint hint of the moon peeked through the rain clouds, illuminating his chiseled face and his strong square jaw.

His boots pounded the wooden steps as he climbed them, then he stopped in front of her, hazel eyes narrowed and full of concern. "Macy?"

The gruff timbre of his tone was her undoing. He reached for her arms, stroked them, forcing her to look at him. The worry reflected in his eyes shattered her resistance.

Choking out his name, she leaned into him, her body trembling as he wrapped his arms around her.

STONE RUBBED MACY'S BACK, gently soothing her. She was a tough agent, but whatever had happened had really shaken her.

Which meant it was bad.

He held her until her trembling slowly subsided, and she pulled away from him.

"I'm sorry about that," she murmured.

"No problem. Talk to me," he said. "What happened?"

She brushed her damp eyes with the back of her hand, then leaned against the railing and gestured toward the dumpster. Though her dark hair was damp from rain, and her clothes dusty, she still was beautiful. "I was cleaning out the house, tossing most everything."

"To get the house ready to sell?"

She nodded. "I got most of the bedrooms and kitchen done. Then I...decided to check the basement." Her voice wavered. "It was dark, and the light was burned out, but I heard water dripping and wanted to see what it was."

"Go on."

She released a labored breath. "I used my phone flashlight and saw water leaking from the ceiling. I went closer and noticed the wall was rotten and there was a big hole in it. And then I saw it."

"The body?"

Macy nodded again, her gaze haunted. "It's inside the wall."

Stone swallowed hard. If the body was in the wall, that meant it probably wasn't fresh. That someone put it there. Not an accident or a loner hiding out. "A man or woman?"

"I don't know. It's decomposed. Just bones."

"So it's been there for a while," Stone said.

"It looks that way. All I could see was the hand and the skull where the plaster was rotted through." Macy rubbed her arms with her hands. "We need a recovery team and the medical examiner."

"And a forensics team," Stone said. "I'll make the call."

Macy turned to look out at the woods as he phoned the medical examiner and the CSI team. Her faraway look made him wonder what was going on in her head.

"I'm going to take a look myself," Stone said when he hung up.

"I'll show you."

"No need for you to go back inside, Macy. I can handle it. Wait here for the crime team and ME."

She murmured okay, then he went to his SUV, grabbed gloves, boot covers and a flashlight, and carried them back to the porch.

"The door to the basement is in the hall," Macy said.

He geared up before entering the house. He'd never been inside Macy's, and she hadn't been back for years. It showed in the dust, the stuffy odor and the weathered furniture. She said she'd cleaned out things, and that showed, too. Except for a tattered orange vinyl sofa and plaid armchair, the living room looked bare. He crossed to the hall, flicked on his flashlight and started down the steps. The stairs gave way in places, hinting at rot, and he gripped the stair rail to steady his footing. The sound of water dripping and pinging off the floor drew his attention toward the far corner.

The acrid odor of mildew and old body decomp hit him, and he covered his mouth with his handkerchief as he reached the landing. Shining his flashlight across the space, he spotted an antique armoire, then the damp wall where plaster had cracked and rot had created gaping holes.

The stench grew stronger as he walked toward the corner, and he aimed his flashlight onto the wall. The grisly sight of the skeletal remains poking through the opening made him halt in his tracks. He couldn't imagine how shocked Macy had felt.

This place had been her home.

Now it was a crime scene.

Chapter Three

Macy's mind raced as various scenarios played through her head. Perhaps she was wrong about her mother's involvement with that body.

Although she couldn't shake the memory of that awful stormy night. Her mother had been in one of her moods and had screamed at her, but she'd done that before.

Hadn't she? Or had that been the first time?

Her memory of the years before that were muddy. For some reason that one evening seemed to be a pivotal moment.

She'd been terrified and alone. But Kate's mother had found her outside and taken her in, and then she and Kate had become best friends.

Her mother had been distant after that.

Had something happened that night? Had her mother known the body was in the wall?

It was possible that someone had put it there before they moved in. That her mother hadn't known. Or that she'd found it and that had triggered her to have a breakdown.

Or maybe you're grasping. Maybe she killed whoever it was and hid him in the wall so no one would find him. Or discover what she'd done.

She closed her eyes, trying to sort through the events of that night again. But the sound of an engine cut through the silence, and she jerked her eyes open to see a van roll into her drive. On the heels of it came a black sedan that she assumed belonged to the medical examiner's office.

The crime investigators slid from the van, the county logo for the crime lab emblazoned on their shirts, then gathered their kits and walked toward her. A young woman with ebony skin and black hair pulled into a bun followed from the sedan, her medical bag in hand.

Macy shut off her emotions and launched into agent mode.

The CSI team paused at the top of the stairs, and the woman followed. Macy introduced herself and flashed her credentials.

"Dr. Latoya Anderson, ME." She extended her hand, and Macy shook it.

The crime investigators introduced themselves as Wesley Moore and Kat Parker. And Stone reappeared, looking grim faced.

Macy explained about finding the corpse. "It's decomposed, just the skeletal remains, indicating it's been there for some time. I haven't been home in years. I was cleaning out things to put the house on the market." Now that plan would have to be postponed. Her childhood home was literally the scene of a possible homicide. "I'm afraid I touched almost everything upstairs when I was going through things."

"Did you see anything that pointed to murder?" Stone interjected.

Macy pinched the bridge of her nose, thinking. "Not that I recall. Mostly it was canned food, trash, magazines, some clothing and old toiletries. But I can hold off on having the dumpster picked up in case we need to search it."

"Probably a good idea," Stone agreed. "You never know if there's a clue in something that seems innocuous."

"True." She turned to the crime team. "My prints are on

file for elimination purposes. But concentrate on processing the basement." She addressed the medical examiner. "We need to be careful excavating the body."

"Do you have any idea who the victim is?" Dr. Anderson asked.

Macy shook her head. "No, nor do I know how long it's been there or how it got there. Identifying the remains will be a start."

"I'll call a forensic anthropologist to assist with the autopsy," Dr. Anderson said. "But it may take a few days before we can get an ID."

Macy racked her brain for some memory of a man or woman visiting, one her mother had had an altercation with. She struggled for a plausible reason, one that didn't involve her mother being a murderer.

Even if she had killed someone, it could have been self-defense. What if someone had broken in and threatened her? Pulled a gun? She could have tried to protect herself, and even Macy, and things got out of hand.

She closed her eyes again, struggling to tap into her memory banks. But her early years were so fuzzy that her life was defined by that rainy night when her mother had thrown her outside in a crazed rage. There had been more episodes after that that she recalled. She'd never understood what triggered them.

Stone's expression was stark, his voice dragging her from the troubling scenarios playing through her mind.

"Your turn to take a look, Doc," Stone said. "I'll warn you, it's pretty gruesome."

"Gruesome is my day job," Dr. Anderson said wryly. "And you two, call me Latoya."

"I'm Macy, then."

"And Stone," he said. "You want me to walk you down?"

"No, I've got it," Latoya said. "I'm sure you and Macy need to discuss the situation."

Macy tensed, and the ME excused herself and headed down the stairs. Stone rubbed her arm. "You okay?"

Macy choked back a nervous laugh. Was she okay? No, hell no. How could she be okay when she'd just found a body in the wall of her mother's house?

When she might have been sleeping in her room upstairs when the person had been killed and enclosed there?

STONE WATCHED AS the CSI investigators searched and processed the basement and house. He had never been to Macy's in high school. It was definitely not the hangout house. But he'd heard rumors that her mother was unstable. Except for Kate and Brynn, he didn't know if Macy had any other friends.

Although she excelled at track, she hadn't joined in on the after-school sports teams get-togethers. He'd never seen her at a school dance or prom and had been surprised when he heard she'd married Trey Cushing. He'd never liked the jerk, thought he was a bully, although at one time he supposed the girls found him charming.

But he'd heard the disrespectful way Trey talked about girls and didn't like it.

Dr. Anderson confirmed that the victim was a male. It took hours for the crime team to process the basement and remove the skeletal remains. The recovery team had to be careful not to damage the bones or destroy any forensics that might have been left behind so the ME could determine cause and general time of death.

"We found hair and fibers of clothing that are partially decayed, but we might be able to get something from them," one of the investigators told Macy. "We also found traces of blood in the wall and on the clothing. We'll send it all to the lab."

Macy showed them the bags of clothing she'd collected from her mother's room, and one of the CSIs went through it, searching for blood or hair fibers, although after so many years, it would be difficult to determine their origin or how long they'd been there.

Dawn was just streaking the sky when they finally finished. Yellow crime scene tape encircled the house with the warning not to enter.

Macy looked pale and shell-shocked, her dark hair a tangled mess where it had escaped her pony tail.

"You can't stay here," Stone said.

"I wasn't planning to," Macy said with a shiver. "I have a room at the inn in town."

"Let me drive you," Stone offered.

"Thanks, but I need my car to get around town." As anxious as she was to get out of Briar Ridge, she couldn't leave until she knew the truth about what had happened here.

EXHAUSTION MINGLED WITH the shock of the night as Macy parked at the Rosebud Inn. In spite of the vibrant red and orange streaking the morning sky, dread curled in her belly as questions needled her.

Dammit. Her mother might hold the answers…which meant she had to visit her. That had not been on the agenda. But she had no choice now.

Her chest clenched as she grabbed her bag and entered the Victorian house that the owner, Celeste, had recently renovated. When Kate pushed to build the new school, it sparked a wave of store owners and businesses that had fallen in disrepair the last fifteen years to make some much-needed updates.

Celeste had added a rose garden, gazebo by the pond and fresh paint on the exterior. She'd also remodeled the rooms inside with themes, hoping to draw tourists back to the area. The mountain ridges rose in the background, sunlight shimmering off the peaks, promising a sunny day compared to the gray storm clouds yesterday.

For a short few days, Briar Ridge had felt a sense of hope in the aftermath of a long storm. The new school was opening. A memorial had been created to honor the fallen students and Kate's mother, who'd died protecting her pupils. Former classmates and residents had started to build relationships and trust again. Tourists were starting to return, renting cabins, camping, hiking and enjoying the outdoor activities the scenic mountains offered.

But that sense of peace and trust was about to end. Soon everyone in town would know about her discovery. Once again, her family would feed the gossip train with whispers and accusations. Tears blurred Macy's eyes as she slipped inside past the front desk. The scent of coffee, pancakes and bacon wafted to her from the kitchen where Celeste was preparing breakfast for the guests.

Her stomach roiled. She was too exhausted to eat. Right now she needed sleep and quiet before she had to face the media frenzy that would start when the news leaked.

Gretta Wright, one of her classmates who'd run a gossip rag in high school, had now joined the professional journalism ranks and was a local newscaster. Like a raptor stalking its prey, she'd lunge on the story—and Macy's possible involvement. She'd already had a field day with the fact that Macy had arrested her ex for giving Ned Hodgkins the gun he'd used to slaughter their classmates.

Before the story broke, though, Macy wanted to find the answers. As soon as she got some rest, she'd visit her mother and make her talk.

As STONE DROVE toward his cabin on the creek, he phoned his deputy to handle the routine work in the office so he could go home and grab some z's. It would take time for the lab to process the blood and forensics, look for a DNA match. Meanwhile, he'd refuel.

Although Macy's pained face taunted him. She'd looked so forlorn that he'd wanted to comfort her, but he reminded himself to remain professional. She'd never intended to stay in Briar Ridge. Had told him from the start that she'd be leaving town after the class reunion and resuming her own life.

No sense in getting too close to her when he knew that. He'd been down that road before, thank you very much. His high school girlfriend Joanna had bolted after graduation, too. Said she didn't want small-town life. She wanted to see the world. Had headed to New York City, and he'd never heard from her again.

Macy would do the same.

But now they had a crime to solve. There was no way she could sell that house until they did.

The road from Macy's toward his cabin was devoid of traffic, but when he turned onto the street outside town he spotted his brother staggering down the road, walking along the shoulder in the direction of his apartment. Worry and anger slammed into him, and he slowly eased up beside him. Mickey stumbled and nearly fell, flailing to keep from falling into the ditch.

Stone gritted his teeth, then pulled over, gravel spewing as he skidded to a stop. He shoved open the door of his squad car, shaking his head as Mickey wove back and forth. Fearing he'd slip or get hit by a car, he jogged to him.

Mickey's eyes were glassy and half-closed as he slowly turned him to face Stone. "What the hell, Mickey?"

His brother grunted, wobbling sideways. "What are you doing here?"

"I was on my way home from a case I worked last night," Stone said, the stench of booze hitting him in the face. "You're drunk, little brother. Come on, I'll drive you home."

Mickey yanked his arm away. "Leave me alone. I didn't ask you to come."

"No, you didn't. But I'm taking you home anyway." He'd already lost enough people in his life. Mickey pulled back and stumbled toward the embankment, and Stone grabbed him just in time to keep him from falling into the rocks. His brother cursed as Stone hauled him to his squad car, opened the door and helped him inside. Before Stone could make it to the driver's seat, Mickey had passed out cold.

Worry knotted his gut, the guilt overwhelming him. He'd promised his father he'd watch out for Mickey. But somehow he'd already let him down.

Chapter Four

Macy slept fitfully for three hours, then jerked awake and stared at the cracks in the ceiling. Ever since she was a child, night had been her enemy. The dark filled her with dread, the uncertainty of her mother's moods plaguing her with anxiety.

Track had become her stress release and she'd been jogging ever since. As soon as she climbed from bed, she dressed in running clothes and shoes and hit the sidewalk outside.

She hadn't seen her mother in years. Today she not only had to face her, but she had to ask her about a dead man.

The midday sun beamed down on her, the humid air making her hair stick to the back of her neck as she jogged into the heart of town. Her ponytail bobbed up and down, her heart racing as she picked up her pace. The town square held a park and walking trail where families and mothers were out strolling with their children, and kids played at the park in the center.

She passed Pearl's Dine & Pie which was packed with the lunch crowd, then Joy's Fabrics & Crafts. As she reached the Cut & Dye she couldn't help but think about Cassidy Fulton, who worked there. Cassidy was another former student, one who'd actually slept with Ned before the shooting and had his baby. She'd kept that secret for years, but it had come out recently.

The place offered full salon services, including hairstyling, highlights, mani-pedis, massages and waxing. The rumor mill usually started there, spreading quickly from one hairdryer to the next. She'd heard Cassidy was moving. The publicity over the fact that Ned Hodgkins had fathered Cassidy's son, and her son had been arrested for trying to hurt Kate, was probably more than she could take.

The tension in Macy's shoulders eased with every mile, and her courage returned. She was a trained FBI agent, had gotten out of a terrible marriage and taken down notorious criminals. She could confront her own mother without falling apart.

With last night on her mind, as she passed the sheriff's office, she decided to check with Stone to see if he'd heard from the lab.

Wiping perspiration from her forehead, she entered the office and greeted the receptionist, Hattie Mae Perkins. While working with Stone the last couple of weeks, she'd learned that Hattie was new on the job but had lived in Briar Ridge all her life. She also liked to bake and kept the break room furnished with cookies and cakes.

"Is Sheriff Lawson in?"

"Not yet. He had a late night."

She knew all about that. Soon everyone else in Briar Ridge would. "Thanks. I'll give him a call."

She ducked outside and jogged back toward the inn, but as she turned the corner past the bookstore, the hair on the back of her neck prickled. She scanned the street, the sense that someone was watching her hitting her full force.

Then she saw a group of ladies hovering, whispering, watching her. Gretta Wright stood talking to them. She looked over at Macy and made eye contact, a twinkle in her eyes as if they were talking about her.

Had someone already leaked news about the murder?

STONE SILENTLY CURSED as he stared at his little brother, who was still passed out on the couch where he'd left him early this morning. A few hours of sleep for him, but now he was back and his brother looked nowhere near ready to get up and work.

He had no idea what was going on with Mickey. For a while after the shooting, he'd been depressed and had a chip on his shoulder.

But school for the visually impaired had helped him adjust and taught him coping skills, and then he'd turned his interest in video games and music into a job by working for an online company.

He nudged him with his knee. "Come on, Mickey. I brought you a breakfast sandwich. I'll make coffee and we can talk."

Mickey groaned, then rolled to his back and pressed his hand over his eyes. "Go away. I'm tired."

"You're hungover," Stone growled. "What about work today?"

"I'll get to it." He rolled to his side and tugged the pillow over his head. "Don't you need to be out playing the hero somewhere?"

"I'm no hero," Stone said, his voice laced with self-disgust. Why did his brother sound bitter toward him? "Tell me what's going on," he said, softening his tone. "I can't help you if I don't know."

"I don't need your help," Mickey snarled.

Stone's cell phone buzzed. Macy.

"I gotta go. Get up, clean yourself up and eat something, Mickey. And call me when you do."

"Yeah, yeah, yeah," Mickey muttered.

Stone clenched his phone and answered as he stepped outside his brother's apartment.

"It's Macy," she said a little breathlessly as if she was running. "Have you heard anything from the ME or lab yet?"

"No, hopefully sometime later today, but that may be pushing it."

The sound of a car honking echoed in the background. "I'm going to talk to my mother," Macy said.

Stone slid into his squad car. "I'll go with you."

A tense second passed. "That's not necessary, Stone. I can handle it."

He heaved a breath. "Macy, you know how this works. It's a homicide investigation and you have a conflict of interest."

"Don't you trust me?" Macy said, anger lacing her voice.

"It's not about trust," he said. "It's about protocol. You know we have to follow the rules and the clues, no matter where they lead us."

Even if it meant he had to arrest her mother.

MACY KNEW STONE was just doing his job. But confiding her family secrets was something she thought she'd never do. Some things needed to stay buried.

Maybe that's what her mother had decided about the body…

But now that it had been exposed, Macy couldn't ignore it or cover it up.

"I'm jogging," Macy said. "Give me thirty minutes for a shower and some coffee."

"Okay. I'll pick you up in a little bit."

She agreed and hung up, looking over her shoulder and all around her as she rushed into the inn. She'd half expected Gretta to follow her or show up any minute. But she breathed out in relief when she didn't see her.

Celeste still had hot coffee and pastries on the buffet in the dining room, so she grabbed a cup of coffee and a Danish and carried it to her room—the Orchid Room. Painted a soft, soothing lilac, the room felt like a retreat from the ugliness of the outside world. She ate, then stripped her running clothes and climbed into the shower. The hot water helped soothe her aching body, and she closed her eyes and scrubbed her hair, but the grisly image from the night before taunted her.

Once again, her mother had found a way to sabotage her life. Anger was the only way she'd survived before, so she latched on to it. She dried her hair, then pulled it back into a ponytail and dressed in a blue T-shirt and jeans. No need to dress the part of the FBI. That would only intimidate her mother and trigger a defensive reaction.

Grabbing her shoulder purse, she stowed her phone and weapon inside, then left the room, locked it and hurried down the steps to the front door. By the time she stepped outside, Stone was parking. She jogged over to his squad car and slipped into the passenger side.

"We're going to Bear Mountain Gardens," Macy said.

Stone's dark eyes flashed with emotions she couldn't quite define. "You ready for this?"

No. Hell no. "Just drive," she said quietly.

He nodded, stepped on the gas and pulled from the parking lot. Macy turned and looked out the window at the passing scenery as he wove through town.

The last time she'd seen her mother, they'd screamed at each other. Her mother had been in one of her manic states, ranting and throwing things and blaming Macy for all her problems.

Sometimes she thought her mother had wished she'd never been born.

TENSION RADIATED IN the silence as Stone drove through the secure gates and parked in the circular drive in front of the main entrance to Bear Mountain Gardens.

Hoping she'd open up on her own, he'd decided not to push Macy to talk.

The assisted living facility was set on ten acres and divided into sections based on the senior's needs. One area served the assisted living, another focused on housing for memory care, and another doubled as a halfway house type situation for those undergoing counseling for mental disorders and addiction. Staff included nurses, doctors, certified nursing assistants, counselors, and occupational therapists. Medications were monitored by the staff.

Social activities were organized for residents in a community center, and the landscape outside provided walking trails and a flower and vegetable garden that the residents themselves tended to.

Macy shifted as he parked, her breath heavy with dread.

"I don't know what happened between you two, but I sense it wasn't pleasant," he said gently.

Macy angled her head to look at him, her eyes swimming in pain. "My mother suffers from bipolar disorder. She's manic one minute and depressive the next. When she took her meds, she was easier to handle. When she didn't, which was more often than she did, she got ugly." She reached for the door handle and opened the door. "That's why she's here. To monitor her meds and keep her stable."

Stone swallowed against the emotions the empty hollowness in her tone stirred. "She hurt you?"

Macy gave a small shrug but ignored the question, then got out and slammed the car door.

Her withdrawal made his chest clench. The rumors he'd heard at school and in town obviously had merit.

Just what had her mother done to her behind closed doors?

Chapter Five

The only time Macy had been to Bear Mountain Gardens was when her mother was admitted. She'd never told anyone about that day. Instead, she'd locked the pain in the darkest corners of her mind out of reach and hopefully forgotten.

But now the memory tumbled through the door and slammed into her with the crushing weight of a boulder.

"You can't leave me here, Macy!" her mother screamed. *"I'm your mother."*

Her mother's doctor, a kind middle-aged woman named Dr. Garrett, had intervened. *"We talked about this, Lynn,"* the doctor said gently. *"You agreed to stay here and undergo therapy so you could get better."*

"It's her fault I'm like this," her mother cried. *"It's Macy's fault."*

"Macy did not make this decision," Dr. Garrett said firmly. *"The court ordered you to undergo treatment in a monitored facility."*

"I didn't do what she said I did!" her mother screeched.

Macy instinctively rubbed a finger over the scar on the back of her neck, the one her mother had given her when she'd knocked her against the corner of the table.

"Give the program a try," Dr. Garrett said. *"You have a chemical imbalance that affects your moods. The medi-*

cation will stabilize those moods and help you live a more productive life." The psychiatrist patted her mother's back. "I'll be with you every step of the way."

But her mother wasn't responding to the doctor's calm tone or assurances. She looked wild-eyed and crazed, and suddenly shoved the doctor away from her with such force that Dr. Garrett stumbled backward and grabbed the wall for support. Then she ran for the door.

Dr. Garrett recovered quickly and motioned to the male nurse at the door, who caught her mother before she could escape the room. She swung her fists at the man, beating him in the chest as she screamed and kicked.

Dr. Garrett gave Macy a sympathetic look, removed a hypodermic from her pocket, then calmly walked over and gave Macy's mother the injection.

Her mother turned a venomous look toward Macy.

"What did I do to you to make you lock me in here?"

Pain nearly choked Macy at the accusation. She'd done lots of things to Macy, but Macy had never told. She'd tried to pretend that they had a normal life.

But nothing in her household had been normal.

She pulled herself from the past. Kate and her mother had known. They'd seen her erratic behavior themselves.

After Macy left town, her mother had gotten worse. She'd received numerous calls from the police where she'd been found drugged and on a rampage.

Not in Briar Ridge, but always close to wherever Macy was living. She'd been stalking her. And then the attack…

A shudder coursed up her spine.

Stone remained a quiet force by her side, yet humiliation washed over her at the idea of airing her family's dirty secrets in front of him.

Pulling her credentials, she identified herself to the nurse's assistant at the front desk and explained she needed to see her mother.

The young redhead called Dr. Garrett and informed her of their arrival. The psychiatrist had sent her reports on her mother's condition the past year after she'd been admitted. Before that, Macy had rarely visited since she left town and then only for holidays or when her mother's doctor called because she'd had an episode. Some days were good. Others she slipped. Dr. Garrett believed that with the right kind of therapy they'd uncover the source of what had triggered her mother's condition to decline and to learn the source of her psychotic break.

Now Macy might have a clue to help fill in the gaps.

STONE FELT FOR MACY, but his job was to uncover the truth about a crime and protect the citizens of Briar Ridge, and he intended to do it.

Even if it meant asking Macy tough questions or keeping her out of the loop.

When Dr. Garrett arrived, Macy introduced them and asked to speak in private.

"Of course." The plump woman led them down a carpeted hallway past several offices, then to her own. Her diplomas and awards hung in frames on the plain beige wall, documenting her degree, residency, fellowships and experience. Yellow gerbera daisies filled a vase on the desk, which was neat and organized.

She offered them coffee, and they both accepted. Macy looked eager for it, or maybe she just wanted something to do with her fidgety hands. Then they claimed chairs in a seating area in the corner of the room, which looked cozy and was obviously meant to make her patients feel at ease.

"What's this about, Macy?" Dr. Garrett asked.

Stone appreciated her direct approach.

"I came home to clean out my mother's house and put it on the market, but I found something very disturbing last night. I need to ask my mother about it," Macy began.

She inhaled sharply, then gestured to Stone. He silently thanked her for letting him take the lead. Maybe she did recognize that she couldn't be objective in this situation.

The doctor narrowed her eyes. "I'm guessing from the fact that the sheriff is with you that this is not just a social visit."

Macy shook her head and Stone cleared his throat.

"Dr. Garrett, last night Macy—Agent Stark—found a dead person's remains in the wall in the basement of her mother's house."

Dr. Garrett's eyes widened in shock, and she glanced back and forth between them. "Oh, my word."

"At this point, we haven't identified the man," Stone explained. "But judging from decomp, we believe the bones have been there for some time."

Macy's face paled. "The state of decomp suggests the body was there when my mother still lived at home," Macy said. "That means we have to question her."

Dr. Garrett's forehead wrinkled as she processed the statement. "Are you suggesting that someone was murdered in the house?"

Stone gave her a grim look. "It's possible. It's also possible that the person was killed elsewhere and stored in the wall afterward, but if Mrs. Stark was living at the house at the time, that would have been difficult to do without her knowledge."

"But her mental state…" The doctor cut herself off. "With HIPAA laws, I can't discuss Lynn's medical history in front of anyone except Macy, her legal guardian. Not unless I have permission. I also can't allow you to question her without my presence."

Stone expected HIPAA to complicate the situation. And for the doctor to insist on being present.

Macy sighed heavily. "I give my permission for you to discuss her condition in front of Sheriff Lawson. No one else but him. We have to find out what happened in that house."

Macy's pained tone tore at Stone, but she was FBI. She knew the drill. And she obviously wanted answers.

Dr. Garrett studied them both for a long minute. "All right. But if Lynn does know about this body, then it could have been the trigger for her psychotic break, so we have to tread carefully. That means you let me lead the discussion. If I sense she's getting too agitated, or that she's repressed memories of a murder, then we stop, and I'll try therapeutic techniques to help her tap into her memories slowly. The last thing we need is to cause more damage to her psyche." She drummed her fingers on her suit pant leg. "There's also the possibility of TMR."

"What is that?" Stone asked.

"Traumatic memory recovery, although there have been instances during that kind of treatment where patients recalled false memories or events. With bipolar disorder and schizophrenic tendencies, that's a possibility."

She made it sound bleak, Stone thought.

But they had to get answers.

MACY WRESTLED TO control her emotions. Stone had no idea how much it cost her to give him access to her mother's condition. That was opening a closed door to the secrets in her life.

Her face heated at the thought. But she had joined the Bureau to see that justice was served, and she couldn't move forward without closing this chapter in her past.

She and Stone followed Dr. Garrett through the building. She chatted about the facility as they went. One section was designated for patients with medium care, meaning they required checkups to monitor medicine and make sure they made their therapy sessions, versus another unit that was highly secured to keep dangerous, potentially violent patients under lock and key.

Her mother had initially been sequestered to that unit but through cooperative behavior had eventually been moved to the less guarded section, offering her more freedom during the days to roam the gardens and participate in the activities meant to help patients heal and blend into society.

The doctor's monologue saved Macy from talking. Her stomach was churning at the thought of facing her mother again. As many sinister criminals as she'd faced the past few years, none of them turned her into the terrified, quivering little child who had borne the brunt of her mother's rages.

After winding past the solarium and community room, they stepped through French doors that led to the garden area where residents were pruning the plants and tending to the colorful flowers. Several patients/residents were pulling weeds and picking the vegetables that had ripened, filling baskets that would go to the kitchen for dinner preparation.

Macy did not see her mother anywhere.

Dr. Garrett's brow furrowed, and she approached one of the nursing assistants and spoke in a hushed tone. When she turned to Macy, her pulse jumped.

"The nurse said your mother refused to come to the garden today," Dr. Garrett said. "Let's check her suite. She could have overslept."

The nerves in Macy's stomach clawed at her.

Dr. Garrett led them back inside, then down another hallway to her mother's suite. Due to her dangerous nature, she hadn't yet earned a kitchenette, but she had a private room and bath and a window that offered a view of the majestic mountains beyond. It was a little pricey but with insurance and her savings, she managed to make it work, although sometimes her money was tight. Selling her mother's house would definitely help with the budget.

Dr. Garrett knocked and when no answer came, used a key to unlock the door. The moment they opened the door, Macy had a bad feeling.

They checked the bedroom and adjoining bathroom, and no one was inside. But things were scattered all across the room, the window was open and the screen had been slashed.

STONE EXAMINED THE window frame and torn screen, then gave the doctor a questioning look. "It looks like Mrs. Stark cut the screen and climbed out the window. Was there some reason she didn't just go out the door?"

The psychiatrist dug her hands into the pocket of her white coat. "She has seemed agitated this week so we suspected she might be ditching her meds. When she stops them abruptly, she becomes paranoid and experiences delusions."

Macy's quickly drawn breath echoed in the air. "Did you think she was dangerous to herself or the other patients?"

The doctor shrugged. "She was erratic. Yesterday she said someone was watching her. She got into it with another resident and when a guard tried to break it up, she tried to stab him with a fork."

Stone didn't like the picture the doctor was painting. Macy's expression remained neutral, a sign she wasn't surprised at the news. Which told him more than if she'd said something.

"When was the last time anyone saw her?" Stone asked.

Dr. Garrett rubbed her temple. "I'll check with her nurse and get an exact time for you."

"We need to search the entire facility and grounds," Stone said. "If she left on foot, she can't have gotten very far."

Macy squared her shoulders. "Find out if any staff member or visitor's car is missing, too."

The doctor pulled her phone and called security. "We have a missing patient. Lynn Stark. Start a thorough search and put the facility on lockdown. Also, make sure everyone's vehicle is accounted for in case she stole a car and drove away."

"I'd like to see security cams," Stone told her as she hung up.

"Let's split up, then," Macy said. "I have a few more questions for the doctor."

Dr. Garrett called a CNA to show Stone to the central security room, and he left Macy with the psychiatrist.

Although doubts crept in. Had Macy simply wanted to manage their time, or did she want to talk to the doctor alone because she was hiding something?

MACY'S MIND RACED. Where the hell was her mother?

"I'm sorry this happened," Dr. Garrett said, worry knitting her forehead. "I promise we'll do everything possible to find her. We pride ourselves on our residents' safety and well-being."

Macy understood the doctor was concerned about liability issues, but she was more worried about what her mother might do while off her meds. The timing of her disappearance was also disturbing.

"Dr. Garrett, during my mother's therapy sessions, did she mention anything about a body in the wall at our house?"

A tense second passed. "You know I can't violate patient-doctor confidentiality."

Macy gritted her teeth. "I understand, but Sheriff Lawson and I are conducting a homicide investigation. If you have information that pertains to that, you have to talk to me."

The doctor's expression gave nothing away. "We've just barely begun to scratch the surface of the inner workings of her mind," she said. "But I can honestly tell you that she has not mentioned a murder or a body in the house."

Macy sensed the doctor was weighing her words carefully. "Do you know what caused her to have a psychotic break?"

"Not specifically." Dr. Garrett folded her arms. "Oftentimes, a traumatic event in childhood triggers a break later in adults. The patient may or may not recall the event. So far, she's been resistant to hypnosis, which might help."

Macy swallowed hard. "I don't know anything about her childhood," she said. "She refused to talk about her parents or my father. But I remember one night when I was five, she flew into a rage and threw me outside. Now I found this body, it makes me wonder if something happened that night to trigger her episode." Macy shifted. "If she was attacked and killed this man in self-defense or murdered him, could that have been the trigger for her break?"

"A traumatic event like an attack could incite a break, yes." The doctor gave her a sympathetic look. "I understand that growing up with a mentally ill mother can scar a child. Perhaps you need to seek counseling yourself to deal with your own trauma."

Macy bit down on her lip. "It's not about me right now. Has Mother talked about running away?"

Dr. Garrett shrugged. "All of my patients talk about running away at some point. They feel trapped and liken being here to prison. Although as you can see, the accommodations and activities are designed to treat the patient physically, emotionally and mentally. But I will go back and study my notes to see if she referenced a specific place she'd go when she left here."

She might come after her, Macy thought. Or go home. She turned to study the room. "I'd like to look through her things. Maybe there's something here that will explain the reason she left."

The doctor agreed, then left to check with security and see if they'd found her on the premises. Macy walked over to the small desk in the corner of the room. Above it hung several pages of sketches, all black-and-whites of monsters, all disturbing.

Were those monsters representative of someone in particular?

Chapter Six

Stone spent the next hour studying camera footage with the lead security officer. Dr. Garrett texted saying Mrs. Stark had been in her room around eight for breakfast, although the CNA stated that she was agitated and refused to eat. She left Lynn inside her room, pacing and ranting that someone had tried to break in the night before. That was the last time anyone had seen her.

"Narrow in on the evening and night," Stone told the security officer. "Let's verify that no one actually tried to break into her room."

The officer rolled the footage, and Stone scrutinized the area outside Mrs. Stark's room and the window. Minute after minute passed, and all was quiet and still. They continued to watch through the night hours until morning, but he didn't see anyone lurking outside the window or tampering with the screen.

"Many of the patients here are delusional and paranoid," the officer said. "We've had them get hold of phones and call 911 from their rooms claiming we're trying to kill them."

Stone grimaced. It was a difficult and sad situation for everyone, including the patients' families.

His admiration for Macy stirred. In spite of the hell

she'd gone through, she was a responsible woman and savvy federal agent.

The guard continued to run the footage, and Stone watched the sun rise outside, slanting across the gardens, then the grounds, until 9:10, when he saw someone inside Lynn's room at the window.

Slowly the camera caught the woman ripping the screen and cutting away enough of the mesh to crawl through.

A second later, she dropped to the ground outside. She lost her footing and hit the grass on her hands and knees, but quickly pushed up to stand. Still, she crouched low and inched away from the building.

"Zoom in on her face," Stone said.

The officer did as he said, and Stone's pulse jumped. He hadn't seen Macy's mother in years, and she'd definitely aged. Her dark hair was choppy as if she'd cut it herself, her eyes glassy-looking, her shirt inside out. She'd obviously dressed in a hurry. She kept glancing all around, scanning the gardens as she sneaked toward the woods bordering the property.

Time passed and a few patients and residents began to drift outside, gathering by the small pond and on the terrace where they enjoyed coffee, snacks, and board and card games. Each time one appeared, Mrs. Stark ducked behind a bush or tree.

Ten minutes later, she climbed the fence at the edge of the woods, then she took off running and disappeared into the shadows.

No one had even noticed she was gone.

SADNESS NEARLY OVERPOWERED Macy as she studied the drawings of the monsters on her mother's wall. The disturbing sketches were obviously her mother's way of working out the demons in her mind.

The minimal furnishings in the room looked bleak as

well. A single bed and wooden dresser. Plain white sheets and green comforter were tangled and twisted. Her pillow lay on the floor. She glanced inside the closet. A few pairs of sweatpants and jeans, T-shirts and long-sleeved shirts. Tennis shoes.

In the dresser drawer, she found plain underwear, socks and a couple of nightgowns. She rummaged through, searching for something to tell her more about her mother, but found nothing.

She returned to the wall of drawings, then sat down at the small desk. Charcoal and sketch paper had been placed on top, ready to use.

She opened the desk drawer and saw a journal inside. Pain squeezed her chest at her mother's random, disturbing drawings. One depicted a naked woman curled on the floor in the corner, her arms wrapped around her legs, her head bent into them as if she were crying.

She flipped to another page and saw a sketch of their house, night shadows casting an eerie feel over the trees and yard, with more monsters lurking in the woods.

Turning to the next page, she found a house again, this time with drawings of snakes climbing the walls and hanging from the roof. The next one depicted vultures attacking the windows. Then another one of bloody footprints on the floor of the wooden porch.

Were the bloody footprints delusions or pieces of memories?

Her phone buzzed. Stone.

"Macy," he said when she connected, "security footage shows your mother escaping through the window and running into the woods. There was no sign that anyone tried to break into her room or that someone assisted her in leaving."

"So she left on foot?"

"Yes. According to the time stamp, it was a little after nine. I got a copy if you want to look at it."

Did she? No, she trusted Stone. Macy glanced at her watch. It was noon now. Her mother had left three hours ago.

"I found a journal of her drawings," Macy said. "I think I may know where she's going."

"Where?" Stone asked.

Macy's stomach churned. "Home."

STONE ISSUED A BOLO for Macy's mother, then drove back to Briar Ridge. Macy sat silently beside him, staring out the window as if lost in another world. Armed with a new understanding of what she'd endured as a child and as an adult, it was no wonder she hadn't returned to Briar Ridge until the reunion. She had nothing good here to come back to.

He didn't blame her for wanting to leave again.

He had his own share of hurtful memories in Briar Ridge. That damn shooting. His brother's injury. His part in not seeing Ned Hodgkins's plans or the pain he was in from being bullied.

But he also had precious memories of fishing with his father and trailing after him when they went hiking. He'd known his father loved him.

That he loved the town. Hell, he'd lay down his life for his family and the residents of Briar Ridge.

Stone felt that responsibility now. He could never walk away from it. Never.

Still, he had a job to do, a case to solve. It would either bring closure for Macy or open up another can of worms that could destroy her life. "Did you learn anything from Dr. Garrett?"

Macy ran a hand over her ponytail. "Not much. It was early in my mom's therapy with her. I asked her to study the notes from their sessions for information about what might have happened at the house." Macy shrugged. "Who knows if it'll yield results? It's hard to know what's real and what's not in my mother's mind."

Stone didn't comment. That was more than she'd ever shared.

Macy turned to look out at the passing scenery, farmland, mountains, green grass and wildflowers dotting the mountain. All peaceful. Yet tension screamed off her, and there was nothing peaceful in her eyes.

He fought against the lump in his throat. "Did you find anything in the room?"

"Just sketches of monsters my mother drew," she said with a crack in her voice. "And the house. There were some of those."

Stone forced his hands to stay on the wheel when he wanted to take Macy's hand in his and comfort her. But that would be a mistake.

He had to keep his mind on the job.

"Let's drive by the house," Macy said. "My mother may have gone there."

"On foot that would take a while," Stone pointed out.

"But she could have stolen a car or hitched a ride."

"True."

He veered onto the turnoff for Main Street, and they fell silent as he drove to the Stark house. Macy's body was coiled with tension, dread in her eyes as he parked. The only car there was Macy's.

Still, they got out and approached the house slowly, then inched up the steps. Shadows cast dark spots about the house, the scent of death and mystery clinging to the dusty walls as they entered.

"I'll take the downstairs," Stone said.

Macy nodded, pausing to listen. The ticking of the clock

and wind whistling through the eaves of the house echoed in the air.

He strode to the door to the basement while Macy combed the main floor and bedrooms.

Five minutes later, they met in the living room. "She's not here," he said.

"No, but she may be on her way," Macy said, her tone grim.

Stone's phone buzzed. His deputy, so he connected. "Yeah?"

"Sheriff, Gretta Wilson is here demanding to talk to you."

Dammit. Gretta had been a pain their backsides ever since high school. Stirring up gossip. Printing everyone's business no matter who she hurt.

If it was up to him, he'd lock her up.

But the first amendment and all the press hype prevented that.

When the blame went around for Ned Hodgkins's shooting tirade, he couldn't ignore the fact that she'd escalated the situation by exposing hurtful things the students had said about Ned.

Why was she at his office now? To make trouble? Get back at him and Macy for not giving her the scoop on Ned's son?

Or could she somehow have found out about the body?

TEN MINUTES LATER, Macy braced herself to remain unemotional as she and Stone climbed from his vehicle and walked toward the entrance to the sheriff's office. Gretta had gotten under her skin long ago, and she'd told her off in high school.

Needless to say they weren't friends and never would be.

Gretta's eyes lit up, and she made a beeline for them, blocking the doorway so they couldn't enter and shoving a microphone in their faces.

"Special Agent Macy Stark, is it true that a body was discovered at your family's home last night?"

Macy curled her hands into fists, wondering where Gretta had gotten her information. She swore the vile woman had cameras—or informants—everywhere.

But she couldn't avoid the inevitable or lie to the people in town, or that would make the situation worse. Taking a deep breath, she spoke calmly. "Yes, a body was discovered in the basement of the house where I grew up. At this time, we have not identified the remains, nor do we have any information to report about the cause of death or how long the body has been there."

Gretta narrowed her eyes. "But your mother lived in that house until recently, didn't she?"

"No comment."

Macy started to walk away, but Gretta stepped in her path. "Agent Stark, your mother suffers from mental illness, correct?"

Macy stiffened, but Stone cleared his throat. "This is Sheriff Stone Lawson. As Special Agent Stark stated, the police and FBI will be running a joint investigation into the situation. We have no further statement at the time."

Gretta opened her mouth to protest, but Stone gently brushed her aside, curved his arm around Macy's waist and hustled her toward the door.

Macy was trembling as they entered the sheriff's office. Mixed emotions pummeled her, and she spun toward Stone.

"I appreciate you trying to protect me, Stone, but now Gretta will make something of you stepping in or hint that something is going on between us and make me look incompetent. I'm a professional. I can take care of myself."

STONE CROSSED HIS ARMS, his jaw tightening.

"Macy, your mother's medical history doesn't reflect on you. And no one is going to think you're unstable just because she was." And he had thought something was going on between them.

Or maybe that was his own wishful thinking.

Macy whirled around on him, hands on her hips. "Don't be naive, Stone. I heard the gossip growing up. Saw the way people looked at me in town when I was with her." Her voice cracked. "Even Brynn's mother didn't like that she and I were friends."

Anger shot through Stone at the unfairness of the situation. "Mrs. Gaines is a snob. Who cares what she thinks?"

But he saw it in her eyes. She cared. Because she'd been a little girl at the time. And in spite of the saying that words could never hurt you, they definitely could.

"I'm sorry," he said. "I don't mean to be insensitive." He heaved a breath. "I know people can be nasty. Judgmental even. But nothing your mother did or does can change who you are."

Macy squeezed her eyes closed for a moment and exhaled. When she opened them, she rubbed the back of her neck. "Sorry. I shouldn't let Gretta get to me."

"She's a troublemaker," Stone said wryly. He reached for his phone. "I'm going to call the ME. See if she has any information."

"Put her on Speaker," Macy said.

He nodded, then rang the ME's office. "Dr. Anderson, you're on speaker with Agent Stark. Do you have anything on that body?"

"No ID yet. But the forensic anthropologist is using PMCT for identification and to determine cause of death."

"Postmortem computed topography?" Macy asked.

"Exactly. It's complicated, but in the case of skeletal remains, it analyzes toxicology, looks for traumatic fractures, surgical dissection of foreign bodies and state of carbonization to determine time, cause of death and previous injuries to the body."

Stone pulled a hand down his chin. "And?"

"The body belongs to a male. Midthirties at time of death. Previous injuries include a broken nose, ribs and arm."

"Someone beat him to death?" Stone asked.

"No, those were older injuries."

"Then what was cause of death?" Macy asked.

"Puncture wounds and scoring on the bone indicate he was stabbed multiple times. Judging from the size and length of the scoring, it could have been done by a hunting knife or a common kitchen knife."

Which her mother could have grabbed in the house. Macy remembered that one of the knives was missing when she was taking inventory of the kitchen. Remembered seeing an image of blood trickling down her arm…

"Ask the crime team if they found a kitchen knife that belongs to the set in the kitchen," she told Dr. Anderson.

His gaze met hers, then he nodded.

"Any guess as to how long he's been dead?" she asked the ME.

"Evidence suggests he was killed at least two decades ago, maybe twenty-five to twenty-seven years."

"So most likely he's been in that wall all that time?" Stone asked.

"Your forensics will have to determine that," Dr. Anderson said. "But there was no evidence that his body was frozen or kept somewhere else and moved there. We're running dental images and DNA results through the system to see if we can make an ID. Hopefully, we'll have more soon."

Stone thanked her, then ended the call. Macy rubbed her temple and sighed.

Stone gave her a sympathetic look. "You okay?"

She shook her head, her eyes pained. "If he's been dead

that long and in that wall the whole time, my mother and I would have been living there."

Stone swallowed. He saw the wheels in her head spinning. If that was true, Macy's mother might know exactly what had happened.

Or…she might have murdered the man herself.

Chapter Seven

Macy couldn't shake the conversation with Gretta. Stone had managed to hold her off, but that wouldn't last long. If Macy didn't find her mother soon, they'd need to run her picture on the news. Then everyone would know she'd escaped the Bear Mountain Gardens and that they considered her dangerous.

The hair on the back of her neck prickled as she and Stone found a booth at Daisy's Diner, a new place that had been built near the bookstore in town. The fifties decor boasted posters of old movies, red checkered tablecloths and a jukebox. With summer break for the schools and tourists returning to the area, it was packed with the lunch crowd today and teenagers chowing down on chili burgers and milkshakes.

Several locals turned to stare at them, whispering and talking in hushed tones. Obviously they'd seen the news and were wondering if a murderer was running loose in town.

The ME's estimated TOD for the man taunted her. It fit with the memory of the first time her mother had thrown her out in the rain.

The waitress, a perky brunette in her twenties with a nose ring, bobbed over to take their orders. Macy wasn't hungry but knew she needed fuel to do the job, so she ordered the special, a cup of Brunswick stew, and water while Stone ordered a loaded burger overflowing with mushrooms and a side of fries.

Mayor Gaines and his wife entered, the woman's cold stare a reminder of how she'd treated Macy as a child. The couple stopped at their table, the mayor's posture rigid.

"I saw your short briefing with that ghastly Gretta Wright," Mayor Gaines said. "Sheriff Lawson, when were you going to notify me that a murder had occurred in my town?"

A muscle ticked in Stone's jaw. "The skeletal remains were only discovered yesterday, Mayor. And I did plan to call you, but I wanted more information first."

"Yet you spoke with Ms. Wright?"

Stone took a long sip of his sweet iced tea. "I have no idea how or where Gretta got her information. And I certainly didn't intend to go public with this case until I clarified a few details."

The mayor buttoned his suit coat. "And have you?"

"As I said to the press, we've only begun the investigation. We don't have an ID on the body yet."

"And where did this murder occur?" the mayor asked.

"That's another question we're trying to answer."

"You're being evasive," the mayor said. "Tell me what you *do* know."

Stone glanced around, then lowered his voice. "I'd rather not discuss this in a public place. There are eyes on us."

The mayor inhaled, then gave a clipped nod. But his wife shot daggers at Macy with her eyes. "Why am I not surprised that there was a dead man in your house?"

Macy's chest clenched. "Well, it came as a shock to me."

"Really? We all know your mother had problems. I heard you finally got her admitted to a hospital."

Macy tensed, but before she spoke, the mayor took his wife's arm. "Not here."

The waitress arrived with their food, and the mayor coaxed his wife to the back of the diner. Macy clutched her water, well aware everyone in the café was watching her and Stone.

Mrs. Gaines's rude comment was only the beginning. Once word spread about the body, she and her mother would be the center of a scandal that Macy wouldn't be able to escape.

STONE WANTED TO throttle the mayor's wife. If he hadn't thought it would embarrass Macy, he would have told the woman off.

Anxious to leave, he and Macy finished their meal in silence. He grabbed the bill and paid it before Macy could, then stood and followed her to the door. But as they stepped outside, Kate McKendrick and Brynn Gaines appeared.

Macy halted, her eyes widening as Kate enveloped her in a hug. "We were going to stop by the house and see if you needed help later," Kate said.

Brynn rolled her wheelchair closer and took Macy's hand. "You okay, Macy? We saw the news."

Emotions flickered in Macy's eyes, and she took a breath. "Yes, but it's a mess. I'll be staying in town until we solve this case."

"Who was the man?" Kate asked.

Macy and Stone exchanged a look. "I can't talk about it here. I'll explain everything later."

Kate and Brynn murmured their understanding, although Stone saw the worry in their eyes. The three had been like sisters growing up. Different personalities but inseparable. Brynn's mother pushed her into beauty pageants and focused on appearances while Kate had been shy and bookish.

When her mother died in the shooting, Kate understandably had a difficult time. But she'd become a teacher and now was the high school principal.

Brynn had suffered as well. Surgery and physical therapy weren't able to repair the damage from the bullet she'd taken and she was partially paralyzed. Mrs. Gaines had smothered her, but after the reunion, he'd heard Brynn moved into her own place.

He was glad the reunion had brought the three women back together. Macy was going to need her friends now.

Rain clouds rolled across the sky, obliterating the midday sun and hinting at a summer storm as they got in his car. Macy remained silent as he started the engine.

"Take me back to the house so I can get my car," Macy said.

"Listen, Macy, I'll go with you to your house."

She shook her head. "I need some time alone, Stone. Or don't you trust me? Do you think I'm going to try to hide something from you?"

The edge to her voice made his jaw tighten. "That's not what I meant. But I understand you're close to this case."

Macy gritted her teeth. "I am, but I also know my mother can be dangerous. If she shows up, I'll keep her there until you arrive." She gave a look of gratitude. "I need you working every clue."

He reluctantly agreed, then his phone buzzed, and he saw it was his deputy so he answered. "Sheriff, I got a call about a stolen car. Thought you might want to check it out in case the Stark woman was involved."

"I'll be right there."

"What was that about?" Macy asked as he headed toward the inn.

Stone decided not to share unless he knew something, so he shrugged it off. "Just routine stuff."

If Mrs. Stark had stolen the car and he had to chase her down, he didn't want Macy to have to be part of it.

When he parked, he caught her arm before she got out. "Even though the crime team is finished, Macy, you know what all was there. Be alert for something they might have missed."

Her eyes darkened, then she got out without responding.

YELLOW CRIME SCENE tape flapped in the wind, the dark rain clouds hovering above the house a grim reminder that Macy's home was now the scene of a homicide investigation. She parked in front of the dilapidated structure, wondering if she should just have it demolished once she solved the mystery of what happened in that basement. The property had some value but not the house, especially with its sordid history now.

Senses alert in case her mother had found her way back, she scanned the front and side yard, then climbed from her car and walked up to the porch. The front door was unlocked, the screen door banging back and forth.

The rickety stairs creaked as she walked up them, and a screeching sound echoed from somewhere inside. Pulling her gun at the ready, she inched into the house. Fingerprint dust covered everything in sight, including the doorways and knob and what little was left of the furnishings.

It looked as if the place had been tossed. But that was partly her doing, partly the forensic team. She'd been rushing like a madwoman to clean out the house so she could hightail it out of town. No telling how long she'd have to stay in Briar Ridge and endure the gossip and stares now. More painful memories would pile up on top of the ones she'd tried to forget since she'd left Briar Ridge. And if her mother was guilty of murder...

The screeching sound jarred her gaze toward the kitchen and back door. Slowly she crept through the living room and looked inside the kitchen. The stench of cat pee hit her, and she spotted the source of the screeching. A stray cat was clawing at the back screen door to get out.

Breathing out in relief, she hurried to open the door. The feral cat hissed at her, then darted outside the minute she opened it. She watched it race into the woods to escape and wished she could do the same.

She reached for the door to close it but caught sight of a shadowy figure moving through the rows of thick pines. Thunder suddenly crackled, and a streak of lightning lit the sky.

Macy hated storms, but she stepped outside, desperate to see who the person was. Dark clothing, hunched over, hugging the trees like an animal. She rushed down the steps, but the figure turned and darted through the woods, disappearing into the shadows of the weeds and brush.

Her heart hammered. Was that her mother?

STONE FLIPPED OFF the siren on his police car as he came to a stop in the RV park.

This place was a popular spot for tourists on a budget who wanted the benefits of the creek and proximity to the hiking trails and canoeing. Except for the rumble of thunder and a dog barking, the wooded area was quiet.

A big guy who looked like a lumberjack stood from where he and a boy about ten were playing horseshoes beside the RV. They both halted when they saw his police car, and the man walked toward him.

"Sheriff Lawson," he said.

"Abel and Matt Young," the lumberjack guy said.

"My deputy said you reported a car missing."

The man nodded and gestured to his son to gather the horseshoes. "Yeah, last night we went camping over on the mountain. When we got back this morning, my Jeep was gone."

He scratched his beard. "First I thought the wife took it into town with my little girl for supplies. But she said she went for a hike to the falls with Jordie, and when she got back, the Jeep was gone."

"What time was that?"

The man glanced at his watch. "Sometime around noon." He pulled a face of disgust. "We picked this place because we thought it was safe to raise a family. Now... not so sure."

Stone hated the distrust crime caused. The shooting years ago had completely divided the town and made everyone suspicious and wary of their neighbors.

"I'm sorry this happened to you," Stone said sincerely. "I will do everything possible to recover your vehicle and get to the bottom of it."

"I appreciate that," the man said. "My wife is a nervous wreck. She wants to pack up and go back to Durham where her mama lives." He gestured toward his son. "But Matt loves it out here."

Stone remembered hiking, fishing and canoeing with Mickey and his own father and nodded. "For what it's worth, I do think you're safe. And if you want, I can help you arrange for a rental car." He glanced around the RV park searching for security cameras. But there were none out here in the wilderness.

"I appreciate it. But we've already contacted our insurance company and they're sending over a rental."

"You gave my deputy the make, model and license of the Jeep?"

"We did," he said.

"We'll get an APB issued for it. I'll let you know if or when it turns up."

The man thanked him, and they shook hands, then Stone headed back to his squad car, considering the possibilities. Some kids could have stolen the vehicle, looking for a joyride.

But considering the proximity to Bear Mountain Gardens, it was possible Macy's mother had made it on foot here and stolen the Jeep. If so and she was headed home, she might already be there.

He pulled his phone to call Macy and warn her.

MACY'S PULSE HAMMERED as she jogged toward the woods to give chase. The clouds opened up, dumping rain, and lightning flashed, striking a tree in the distance. Her phone was ringing on her belt, but she ignored it and fought through the rain to reach the edge of the woods.

Rain pummeled her, the thick downpour clogging her vision and slowing her as the wind picked up and blew leaves and debris around her. She zigzagged through the massive line of trees, weaving back and forth in search of the shadowy figure. But it had disappeared.

Heaving a breath, she wiped rain from her face and trudged on. Her shoes sank into the muddy ground as she dodged a falling limb and jumped over twigs that snapped off from the force of the wind.

She ran half a mile, searching, looking, stopping to examine the brush, but the heavy downpour made it impossible to track. Frustrated, she halted and turned, scanning all directions, but everything was a foggy blur.

Another crack of lightning and a tree falling in the woods made her turn and jog back to the house.

Battling the storm took all her energy and by the time she arrived at the house, rain drenched her clothing and hair, and she felt chilled to the bone. She rushed up the back steps and into the house to escape the weather, then checked her phone. A voice mail from Stone.

"Car stolen within five miles of Bear Mountain Gardens. Issued an APB. Be on the lookout for a 2020 Jeep Cherokee. Navy blue."

Her mother could have escaped and stolen the car and be here now.

She hurried to the front door. The headlights of a dark sedan nearly blinded her, and she froze, a hand on her gun as she waited to see who was behind the wheel.

SHE WATCHED THE HOUSE, a fine sheen of sweat coating her skin. Macy was back in town. And she'd found a body in the damn house.

She'd heard the news in the car on the way out here. At this point, the police knew nothing. It had to stay that way.

But Macy was FBI now. What if she figured out what happened?

What if she remembered?

Fighting panic, she opened her pill bottle, popped a Xanax into her mouth and swallowed it down.

She couldn't take that chance.

Chapter Eight

Macy clenched her weapon and started outside to confront whoever was in that car, but as soon as she stepped onto the porch the vehicle moved on.

Probably just some rubbernecker wanting to see the house where a dead body was just discovered.

Breathing out in relief, she went back inside and closed the door. Dammit, this place was spooking her.

She wanted to be done with it. But that couldn't happen until she learned the truth. Deciding to take another look around in case she'd missed something, she hurried to her mother's room and searched beneath the bed, then the closet again. She stood on tiptoe and raked her hand along the top shelf and her finger brushed something. She strained to reach it but couldn't so she dragged the desk chair in the corner to the closet and climbed up on it. Shining her flashlight across the shelf, she saw a photo album and a box.

She pulled them both down, set the box on the floor, then sank into the chair to look through them. First the photo album. Macy had never seen the album before. She had no idea her mother had even kept one. Lynn Stark hadn't exactly been the sentimental, doting mother.

Her mother had refused to tell her anything about her

father. Macy had long ago decided it didn't matter. If he'd wanted to be part of her life, he would have.

But if he'd stayed in touch, he might know what happened here. Maybe she'd find a clue in here, a picture or a love letter.

She opened the book and found dozens of pictures of her when she was an infant. She was swaddled in a pink blanket and wore a big pink bow. In other pictures, she was in a crib with purple polka-dot sheets and a stuffed bear propped in the corner. She flipped the pages, surprised that her mother had chronicled her development.

There was her first Christmas where she was sitting on Santa's lap, then Easter in a pretty yellow dress and bonnet. Her first birthday where she'd dug her whole pudgy little hand into the cake. And Halloween when she dressed up like a unicorn.

The pictures continued, marking her first year, then second, third and fourth. The day she'd gotten her first soccer ball, her jump rope, swinging at the park, her first missing tooth.

Her heart stuttered at the sight of a picture of her mother cradling her and rocking her. The tender look on her mother's face was not one Macy remembered.

But her eyes glowed with love and affection.

A well of sadness opened up inside Macy, and tears blurred her eyes. Macy struggled to recall those moments when she looked happy and loved. But the pictures stopped abruptly at age five, and so had any pleasant memories.

Had her mother loved her at one time?

If so, what had happened to make her stop?

STONE CLENCHED HIS jaw as the interview with him and Macy replayed on the news. That damn Gretta Wright was such a pain in the butt. He hoped she didn't destroy Macy.

"Police are now looking for a 2020 navy blue Jeep Cherokee which was stolen this afternoon from an RV park. They suspect that a woman named Lynn Stark took the vehicle after escaping the psychiatric facility where she is undergoing treatment. Ms. Stark owns the house where the body was found in the wall by her daughter, Special Agent Macy Stark, and is wanted for questioning in what they believe was a homicide."

He glanced at his deputy. "Where the hell does she get her information?"

Murphy shrugged, then looked back at his computer. "People talk. Can't hide the truth from the public."

Stone narrowed his eyes. "Did you tell her?"

His deputy shook his head. "It's a small town, Sheriff. The residents have a right to know if a criminal is on the streets."

Stone stiffened. "First of all, we don't know that Lynn Stark had anything to do with the corpse or even with the murder itself. And we are not going to accuse someone publicly without evidence."

Murphy made a clicking sound with his teeth. "All the more reason to use every resource to get the word out so we can find her."

His lungs squeezed for air. Murphy was right, although sympathy for Macy welled inside him.

You can't let that stop you from doing your job.

"You think Macy knows what happened and just isn't talking?" Murphy asked.

Stone swallowed hard. "The man has been dead over twenty-five years," he said. "Macy would have been a little girl then. So no, I don't think she knows. She was in shock when she called me and I got to the house."

The chair creaked as Murphy leaned back in it. "Maybe so. But the real question is would she cover for her now? For all we know, she could help her mother hide out. With her experience as an agent, she'd know how to do it."

Stone didn't like the direction of the conversation. "Do not go around stirring up those kinds of questions," he snapped. "Macy has enough on her shoulders without gossip."

"I'm not," Murphy said. "But people are going to wonder."

Stone's temper flared. His deputy was right. But he didn't like it. "Because she's had psychological issues, she also would be a good scapegoat."

"True," Murphy said. "But hard to believe she was living in that house and didn't know a dead man was in the wall."

"Let's just concentrate on doing the job and finding her," Stone said.

Hopefully Forensics would have something useful to add, too. Concrete evidence, not just speculation.

His gut churned as he stood. He didn't like the doubts creeping through his mind. Macy did have secrets. And a troubled past with her mother.

She'd gone to the house, and he hadn't heard back from her. What if her mother had shown up?

He had no idea if she'd hurt Macy or not.

He pulled his keys from his pocket. He'd take a ride out there and see what was happening.

EMOTIONS CLOGGED HER throat as Macy closed the photo album. There was nothing of her father inside, although now she knew that at one time her mother had a tender side for her.

Next she opened the box and realized it held items from her childhood. The pink baby blanket. The little white teddy bear. Several hair bows, frilly socks and a pair of black patent leather toddler shoes.

Faded tissue paper had been wrapped around other

items. She pulled it away and found two dresses that looked as if they'd been hand smocked.

A memory tickled her conscience—her mother humming along with the buzz of a sewing machine. Fabric swatches littering a table. Her standing on the table while her mother pinned the hem of the Easter dress she was making.

The memory disappeared as quickly as it had come, and an image of her mother screaming at her because she spilled milk on the floor took shape. Then her mother threatening to spank her with a switch she cut from the cherry tree out back. She was six at the time, and she'd run and hidden in the closet, terrified of a beating.

A knock on the front door startled her, and she set the dresses back inside the box and hurried to the living room. She half hoped it was her mother so they could talk, but her mother wouldn't knock. And if she was on the run and off her meds, she might be incoherent.

Bracing herself in case it was her and she was in one of her irrational states, she checked through the window.

Stone stood on the other side. "Macy?"

Relieved, she exhaled and opened the door. The rain had stopped, but the sky was still dark, the clouds ominous, and the wind shook raindrops from the trees.

"Did you find that Jeep?" Macy asked.

"Not yet. Gretta is running it on the news."

Her mouth tightened at the mention of the reporter's name. "I thought I saw someone in the woods earlier and gave chase but didn't catch up. If it was my mother, she could have parked the Jeep somewhere and then sneaked up through the back."

"We'll find it and her," Stone assured her as he stepped inside.

"There was also a sedan that slowed in front of the

drive. I didn't see the driver, so it may have been nothing. But she could have ditched the Jeep and changed vehicles."

Stone shifted. "Did you get the license plate of the sedan?"

"It was too dark, and the lights were blinding." She shrugged. "Of course since the news ran, there's bound to be curiosity seekers driving by. And with school on summer break, I half expect teenagers to try to come in and get a peek. Just the kind of dare they might pull."

"True. I can post a guard here if you want to protect the property."

Macy scrunched her nose, considering it. "I don't think that's necessary. There's nothing valuable here. But maybe the night deputy should do routine drive-bys to prevent vandalism or in case my mother shows up."

"I'll put him on it," Stone agreed. "You know you can't stay here. Now the news aired, if your mother didn't kill the man, whoever did could come back."

"I know. I'm going to take another look downstairs and then head to the inn for the night."

Stone's eyes darkened. "You sure you want to do that?"

"I have to make sure we didn't miss anything."

He studied her for a long minute. "I'll go downstairs with you."

Reluctantly she agreed. Clenching her flashlight with a clammy hand, she inhaled a deep breath and made her way to the basement door. The wood floor creaked as Stone followed her down the rickety stairs. The stench of death blended with the moldy smell, and she had to drag in a breath to stem the nausea.

"If this man has been here over twenty-five years, you would have been about five to eight years old at the time," Stone said out loud.

Macy nodded, but his voice faded as the sudden sound of pouring rain beat down and she was launched back in time.

"MACY?" STONE STUDIED HER pale face, then quickly realized her mind was somewhere else.

"My mother never let me come down here," she said in a distant voice. "She kept it locked and said it was off-limits."

"Did she explain why?" Stone asked.

She shook her head, reached the bottom of the staircase, then paused and stared at the hole in the wall.

The plaster had been rotting when she'd found the body, but after dusting it for prints and taking trace samples, it had been ripped apart in sections for the recovery team to remove the skeleton.

"Just that there were rats down here," Macy murmured.

Maybe she had meant human ones.

"I used to have nightmares about them crawling through the eaves of the house and vents and dropping from the ceiling."

Stone held his tongue. While Macy had been having nightmares, he'd been camping and fishing with his father and Mickey. They'd had a good childhood with loving parents until the high school shooting blew up their lives.

The urge to comfort Macy tugged at him. "Maybe she was protecting you by warning you away from down here."

"Maybe," Macy said, although she didn't sound convinced, making him wonder what secrets she'd kept.

The ties between parent and child ran strong. Kids craved love and would forgive and forget in order to get it. Some children of abusive parents or ones with addictions and mental diseases often lied to cover for their folks. He'd seen it on the job a couple of times on domestic calls when he'd had to call social services, and he felt for those kids.

Had Macy lied and covered for hers? Would she do so again now if she thought her mother was guilty of murder?

"You said you didn't know your father, didn't you?" he asked quietly.

"I didn't," Macy said. "She never told me his name. I assumed if he didn't want me, why should I care?"

As much as she presented a tough front, he heard the hurt in her voice. Not knowing had to have eaten at her.

"Have you seen your birth certificate?"

"Yeah, I found it in the desk. But my father's name is not listed on it."

"Was your mother always ill?"

Macy looked at him, confusion in her eyes. "I thought so, at least as far back as I can remember. But…now I don't know."

"Why do you say that?"

Macy heaved a breath. "Because I found a photo album filled with pictures of me when I was little. Shots of me on holidays and birthdays and one of her holding me with love in her eyes."

Dammit. Not only had her father been absent and she'd thought he didn't want her, but she'd thought her mother didn't love her.

"I'm sorry, Macy. It sounds like you had it really hard…"

She lifted her chin. "I don't want your sympathy, Stone. I want to know what the hell happened. I can't leave here until I do."

Chapter Nine

Macy battled her emotions. Kate was the only one who'd ever witnessed her mother's erratic behavior and how terrified she'd been as a child.

Exposing her painful secrets to Stone made her feel more vulnerable than she'd ever felt in her life.

But she had to face the truth, no matter what it was.

If her mother was guilty of homicide, she'd deal with it. If she was innocent, she needed Macy's help.

"Your mother was young back then. Did she have a boyfriend or date anyone?"

"You heard the rumors," Macy said. "My mother was crazy. What man would want to deal with that?"

Stone walked over and rubbed her arm, forcing her to look at him. "I know she was troubled, Macy. But that doesn't mean she didn't have male friends. Even if it was no one serious, do you remember a man coming around here? Someone she may have been involved with, even if it was just for a night or two here and there?"

Macy rubbed her temple. "She did bring a couple of men home, but I never met them." Because her mother had either locked her in the closet or thrown her outside while she entertained.

"Did she leave you with a sitter or go out when you were playing at a friend's?"

Macy's throat closed. "I didn't have playdates, Stone. At five, my mother was a mess. When she was home, she didn't spend time with me or drive me to see a friend. And I never wanted anyone to come over."

A muscle ticked in his jaw. "Because you didn't want them to see what was going on?"

"Exactly." Refusing to keep diving into her humiliating past, she turned and ran up the stairs. The only one who knew and had seen the truth was Kate.

But soon everyone was going to know.

STONE FOLLOWED MACY back up the stairs to the kitchen and found her leaning her hands on the counter and drawing in a deep breath.

"I know this is difficult," he said. "We should call it a night and start fresh tomorrow."

She nodded. "Maybe the ME will have an ID on the body then."

"Hopefully so." Then he could get to the bottom of this case and give Macy some peace. Only finding the truth might do the opposite.

"Did your mom have any close friends she might have confided in?"

Macy made a wry sound. "I don't remember her having any friends. Ever."

"How about her folks?"

"My grandparents died before I was born."

So Macy had had no one except an unstable mother.

"What about a job?"

"She managed to put food on the table by cleaning houses for folks around town."

"Do you know who she worked for?"

Macy shook her head. "I heard her mention a couple of names. But she kept a calendar somewhere to keep up with her jobs. I think I saw it when I was cleaning out her things."

"Did you throw it away?"

"No. There were other papers in there and I decided I'd tackle it later in case there was something important in the paperwork." She went to the desk in the corner, opened the top drawer and removed a folder and then several day planners. They dated back fifteen years but stopped about five years ago.

"Let me take these and I'll make a list of names of people we can talk to," Macy said.

"Let's divide them," Stone suggested. "We can meet tomorrow and start following up."

Macy hesitated. "If you don't mind, I'd like to look through them myself first. There might be something in there that will jog my memories."

Stone shifted onto the balls of his feet. "As long as you share what you find, Macy."

Anger flared in her eyes. "Don't worry. I intend to face whatever happens."

Stone wanted to reach out and comfort her. But held his hand back. "It's natural to have allegiance to your mother," he said softly.

Pain streaked Macy's face. "It's complicated," Macy said. "But I'll do whatever needs to be done."

He gave a nod. He just hoped the truth didn't destroy her.

THE NEXT MORNING Macy got up early and skimmed through the calendars her mother had kept, jotting down the names of the people her mother had cleaned for. She had no idea how many of them still lived in Briar Ridge, but there were seven names within a five-year time span of when the man in the wall would have been murdered, so she focused on those first.

She needed to discuss the list with Stone, but first she met Kate and Brynn for breakfast at Daisy's Diner. Whispers and stares told her that the rumor mill hadn't missed a beat. And now she and her mysterious mother and their connection to a murder were at the heart of it.

Her friends had already ordered a pot of coffee and platter of assorted pastries for the table. They both gave her tentative smiles when she slid into the booth to join them.

"How are you doing?" Kate asked as Macy poured herself a cup of coffee from the pot.

"As well as I can," Macy said honestly.

Brynn stirred sweetener into her tea. "Did you get any sleep?"

Macy shrugged. "Not much." And when she'd finally drifted off, she'd had fitful nightmares of the bones and the man's deep, hollow eye sockets.

"Why don't you come and stay with me while you're here?" Kate offered.

Macy shook her head. "I'm not going to impose on either of you," Macy said. "Besides, aren't you and Riggs planning your wedding?"

A sheepish grin tugged at Kate's mouth. "We're starting to," Kate admitted. "We've set a date for end of summer and decided to have it outdoors at the Bear Mountain Resort."

"That's so exciting," Macy said. "I'm really happy for you."

Brynn squeezed Kate's shoulder. "You deserve it, Kate."

Kate pulled both their hands into hers. "We all deserve to be happy. And Macy, you could never impose. We're spit sisters, remember?"

A blush climbed Macy's neck as she recalled the three of them spitting into their hands and rubbing them together. "Thanks, both of you. But I'm okay, really. I'm staying at the inn, which is lovely now it's been redone. And part of that is due to you, Kate, and the rebuilding of the high school."

Kate looked sheepish. "I'm just glad folks in town are renovating and sprucing up their businesses. The town has been depressed for too long."

"I hope finding this body doesn't send everyone back into a spin," Macy said.

"Don't worry about that," Brynn said. "Just tell us how we can help."

Macy squeezed their hands, then thanked them and reached for her coffee, inhaling the rich pecan scent. They all dived into the pastries then as more customers slipped into the diner. Two older women stared at her while a couple of her former classmates she'd seen at the recent reunion gave her sympathetic looks.

She ignored them and finished her coffee, anxious to leave. "I'm meeting Stone at his office in a few minutes," she said as she waved the waitress over for the check. "Last night I found my mother's cleaning calendar. We're going to talk to her employers and see if she shared personal information with them."

Kate grabbed the check and wagged her finger at Macy, indicating she was covering the bill. "Do you have any idea who the dead man is?"

"Not yet," Macy said. "You know my mother never had a serious boyfriend."

"But she brought men home sometimes, didn't she?" Kate asked.

Macy shuddered. "A few times, but I stayed away from them."

Brynn bit down on her bottom lip. "Macy, I hate to suggest this, but…do you think it could be your father? That maybe he came by one night and he and your mother argued, and something happened between them?"

STONE DROPPED BY to check on his brother on the way to his office. But Mickey slammed the door in his face and told him to butt out of his business. He also smelled like booze again.

A sense of foreboding overcame him. He was losing his little brother. Hell, he'd been losing him for years.

And he had no idea what to do about it.

Gray rain clouds drifted across the sky as he parked at the sheriff's office. The moment he stepped inside, his deputy looked up at him. "Tip came in. That stolen Jeep was spotted at a gas station near the motel off the main highway. I was going to check it out."

"Go home and get some rest. I know you did drive-bys last night at the Stark house. See anything?"

Murphy shook his head. "Just a couple of teenage boys looking through the windows. I warned 'em that place is a crime scene and if they or any of their friends went inside, I'd lock 'em up."

Murphy was a big guy with a deep baritone voice. Couple that with his badge and gruff exterior, he could put the fear of God in someone with just one look.

Stone thanked him, then texted Macy about the Jeep. She responded saying she'd be there in five minutes, so he went to his office and phoned the ME. "Dr. Anderson, do you have an ID for me?"

"Not yet," she said. "I sent DNA to the lab and am waiting on results. I'll let you know as soon as I do."

He pulled up the CSI team's report and skimmed their notes. Several pairs of fingerprints upstairs, only two downstairs. Hair and fibers of various sorts, which were being analyzed. No guns in the house. They had found the knife set on the kitchen counter and were analyzing those for blood, but they had not found the missing knife.

Was that the murder weapon?

A knock sounded, then Macy poked her head in the doorway. "Stone?"

"Yeah, let's go." He stood, grabbed his keys and they rushed outside to his squad car.

"Where is the Jeep?" Macy asked.

"It was spotted at a gas station near a motel on the highway heading toward Bear Mountain Resort." The morning sun splintered through the storm clouds, beating down on the pavement.

Families were already gathering at the park, kids playing chase on the playground, walkers and joggers taking advantage of the temperature before the heat rose today. Already signs had been posted advertising the Fourth of July parade and festival planned for the holiday celebration. Arts-and-crafts booths, face painting for the children, a bicycle parade for kids who decorated their bikes, floats, and food trucks would provide entertainment for the day, and a stage had been set up for music guests. Come dark, they would have a fireworks show.

He flipped on his siren to maneuver past the slower traffic. If Macy's mother was in that Jeep, and if she'd seen the news, she might be on her way out of town. They passed farmland as he exited the city limits and he wound around the mountain road for three miles, then turned right at the fork onto the highway leading toward the resort.

Another mile down the road, and he reached the gas station. It was connected to a convenience store, but the Jeep was not in the parking lot.

"She could be miles and miles from here by now," Macy said.

Stone parked and opened his car door. "Let's go see what the store clerk has to say."

Macy got out and they walked up to the door together, then went inside. A family with toddler twins was checking out at the register, armed with fruit drinks and snacks.

Stone waited until they finished paying, then stepped up to the register. A kid in his twenties with a tattoo of a tiger on his forearm looked up at them.

Stone identified himself. "I got a call that someone spotted at 2020 navy blue Jeep here."

"Yeah, that was me," the kid said. "Saw on the news you were looking for it."

"When was it you saw the Jeep?"

"Last night about six. But I didn't see the news till this morning. Soon as I did, I called."

"Did you see who was driving it?" Macy asked.

The young man tugged at his earring. "Looked like a woman, but I didn't see her face. Gassed up, used the john and sped away."

The bell on the door tinkled and another family entered, fanning out to comb the aisles for their beverage and snack choices. A guy in his forties followed them in, walked straight to the refrigerated section and grabbed a twelve-pack of beer.

"Do you have security cameras?" Stone asked.

The boy coughed into his hands. "No, manager said we don't need 'em."

You never needed them until there was a crime, Stone thought wryly.

"Which direction did the driver go when she left?" Macy said.

The kid pointed north toward the resort and the stretch where he knew there was a motel, and Stone and Macy hurried to his car. Stone peeled from the parking lot knowing every minute counted.

If Macy's mother had stayed at the motel, maybe she was still there.

Chapter Ten

Macy's nerves teetered on the edge as Stone sped north. The mountains rose with stiff peaks and ridges; rustic cabins and houses perched on hills that overlooked the creek and river.

The motel looked outdated and sat off the road near a truck stop. Mud splattered the concrete structure, and the low windows were coated with grime.

She cringed at the idea of her mother staying here, hiding out like a common criminal.

Stone parked in front of the motel entrance, and she scanned the parking lot. Two pickup trucks, a Range Rover, another truck with a pop-up camper and a minivan. The navy blue Jeep was parked at the end of the row of motel rooms in plain sight.

"Stay in the car," Stone said softly. "Let me handle this."

She shook her head and reached for the door handle. "If my mother is here, she might respond better to me than you."

His brows arched as if he wondered if she was playing him, but he refrained from expressing his doubts out loud.

"Let's split up," she said. "Go talk to the desk clerk, see what you can find out and get a key. I'll stake out the room in case she's holed up in there and spots us and tries to run."

"Are you sure about this, Macy?" Stone asked.

Her gaze met his, the questions in his eyes haunting her. She thought she'd earned his trust and respect when they'd worked together recently, but if she were in his shoes, she might ask the same questions.

"I'm not going to let her get away or help her escape," she said. "I told you. I want to know what happened in that house." And if her mother was a murderer.

He exhaled, then headed for the entrance. Macy shut the car door as quietly as possible, then eased toward the front side of the building and crept along the wall of rooms. Two families exited their rooms, children chatting excitedly about their plans to go swimming for the day.

Senses honed, she glanced all around her and inside the rooms with open curtains and saw two rooms were empty. In the other one, a couple was watching TV. She crept toward the Jeep and peeked inside, but there was no one in the vehicle. The Jeep belonged to a family who'd been camping, and hiking gear had been stowed in the back.

Nothing to indicate her mother had been in there. Although her mother had run from her room to escape, and they had no indication that she'd taken anything with her.

She moved to the next room and noted the curtains were closed so she couldn't see inside. Knowing there were no back door exits, she raised her fist and knocked on the door. "Housekeeping."

She stepped to the side of the door, tapping her foot as she waited and listening for sounds of someone inside. The cheap rooms had window air conditioners, and the hum of it was so loud that if anyone were inside, the machine might drown out the sound.

"Housekeeping, I have clean towels," she said as she knocked again.

Again no one answered, so she jiggled the door, but it was locked.

She decided to try a different tactic and knocked once more. "Mom, it's me, Macy. If you're in there, please open up."

STONE IDENTIFIED HIMSELF to the desk clerk, a sixty-something man named Everett. His gray hair was thinning; his teeth were stained yellow from years of smoking, his hands pocked with age spots.

"We had a call about that navy Jeep out there," Stone said. "It was stolen yesterday. Did you see who was driving it?"

The man adjusted his thick Coke-bottle glasses. "Some lady, I think."

Stone showed him a picture of Macy's mother, although it was an older photo Macy had given him when the woman was ten years younger. "Was this the woman?"

Everett squinted as he studied it. "I can't say for sure. Eyes ain't what they used to be."

Judging from the man's thick glasses, Stone had expected as much. "How about checking the registry? The woman we're looking for is Lynn Stark."

He ran a hand over his bald spot, then glanced at the registry. "Don't see that name here."

"She could have checked in under a different name. Look for a woman traveling alone."

He checked again, then shook his head. "Got a couple of families and group of hikers. Four empty rooms." He tapped the desk with his finger. "Oh, someone did report a noise in room eight on the end, but nobody was in that room."

Ms. Stark could have broken in and spent the night there.

"Can I take a look at that room?"

"I reckon so." He hobbled around the desk with a metal key ring. He handed Stone the keys. "I'd show you, but my arthritis is acting up this morning. Knees hurting. Just bring the keys back when you're finished."

Stone nodded, then took the ring of keys and strode back outside. He glanced at each room as he passed but saw nothing suspicious although decided to check the empty ones after he looked in room eight.

He found Macy outside the room. "No single female registered. Desk clerk said there was a noise in this room last night but no one registered."

"I knocked but no one answered," Macy said.

Stone inserted the key and turned the lock. The door squeaked as he opened it and looked inside. At first glance, no one was inside.

Macy crept into the doorway and flipped on a light. The room was early eighties decor with a queen bed draped in an orange floral bedspread that was tangled from where someone had slept in it.

"Someone was here," Macy said.

"Looks that way." Stone strode to the bathroom and glanced inside. "Whoever was here took a shower. Towel is wet, and shampoo and soap have been used."

Macy heaved a breath. "If it was my mom, she broke in and slept here last night. Then she ditched the Jeep."

"There's one way to find out," Stone said. "I'll call a forensic team to dust for prints."

Macy rubbed her temple. "The question is—where is she now?"

WHILE THE CSI team processed room eight, Macy and Stone checked the other rooms but found nothing suspicious. She told the investigator to compare DNA and prints from the room to the ones at her mother's house.

On the way back to town, Macy and Stone stopped at Pearl's Pie & Dine for lunch and to plan their next move. Macy ordered the special, chicken and dumplings, while

Stone ordered meat loaf, then they finished off the meal with fresh peach cobbler and vanilla ice cream.

"Did you look through your mother's calendars?" Stone asked.

Macy washed the delicious, sweet fruity dessert down with coffee, then pulled the list of names from her phone.

"Yes. I made a list of people she was working for around the time of the man's death," she said. "There are eight names, but I don't know how many of these folks still live around Briar Ridge."

"Let's go through them, and I'll see if I can help."

Macy took another sip of coffee before she began. "First there's a woman named Beverly Jones."

"Miss Beverly still lives on Main Street," Stone said. "She's in her seventies now, sings in the church choir, makes blankets for the children's hospital."

"She sounds special," Macy said.

"Yeah, everyone in town loves her." Stone pushed his empty plate away and wiped his mouth. "Who else?"

"Pat and Ken Dansing."

"They moved away years ago to Charleston, South Carolina, to be closer to their daughter and her family. If we need to, I can find a way to get in touch with them."

Macy shrugged. "May be worth a phone call. Next is Troy and Shirley Cregan."

"Troy and Shirley run the local butcher shop."

Macy nodded. "Dodie Lewis?"

"Sorry to say Dodie passed away a while back. Cancer."

Macy deleted her name. "What about Loretta Pruitt?"

Stone whistled. "Loretta's still around. She used to run the day care in town, but she's retired now."

"Vicki Germaine?"

"Property manager for those cabins on the creek."

Macy drummed her fingers on the table. "Last one is

Adeline and Prentice Walkman." Macy hesitated. "Prentice Walkman—he's running for senate, isn't he?"

Stone pulled a hand down his chin. "Yes. They haven't lived here in ages. Sad story there. They had a son, but he got hit by a car when he was seven. They moved after that. I guess it was just too painful for them to stay."

"I can understand that," Macy said. After all, she'd run from Briar Ridge to escape her own painful memories.

STONE PAID THE bill and drove Macy to Beverly Jones's house, a small craftsman bungalow that looked as inviting as the sweet lady who lived there.

She leaned on her cane as she opened the door and invited them in, then offered them iced tea, but he was still full from lunch and Macy politely declined.

She led them through the entryway past a craft room to the right where shelves held baskets of colorful yarn and a table was laden with blankets she'd already knitted for the hospital. The living room was cozy with a couch and a rocking chair, which was where Ms. Beverly sat, her knitting needles and a work in progress in the basket beside the chair.

Her wavy hair was white, her body trim, her smile tentative as if she knew the reason for their visit.

"I saw the news." Beverly's eyes glimmered with compassion when she looked at Macy. "I know you've been through a lot, dear. That must have been some shock."

"It was," Macy said softly. "We're trying to figure out what happened. I found a list of people my mother used to clean for and your name was on it. I was hoping you could tell me more about her."

Beverly picked up the blanket and began working the knitting needles as if she needed to do something with her hands. "Lordy, that was a long time ago. My Lamar and I had just been married two years when we moved here. He worked at the factory, and I had a job as a secretary. I met your mama at the thrift store. She was trying to buy you some baby clothes but was short on money. So I offered her a job and let her clean once every couple of weeks." A faraway look settled in her eyes. "You were just a baby, Macy. She brought you with her."

Macy's mouth tightened. "How was she back then?"

The older woman's eyes lips twitched with a tiny smile. "She was good. Doted on you, she did. Was always stopping and kissing all over you."

"Really?"

"Surely did," Beverly said. "Didn't want to leave you for a second."

Macy inhaled sharply, the pain in that sound tearing at Stone. What had happened to make her mother's behavior change?

"Did she ever mention my father to you?" Macy asked.

Beverly shook her head. "No, and I didn't ask. Didn't figure it was any of my business."

"So you don't know if she had a man in her life or if she was dating anyone?"

"No, all she talked about was you, dear." Beverly set her needles down with a sigh. "Then my Lamar lost his job and took sick, and I had to let her go. I hated it, but I couldn't afford to keep her." She reached out and squeezed Macy's hand. "I'm sorry I can't tell you more. I gave her name to a couple of other folks, though, and they hired her. Then later I heard rumors about how she was acting out, leaving you alone at all times of the night, how she got volatile with Shirley Cregan, and I couldn't believe it. That wasn't the Lynn I knew."

Macy's breath whispered out, anguish riddling it. "Did you talk to them? Did they tell you anything that might have triggered a change in her?"

Beverly shook her head. "I wish I knew. If I had, maybe I could have helped her."

MACY THANKED BEVERLY, a bittersweet feeling flooding her. The Lynn Beverly described was the one she'd seen in those early photographs of the two of them.

So what had happened to turn her into a monster of a mother?

"I know this is hard, Macy," Stone said when they settled into his car. "I can handle the other interviews if you need to take a break."

"Thanks, Stone, but I need to hear what these people have to say. Who's next?"

"Let's talk to the Cregans."

Macy pulled her tablet from the seat. "I'll see if I can locate the Dansings' phone number while you drive."

Stone turned onto Main Street and drove toward the butcher shop, which was located on the opposite side of the town square. Macy searched DMV records in Charleston and by the time they reached the butcher shop, she had a phone number.

She called the number, and it rang four times, then went to voice mail. She left a message asking them to call her, then hung up just as Stone parked. The butcher shop was in a concrete building that had just gotten a fresh coat of white paint. A middle-aged couple was leaving as they entered, carrying a bag of meat.

For a brief second, Macy wished for that normalcy instead of a life revolving around murder.

The bell over the door tinkled as they entered. A glass-enclosed case faced them, full of various assorted cuts of beef, poultry and pork. A refrigerated case to the side held fresh and frozen meats along with premade meals for easy pickup.

A chunky man with thick silver hair wearing a butcher's apron was working behind the counter while a thin brunette woman in an apron was restocking a basket holding freshly baked bread for sale. The couple looked to be midfifties.

Stone headed to the counter to talk to the man while Macy approached the woman. "Mrs. Cregan? I'm Special Agent Macy Stark."

She nearly dropped a loaf of bread but managed to hang on to it. "I know who you are."

Or course she did. Between the news and the rumor mill, everyone in town knew she and the sheriff were investigating the mysterious skeletal remains.

"Is there some place we can talk?" Macy glanced at the door, where two men were lumbering in.

"Sure. Troy can handle it out here." She motioned for Macy to follow her into the back, and Stone stepped to the side as the men reached the meat counter. The woman looked at her warily as they settled into chairs in a small office that was cluttered with paperwork.

"I'd like to ask you some questions."

Mrs. Cregan cut her eyes away as if nervous. "I don't know anything about that body, if that's why you're here."

"I understand," Macy said. "My mother disappeared from the psychiatric facility where she was undergoing treatment?"

Mrs. Cregan nodded. "Yes, I heard."

Macy gritted her teeth. "I found my mother's work calendars when I was cleaning out her house," Macy said. "And I saw that she used to clean for you." According to the dates, Macy would have been seven at the time.

"She did for a short while."

"Do you know if she was seeing anyone? Did she ever talk about a man, maybe problems with someone?"

Mrs. Cregan shook her head. "I'm afraid not. But like I said, she just worked for us a short while. Weeks, really."

From her tense tone, Macy detected there had been trouble. "What happened?"

The woman looked down at her hands. "I don't want to talk bad about your mother, Macy."

"Trust me, I haven't worn blinders with her since I was little. I know she had issues. Just tell me what happened."

The woman sighed. "We noticed that she acted erratic sometimes and wasn't always reliable. Showed up sometimes on time and other times didn't show at all. One time the house would be neat and clean, but once it looked as if it had been ransacked."

"That sounds about right. She's bipolar," Macy said.

"Then Troy caught her stealing some of the Hydrocodone he took for his back after he had infusion surgery. We had to let her go then."

Macy took a deep breath. "I'm sorry, Mrs. Cregan. I appreciate your honesty."

The woman squeezed Macy's hand. "I hope you find her and figure out what happened. Things like that can haunt a person."

She had no idea how truly haunted Macy was.

Chapter Eleven

Stone followed Macy to the car, disturbed by the things Troy Cregan had painted of her mother.

Judging from the tight expression on her face, it hadn't gone well with Troy's wife, either. "Macy?"

"She said my mother only worked for them a short time, that she became unreliable. Sometimes cleaned, then sometimes left the house in chaos. They caught her stealing pain meds and let her go." She turned to Stone. "What did Troy say?"

"Do you really want to know?"

Macy crossed her arms. "Stone, I lived with the woman. Nothing you can say is going to surprise me."

He cleared his throat. "He said the same thing, only he wasn't quite so nice about it. Said when he confronted your mother, she became belligerent, picked up a fire poker and swung it at him."

"Good God," Macy said. "Did he report it to the sheriff?"

That would have been Stone's father. "Said he threatened to if she ever came back to their house. Before she left, though, she overturned furniture and broke lamps."

Macy turned to look back at the butcher shop as he pulled from the drive. "She was lucky they didn't press charges."

Stone's heart squeezed for her. "Let me talk to the others. You don't have to put yourself through this."

"Yes, I do," she said stubbornly. "I can't possibly rest until I know the truth about what happened in that house." She massaged her temple, and he turned onto the side street, then drove to Loretta Pruitt's house. She lived across from the Love 'n Learn Day Care, which she'd run for thirty years but had retired two years ago, and her daughter had taken over the business.

Five minutes later, they knocked on Loretta's door. The plump woman greeted them with the same smile she graced everyone with. She'd never met a stranger and volunteered at the pet rescue shelter, as evidenced by the three cats stretching lazily on the furniture as she invited them in. In the kitchen, she insisted they have a glass of homemade lemonade.

Stone introduced Macy, but Loretta waved off the introduction. "I remember you from when you were little," she said. "Your mother used to clean the day care for me. Brought you along with her. You used to love playing with the blocks and puzzles. Wasn't much into dolls, though."

A tiny smile flitted in Macy's eyes. "That's true. I was more of a tomboy. Into sports."

Loretta fluttered a hand to her chest. "I'm so sorry to hear your mother hasn't been well these last few years."

Macy's expression softened. "Thank you. Most people aren't so kind."

Loretta took Macy's hand. "We're supposed to love our neighbors and help them when they need it."

Macy pursed her lips, her eyes watering. "Thank you again. Can you tell me what you remember about her?"

Loretta sipped her lemonade. "What do you want to know?"

"How was she when she worked for you? And how old was I?"

The woman frowned. "You were about four, if I remember right. Your mama seemed real sweet, a little shy and nervous sometimes, but she took good care of you. At least back then." Her voice cracked. "Later, I heard she left you alone too much. Once when you were about six, I saw her screaming at you in the park. Then she went off and left you."

Stone didn't like the picture he saw in his mind. So far two people described her as loving and kind when Macy was small. But her behavior had become more disturbing, bordering on abusive.

Or *had* it been abusive?

What exactly had gone on behind closed doors?

MACY'S PHONE BUZZED as she and Stone left Loretta's. Pat Dansing's name appeared on the screen, so she answered and put her on Speaker. She didn't want Stone to accuse her of hiding anything.

Stone steered the car in the direction of the cabins on the creek while she explained the reason for her call.

"Yes, I remember your mother," Pat said, her tone cautious.

"She worked for you for a while?" Macy asked.

"Yes, but not for long."

"What happened?" Macy asked. "And please be candid, Mrs. Dansing. She's missing right now, and anything I can learn about her may help find her."

"The truth was that your mother scared my daughter."

Macy's stomach knotted. "What happened?"

"Lucy was five," Pat said. "She was about the same age as you, Macy. We owned the hardware store, and when Ken was out on a buying trip, Lucy would come to the store with me. One day you came in with your mama, and Lucy wanted to play with you, but you touched some of the tools and your mama went crazy. She locked you in the bathroom and started screaming and wouldn't let you out."

Pat hesitated.

"Go on," Macy said.

"Lucy was terrified and crying. Finally, Ken got there, and he unlocked the door and threatened to call DFACS. She dragged you out of there." Her voice trembled. "I…had to calm Lucy down, and Ken told your mother she couldn't come back. But… I…we should have called DFACS right then, but Ken was afraid of what she'd do to retaliate, that she might hurt Lucy." She released a strangled sound. "I've never forgiven myself for not calling and reporting her, though."

Macy swallowed back emotions. "It's not your fault," she said softly. "Social services did come out a few times, but my mother could put on a good act, and they just dismissed it."

The damn system was flawed, Macy thought. Kids got lost in it all the time. Shuffled around from one foster home to another. Sent back to abusive homes where the abuser exercised their anger at being reported on the child.

Thank God for Kate and her mother.

"Mrs. Dansing, did you ever see my mother with a man or hear about her dating someone?"

"No," the woman replied. "After that day, I never talked to her. Truth be told, I avoided her and you. I was too ashamed."

STONE SCRUBBED A hand down his face. They had to keep checking with everyone on the list. Vicki Germaine was next.

But he didn't know how much more he could stand to hear. The picture of Macy as a little girl being abused made him clench the steering wheel in a white-knuckle grip.

Anger churned through him as he maneuvered the switchbacks and climbed the steep incline winding around the mountain. The cabins offered scenic views of the countryside and valley below and private nooks for roman-

tic getaways or families wishing to escape the hustle and
bustle of the city.

He turned onto the winding narrow road that led to the
rental office, Macy's silence worrying him. So many of
their classmates and their families had fallen apart after
the school shooting.

But how had she survived her mother's mental instabil-
ity and not caved beneath the weight of it and the school
massacre?

His admiration for her rose notches.

He parked at the rental office, and Macy climbed out in
silence, the weight of what she'd heard today obviously sitting heavily on her shoulders. An SUV was parked in front,
but the family came out of the building with keys and left.

Together he and Macy walked up to the entrance and
ducked inside. Pamphlets for tourist activities including
scenic mountain sights, biking and hiking tours, white-
water rafting and seasonal festivities filled a wall on one
side. Maps of the area occupied another and Vicki Germaine, a white-haired lady with bright green eyes stood
behind the reception desk.

"Vicki," Stone said in way of greeting. "This is Special
Agent Macy Stark."

"I figured you might show up at some point," Vicki said,

Five minutes later, they were seated in a break room
with Vicki sipping coffee while a young girl named Tory
manned the desk. Stone explained about the investigation, and Macy relayed that she needed to know about her
mother when she worked for the rental company.

"That was a long time ago," Vicki said. "But I do remember her."

Stone ground his teeth as Macy asked about Vicki's experience with her mother.

"Lynn Stark was a troubled woman," Vicki said. "She

was like two different people. Sometimes she did a good job, and I needed the help, but I had to let her go."

"Why?" Macy asked. "Was she stealing? Doing drugs? Violent?"

Vicki shook her head. "When we had a free room, she used it to bring her lovers there."

Macy's face paled. "Her lovers?"

Vicki nodded. "Don't know any of their names. But one of the handymen walked in on her, and she went off on him. I let her go the next day."

"Is this handyman still around?" Stone asked.

Vicki shook her head. "Passed away last year. Car accident."

"And you had no idea who any of the men were?" Stone asked.

Vicki shook her head. "I never saw them. She always made sure to use a room that wasn't booked and cleaned it so I wouldn't find out."

One of those men could be Macy's father. Or the corpse in the wall in her house.

Stone thanked Vicki, and he and Macy walked back to his car.

"My mother was a piece of work, wasn't she?" Macy muttered as she fastened her seat belt.

Stone made a low sound in his throat. "She was ill," he said. "That doesn't excuse her behavior, but she wasn't in her right mind when she did some of the things she did." Still, Macy had suffered. "It sounds like she loved you as a baby."

Was that enough to make up for the pain and suffering she'd caused Macy the rest of her life?

MACY CLOSED HER EYES, her mind swirling with confusion. If her mother had multiple lovers, maybe she didn't know who had fathered Macy. And any one of them could have come to the house, had an altercation with her mother and ended up dead.

She had a sinking feeling the changes in her mother's behavior had to do with what happened at her house that rainy night.

She struggled to recall her mother mentioning a man, but she'd kept that part of her life private. When she'd asked about her father, her mother had become irate and told her never to ask again.

She hadn't. She'd been too afraid to.

Stone's phone buzzed. "It's the ME," he said, then connected through his hands-free Bluetooth and put it on Speaker. "Sheriff Lawson."

"Sheriff, I know you wanted this ASAP, so I called in a forensic specialist, Dr. Diane Song. She analyzed the bones recovered at the Stark house and confirmed that the body is a male. He was midthirties at the time of death, which was approximately twenty-seven-years ago. I mentioned that he suffered other injuries and ran his DNA in the system."

"Do you have an ID? And why was his name in the system?" Macy asked.

"Because he served time in prison," Dr. Anderson said. "His name is Voight Hubert."

Macy's heart hammered. "What was he in prison for?"

"That's as far as I got. The rest is up to you. I have another body on my table now that I have to get to."

More questions nagged at Macy as they ended the call. Was Hubert the lover her mother had been romantically involved with?

As Stone drove back toward the sheriff's office, she pulled out her tablet. Seconds later, she accessed prison records and found Voight Hubert's name. He had been arrested thirty years ago on felony charges for assault with a deadly weapon and attempted murder.

She pulled up the police report and skimmed it, then

found an article about the trial and read it aloud to Stone. Stone pulled into the parking space at his office and cut the engine. Night had fallen, the clouds obliterating the stars tonight and casting a grayness over the town.

"Evidence proved that banker and financial adviser George Billman paid Voight Hubert twenty thousand dollars to kill Billman's wife. Billman was indicted on fraud and conspiracy to commit murder charges. In exchange for his testimony against Billman, Hubert received a lighter sentence."

"Hubert was a hit man?" Stone asked.

"Yes. He was released from prison twenty-eight years ago, so that fits the timeline." Macy chewed the inside of her cheek. "But it makes no sense that he'd tried to hurt my mother. She had no money or enemies that I know of, not anyone who'd hire a hit man to come after her."

"He could have been the man she met at those cabins," Stone suggested.

"I thought of that. But how did he end up dead?"

"Lovers gone awry," Stone said. "It happens a lot. They got in a fight. Things became violent. Physical. He had a record of assault. He could have attacked her."

Macy pursed her lips. "That makes sense, especially with her history." Another disturbing thought occurred to her, and she called Dr. Anderson's number. "It's Special Agent Stark. I need you to do something for me."

"What is it?" Dr. Anderson asked.

Macy inhaled a deep breath. "Run a DNA comparison between Hubert's DNA and mine." If Hubert was her father, she had to know.

Chapter Twelve

Possible scenarios raced through Macy's head.

Lynn Stark could have slept with Hubert years ago, then given birth to Macy. Hubert may or may not have known she was his child. And if he did, he may or may not have wanted to be part of her life.

Her mother could have kept in touch, visited him in prison, or reconnected with him when he was released. If he hadn't known he had a daughter and discovered she was his, he could have been angry with her mother and they'd fought. Or hell, her mother might have been desperate and turned to him for money.

"Macy, do you want to talk?" Stone asked.

She gripped the door handle. "It's been a long day. I just want to turn in."

Indecision played in his eyes. "Are you sure you want to be alone? We could grab dinner."

"Thanks, but I'm going to keep looking through my mother's day planner and see if there's any mention of Hubert."

"All right. Call me, though, if you change your mind."

She murmured she would, then climbed out and walked to her car. On the way back to the inn, she picked up a sandwich at the diner, then carried it to her room. Her classmates who'd stayed at the inn during the reunion were gone now, and families and couples occupied the space, their chatter and laughter a reminder that she had no family of her own.

Stone's invitation to dinner taunted her. He was strong, handsome, a hero in town. An alpha man with heart and soul. The kind of man a woman could count on.

But she'd allowed herself to lean on Trey Cushing when she'd been vulnerable, and that had been a huge mistake.

She and Trey never should have gotten married. But she'd been hurting and traumatized and vulnerable after the shooting, and Trey had offered a strong shoulder to cry on. He'd also been charming.

But that charm disappeared after they were married, and he'd become controlling. He also had anger issues that emerged when she stood up to him. Within months, she'd known she had to get out of the marriage.

But an unexpected pregnancy had made her try to work it out.

Trey hadn't wanted a family, though, and asked her to make it go away.

She knew what it was like to grow up unloved and refused his demands. Had vowed to raise the child alone and make certain her baby felt wanted and loved every single day of his or her life.

Anguish tightened her chest. But at seven weeks, she'd had a miscarriage.

Trey had been relieved. She was devastated. But it was the catalyst she needed to make the split.

Stone was nothing like Trey. But she couldn't get involved with him now. Not when her life was such a mess.

STONE COULDN'T TAKE his mind off Macy's troubled childhood. She had all the reason in the world to be bitter or have a chip on her shoulder, but she'd made something of herself and used the trauma of her past to help shape her into a good, caring citizen.

His own childhood seemed cushy compared to hers.

He shouldn't have been surprised that she'd requested a DNA comparison to Hubert. He should have thought of it himself.

How would she feel if she learned her father was an ex-con?

The streetlights illuminated the cars and people out wandering the stores and enjoying dining out. His deputy was back at the station, so he could take a break. The new coffee shop, the Grind, sat on the corner across from Daisy's Diner and was overflowing now that it offered wine, beer and specialty after-dinner drinks and desserts.

He was tempted to stop for a beer but decided to go home instead, just in case Macy changed her mind and wanted company. But just as he turned onto the street leading to his house, a call came in.

"Sheriff," his deputy said when Stone responded. "Got a call from Blues & Brews. Bar brawl just broke out. I'm on my way there now." Tension stretched over the line for a minute. "Your brother is involved."

Dammit. "I'll be right there." Stone spun the squad car around, flipped on the siren, then sped toward the pub. Blues & Brews was at the edge of town and offered bar food, drinks and live music. Tonight was open mic night. He'd encouraged Mickey to play and sing one night, but his brother had shut down and left in a huff.

The neon lights of the giant beer mug boasting the name of the bar shone bright against the dark sky. The parking lot was full, so he swung into a space across the street. Blues music flowed from the speakers and bled outside, the hammering of boots pounding the floor indicating the dance floor had opened up.

Just as he approached, the door opened and two men

tumbled out the door, swinging fists and rolling across the ground. Stone cursed and jogged over to the scene. A few patrons had stepped outside, gawking, while two brawny men were trying to break it up.

He saw Mickey throw a punch and miss, his voice slurred as he yelled. The two of them fell to the ground together, grinding into the gravel as they traded blows. He quickly scanned them both in search of weapons and was relieved when he didn't spot a gun or knife.

"Get back!" he shouted at the spectators, then strode to the men and shouted at them to stop.

Mickey bellowed at him, but Stone grabbed his arm to pull him off the other man. His deputy arrived then and yanked the other man to his feet. He was staggering and swaying, mumbling obscenities.

Mickey jerked at Stone. "Let me go!"

"Not until you settle down, little brother," Stone said, well aware that everyone was watching.

"Give it up, man," his deputy growled at the drunk.

Stone addressed the growing crowd of spectators, "Show's over, folks. Go on back inside." He glanced at the bartender. "What happened?"

He gestured toward the man Mickey had been fighting. "I don't know. One minute they were talking football, the next shouting and throwing fists."

Stone thanked him, then motioned for him to go inside. "We've got it. Sorry about this. If there are damages inside, let me know."

"Thanks, Sheriff." The bartender nodded, then ducked back inside.

"Take him home," he told Murphy. "I'll drive Mickey home myself."

The crowd dispersed, Murphy hauled the drunk toward his police car, and Stone yanked at his brother's arm.

"Go away," Mickey muttered.

Stone steeled his jaw to control his anger and dragged Mickey across the street to his car. He yanked open the door and pushed his brother inside.

"I can take care of myself," Mickey mumbled, his voice slurred.

"To hell you can. Just get in and shut up," Stone growled.

He slammed the door, then got inside and headed toward Mickey's. Something had to change. His brother needed help.

BEFORE MACY TACKLED looking through the remaining day planners, she decided to call the Walkmans. They were the only ones from her initial list that she hadn't spoken with. Their personal number wasn't available to the public, but she finally got the number for Mr. Walkman's administrative assistant, a man named Ryan Barkin.

"Mr. Barkin, I'm trying to reach the Walkmans, either Mrs. Walkman or Mr. Walkman. I need one of them to call me back ASAP."

"What is this about?" Barkin asked.

"I'm investigating the death of a man who was found dead at my mother Lynn Stark's house in Briar Ridge. I'm talking to everyone who knew her at the time. She cleaned houses for the Walkmans, so I just have some basic questions to ask them about her state of mind when she worked for them."

"I see," Barkin said. "The Walkmans have a busy schedule with the campaign, but I'll relay the message."

Macy thanked him, then hung up and turned back to the calendars. She spent the next two hours scouring the calendars and made a second list consisting of five more names and calling them. Two were single women who both stated they felt sorry for Lynn but couldn't handle her mood swings. One couple used to own an antique store and admitted that Macy's mother broke several items in the store and appeared to be intoxicated or on drugs, so they fired her.

Another man, whose wife had died of heart failure, had dementia himself and was now in a nursing home, so she dismissed him as not being able to help.

Frustrated, she decided to look into the social worker who'd visited the house. She put in a call to find her name but with the late hour, had to leave a message.

Next, she dug deeper into Hubert. She found records indicating he'd been in juvie, but the records were sealed. Another assault charge had been placed but withdrawn by the female who'd reported a break-in at her house.

She scratched her head wondering why the woman had dropped the charges. Maybe a domestic situation? Women often recanted charges out of fear or because they were involved with the assailant and softened, then took him back. Others knew the arrest would only trigger more violence and backed out, blaming themselves and opting to remain in an abusive relationship.

She searched for the woman's name and found it listed as Angie Wickins. A quick background check revealed that she owned a gardening shop outside Briar Ridge.

Macy made a mental note to talk to her tomorrow. She'd also call the prison where Hubert had been incarcerated and find out his cellmate's name. After twenty-seven years it was a long shot, but she had to pursue every angle.

Exhausted, she tucked the files away, dragged on a tank top and cotton pajama pants and crawled in bed. The lavender color was soothing and spa-like, the flowers on the table wafting sweetness and summer.

Yet when she closed her eyes, the beauty faded and all she saw was the dark dungeon-like basement at her mother's and Hubert's bony hand protruding through the broken plaster.

Her phone buzzed, and she snagged it from the nightstand and checked the number, expecting Stone or maybe the Walkmans. But the screen read unknown.

Clenching the phone with a shaky hand, she pressed Connect.

A muffled voice spoke. "Stop asking questions or you'll end up dead, too."

"MICKEY, YOU'RE KILLING YOURSELF with this binge drinking," Stone said as he escorted his brother inside his house. "You have to stop."

"What do you care?" Mickey snarled as she staggered to the sofa and dropped down onto it.

How could he get through to his brother? "Of course I care. You're all I've got."

"I don't need you," Mickey said, then closed his eyes and laid his hand over his face with a groan.

"Maybe not. But you need a program," Stone said. "There's an AA group that meets at the church on Wednesdays. If you want, I'll go with you."

"I'm not going to go listen to a bunch of whiners," Mickey said. "I'm not like them."

But he was. "Maybe not," Stone said. "But they could help you figure out why you drink so much. Why you're throwing away your life like this."

"I know you like to play hero, but I don't need you to rescue me."

"You resent me because I should have taken that bullet instead of you," Stone said. "I wish it had been me. I'll never forgive myself for not stopping what happened."

"There you go, thinking you're supposed to save everyone," Mickey said, his words slurring. "But you can't. You can't save me…"

A knot of fear tightened Stone's belly. "I'm not giving up on you, little brother. I'm not."

Angry and frustrated, he strode outside before his temper got the best of him. He'd wait until Mickey was sober, then he'd try again.

His phone buzzed as he got in his car. Macy. Pulse jumping, he answered.

"Someone just called and threatened me," Macy said.

Stone's breath caught. "Male or female?"

"I couldn't tell," Macy said. "The voice was muffled. But it was a warning—stop asking questions or I'd end up dead."

Stone muttered a curse. "I'll be right over."

"I'm fine, Stone," Macy said. "I've already called to put a trace on my phone. If the caller phones back, maybe we can trace the call."

"To be on the safe side, I want to be able to track your phone, too," Stone said. "Is that okay?"

"I guess that would be smart," Macy agreed, although she sounded reluctant. Her pride be damned. Her safety was more important.

"Where are you?" Stone asked.

"At the inn. Don't worry, I'm inside for the night."

Stone glanced back at his brother's house. He was worried to death about Mickey and hated to leave him. And now Macy... He wanted to go to her and hold her in his arms. To make sure she stayed safe all night.

But she'd built walls around herself just like Mickey. And just like he had years ago.

He was already losing Mickey.

He couldn't stand to care too much about anyone else and then lose them, too.

THE NEXT MORNING, Macy met Stone at the station, explained about Angie Wickins, and he drove them to the gardening center where Angie was employed. He looked a little rough around the edges, as if he hadn't slept much. Neither had she.

"Are you all right?" Macy asked as he wound up the mountain.

Stone's dark gaze met hers, emotions flickering for a second before he wiped them off his face and maneuvered another turn. "Fine. Did you hear about the trace?"

"Came from a burner phone, just as I expected," Macy said.

"Figures. Someone knew those are almost impossible to trace," Stone said.

A thick silence fell between them as he drove, the case weighing on Macy. Her mother's face had taunted her all night. She thought she'd seen her outside the window. Saw her running through the woods behind her house, a bloody knife in her hand.

The sun was struggling to break though the storm clouds but failing, and gray streaked the sky, adding a dreariness to the day and making her want to crawl back in bed and bury herself beneath the covers.

For a split second, she closed her eyes and imagined she wasn't alone in the world—or in that bed. That Stone had crawled in beside her and was holding her tight. She felt safe and cared for and her heart pounded as he touched her cheek, then pressed his lips against hers.

They hit a pothole, jarring her back to the present, and Stone veered up the graveled drive to the gardening center. Several pickup trucks and SUVs sat in the parking lot, customers already filling the cabs and trunks with assorted plants and flowers.

The bright red, purple, yellow and pink perennials dotted the landscape with color. Marigolds and sunflowers drew her eye with their cheery blooms.

Together she and Stone walked up to the front of the

store, which held potting supplies, ceramic pots, bird feeders and other essentials. Two workers strolled through the outside area where customers combed the aisles.

A fortysomething auburn-haired woman wearing a gardening apron was working the register, her name tag reading Angie. Her hair was piled on top of her head in a messy knot, and dirt stained her apron as if she lived and breathed her work.

She and Stone exchanged a look as they approached the counter. Her eyes widened in recognition when she saw them, then confusion flashed across her slender face.

"Can we talk in private?" Stone asked.

She nodded, as if she didn't want to discuss whatever they'd come to talk to her about in front of her customers. Then she waved a young twentysomething girl over. "Rachel, can you work the register?"

"Sure." Rachel left the stack of birdseed she'd been arranging for sale and sauntered over, smiling as she took Angie's place at the register. Angie motioned for them to follow her through the back section to a small office and closed the door.

She fidgeted with her hands, then picked up a packet of flower seed and tapped it in her palm. "What is this about?"

"Have you seen the news about a body being found in a house in Briar Ridge?"

The seeds rattled as Angie continued to tap them. "I saw it. But what's that got to do with me?"

Macy licked her dry lips. "We identified the dead man as Voight Hubert," Macy said.

Angie gasped, surprise flitting across her face.

"I don't know anything about that," she said, her voice cracking.

Macy's instincts surged to life. "But you did know Voight Hubert, didn't you?"

She stiffened, working her mouth from side to side. "Why are you asking?"

Stone cleared his throat. "Because we know that he was arrested for assaulting you, and that you dropped the charges."

Angie closed her eyes for a second as if to stem her emotions. Or perhaps to give herself time to concoct a lie.

Macy softened her tone. "Angie, this is obviously painful for you to discuss. But I need to know what happened. Did he assault you?"

She gave a tiny nod of her head. "But I don't want that to come out again. It was hard enough the first time."

"How old were you?" Macy asked.

"Eighteen," Angie said. "I was at a club with some friends and didn't notice that he was watching me. I went out to my car to leave and he cornered me. He grabbed me and dragged me into the woods…" Her voice broke, and Macy squeezed her hand.

"Take your time," Macy murmured.

"I screamed and fought him," Angie said. "I even bit his hand, but he was strong and drunk and…"

"He raped you?" Macy asked.

She shook her head and fidgeted with her hands. "He was going to, but this other guy in the parking lot heard me scream and came running. He knocked the creep off of me and punched him, then called 911."

"A Good Samaritan," Stone said.

"Sure was." Angie nodded with a tiny smile. "I ended up marrying him."

Macy smiled. "Is he here now?"

Sadness flickered in her eyes. "I lost him three years ago to a drunk driver," Angie said. "He and I took this place over when my daddy retired. Every time I plant seeds or see the flowers blooming, I think of him."

Macy's heart squeezed at the love in her tone. "Why did you drop the charges?" she asked.

Angie cut her eyes away. "My father. He flew into a rage and said everyone would blame me because I was underage and had a beer. It was so stupid of me…"

"It was not your fault," Macy said.

"But what he said was true. People would have talked, gossiped," Angie said, a wary acceptance in her voice. "Stared at me."

Macy understood about that. Sexual assault victims were often treated like criminals themselves. No wonder so many didn't follow through in court.

"Anyway, Daddy said he wanted to protect me, that they'd make me out to be a tramp. And I just wanted it to go away," Angie said. "So I agreed." She cut her eyes away again, and Macy sensed she was holding back.

Macy rubbed her arm. "What aren't you telling us? *Did* Hubert just go away?"

"He actually showed up at my house one night about a month after that, was outside watching me through the window. My father caught him and threatened to kill him if he ever came near me again."

Chapter Thirteen

Stone balled his hands into fists. He'd heard similar stories before, but they enraged him every time. His father had taught him to respect women. To protect them. "What happened after that? Did Hubert ever come back?"

"I never saw him," Angie said. "And my father and I never spoke of it again."

Stone's breath eased out. "Where is your father now? We'd like to talk to him."

"That's impossible," Angie said. "He died ten years ago."

"Angie," Macy said. "Do you think your father would have made good on that threat?"

The woman wiped her hands on her jeans. "I don't know. Why? Are you trying to say he killed that vile man who attacked me?"

"I don't know what to think." Macy softened her tone. "What about the man you married?"

"What about him?" Angie's voice turned defensive.

"Did he ever talk to Hubert?" Stone asked.

"You're not pinning that vile man's death on my daddy or on my sweet husband." Angie stood. "I've said too much already. I have to get back to work."

Her posture rigid, she gestured for them to leave her office.

Macy pushed a card into her hand. "If you think of something else, please call me."

Angie stuffed the card into her pocket and gave Macy a dark look.

Stone followed Angie back through the gardening shop. He and Macy waited until they'd settled in his car before he spoke.

"Interesting story. If Angie's father or husband had anything to do with Hubert's death, she obviously doesn't intend to tell us."

"No, she's protective of them." Macy buckled her seat belt. "Considering what happened, I can't say as I blame her. After all this time, with both men deceased, it'll be hard to prove their involvement."

"And if one of them murdered Hubert, how did he end up in your house?"

"Good question."

Stone's mind raced. "Do you remember if your mother ever went to that gardening center? Maybe she had a delivery or gardener come out to tend the yard?"

Macy pinched the bridge of her nose as if struggling to recall. "I don't remember her gardening as I got older, but she may have when I was young. When I was looking at old pictures, there was a flower garden out front. But she must have let it all die later on after her break. And she never hired anyone to help. We didn't have the money." She angled her head to look at Stone. "What are you thinking?"

"Just looking at every possibility," Stone said. "Both Angie's father and her husband had reason to hate Hubert."

"True, but they work in the gardening business," Macy said. "Why wouldn't they have just buried him somewhere? That would have been easier than putting him in a wall where he might be found."

Stone considered that. "That makes sense." Only it put them back to square one.

MACY CONTEMPLATED OTHER possibilities as Stone started the engine. If Angie's father or husband knew her mother was unstable, they could have decided she'd make a good scapegoat if the body was ever discovered. After all, who would believe a psychotic woman?

If that was the case, what if her mother came home and found them or the body, and that triggered her break?

You're grasping at straws. Trying to justify any way you can that she was not at fault or directly connected to the man's brutal murder.

Stone drove back toward town, and Macy's stomach knotted when she spotted Gretta's BMW parked in front of the station.

"The vulture's here," Stone muttered.

"I guess being a predator is a necessary evil to do her job."

A wry smile curved his mouth. "I'll handle her if you want to hide out in my office."

Macy shook her head. "I can't run from it," she said. "I tried that before, yet here I am now."

Stone squeezed her hand, and they got out and walked into the station. Gretta was talking to Deputy Bridges when they entered, a flirtatious gleam in her eyes as she leaned close to him.

Macy rolled her eyes. The woman could be charming—when she wanted something. Maybe the deputy had fallen for it and was feeding her information.

Gretta straightened when she saw them and gestured toward her sidekick, a cameraman named Rickey. "Sheriff Lawson, Special Agent Stark, do you have an update on the investigation into the homicide?"

Stone squared his shoulders. "We have identified the man as an ex-con named Voight Hubert who served time in prison for being a hired hit man. At this point, we don't know how he ended up at the Stark house. He was killed approximately twenty-seven years ago. Anyone with information about him should please call the sheriff's office."

Gretta pushed the mic toward Macy. "Special Agent Stark, any word on your mother who escaped the psychiatric hospital?"

Macy's lungs tightened. Gretta seemed to take pleasure in pointing out her mother's mental illness. "No word at this time. Again, we're asking anyone who sees or speaks to her to report it to the police."

Gretta narrowed her eyes, scrutinizing Macy. "Do you think that your mother is dangerous?"

Macy swallowed hard. Did she? "We have no reason to believe that at this time, but she is wanted for questioning."

"But you grew up with her, Agent Stark," Gretta said sharply. "Did she exhibit violent behavior when you were a child?"

Macy struggled not to react, but Stone stepped in. "We are not here to speculate, but to find facts. Agent Stark's personal relationship with her mother is not up for comment."

Stone took Macy's arm and ushered her back toward his office. "That woman," he growled.

Macy blinked back unwanted tears. "She's just doing her job."

"Don't defend her. She enjoys putting people on the spot," Stone said, his tone angry. He paced to his desk and looked out the window. "I think Bridges is leaking her information. If I find out that's true, I'm going to have his head on a platter."

Macy moved to the table in the corner and pulled her laptop from her shoulder bag, and Stone went to grab coffee. Her phone buzzed, and the name Walkman appeared on her screen. She answered the call and introduced herself.

"This is Adeline Walkman," the woman said. "I was

asked to call you. I just saw the news about your mother and that man's murder."

"Yes," Macy said. "I understand that Lynn Stark cleaned house for you at one time."

"That's true," Mrs. Walkman said, a note of sympathy to her voice. "But that was years ago, and we haven't had any contact with her since. I'm sorry to hear she's been in a psychiatric hospital."

Macy swallowed to tamp down an emotional response. "Thank you so much, Mrs. Walkman."

"Please call me Adeline. Now, how can I help?"

"I'm looking for any information you can give me about her."

"Well, it's been a long time, and she only worked for us a couple of months. We lost our son to an accident and decided to move. Too many painful memories in Briar Ridge."

"I understand that, and I'm so sorry for your loss," Macy said. More than the woman knew. "Did she happen to ever mention having a boyfriend?"

A heartbeat passed. "I'm afraid not. We didn't discuss personal things at all. I was working for a nonprofit back then, so she usually came to clean when I was out of the house. I left a check for her, and she was gone when I returned home."

Macy exhaled. "Thanks for returning my call. If you think of anything else, please let me know."

"I will. And I hope you find her and get her the help she needs."

Macy thanked her again, hung up and turned back to her laptop just as Stone loped in with two cups of coffee.

"Thanks," she said as she took the cup. "Just talked to Adeline Walkman. That was a dead end."

"Sorry, Macy," Stone said.

Macy shrugged. "It was a long shot. It's not like Mother

had any real friends she'd confide in. "I'm going to look into Hubert more," she said. "See if he had family or if anyone reported him missing."

She spent the next half hour checking missing persons reports while Stone called the prison where Hubert had been incarcerated to inquire about his cellmates.

"No one reported Hubert missing," Macy said.

"Did he have family?"

"Let me check." Next, she ran a search into Hubert's past in search of relatives. "No surviving family members, and he never married. His mother was a cocaine addict. Voight was removed from her custody and placed in foster care at age three, where he was tossed around from one home to another."

So he wasn't close enough to anyone that they would have missed him.

STONE TOOK A long sip of his coffee. "Warden said Hubert had two cellmates. Man in for beating his kid to death with a baseball bat. Died in a prison fight a few months after Hubert was incarcerated."

"Sounds like he got what he deserved," Macy said.

Stone nodded. "Second cellmate was a man named Bubba Yates. Did time for a hit-and-run. Downed a half pint of whiskey, then got behind the wheel." At least with Mickey's loss of sight, he couldn't drive. Stone had always hated that loss of independence for his brother. At the moment though, he was glad he couldn't get behind the wheel and hurt himself or anyone else. "Served seven years for vehicular manslaughter."

Macy plugged the man's name into her laptop and ran a search. "Looks like he lives outside Hendersonville. Let's go talk to him."

Stone grabbed his keys. "We'll grab lunch on the way." Stone told Murphy where he was going as they left the station.

The temperature outside was climbing to the eighties, but a slight breeze stirred the trees and gave some relief. They stopped for barbecue sandwiches, then Stone wound through the mountains, the heart of the apple houses where people flocked in the fall to pick apples and purchase homemade apple jellies, pies, breads and apple butter.

Macy searched for more information on Yates and learned he worked at a hardware store. She called the owner, who relayed that he was at work, so they drove straight to the store.

The sun was beaming down hotter as they parked and went inside. Stone identified himself to the clerk and asked for Yates. He was a rail-thin man wearing a shirt emblazoned with the hardware store's name.

Stone asked him to step outside with them, and the man's look turned wary.

"Am I in trouble or something?" Yates asked.

Stone shook his head, then explained they wanted to talk about Hubert.

"That's a name from the past." Yates pulled something from his pocket and rolled it around in his palm. "I haven't seen or talked to him since I got out of prison."

"You never reconnected when he was released?"

"No way." He opened his palm to reveal a sobriety chip. "I found God in prison, joined AA and been sober ever since." A sadness tinged his eyes. "Don't change what I did, though. Have to live with that guilt every day."

Stone understood about guilt.

"Mr. Yates, Hubert's body was recently found in Briar Ridge," Macy said. "He's been there for twenty-seven years."

Yates's brows shot up. "I swear I never talked to him or saw him after I got out. He was trouble, and I didn't want anything to do with him."

"We understand that he served time for taking money to kill a woman," Stone said. "Did he talk about that?"

"Just that he was sorry he got caught. I'm telling you, he was a mean one."

"Did he have any visitors that you remember?" Macy asked.

The man ran his thin hand over a scar on his cheek. Stone wondered if he'd gotten it in the accident or in prison. "Heard him talking to another inmate about some woman visiting him. But he never mentioned her name, and I didn't ask."

"Was it a romantic visit? Someone he knew?" Macy asked.

Yates shrugged. "Don't think so. Said he was going to get a big payday when he was released."

Stone glanced at Macy. Sounded like he might have been planning another job. Who had he been hired to kill?

WHILE STONE DROVE them back to the station, Macy called the prison warden and identified herself. "We spoke with a former cellmate of Voight Hubert. He said Hubert had a visit from a female before his release. Can you look back at the visitor logs and find out who she was?"

A long second passed. "That was a long time ago."

"It's important," Macy said impatiently. "We're trying to solve a murder."

"Why the big rush? It's been over two decades," he said.

Macy tightened her fingers around the phone. "Two reasons. One, the man's body was found in my own house. And we have reason to believe that visitor may have hired Hubert to kill someone else. That happened on your watch."

The man cursed. "All right, but it'll take some time. We weren't digitized back then, so logs will be archived. I'll get my assistant to see if she can dig up those records."

"Do you have security footage of the visitors where we might get a look at her?"

"I'll see what I can find."

"Check his mail, too, for anything suspicious. And see if anyone put money into his account while he was there."

"If a piece of mail was suspicious, we would have reported it. Otherwise after all this time, it would have been discarded," he said. "But I'll see if there's a record of anything suspicious filed and look into his account. I'll get back to you ASAP."

BACK AT THE SHERIFF'S OFFICE, Stone looked up as his deputy poked his head in. "Sheriff, a call just came in. Neighbor was driving by the old Simmons place and thought she saw someone breaking in. I'll check it out."

Stone stood. "Agent Stark and I will go. I want you to look around at any abandoned properties or rentals not being used, in case Lynn Stark is hiding out in one of them."

Murphy gave a nod. "Copy that."

Macy gathered her laptop and shoulder bag. "Let's go."

Dusk was falling by the time they reached the Simmons place, an old farm with chicken houses that had fallen into disrepair years before.

"Do you recall Martha and Tim Simmons?" Stone asked.

"Yes," Macy said. "Their daughter ran track with me."

"They moved after the shooting," Stone said. "Couldn't sell the place. Farm went into foreclosure."

"No one wanted to move to the town where kids got slaughtered," Macy said.

Stone nodded grimly. "Thankfully that's changing now with the new school in the fall."

"Kate was pretty amazing," Macy said, her voice filled

with affection and a tinge of sadness. "I never would have survived growing up without her and her mother."

Stone laid his hand over hers. "I'm glad you had her, Macy. And sorry we weren't friends back then."

"I wasn't exactly the social type," Macy said.

And now he understood the reason.

Storm clouds moved across the sky, painting the mountains a gloomy gray. In the distance, he could see it raining on top of Bear Mountain, the trees shivering with the wind. He and Macy scanned the property as he maneuvered the narrow graveled drive.

There were no cars in sight.

If Macy's mother was here, how had she gotten this far? Had she stolen another vehicle and ditched it? Or maybe she hitchhiked?

"It looks sad and run-down," Macy said.

"A lot of properties around here do," Stone said. "But it could be revitalized if someone ever wanted to buy it and turn it back into a working farm."

He slowed as he approached the white farmhouse and glanced at the ripped screens and peeling paint, then to the right where two chicken houses were abandoned. A rotting barn was missing a roof.

He parked, and Macy climbed from the vehicle and quietly closed the door, her face strained with anxiety. Still, she was focused.

Together they started up the drive but suddenly a noise to the right jerked his attention to the window, and then a gunshot rang out.

Macy ducked behind an oak tree, and he darted beside her, both pulling their guns. He pivoted to the left and she went right, visually sweeping the property to see where the shot had come from.

Chapter Fourteen

Macy gripped her gun at the ready and peered around the edge of the tree in search of the shooter. Another shot rang out, whizzing past her, and Stone motioned that he'd spotted someone at the window. The screen was torn, the glass broken, and a shotgun poked through the hole.

"Police, put down the gun!" he shouted.

"Mom, are you in there?" Macy yelled. "If you are, drop the gun and let's talk."

The barrel of the gun bobbed, but the door remained shut.

"Open up and put the gun on the porch!" Stone shouted. "No one has to get hurt. We just want to talk."

Macy eased along the bushes, taking cover, and he picked up a rock and threw it against the woodpile to create a distraction. She ran for the back of the house and crept up the steps to the back door. Inching slowly, she kept her eyes peeled in case the shooter realized she was coming in from the back.

The wind whistled through the trees in the back, the rotting boards of the back stoop creaking. She eased open the screen door, sweeping the interior as she tiptoed inside. The house was dark and smelled of must and mold. Except for a rickety pine table, the outdated kitchen looked empty, floral wallpaper peeling from the dingy walls.

She eased through the room into a hallway, then spotted the living room, which held a dusty-looking plaid sofa and a coffee table that listed to one side from a broken leg.

She plastered herself against the wall and peered into the room from the door and saw a hunched figure at the window holding the shotgun.

A man, not her mother.

"Lower the gun and step away," Macy said firmly.

At the sound of her voice, he swung around, the shotgun waving in his shaky hands. His eyes looked crazed as if he was high, and he swayed. She guessed his age to be midsixties. An empty liquor bottle sat on an end table with several bottles of pills.

"Please put the gun down," Macy said softly. "I don't want anyone to get hurt."

He looked confused when he glanced down at the gun, as if he didn't know what he was doing. She inched closer to him, holding up her hand to indicate she wasn't going to shoot.

The weapon bobbed up and down, but he slowly lowered it to his side. "I ain't done nothing wrong," he said, his words slurring.

"Then you don't have anything to worry about," Macy said. "I came here looking for my mother. I thought she was in here."

"Ain't nobody here but me."

"What's your name, sir?" Macy asked.

"Floyd. Floyd Gleason," he muttered.

"Listen Floyd. So far you haven't done anything wrong. I'm sure you fired that shot to protect yourself," she said in a soothing tone. "But if you shoot again or don't give up the gun, I'm going to have to arrest you."

His expression was confused as he looked up at her, and she gave him a nod of encouragement. "Please. Just lower it."

He slowly laid the gun on the floor, and she shouted at Stone to come in. He entered cautiously, taking in the scene.

"What are you doing here?" Stone asked.

"Just sleeping," the older man said. "Wasn't hurting anyone. Ain't nobody lived here in forever."

Stone checked the pills on the table. "Oxy."

"For my back," the man said. "Got so much pain I can hardly walk."

"Do you have any family we can call?" Macy asked.

Emotions streaked the man's face, and he shook his head.

Sympathy for him welled inside Macy. This man didn't pose a threat. He was just homeless and lonely. "Let us take you to a shelter," Macy said. "You can get some help there, a hot meal and a bed."

"Just let me be," the man said.

Stone stepped forward. "Come on, I know a place where you can go and be with some friends."

The man reluctantly agreed, and Macy took his weapon while Stone helped him to the car.

Thirty minutes later, they dropped him at a group home for men run by the preacher at the community church. Stone looked troubled as they left.

"Let's call it a night," he said when they reached the station. "I need to check on my brother."

"Is he okay?" Macy asked.

Stone shrugged. "Not really."

Macy's phone buzzed with a text from the ME.

DNA from Hubert is not a familial match to yours.

A sliver of relief flitted through Macy. At least her birth father wasn't a hired killer.

But if Hubert wasn't her father, then who was? And why had Hubert been at her mother's house?

STONE COULDN'T SHAKE his nagging worry about Mickey. If his brother didn't get some help, he might end up like the man he'd just dropped at the group home.

He left Macy at her car, drove by and picked up burgers, then headed to Mickey's. When he arrived, he noticed the house looked dark. He started to leave but knew he wouldn't sleep unless he saw his brother, so he grabbed the bag of food and carried it to the door.

He knocked, then twisted the doorknob. "Mickey, are you here?"

No answer. "Mickey!" he called as he strode into the living room. "Hey, man, I brought burgers." He dropped them on the kitchen counter, then strode to Mickey's office, hoping to find him at work. The desk was a mess, his laptop was open, but Mickey wasn't inside the room.

He went to the bedroom next and glanced inside. Dammit, his brother was piled in the bed, snoring. A half dozen beer cans sat on the dresser, an open one on his nightstand. Stone crossed to the bed and nudged him.

"Mickey, wake up, man. Eat something."

Mickey grunted and pulled the covers over his head.

"Come on, little brother. We have to talk."

"Go away," Mickey growled.

"I'm trying to help you. If you don't get your act together, you're going to lose your job."

"I already did," Mickey said. "Now get out."

Frustration filled Stone. "I'll leave, but I'm going to make a pot of coffee. There are burgers on the counter."

His heart heavy, Stone turned and strode from the room. He sat for a half hour watching the house, hoping Mickey would turn the lights on and get up. But the house remained dark, and he saw no movement inside.

Another half hour, and a helpless feeling engulfed him as he drove away.

MACY DECIDED TO search her mother's house again, this time focusing on something that might lead her to her father or a connection to Hubert.

Just as she parked, though, the warden called. "The name on the visitor log was Nellie Norris," he said. "Sorry, but I couldn't find a photo or video of the visit. The archived records room is a mess. Had some flooding a few years back, so some of them might have been thrown out if they were damaged."

Macy sighed. "I appreciate you looking," she said. "I'll see what I can find on Nellie Norris."

Macy thanked him again and hung up. Then, anxious for information, she pulled her laptop from her bag, booted it up and ran a search for the woman. First, she checked DMV records and found two women by that name. The first lived in Raleigh and was twenty, so her age didn't fit. The second was a thirty-five-year-old, which also didn't fit. Twenty-seven years ago, she would have been eight.

She deepened the search and found another Nellie Norris who died at the age of eighty the year before. It was possible she could have been the woman who'd visited Hubert, but if so, she would be no help now.

If her mother had visited him, her age didn't fit with any of these women, either.

A dead end.

Or was it possible that the woman had faked her identity to see Hubert? There were security measures in place to prevent that from happening, but a smart person with connections could find a way to circumvent them.

Gritting her teeth, she shut down her laptop and stowed it back in her bag.

Thunder rumbled, the storm clouds gathering on the horizon threatening rain. She opened the car door and hurried up to the house before the downpour started. The crime scene tape flapped in the wind. Her hand trembled as she entered, the musty odor mingling with the scent of her own fear.

Whispers of evil echoed through the eaves of the old house, and the thin walls shook as the rain outside began. Memories of hiding in the closet bombarded her, her mother's erratic screams drifting to her from the place in her mind where she thought she'd locked them away forever. She pictured her mother in the kitchen in a thin cotton gown, her hands shaking as she lifted a water glass to her lips and took a sip, washing down a handful of pills.

Another memory surfaced—country music played on an ancient radio, her mother taking her hands and dancing in the kitchen, singing and swirling Macy around in a dizzying rhythm. A smile tilted her mouth. She'd forgotten that occasionally she had a pleasant moment or two. The painful memories seemed to have washed away those times like a heavy rain crushing the pansies her mother had planted during one of her good days.

Pulling herself from the memory, she decided to check the hall closet. A couple of her mother's old coats were still inside, so she checked the pockets and found a few receipts from the drugstore, a gum wrapper and some loose change. A pair of rain boots sat on the floor, and a shoebox was on the top shelf. She brought it down and looked inside. Folders with assorted bills, then several old checkbooks and statements were inside.

A streak of lightning zigzagged across the sky, illuminating the foggy window, and took her back to that horrible night when the storm woke her.

A tree branch scraped the window, clawing at it like sharp fingernails. The limbs looked like giant hands reaching for her. Glass rattled, then shattered and rain blew in, the wind roaring like an animal.

She screamed and dragged the covers up to hide, but the floor creaked and she suddenly smelled a musky odor. Clenching the covers in her hands, she peeked and saw a shadow looming above her bed.

She screamed, thunder drowning out the sound, then she heard footsteps and her door squeaking open, then closing. Shaking in terror, she slid from beneath the covers, then crawled under the bed and covered her mouth with her hand. She lay still, afraid to move, afraid the man would return and get her, but she kept her eyes peeled toward the door.

Seconds ticked by. The rain beat down. The lightning popped.

Then she heard the noise in the hall. Footsteps. Something banging. Her mother screaming...

Macy gripped the wall to steady herself as the memory slowly blurred and reality returned. Thunder boomed outside, sending a shudder coursing through her. Suddenly the monsters were everywhere in the house, shadowy figures floating through the walls, darting across the ceiling, eyes piercing her.

She didn't want to spend another minute in this house. Not tonight.

Heart hammering, she rushed to the door, ran outside to her car and stored the box in the back seat. Brush crackled behind her and she spun around and thought she saw someone move, going into the house.

Was it her mother?

Exhaling a shaky breath, she jogged back to the house, raindrops splattering her. If her mother was inside, she'd make her talk.

She paused at the doorway, then crept forward and peered inside. "Mom?"

The floor creaked and she pivoted, but suddenly something hard slammed against the side of her head. Macy staggered and grabbed at the wall, then her attacker's arm. But the room spun and stars danced behind her eyes.

She blinked, struggling to stay on her feet, but the dizziness overcame her as pain shot through her skull, and she collapsed into the darkness.

SHE DRAGGED MACY across the floor, cursing herself for letting things get this far.

She should have killed her and burned down this damn house a long time ago. Her secrets were meant to stay hidden, just like that body in the wall, but now Macy was messing it all up.

Her lungs strained for air with the weight of Macy's limp body as she pulled and yanked her to the closet. She opened the door and pushed Macy inside. Huffing to catch her breath, she slammed the door shut, then ran out back where she'd left the gas can earlier.

The thunder still rumbled, but the clouds seemed to be moving on. Wiping sweat from her forehead with one hand, she carried the gas can inside and poured it around the living room and kitchen.

Stepping back, she set the can beside the closet door, then removed the book of matches from her pocket. The first one struck quickly, and she tossed it toward the old sofa, then struck a few more and threw them onto the gas.

Flames burst to life, then began to catch and creep across the wood floor, eating the rotting wood like kindling.

Chapter Fifteen

Stone was almost home when the 911 call came from the couple who'd bought Kate's former house. A fire had broken out at the Stark place.

He flipped on his siren, then sped toward the house, punching Macy's number as he maneuvered around a pickup and slower traffic. He honked at a car that started through the intersection, then whipped his car to the right to avoid hitting it.

Macy's phone rang four times, then went to voice mail. Dammit, where was she?

Fear clawed at him. Hopefully not at the house…

He hung up and tried her number again but got her voice mail. He glanced at the diner as he passed, looking for her car, scanning the streets and other businesses, but didn't see it anywhere. On the chance she just wasn't answering her phone or the battery was dead, he called the inn.

Celeste answered. "It's the sheriff. Is Macy Stark there?"

"I haven't seen her come in tonight," Celeste said.

Disappointment made him curse. "If she does, have her call me."

Celeste agreed, and he hung up and rounded the turn to the Stark house and barreled up the driveway. Flames were shooting into the dark sky, smoke curling in a gray cloud out a broken window. His pulse jumped when he spotted Macy's car in the drive.

Panicked, he jumped out, shouting Macy's name as he ran toward the house. He couldn't wait for the fire department. Macy might be inside.

"Macy!" Hoping she'd escaped, he glanced all around the outside but didn't see her anywhere. Shouting her name again, he jogged up the steps. The door felt warm but not hot and was ajar.

He looked through the front window and saw flames rippling along the far wall of the living room and in the kitchen. Patches danced around the vinyl sofa and chewed at its legs, climbing upward.

He didn't see Macy in the front. The hall didn't appear to be in flames yet. He eased the door open, the heat and scent of gasoline assaulting him as he stepped inside. "Macy!"

Quickly he scanned the room, then the kitchen. No Macy. Smoke blurred his vision as he darted down the hall, and he coughed, covering his mouth with his hand to keep from inhaling it. He jumped over patches of flames and dashed into the bedrooms but didn't see Macy anywhere.

Fear pulsed through him. Where the hell was she?

Panicked, he checked the closet and bathroom. Empty. The fire was crawling closer, though, the heat growing more intense.

"Macy, where are you?"

Maybe she'd escaped out back.

Judging from the gasoline can, the fire had been set intentionally. She could have caught the person during the act and given chase outside into the woods.

He had to make sure the house was clear, though, so he darted through more shooting flames to go to the basement. But the closet door caught his eye. He pulled at it, but the door seemed stuck. He banged on it and called Macy's name again, beating at the fire eating the floor and door.

He slammed his shoulder into it, then yanked it again and the door finally swung open. His heart stuttered when he spotted Macy slumped on the floor unconscious.

Cold fear knotted his stomach, and he stooped down and scooped her into his arms. He pressed her face into his chest to keep her from being scalded or from inhaling more smoke, then raced through the burning room, dodging plaster crumbling down from the ceiling.

A siren wailed outside, the fire engine roaring into the drive as he ran with her, carrying her away from the inferno. She hung limp, her hair draping his arm as he knelt beneath a tree and gently laid her on the ground.

His heart raced as he felt for a pulse.

MACY'S HEAD THROBBED as if someone was pounding her skull with a hammer. She felt movement and nausea roll through her, then heard a gruff voice calling her name.

"Macy, honey, wake up."

A soft stroke of her hair, and she tried to open her eyes. Loud voices echoed around her. A siren. The wind. Wood popping and crackling.

"Macy, it's Stone. The medics are going to take you to the hospital."

The world blurred, smoke stinging her eyes as she felt herself being lifted. A blanket over her. Gentle hands turning her head, parting her hair, talking over her.

Stone squeezed her hand. "What happened, Macy?"

Confusion clouded her brain, but snippets of her memory returned. "Someone…at the house…hit me."

"Did you see who it was?"

She shook her head, or at least she thought she did. The movement sent another wave of nausea over her, and she swallowed back bile.

"Male? Female?"

"Just a shadow," she whispered.

"Okay, take it easy." He noticed bruises on her hands and arms and wondered if she'd fought her attacker. "I'm going to call a crime team, then I'll meet you at the hospital."

Macy felt his hand squeeze hers, then she was jostled around as the medics loaded her into the ambulance. The siren fired up, screeching and jabbing at the pain in her head like dozens of needles.

She closed her eyes to drown it out and let the darkness pull her under again.

STONE PULLED THE hood of his rain jacket over his head as he watched the firefighters work to extinguish the blaze. He was grateful for their quick action. The clouds had finally unleashed a deluge of rain, which helped to douse the flames, and everyone was soaked.

"We managed to contain the damage to the living room and kitchen," his friend and the chief arson investigator Riggs Benford told him. "Although the smoke and water damage will be significant to the other rooms. What happened?"

His jaw tightened. "Someone knocked Macy unconscious, then put her in the closet and poured gasoline around the room."

Riggs eyes darkened. "They tried to kill her?"

Stone nodded. "Someone doesn't want her investigating the murder that happened here. She received a threat earlier."

"Damn," Riggs said. "Is she okay?"

"She took a hit to the back of her head and probably has a concussion," he said, worry gnawing at him. "But I didn't see any burns. I'm headed to the hospital when I leave here."

The Evidence Response Team arrived, three investigators exiting their van with their kits.

"Fire will have to cool down before we can do much," Riggs told him. "But I'll hang around and oversee the team."

"Thanks. I saw a gas can in there. Maybe you can get some prints."

The ERT approached and Stone explained what had happened. He glanced at the graveled drive and saw tire prints from Macy's car. But no other. "That car belongs to Special Agent Macy Stark," he said. "She was trapped in the closet in the fire and is on her way to the hospital. Look around out here for signs of another vehicle." He pointed to the woods behind the house. "It's possible whoever attacked her left on foot through the woods and had a car parked on the street on the other side."

"We'll be thorough," the lead ERT officer said.

"I'm going to question the neighbor and see if anyone saw a car or person here."

The team began to disperse while the firefighters began stowing their equipment. Smoke still drifted from the debris, the odor of charred wood mingling with the scent of rain.

Stone wiped water from his face, told Riggs to keep him posted, asked him to have one of the officers drop Macy's car at the inn, then he climbed in his squad car. He drove the short distance to the neighbor's house, the one that had once belonged to Kate and her mother. After Kate graduated from college, she'd decided to sell and had bought a new build to start over.

The rain was slacking off as he parked at the ranch house, noting the new owners had done some updates by painting the brick white, adding black trim, and planting colorful flower beds. Kate must be pleased that they were taking such good care of her mother's home.

He walked up to the front door and knocked, Macy's pale face as he'd carried her from the burning house haunting him. A few minutes later, and he would have been too late.

Footsteps sounded inside and the door opened, revealing a young woman holding a toddler on her hip. The little redheaded girl was licking a red Popsicle, the juice dripping down her chin. He'd seen the family around town and knew they had two other children. The father worked at the bank.

"Sheriff?"

"Hi, Mary Sue," Stone said. "I guess you saw the smoke at the house next door."

"I did and called 911," she said. "What happened?"

Stone explained that Macy was there.

"Oh my goodness, is she okay?"

"She's at the hospital," he said, the urge to be with her growing stronger. But Macy would want him to ask questions, find out who'd tried to kill her. "Did you see another vehicle over there tonight? Or a person on foot maybe?"

Mary Sue shook her head. "I'm afraid not. Little Amelia has been sick, so I've been inside with her all day and evening. And Johnny isn't home yet."

Stone gave a quick nod. "How about any time over the last few weeks?"

The toddler rubbed at her eyes as she finished the treat, and Mary Sue took the sticky Popsicle stick. "Sorry, but I haven't. I was shocked to hear about that body being found."

"When Lynn Stark was still living here, did you ever see anything suspicious going on there?"

The woman wrinkled her brow. "I hate to talk ill of her, but I thought she was troubled, so we kept our distance." Her voice cracked. "I guess I wasn't a very good neighbor."

"You were just taking care of your family," Stone said.

She bit down on her lower lip, then released a breath. "Actually I might have seen something. I should have called it in, but I felt bad for not trying to help that woman out. But now..."

"What are you talking about?" Stone asked.

"I think I saw Lynn at the house earlier today."

Stone's gut clenched. If Macy's mother had been there, could she have set the fire? Would she try to kill her own daughter to keep her secrets?

"Thank you." He hesitated. "If you think of anything else, please give me a call."

She murmured she would, and he rushed back to his car. Fear for Macy made him speed toward the hospital.

If whoever wanted her dead realized Macy had survived the fire, she was still in danger.

MACY ENDURED THE CAT scan and stitches, managing not to pass out again, but her head throbbed, her eyes were burning, and her throat felt raw.

Finally she was settled into a room for the night. As much as she hated hospitals and had asked to go home, the doctor insisted she stay overnight for observation.

The steady sound of machines beeping and medicine and food carts clanging down the hall blended with the staff's voices, and she felt her eyes closing again, the bliss of sleep pulling at her.

In her mind though, flashed an image of the house she'd grown up in and those last few minutes before she'd lost consciousness. The sound of a footstep, the shadow moving across the doorway...had it been a man or a woman?

She clenched the edge of the sheet in frustration, willing some detail to come forward. An image that would give her the answer.

The scent of alcohol and antiseptic from the hospital

wafted to her, then the smell of lavender. No...not here. Back at the house when she started inside...

Lavender...her mother used a lavender scented lotion. Once when she was small, she'd gotten into the bottle and slathered her arms and legs with it. For her birthday, when she was four, her mother had given her a bottle all her own.

She clung to that sweet memory as she drifted to sleep, yet the nightmares returned. In that rainstorm...the man in her hallway...her mother screaming, the man's voice...

The next day, her mother staring blankly into space... wailing...yelling at her to go away...

A noise startled her awake, then a soft, husky voice. She opened her eyes, squinting in the dim light, looking up to see Stone's handsome, worried face, his dark eyes studying her. He reached out and brushed her cheek with the back of his hand.

"How do you feel?"

His tenderness brought tears to her eyes. How long had it been since anyone had really cared about her? Her ex certainly hadn't.

"Macy?"

She swallowed to wet her dry throat. "A headache, sore throat. I'll be okay."

A small smile of understanding passed across his broad chiseled face. "What did the doctor say?"

"A slight concussion. I wanted to go to the inn, but he insisted I stay for observation." She tried to sit up and winced, a coughing spell overcoming her.

Stone handed her the cup of water on the bedside table, and she took a long, slow drink. The water felt good on her throat as it went down.

Stone took the cup when she was finished and she sank back, exhausted. "Did you find anything at the house?"

"Forensics are processing the scene now, and Riggs is overseeing the arson investigation. There was a gas can left there. Maybe it'll yield something." He ran a hand through his hair. "Do you remember anything?"

"I took some of my mother's papers out to the car to look through later. When I turned, I saw a shadowy figure in the house and went to check it out." She paused, struggling again for details. "I couldn't tell if it was a man or a woman. But… I think I smelled lavender."

"Lavender?"

Macy nodded. "My mother used to have lavender lotion. The strange thing is that I hadn't smelled it before in the house since I got back."

His eyes narrowed, worry flickering in the dark depths.

Macy's pulse jumped. "What is it? Do you know something you're not telling me?"

Stone looked away. "We can talk about it tomorrow after you're feeling better."

Macy reached for his hand. "Tell me, Stone. Don't hold back."

He cleared his throat, his eyes filled with concern. "The lady who bought Kate's house said she saw your mother at your place earlier today."

Macy's chest clenched. Had her mother set the fire and tried to kill her?

Chapter Sixteen

Stone hated the pain in Macy's eyes. He should have kept his mouth shut tonight. Given her time to recover before he dropped that bombshell.

The very idea that her own mother would try to kill her had to come as a shock. Or had she already considered the possibility? What else wasn't she telling him about Lynn Stark?

"Do you want to talk about it?" he asked.

She shook her head. "What is there to discuss? I know my mother has personality disorders and can be violent. If she's scared now of getting caught for something she did years ago, it could push her over the edge."

"But to lash out at you?" he said, unable to keep the disbelief from his voice. "She's your mother, for God's sake. There has to be another explanation."

Macy rubbed her temple, her eyes drooping, and he tamped down his outrage. "I'm sorry, Macy."

She looked up at him with such emotion that his heart squeezed, and he gently stroked her cheek. More than anything he wanted to make things right for her. But he had no idea how to do that.

Maybe you can find Lynn and prove she didn't try to burn down the house with Macy inside.

But what if she had? How in the world would Macy live with that?

"You need to rest now," he said softly. "We can talk tomorrow when you're feeling better."

"I am tired," she admitted. "You can go."

He stroked her cheek again, and her eyes fluttered, then closed. He didn't intend to leave her alone, not knowing someone had tried to kill her. If the culprit realized she'd survived, he or she might come back to finish the job. "Just rest, Macy," he murmured.

Although he didn't think she heard him. She'd already drifted to sleep.

He stared at her for a long minute, his heart hammering with admiration and worry. Macy acted tough, but she had a vulnerable side. She just covered it up because she'd had to in order to survive.

In his mind, he saw her as a teenager. Quiet. Studious. An athlete. He'd watched her run track and remembered she was fast, that she blew by some of the other girls. The hundred-meter was her best event, and she always brought up the rear in the relays. She'd taken the school to the state championships. She'd been humble when praised, but she'd had a dogged competitive spirit and intense concentration.

Maybe because she was blocking out her terrible home life.

At least on the track she'd found accolades. Although he never saw her hanging out with the other girls afterward.

His phone buzzed. A text from Forensics: Prints on the gun case and rock used to break the window at the pawnshop belong to Lynn Stark.

He ran a hand over his face, his stomach churning. So not only had she been seen at the Stark house today, before the attack on Macy, but she'd stolen firearms after she'd escaped the psychiatric center.

Which meant she was armed and dangerous.

THE NIGHTMARES AND memories assaulted Macy in confusing snippets as she slept. She saw her mother slipping into the shadows of the house earlier. Heard her whispered warnings not to go in the basement. Saw her passed out on the kitchen floor half-naked with a bottle of pills beside her.

But even in her dreams with the haunting realization that her mother had actually been at the house, she fought the ugly possibility that her mother had dragged her in that closet and planned to burn her alive.

She moaned and rolled to her side, nausea building. Her eyes opened and then closed, the pain in her head so intense she begged for sleep to sweep her away again.

Another memory floated through her subconscious, launching her back in time. *She was seven years old, and she woke up to the sound of her mother's voice. When she tiptoed to the kitchen, her mother was dancing around and singing into the rolling pin as if it were a microphone. When she saw Macy, she laughed, took her hands, and they danced around together in their pajamas. Then they ate pizza and had Coke floats for breakfast on a picnic cloth in front of the TV and watched cartoons.*

"We're going to the carnival now," her mother said. "And then we'll get ice cream and go shopping and buy you the prettiest dress you've ever seen."

Macy didn't want dresses, but her mother was so happy and excited that she didn't dare say so.

They got dressed quickly, then drove to the carnival, and her mother squealed and laughed like a child as they rode ride after ride, and then her mother won a giant panda bear for her in a ring-toss game. They gorged on ice cream and cotton candy.

But when they went to town and walked toward the dress store, they passed a coffee shop and her mother sud-

*denly halted. For a long minute, she stared through the
window at a couple inside laughing and holding hands.*

*Then suddenly a dark shadow fell over her. She stiff-
ened, snatched Macy's hand and dragged her away. She
squeezed Macy's hand so tightly Macy cried out. But that
only made her mother madder, and she yelled at Macy to
shut up.*

*"Don't be a baby," her mother snapped as she yanked
her to the car.*

*Macy's lip quivered as tears trickled down her face,
and she couldn't help but cry.*

"I said shut up!" her mother screamed. "Shut up!"

*Macy buried her head into her hands and pressed her
fist to her mouth to keep from sobbing out loud as her
mother drove like a maniac home. When they got there,
her mother threw the panda bear in the trash outside, and
shoved Macy into her room and locked the door.*

Macy jerked her eyes open, disoriented, a sick feeling
overwhelming her. A low sound echoed around her, and
for a moment, she was so disoriented she struggled to recall where she was.

But slowly reality returned and the ugly truth hit her.
She was in the hospital. Someone wanted her dead.

Pulse quickening, she rolled to her back again, then
looked up and saw Stone in the recliner beside the bed,
his head lolled to the side. The noise she'd heard was his
soft snoring.

A five-o'clock shadow grazed his wide jaw, his button-
down shirt stretched across his thick muscled chest, ac-
centuating his broad shoulders, and a lock of his brown
hair fell across his forehead.

She should wake him and tell him to leave. But the fear
pounding her chest was relentless, and he looked so sexy
in that chair, that he made her feel safe.

It had been a long time since she'd felt safe.

So she closed her eyes again and allowed sleep to claim her, praying that the nightmares would leave her alone for a little while. But she knew they'd be back.

Still, she'd face them in the morning.

STONE WOKE THE next morning with a crick in his neck, the sound of medicine carts, nurses' voices and hospital machinery echoing from the halls.

He'd kept one eye half-open most of the night in case Macy's attacker showed up, but thankfully no one except the staff had come into the room. And they had been in plenty of times to take Macy's vitals. How anyone rested in a hospital was beyond him.

He rolled his shoulders and neck to work out the knots. But one look at Macy's pale face as she tossed and turned in the hospital bed and he knew staying with her had been worth it.

At least she was safe.

Although she appeared to be in the throes of a nightmare.

"No…" she cried. "Please stop…"

The pain in her cry tore at him, and he rubbed his hand over his bleary eyes, then gently stroked the hair from her forehead. "Macy, wake up, honey," he murmured. "You're having a bad dream."

She clenched the sheet in a white-knuckle grip, drawing his attention to the bruises on her hands and arms again as she slowly opened her eyes. He hoped to hell the forensics team found the attacker's DNA beneath her nails. Then he could track down the animal who'd hurt Macy and lock him or her up.

"You stayed all night?" Macy said in a raw whisper.

She sounded surprised.

"Of course," he said. "I'm not leaving you alone again until we find the person who set that fire."

Emotions glittered in her eyes, but the doctor came in before she could speak.

"How are you feeling this morning?" the doctor asked as she reviewed Macy's chart.

Macy lifted her chin. "Fine. I'm ready to be discharged."

The doctor quirked a brow, a glint in her eye. "I'm sure you are. But you did sustain a contusion on the back of your head." She tapped the chart. "Your vitals look good, but you need to rest another day. If I release you, I don't know that will happen."

Macy opened her mouth to argue, but Stone cut her off. "She will. I will watch over her myself."

Macy shot him a venomous look, but he simply graced her with a challenging smile as if to say it was the hospital or him. Her choice. The only way to deal with her, he realized. She did not like to be out of control.

He could relate to that.

"Macy? You are coming home with me—" he paused for emphasis "—under protective custody, of course."

That earned him another glare, but she released a resigned sigh. "All right. I just want to get out of here. Who the hell can sleep with people coming in all hours of the night waking you up to make sure you're breathing?"

Her exasperation made his lips twitch with a tiny smile, but he didn't dare comment. He liked the fire in Macy, liked her athleticism and grit.

"Fine," the doctor said. "I'll sign release papers. But if you experience dizziness, nausea or disorientation, give me a call."

"I know the drill," Macy said drily. "It's not the first concussion I've had."

New concern flickered in the doctor's eyes. "Then maybe we should run more tests."

Macy was already pushing the sheets away. "I only meant that I understand the symptoms. And of course I'll call you if I have problems." She gave the doctor a saccharine smile that neither the doctor nor Stone was buying.

All the more reason he would not let her out of his sight for the next few days. He didn't intend to let anything happen to Macy on his watch.

MACY KNEW SHE was being stubborn, but she hadn't survived her life by being a wimp, and she didn't intend to start now. She wanted answers, and she was damn well going to get them. Even if it meant putting up with Stone's protective attitude a little while longer.

Her ex had never been protective. Trey was a taker, not a giver. She'd been a fool to believe anything else.

Stone excused himself to make a call while she signed dismissal papers. The medics or nurses, she couldn't remember which, had stripped her clothes and she knew Stone would have sent them to Forensics, which she would have done herself. So she was wearing scrubs back to the inn.

Maybe she could convince Stone to leave her there.

He looked somber when he returned and lapsed into a brooding mood as he drove her back to the inn.

"Stone, I'll really be fine here at Celeste's," she said as he escorted her to her room.

"You're staying with me until we catch whoever attacked you," he said. "You know two heads are better than one. I may be more objective than you."

She tensed, an argument building in her mind.

"And before you say I'm being controlling," Stone said, "remember that we worked well together to uncover the person threatening Kate and what really happened with Ned Hodgkins. I also vowed to protect the citizens of Briar Ridge, and that means anyone visiting or passing through, too."

Damn, he made a compelling case. She blinked, biting

her tongue. But she didn't like exposing herself and her family secrets.

What other choice did she have, though? He *had* saved her life. And although her mother had hurt her, her emotions were all over the place. She might have a blind spot when it came to her.

She could not afford that.

Her job was all she had left.

"All right. But let me get those papers out of my car," she said, grateful she'd confiscated them before the fire.

The hair on the back of her neck prickled. Then again, if the papers held a clue, it was possible that whoever set that fire could have wanted to dispose of them.

Hope battled through the hazy fog of despair eating at her. She'd look at them as soon as they reached Stone's house.

Chapter Seventeen

"Pack everything you'll need for a few days," Stone said as he stood at the door to Macy's room. "You can stay at my place as long as you want. And in case you're worried, I have two bedrooms, so you'll have your own room and bath."

Macy's heart fluttered. She'd wondered about that. She entered the room, still hesitant. "Stone, I would be safe here."

"Don't argue with me," Stone said. "I can't work if I don't know you're safe. And...there's something else I have to tell you."

Her heart skipped a beat at the intensity in his eyes. "What is it?"

"Prints from the pawnshop where the guns were stolen match your mother's."

Macy's breath caught. "Then she's armed."

He nodded. "Armed and maybe panicked. You know what a dangerous combination that is."

Macy stewed over that information. "If she had a gun, why set fire to the house? Why not shoot me?"

"To get rid of forensics," he said matter-of-factly.

A shudder rippled through her. She didn't want to believe that her mother would kill her, but she couldn't ignore facts.

Resigned, she went to the bathroom and packed her toiletries, then gathered her suitcase. Stone insisted on carrying it outside.

"I'll take my car," Macy said as she reached for her keys.

"You're not driving today, not after the head injury," Stone said bluntly. "Besides, leaving your car here could throw off whoever is looking for you. If they see it at my place, they'll know where you are."

He had a point.

"Okay, let me get those papers and the notes I've made on the case so far."

He stowed her luggage in the trunk of his police car while she grabbed her computer bag, her notes on the investigation and the box of paperwork she'd taken from her mother's house.

Her head was throbbing as he drove away from the inn, and she stayed in the car as he stopped at the diner to pick them up breakfast and coffee. The sidewalks were already filling with locals and tourists for the upcoming Fourth festivities, and children laughed and chased each other in the park in the center of town.

Across the street, she spotted a woman with curly brown hair pushing a swing with a young girl in it, and it took her back to her childhood. Except she didn't remember her mother ever bringing her here. Kate's mother had.

Another woman caught her eye as she slipped into the shadows, and her pulse quickened. Was that her mother ducking into a side street?

She reached for the door handle to climb out and give chase, then the woman turned, and Macy blinked her into focus. Not her mother.

Good grief. She was being paranoid.

Stone returned a moment later with bags of food and hot coffee, and she inhaled the rich scents, then added sweetener to her coffee. One swig and her throbbing head already felt better.

Five minutes later, Stone pulled down a long drive to a log cabin on the creek that looked rustic and charming with the pines, live oaks and mountains in the background. Crepe myrtles and hydrangeas added color to the landscaping, and the front porch held rocking chairs.

"This is beautiful," Macy said.

Stone's look turned sheepish. "Thanks. I had it built a few years ago. Needed to be close to town but not in the house where I grew up."

Macy nodded in understanding.

They got out in silence, and she carried the food and her computer bag while he snagged her luggage. When Macy entered, she was struck by the ten-foot ceilings, floor to ceiling windows across the back of the living room that offered a view of the steep ridges and overhangs of the mountains. His furnishings were simple: leather sofa, comfy club chairs, a blanket tossed across the back of the couch. The space was open concept with granite counters, rich wood cabinets, a large breakfast island and rustic beams.

"Wow," she said, impressed. "This is really nice." And very private, she thought. Much like Stone himself.

Stone shrugged. "I like it." He gestured toward the right. "Guest room is on that side. Mine is on the other."

Macy followed him to a bedroom that held a black iron bed covered in a log cabin quilt with an adjoining bathroom. A claw-foot tub was the centerpiece. Both spaces looked as if they hadn't been used, suggesting he rarely had guests.

He placed her suitcase on a luggage rack in the corner of the bedroom, then paused at the doorway and gestured toward his clothes. "I reek of smoke, and I'm sure you'd like a hot shower."

She looked down at the scrubs, still feeling dirty from

the attack the night before. Her hair smelled like smoke and was matted from where she'd bled. "That would be great. Then we can eat and look through those papers."

"Sounds like a plan."

He stepped from the room, and Macy rolled her shoulders, then closed the door. She pulled fresh clothes from her bag, settled her toiletries in the bathroom, then looked at the tub that beckoned. A long hot bath would soothe her aches and pains.But she didn't have time to indulge herself. For now she turned on the shower water, stripped and climbed inside. But as the water sluiced over her, she closed her eyes and tried to recall more details about the attack.

The scent of the lavender...the neighbor had seen her mother at the house. Her mother with a gun...

A dead hit man in the basement. The fact that her mother had taken lovers—or a lover—who she knew nothing about.

Suddenly antsy to get back to work, she dried off, combed through her damp hair, and dressed in a pair of jeans and a T-shirt. Then she hurried into the kitchen for more coffee, food, and to look at those papers her mother had held on to.

But when she entered the living room, Kate and Brynn were there. Stone gave her an apologetic look. "They heard about the incident at your house." He gestured to the coffeepot. "Help yourself. I'll be back." He disappeared into his bedroom, and Kate rushed to Macy and pulled her toward the sofa. A peacefulness fell over Macy like a warm blanket. Macy had loved Kate the minute she'd let her sleep in her room that first night she'd found her outside her house in the storm. Although Kate had always been self-conscious of her curves, Macy thought they were gorgeous, and her auburn hair was as glassy as a pony's.

Plus she was loving, kind and compassionate, just like her mother had been.

Brynn had already parked her wheelchair beside the couch and held a mug of coffee. Even though she looked worried, her blond hair made her look like an angel. In spite of her mother's ill attitude, Brynn had always been pretty on the inside as she was on the outside. "We've been worried sick about you," Brynn said, her voice cracking.

Kate squeezed her hands, and Macy fought tears.

"Are you okay, Macy?' Brynn asked. "Riggs told me what happened last night."

Macy breathed out, glad she'd at least showered the stench of smoke and blood off her. "I'm fine. But it was a long night."

Kate went and poured the two of them coffee, and Macy cradled the cup between her hands.

"What happened?" Brynn asked.

Macy inhaled a fortifying breath and explained the information she'd gleaned so far.

Kate's expression faltered, and Brynn glanced at Stone's closed door. "Is there something going on between you and Stone?"

Macy's heart fluttered. For a brief second as she glanced around the cozy home and thought of Stone staying with her all night, she longed for more. But she gave a small shake of her head. "He's just doing his job, assigned himself as my bodyguard."

A heartbeat passed, and Kate leaned forward. "I know your mother had issues, Macy. But I can't believe she'd actually try to kill you. Have you considered that Trey might have tried to hurt you?"

Macy jerked her head up. "I guess it's possible. He was furious over the divorce and the arrest."

"Has he threatened you?" Brynn asked.

Macy hesitated. "He's left angry messages, but I assumed it was all smoke." Maybe she should have taken the threats more seriously.

"Did you tell Stone?" Kate asked.

Macy shook her head. "I've been so caught up in finding my mother and what happened with that body that I just blew it off."

But the wheels in her head started spinning. If Trey had seen the news about the murder at her house, he could have come after her for revenge, knowing she'd be looking at the dead body and her mother for answers, and not at him as a threat.

STONE HADN'T MEANT to eavesdrop, but he heard Kate ask Macy if anything was going on with the two of them, and she'd denied it.

He wasn't so sure about that. Although maybe the attraction was all one-sided.

But the question about her ex disturbed him. He'd been so caught up in the murder at the Stark house and Macy's mother's disappearance that it hadn't occurred to him that Trey might have retaliated against Macy.

And why hadn't she told him about the threats?

He showered quickly, then dressed in clean jeans and a button-down white shirt and decided to find Trey. He made a quick call to his deputy. "Bridges, see if you can locate Trey Cushing. I want him brought in for questioning."

"Cushing? Isn't he that special agent's ex-husband?" Murphy asked.

"He is," Stone replied. "She arrested him a few weeks ago, but he was released. Apparently he's been leaving her threatening messages."

"You think he may have attacked her at that house and set the fire?"

"I don't know," Stone said. "He has a temper and told her she'd be sorry for humiliating her. Call the lab and asked him to compare his DNA with forensics they found at the Stark house."

"Copy that. Any ideas where Cushing is?" Bridges asked.

"No, but call local motels. He didn't have any family left in town, and he sure as hell didn't have friends. Also check DMV records for an address in case he has property somewhere in the area." He drummed his fingers on his thigh. "He drives a black Ford truck. I'm not sure about the license plate, but see if you can find it."

"On it," Bridges agreed. "By the way, Gretta has already called, demanding an interview about the fire and the murder case."

"Stall her," Stone said. "Macy needs time to recover, and I need time to investigate without Gretta breathing down my neck. She'll just create panic in town."

Bridges agreed, and Stone ended the call, then went to join Macy and her friends.

"When this is over and you're safe, we need to look for bridesmaids dresses," Kate said. "I was thinking that you and Brynn can wear a little black dress, any style you like."

Macy gave Kate a smile, although she was tracing her finger along the rim of her coffee mug as if distracted.

"I'm sorry," Kate said. "I guess it seems insensitive for me to talk about wedding plans when you're going through so much."

Macy shook her head. "No, we spent too much time apart. I'm happy for you, Kate. Planning your wedding is something to look forward to."

Stone wondered about her own wedding to Cushing. What had gone wrong? Would she ever consider marriage again?

He shook away the thoughts. Now was not the time to consider a personal relationship. He had to protect her and help her put her life back together.

Then she'd leave. But at least when she did, he'd know she was safe. That would have to be enough.

As SOON AS Kate and Brynn left, Stone heated their sausage and biscuits, and they devoured them. Macy was surprised that she was hungry, then realized she hadn't eaten the night before.

"Why didn't you tell me about Cushing's threats?" he asked.

Macy paused, her coffee cup halfway to her mouth. "I guess I didn't think he'd follow through," she said. "You know Trey is a lot of talk and posturing."

"But threats?" Stone's dark gaze met hers. "Considering the circumstances, Macy, we have to consider that he meant them. Getting arrested in front of our class could have put him over the edge."

Pain clenched her chest. "I know that."

"Do you think he's capable of violence?"

Doubts assailed her along with memories of his outbursts when he didn't get his way. "He does have a temper. Maybe we should talk to him."

"I've already asked my deputy to find him and bring him in for questioning," Stone said. "And Macy, we're working together. You have to trust me. Don't keep anything else from me."

Macy gave a little nod, although it was still difficult for her to talk about Trey. She'd been so foolish...

Turning back to the case, she opened the box of her mother's papers and organized them into piles. "There are bills, bank statements and checkbooks going all the way back thirty years," she said. Her mother had been a pack rat.

"Your mother kept all this?" Stone said.

Macy made a low sound in her throat. "She wasn't exactly organized," she said, thinking about her chaotic ways.

"At least here's the deed to the house," she said, then studied it. "It was paid off."

Stone arched a brow. "That surprises me. How did she do that on a housekeeper's salary?"

Macy shook her head, curious herself. "Good question. I know she worked when I was little, but in high school, I don't remember her being employed on a regular basis. By then, she was too…unstable."

"I'll look through her bills if you want to start searching her financials," Stone offered.

Macy nodded and began sorting and stacking the bank statements in order of month and year to make comparisons. She used a legal pad to list names of accounts and amounts paid to her mother in one column, then in another column listed payments her mother had made.

On another sheet she wrote the names of everyone she knew of that her mother had cleaned for and the years she'd worked for the clients so she could match those names to the ones in the bank statements.

It was a painstakingly slow process as she combed through statement after statement. While some of her clients had paid with a check, there were cash deposits that she couldn't trace.

The list of clients:

Beverly Jones
Ken and Pat Dansing
Vicki Germaine
Troy and Shirley Cregan
Dodie Lewis
Loretta Pruitt
Prentice and Adeline Walkman

She searched for discrepancies and found payments from Beverly, the Dansings, the Cregans, Loretta Pruitt and the Walkmans. There was nothing from Dodie Lewis, suggesting she probably paid in cash. The payments were what she would have expected for a maid, although it appeared the Walkmans had paid almost double the others.

It could have been due to the fact that their house was larger, she supposed. Or perhaps she did more in-depth cleaning for the couple. They also seemed more consistent, and she'd been paid weekly whereas the others ranged between twice a month and once a month.

The time frames and payments coincided with what her clients had told Macy. She'd begun working for the Walkmans the year before Macy was born.

Their son had died earlier that same year.

Her skin prickled with unease. Something about the dates seemed curious. But it made sense that if they'd lost a child, they would have been distraught and needed help around the house.

Her eyes grew blurry from studying the numbers and she stood and stretched, then went and got more coffee. "Do you want another cup?" she asked Stone, who was still scouring the stacks and stacks of bills.

"Yeah, thanks," he said.

Macy poured them both a mug and carried it to him. The gesture and close quarters felt somehow intimate, although Stone seemed oblivious. Instead, his brow furrowed as he opened another envelope, removed the contents and studied them.

Macy looked over his shoulder. "What is that?"

"Paperwork noting that your mother's house was paid off." He pointed to the date. "It looks like a lump sum of seventy thousand dollars was sent to the mortgage company."

Macy leaned closer and noted the date, and her heart

hammered. "It was paid off on my first birthday." She glanced at Stone. "The question is—where did she get that kind of money?"

Chapter Eighteen

Stone didn't know Macy's mother well enough to be able to answer that. But the large cash deposit was definitely suspicious. "Did your mother have any family? Perhaps a relative who passed who might have left her the money?"

Macy rubbed her forehead in thought. "Not that I know of. She said her parents died when she was sixteen and she became a ward of the state. And I don't remember her ever talking about other relatives."

"Maybe she did but they were estranged," Stone suggested.

"With her condition, that would make sense," Macy agreed.

"Let me keep looking through her papers," he said. "I'll also search county records to see if she received any kind of inheritance."

"An inheritance wouldn't have been paid out in cash, though," Macy pointed out.

Stone stewed over that. "True. Unless it was paid to a second party, say a relative or sibling who divided it up and gave your mother her share in cash."

"Look into it," Macy said, although she didn't seem convinced. "There's another answer, you know."

Stone's gaze met hers, turmoil darkening her eyes. "Your father?"

"It would fit. He didn't want anything to do with me, so he paid her to keep quiet."

"Yet he provided the two of you with a home," Stone said in an attempt to soften the blow.

Macy shrugged. She couldn't really call that house a home. "I'll keep looking through the bank statements and her calendar to see if she might have visited the prison to see Hubert."

They settled back in for another hour, then Stone stepped onto the back deck and phoned County Records. He asked to speak to Tammy, whom he'd known for years, and explained that he needed information on Lynn Stark, specifically if there were records of her receiving any kind of inheritance.

"I'll see what I can find out and get back to you," Tammy said.

He thanked her, then returned to his computer and ran a background search on Lynn Stark, looking for her birth certificate. She was born in Asheville to Tim and Betty Stark on November 1. Father worked at the carpet mills and mother worked as a cashier at a quick mart.

Just as she'd told Macy, her parents died when she was sixteen and she'd become a ward of the state. At eighteen she'd left the group home and…there wasn't much of a paper trail after that. She had worked at a grocery store for a while, then moved to Briar Ridge, where she'd given birth to Macy at Briar Ridge Hospital.

"When do the checks for housekeeping services start?" he asked Macy.

She checked her list. "The year before I was born." Macy thumped her finger on one of the statements. "You know this is strange."

"What?" Stone asked.

She glanced at her notes, making comparisons between the spreadsheets she was creating. "There are two payments from the Walkmans that were entered after they said they moved away."

Stone frowned. He didn't know what that meant, but it was worth asking about.

His phone buzzed. His deputy. "I need to answer this."

He left her studying the statements while he answered the call. "Sheriff."

"I found Cushing," Murphy said. "I'm bringing him in."

Stone's stomach clenched. "I'll be right there."

THE NUMBERS AND timing of payments were still bugging Macy, but her head was throbbing again so she downed two painkillers and chugged a glass of water.

"My deputy brought Cushing in," Stone said as he hung up the phone. "I'm going to talk to him now."

Macy sucked in a breath and stood. "I'll go with you."

Stone's gaze met hers. "Are you sure that's a good idea? I can handle it."

"I've known Trey a lot longer. I can tell when he's lying." And if he wanted to kill her, she wanted to confront him. She deserved that after putting up with his moodiness during that first year of marriage. And then his overbearing attitude when they'd split. He'd thought he could bully her into coming back to him.

But once she'd made up her mind, there was no turning back.

Stone conceded, and she grabbed her purse and weapon and strapped it on, then followed Stone outside to his car. The bright sunlight hurt her eyes, and she closed them as he drove to the police station.

"Are you sure you're okay, Macy?" he asked gruffly. "If you need to go back and lie down and rest, you can."

"I'm fine," she said, although the winding road was making her slightly nauseated.

Five minutes later, he parked at the station.

"Dammit, Gretta is here," Stone muttered.

A frisson of nerves danced up Macy's spine as she spotted the reporter's BMW. "I swear that woman knows when a crime happened before it happens."

Stone chuckled, and they got out and walked up to the entrance. She squared her shoulders as they entered, bracing herself to contain her emotions as the vulture of a woman made a beeline straight toward her. Deputy Bridges stood from behind his desk with a shake of his head as if to say he had no control over Gretta.

"Macy, are you okay? I heard someone tried to kill you last night. That's horrible," Gretta said, her tone concerned.

Macy recognized her fake smile for what it was. A ploy to finagle information from her.

"I'm fine," Macy said with a curt smile.

Stone interceded. "If you're here for a news report, we can't comment on an ongoing investigation."

Gretta feigned an innocent look. "Well, the public does deserve to know what's going on," she said, her eyes sparking with determination. "If there's a predator in town, they should be warned."

Macy gritted her teeth. She couldn't argue with that, but she knew it was Gretta's way of manipulating them into talking.

"Gretta, we have work to do," Stone said. "We'll let you know when we're ready to give a statement."

She turned to Macy with an eyebrow raise. "Special Agent Stark?"

Macy folded her arms. "As the sheriff said, we will contact you when we have a statement."

She gave Gretta a saccharine smile, then pushed past her. A gleam of approval flickered in Stone's eyes as he gestured to his deputy to get Trey. He led her past his receptionist's desk, then through a set of double doors to an interrogation room.

A minute later, the deputy escorted Trey inside. He was fuming as he strode across the room. "What the hell are you doing?" he shouted at Macy.

"Sit down," Stone said. "We just want to talk."

Trey flung his hands angrily. "Then why drag me here and put me in a holding cell?" Trey bit out. "Humiliating me in front of the town wasn't enough for you, Macy? You want revenge because your bogus charges didn't stick?"

Macy schooled her reaction by squaring her shoulders. "Where were you last night, Trey?"

He narrowed his eyes. "What? What business is it of yours? You divorced me, remember?"

Stone's boots clicked on the floor as he crossed to stand in front of Trey. "I said *sit down*. This won't take long."

Trey glanced back and forth between them, tension radiating from his rigid movements. He sank into the chair with a thud. "What the hell is this about?" Trey barked.

Stone leaned over Trey and pinned him with an intimidating look. "Answer the question. Where were you last night?"

Trey heaved a long, labored breath, his look seething. "I knew you were a cold bitch, Macy. But not cold enough to try to pin attempted murder or arson on me."

Macy crossed her arms. So he did know about the fire and that she'd been assaulted. "*Where* were you?"

He cut his eyes toward Stone, then back at her, his jaw clenched. "As a matter of fact, I was in bed with another woman." His eyes flickered with satisfaction as if he thought she cared.

He was wrong. She pulled a small notepad from her pocket and pushed it toward him. "Write down her name and contact information."

"You jealous, babe?"

Macy gave a wry laugh. "You wish. All I want is the truth, Trey. And to get you out of my life for good."

He angled his head toward her. "And that's all I want from you. To be rid of you for good, too."

The underlying threat in his tone was meant to frighten her. But Macy had long ago stopped being afraid of Trey. Although she would check into his story.

And if he'd taken advantage of the murder investigation to try to kill her, she'd make sure he was locked up tight.

STONE HAD NEVER liked Trey Cushing, but his opinion of the man kept diving lower and lower. He liked to bully those smaller and more vulnerable than him. He always had.

At least Macy had stood up to him.

But at what cost?

Would Cushing actually try to kill her?

Some men were so obsessive about a woman they would do anything to keep her from being with someone else. Was that what had happened here?

Cushing scribbled down the name Desiree Memes and her cell phone number, and Macy reached for it.

"Who is she, Trey? Another hooker?" Macy asked drily.

That told Stone a lot about their marriage. Not only was Trey a bully but a cheater.

"Don't *you* want to know," Trey teased in a singsongy voice.

Macy shook her head in disgust, and Stone motioned for her to follow him. He'd let Cushing stew while he verified his story.

In the hall, Stone took the name from Macy. "I'll follow up on this."

"Stone, I can do it," Macy said.

"Let me do this for you, Macy." He squeezed her arm gently. "Take my office. Keep working on the case."

Macy nodded, relieved she wouldn't have to hear the sordid details of Trey's night with his lover. That is, if he was telling the truth and his alibi checked out. Knowing him, he could have persuaded some woman to cover for him.

She carried her computer bag and the files she'd been looking at into Stone's office and settled behind the small table in the corner. The payments from the Walkmans that had continued after she was dismissed still perplexed her. Although the family could have simply been generous and given her some kind of severance pay.

The lump sum payment also stumped her. None of the people she'd cleaned for would have had that kind of money. Except for the Walkmans.

But why would they pay off her mother's loan? She'd seen them campaigning for senate and they were all over the place raising money for children's charities, a passion they'd obviously developed after they'd lost their son. Had they felt sorry for her mother and adopted her as a charity project back then?

She wished she could take a look at their financial records, but that would require either a warrant, which she had no justification for, or hacking into their accounts.

She couldn't justify a desperate move like that at this time.

Deciding to find out more about the couple, she called Loretta Pruitt, the woman who'd run the day care.

"What can I do for you?" Loretta asked.

"I'm still talking to everyone my mother worked for. I wondered what you could tell me about the Walkmans. Was my mother working for them when they lost their son?"

A heartbeat passed. "No, she started there a few months after. A young girl named Esme cleaned for them before that. But a couple of months after they lost their child, Esme left for some reason. That's when they hired your mama."

"Does Esme still live around here?" Macy asked.

"Last I heard she got married and moved about thirty miles north."

"Do you know her married name?"

Loretta hesitated. "Frances. Man's first name was Buddy." She gave a soft laugh. "I remember thinking Frances was unusual for a last name."

"What did you think of the Walkmans themselves?"

Another heartbeat. "I'm not sure why you're asking all this. But they seemed like a nice couple. Were devoted to that little boy. It nearly destroyed them when they lost him."

Macy thanked her, then ended the call and used her laptop to run a search for Esme and Buddy Frances. She ran a background check but neither had a police record. DMV found them both. They were still married and lived in an area of the mountains called Woody Creek.

A further search and she found they owned a food truck called Nacho Mama's. She punched the number for the truck and a man answered. She could hear pans banging and voices as if they were busy.

"May I speak to Esme?" Macy asked.

"Sure, hang on," the man said.

More voices and clatter in the truck, and several dings signaling an order was up. Finally Esme answered. "This is Esme. You want to place a to-go order?"

"No, thanks," Macy said, then identified herself. "I'm just looking for some information about Adeline and Prentice Walkman."

"Listen, if you're a reporter, I got nothing to say," Esme said, her voice agitated. "I know how this goes. Press trying to dig up dirt on them because he's running for senate."

"I'm with the FBI and am investigating a cold case in Briar Ridge, which involved a woman named Lynn Stark. I understand that years ago she cleaned for Adeline and

Prentice Walkman, and that you worked for them before she did."

Esme's breathing rattled over the line. "I don't understand."

"I'm just collecting background information. I know they paid Ms. Stark well and wondered if you had the same experience."

A tense second passed. "They paid me for cleaning. That's all."

Macy went still, her choice of wording striking her as odd. Was she implying that they paid her mother for something else?

"I was sorry to hear that they lost a child," Macy said, trying another tactic. "I'm sure that was a difficult time."

"It was terrible," Esme said, her voice filled with sympathy. "As expected, they both took the boy's death extremely hard. Lots of guilt and blame going around. Mrs. Walkman became depressed and withdrawn. Her husband tried to reach her, but his wife seemed too deep in grief to accept comfort."

"That is sad, but it's not uncommon for couples who lose a child to drift apart." She waited, hoping Esme would offer more, but she seemed hesitant to speak. "Why did you leave, exactly?"

"I…really can't say," Esme said. "I just needed a change." Someone shouted in the background, and Esme cleared her throat. "Sorry I can't help you. I have to go. We're really busy right now. Got a line a half mile long for lunch."

Macy thanked her, but her mind was churning as she ended the call and replayed the conversation in her head. As an agent, she'd become adept at reading the nuances of people's gestures, inflections in their tones and the things they didn't say.

Esme was holding something back. To protect herself or the Walkmans?

Chapter Nineteen

Stone halfway hoped Trey's alibi did not check out. He wanted to lock the bastard up for threatening Macy and make sure he stayed away from her.

But he was a lawman, and if he crossed the line, he'd lose the respect of the town. And himself. And possibly Macy.

And that was starting to matter to him more than he wanted to admit.

So he left Cushing to sweat it out, stepped into the second interrogation room and called the number Trey had given. The woman's name was Desiree Memes. Seriously.

At least his deputy had taken Cushing off guard so he hadn't had a chance to call and give the woman a heads-up.

Although if Trey had planned his revenge on Macy, he could have orchestrated an alibi in advance.

The phone rang three times before a woman picked up and said hello.

"This is Sheriff Lawson in Briar Ridge," Stone said. "Is this Desiree?"

A nervous cough echoed back. "Yes. Am I in trouble, Sherriff?"

"I don't know. Are you?"

"No, I mean I haven't done anything wrong."

Still, anxiety laced her voice. "I need you to tell me where you were yesterday from 5:00 p.m. on."

An awkward pause. "What is this about?"

"Just routine questions," he said bluntly. "You can answer now, or I can pick you up and bring you in to the station and we can talk here."

A voice echoed in the background, someone calling her name.

"Listen, my husband is home. He can't hear this."

Stone shook his head in disgust. "Then tell me the truth."

Her sharp intake of breath echoed back, a breath filled with apprehension. "I was with Trey Cushing," she said. "We…met after the reunion in town a few weeks ago and have been seeing each other since." Her voice cracked. "But please, you can't tell my husband. There's no telling what he'd do."

Dammit. She truly sounded scared. But she'd just admitted to having an affair and given Trey Cushing an alibi at the same time.

"You were with him all evening and night?" Stone asked.

Another awkward second passed. "Yes, he got a room at the motel outside of town. My husband was on a long haul and just got back."

Did no one treat their marriage vows as sacred anymore?

"If I learn you're lying," Stone said sharply, "your husband finding out will be the least of your worries."

She gasped and he hung up. Dammit to hell, he believed her. Which got Trey off the hook.

And put them back on the path to viewing Macy's mother as a suspect.

MACY WAS STILL stewing over Esme's cryptic response when Stone returned.

"Trey's alibi checks out," he said. "I guess we have to cut him loose."

Macy sighed, relieved that her ex actually hadn't tried to murder her in cold blood. Although that pointed the finger back at her mother, which would be even more difficult to accept.

"I'll get him," Stone said. He disappeared through the back, and a couple of minutes later, returned with Trey. Belligerence radiated from her ex as he glared at her.

"I told you I was innocent, so stop trying to pin everything bad that happens to you on me," he growled. "Did you ever think that you bring these things on yourself?"

His comment felt like a punch in the gut. Stone gripped his arms and shoved Trey against the wall. "Listen to me, Trey, and listen good. Stay away from Macy. If you so much as make a phone call to her or come within twenty-five feet of her, I'll arrest you for stalking and attempted murder."

Trey raised his chin in challenge. "Good luck making that stick."

"Even if it doesn't," Stone said with a menacing smile, "it'll make your life hell. And I'll enjoy every minute of it."

Trey jerked his arm away from Stone, shot Macy a venomous look, then strode across the room. The door slammed as he exited, the air in the office fraught with tension.

Macy's phone buzzed. The Franceses' number. Her breath quickened. Had Esme decided to talk?

She connected the call. "Special Agent Macy Stark. Esme?"

"No, this is her husband, Buddy." His voice was low, muffled. "She told me about your call, and she doesn't know I'm talking to you. I'd like to keep it that way."

Macy stiffened. "I'm listening."

His uneven breathing filled the silence for a moment. "You wanted to know about the Walkmans?"

"Yes."

"Everything Esme told you is true," Buddy said. "But she had a soft spot for the couple, felt really sorry for them after they lost the boy."

"That was tragic," Macy murmured.

"It was," Buddy agreed. "But after a few months the wife was really depressed and her husband…well, he was having a hard time."

"That's understandable," Macy said, unsure where this was going.

"What I'm trying to say here, and I'm not trying to malign his character, and Esme doesn't want the press to get hold of this, but…well, he tried to seduce Esme."

Macy's breath caught.

"She turned him down, and he put pressure on her, but we were dating and she told me and…so she cut ties."

Now the conversation with Esme made sense. "I see. How did Mr. Walkman handle the rejection?" Macy asked.

"He was miffed, but he offered her a nice severance, and she agreed to keep quiet about it because, like I said, she felt sorry for the couple and didn't want his wife to find out."

The hair on the back of Macy's neck prickled. If Prentice Walkman had been looking for comfort with Esme, he could have looked for it after she left.

Her mother came to work for the couple shortly after Esme left. What if he'd tried to seduce her?

STONE SAW THE discomfort on Macy's face as she ended the call. "What is it?"

Macy tapped her fingers on her arm. "I talked to Esme Frances and her husband. She cleaned for the Walkmans before my mother went to work there."

"I gather that she had something interesting to say about the Walkmans," Stone said gruffly.

Macy nodded, then relayed her conversation with

Buddy. "Esme kept quiet to protect the couple out of compassion for their situation."

Stone's jaw tightened. "So while his wife was grieving, he was going to cheat on her with the housekeeper."

Macy didn't like it, either. "A real stand-up guy," she muttered.

"And one who wouldn't have wanted that to come out," Stone said.

"According to Esme's husband," Macy said, "he gave her a nice severance so she would keep quiet."

Stone grunted in disgust, but the jumbled pieces of the puzzling case were shifting, maybe into place. "Are you thinking what I'm thinking?"

Macy raised a brow. "That if he tried to seduce Esme, he might have done the same thing with someone else." Emotions glittered in her eyes. "Like my mother." She swallowed back emotions. "And what if he succeeded? Mom was young and vulnerable and alone. Maybe she gave in. Or…maybe he paid her for sex." The statement felt sour on her tongue, but she couldn't ignore the possibility.

Stone ran his hand through his hair. "He could have paid her to keep quiet."

Macy paled, and he realized where her mind was headed.

"The timing, when my mother worked for the couple…" Macy said, pushing the papers around as she looked at dates. "She went to work for them the year before I was born." She searched another set of papers, frown lines deepening her forehead. "And the house was paid off around my first birthday."

She leaned her head into her hands. "Good God, Stone. We wondered if my real father paid off that loan. What if that man is Prentice Walkman?"

Stone's heart pounded. Walkman was a well-known and respected attorney. He was also running for senate.

If he had an illegitimate child, he wouldn't want that to come out now, not with the upcoming election. "Dammit, Macy. I don't like this. We have to talk to the Walkmans."

Macy felt sick to her stomach. Was it possible Prentice Walkman was her father?

All these years she'd wondered…had looked at men on the streets or in stores or restaurants and wondered if he might be right in front of her. If he lived in Briar Ridge.

If he'd kept in touch with her mother.

If he'd known her mother was ill and hadn't cared enough to try to save her.

And now…to think he might be an established attorney, a man running for senate…that he had known and paid her mother to keep his dirty little secret.

"Excuse me." She stood and rushed toward the restroom, a dizzy spell clawing at her. Inside, she closed the door and staggered to the sink, then ran cold water and splashed her face. Nauseated, her hands shook as she snatched a couple of paper towels and dampened them, then pressed them to the back of her neck. Her body was trembling, anger and disbelief making her stomach seize into a hard knot.

A sob wrenched her gut, and for a moment, she allowed the tears to fall before she pulled herself together.

Then a seed of doubt bled through her emotions.

She could be wrong. Could be jumping to conclusions.

Drying her face with another paper towel, she straightened and finger-combed her hair, then exhaled.

Stone was right. They had to question the Walkmans. It wouldn't be an easy conversation, but now that the ugly thought had planted itself in her mind she couldn't let it go without following through.

Her mother had definitely been working for the Walkmans when she was conceived. If Prentice wasn't her father, he and his wife might know who was.

Pinching her cheeks to bring back the color, she tossed the paper towels in the trash, then opened the door. Stone was waiting in the hall, his eyes dark with concern.

"Macy?"

"I'm fine," she said quickly.

He jangled his keys in his hand. "I called and Mrs. Walkman is home. I told her I needed to speak to her and her husband. If you want to stay here, I'll go alone."

Macy shook her head. "I want to see their faces when we confront them."

Stone muttered that he understood, stopped at the reception desk and told Hattie Mae Perkins he'd be out for a while, then they walked outside together.

Macy lapsed into silence as Stone drove them through town. The stores and street signs were decorated for the Fourth with red, white and blue streamers, and flyers advertised the parade and kids' bicycle decorating contest.

Macy faintly remembered the town's celebration when she was younger. Vendors selling handmade crafts and jams and jellies pitched tarps to hawk their wares, and food trucks set up in the town square while the covered pavilion became a stage for local musicians. Bluegrass and country music bands were featured along with cloggers and the kids' dance teams in town performed. American flags hung everywhere, and she saw a group of high schoolers gathered working on the float for the parade.

She tried to remember if her mother had ever brought her to the parade, but the only faces she remembered were Kate's and her mother's. God, she missed that woman.

Halfway to the Walkmans' house, which was miles and miles out of town and near Asheville, Stone stopped at the Barbeque Pit, and they went inside and ordered sandwiches and sweet potato fries. The smoky scent of pulled pork, chicken and brisket filled the quaint restaurant, and Stone dug into his as if he hadn't eaten in days.

Macy nibbled on hers, although she barely tasted the food.

"If Walkman did have an affair, or affairs," Stone said as he licked sauce from his fingers, "I wonder if the wife knew."

Macy's chest clenched with guilt as she thought of the timing and that the woman had just lost her son.

If Mrs. Walkman was unaware of her husband's extramarital activities, Macy was about to blow Adeline's world up again.

THIRTY MINUTES LATER, Stone pulled down a long oak-tree-lined driveway to the Walkman estate, a stately Georgian home with its own tennis courts, pool and pond. An afternoon rain cloud rolled in, casting the property in gray, the balmy temperature outside dropping slightly as a breeze stirred the air.

He took one glance at Macy, though, and knew the scenery was lost on her. He couldn't begin to imagine how she felt.

Together they walked up to the door, and he rang the bell. A woman in a maid's uniform opened the door and greeted them, then showed them to a formal living room with a white sofa, wingback chairs in an ocean-blue color and a stone fireplace that added warmth.

Across the hall, Stone noticed a dark-paneled office that obviously belonged to Mr. Walkman. Odd how different the two spaces were.

Mrs. Walkman looked up from one of the wing chairs as they entered, brushing her hands over the legs of her slacks. Stone introduced them, and Macy forced a smile, although he could feel anxiety radiating from her in waves.

Mrs. Walkman greeted them with a hesitant smile, eyebrow lifted as she spoke. "You made this sound like it was important," she said to Stone. "I called Prentice. He'll be here shortly." She gestured toward the pitcher of iced tea in the center of a tray on the cherry coffee table. "Would you like some tea? Coffee? Water?"

"No, thank you," Stone said. "We just ate lunch."

She turned her attention to Macy and gestured toward the pitcher. "Agent Stark?"

Macy shook her head. "We just want to talk."

"Then sit down." She poured herself a glass of tea, then took a sip. "Is this about my husband's campaign?"

Macy seemed to be staring at the woman in a silent debate over how to proceed. He'd never seen her look so uncertain.

"No, ma'am," Stone said, taking the lead. "I assume you've seen the news about what's going on in Briar Ridge this last week. That the body of a man was found in a house that belongs to a woman named Lynn Stark."

Mrs. Walkman fluttered a diamond-clad hand to her chest, her eyes sparking with some emotion Stone couldn't quite define. "I'm sorry, but I haven't kept up. I've been so busy running my children's nonprofit and campaigning with Prentice that I haven't seen much of the news."

Macy cleared her throat. "We know that Lynn worked for you at one time. And as I told you when I phoned before, I'm her daughter. Do you remember her, Mrs. Walkman?"

The woman's face blanched slightly as if she was uncomfortable, then she gave a tiny nod. "Yes, poor Lynn. It was such a long time ago, and we've had several different housekeepers since over the years." Her voice wavered slightly, and she rubbed the gold locket dangling over her chest between her fingers. "My mind is a blur about that time in our life. We were grieving over my son's death when she worked for us."

"I'm truly sorry about your loss," Macy said.

"So am I," Stone said. "I'm sure it was traumatic."

"You never get over losing a child. Parents are just not supposed to have to bury their children," Mrs. Walkman said, sadness tingeing her voice. "That's the reason I started the nonprofit. It's in Charlie's name. I wanted to help other children who might need help. I couldn't save my son, but at least we help provide grieving families with a support group."

"That's very admirable," Macy said, her expression still torn. "But I'm trying to learn all I can about my mother. She disappeared from the in-house treatment program where she was staying, and it's important I find her."

"Oh, yes, of course dear." The ice in the woman's tea clinked as she lifted her glass. "I wish I could help you, but I haven't talked to or seen Lynn in years."

Stone studied the woman's reaction. She seemed so nice and caring, just as she appeared on-screen.

Macy cleared her throat. "I've reviewed my mother's financials from that time. That's the reason I'm here. The salary you paid her was more than twice what her other employers did, and you even paid her after she left your employ. Can you explain that?"

"Well," Mrs. Walkman said softly. "Your mother was kind to me when I was going through a rough time. I figured she needed some help, so we gave her a few weeks' pay after we moved to help her until she could find more work."

"Mrs. Walkman," Macy said after a minute. "Did you ever notice my mother and your husband being friendly together?"

Mrs. Walkman curled her fingers around the arms of her chair. "My husband is friendly and nice to everyone. That's his nature."

"But were they ever alone?" Macy pressed.

Anger flared in the other woman's eyes. "Exactly what are you trying to say?"

"I don't mean to be blunt, but I need the truth. Around my first birthday, my mother received a lump cash amount to pay off her mortgage. I have reason to believe that she had an affair with your husband and that he paid her to keep quiet."

The woman's eyes widened in shock, and her glass slipped between her fingers and hit the floor. Glass shattered and tea spilled, trickling all over the pristine wood floor.

Chapter Twenty

Macy studied Mrs. Walkman's reaction, but the usually unflappable woman she'd seen on TV was difficult to read. She obviously was upset by their line of questioning, but was she upset because she'd known her husband had cheated on her and wanted to keep it quiet? Or because she was shocked at the suggestion of an affair?

She and Stone allowed her a moment to process the information, then Mrs. Walkman's expression turned steely. "I don't know where you got our information," she said, a bite to her voice. "Or if you're trying to malign my husband's character because of some secret political agenda, but I can assure you Prentice did not have an affair with that woman."

"Are you certain?" Macy asked. "We understand that you and your husband were having a difficult time back then," she said as gently as possible. "Losing a child often tears couples apart. Maybe he needed comfort elsewhere, and you even forgave him because you were so distraught and grief-stricken yourself."

Perspiration beaded the woman's forehead as she clenched her hands together in an effort to control her anger. "Yes, we were grief-stricken, but my husband and I love each other, and he would never have stepped out on me."

Suddenly footsteps echoed in the foyer, and a door slammed in the background. A minute later, Prentice Walkman appeared in the doorway, his expression wary as he paused to take in the scene.

"What's going on, honey?" he said to his wife.

The couple exchanged a look, and Mrs. Walkman's shoulders sagged in relief. "Thank God you're here, Prentice. This sheriff and FBI agent…you won't believe what they came here saying."

The senatorial candidate went still, his manicured hand automatically adjusting his red power tie. His eyes darkened, and Macy imagined his lawyer's mind already creating a defensive strategy. The best way to learn the truth was to catch him off guard.

But the idea that he might have slept with her mother, that he might actually be her father, caught *her* off guard. Was she looking at the man who'd gotten her mother pregnant, then abandoned them to preserve his marriage and career?

Stone read the sudden emotions in Macy's silence and understood the reason, so he cleared his throat to give her time to recover. "Mr. Walkman, please sit down. We have some questions for you and your wife."

His rigid posture as he crossed the room made Stone wonder if he knew the reason for their visit. He might be running for senate, but if he was Macy's father and he'd abandoned her years ago and covered it up, he had no respect for the man. Especially knowing how Macy had suffered growing up.

Nothing pissed him off more than a man in power taking advantage of a vulnerable woman.

Walkman sat down beside his wife and clasped her hand in his. "So what is this about?"

Stone explained that they were looking for Lynn Stark and that they knew she'd worked for the couple years ago.

He reiterated that they were sorry about the couple's son's death, then he mentioned the payments made to Macy's mother.

"We know Lynn received a large lump sum payment around her daughter's first birthday to pay off her house, and are wondering about your personal relationship to Lynn Stark," Stone said.

Mr. Walkman's expression remained unfazed. "The only relationship my wife and I had with Lynn Stark was as her employer," he said. "And that was not for long. I'm sorry to say your mother was slightly unstable, and then we moved and had no need for her services."

"She became pregnant while she worked for you, didn't she?" Stone asked.

"Yes," Mr. Walkman murmured. "She told us that the father of her baby was dangerous, and that she didn't know how she was going to make ends meet." He squeezed his wife's hand. "Adeline felt sorry for her, so we gave her a nice severance check to hold her over once we moved away." He stood. "Now, we've answered your questions," he said. "I think you should go. Talking about that time brings up painful memories for my wife." His voice softened. "You understand."

He was smooth, Stone thought. Maybe too smooth. "One more thing. Lynn's financial records showed that she received a large cash payment around her daughter's first birthday to pay off her house. What do you know about that?"

"Nothing," Mr. Walkman said. "Maybe she had family who stepped up. Or maybe she lied about the baby's father, and he decided to help her out."

"You see, that's exactly what we're thinking," Stone said. "That the father may have paid her to keep his identity quiet."

"I wish I could tell you more," Mr. Walkman said. "But I can't."

Macy folded her arms. "I suspect you can."

He angled his head toward her, his green eyes piercing Macy's. "Excuse me?"

Macy lifted her chin. "Did you have an affair with my mother?"

MACY HELD HER breath as she waited on Walkman's response. For a fraction of a second, surprise, then a sliver of anger appeared before his eyes softened.

"I'm sorry, Agent Stark, I can see that you're looking for answers and grasping, but the answer is no." He patted his wife's hand, and she gave him a doting smile. "I love my wife and always have. I would never be unfaithful."

Macy remembered Esme's statement, more specifically her husband's, and knew he was lying. But she refused to throw Esme under the bus for fear he might retaliate against the woman. She'd stepped away from his employ out of respect for herself, her husband and Mr. Walkman's wife.

Macy raised a brow. "Then if I asked other housekeepers who've worked for you over the years, they will confirm that your relationship with them has always been aboveboard?"

"Absolutely," Mr. Walkman said.

"I can assure you that our marriage is solid now and always has been," Mrs. Walkman said.

"Then you won't mind providing me with a list of your other housekeepers over the years?" Macy said with an eyebrow raise.

The couple exchanged looks. "I'm afraid not," Mr. Walkman said. "For all I know, you want to smear my campaign. But you have no right to invade people's privacy because you're on a witch hunt to malign me."

Macy gave him a deadpan look. "If you've been faithful as you say, you have nothing to worry about."

A muscle ticked in Mr. Walkman's jaw. "Unless you have a warrant, I don't intend to open up my private life for you to dissect," Mr. Walkman said. "We're done here. If you have more questions, I'd prefer to have my attorney present."

Macy gritted her teeth. She just bet he would.

Stone stood. "Thanks for your time. If you think of anything else that might help us, maybe where Lynn Stark would go or someone she might turn to for help, please give me a call."

"We haven't heard from that woman or seen her in over two decades," Mr. Walkman said. "So we have no idea where she is or where she'd go."

Macy forced an even expression. "One more question, Mr. and Mrs. Walkman. Did either of you know a man named Voight Hubert?"

Mrs. Walkman's eyes narrowed, and she shook her head. Her husband's mouth tightened into a thin line. "No. Who is he?"

"He was an ex-con," Macy said, still gauging their reactions. "He was also the man found murdered at my mother's house." Macy glanced at the husband. "Are you sure you don't recognize the name? Maybe through your law practice at some time."

"I'm quite certain I don't." Walkman stood, adjusting his tie. Dismissing them.

Mrs. Walkman offered Macy a sympathetic smile. "It must have been difficult growing up with an unstable mother. I hope you find what you're looking for, dear."

Macy's gaze met hers. The woman's tone sounded sincere, yet the dig about her mother hurt. "All I'm looking for is the truth," she said frankly. "And I won't stop looking until I find it."

She noticed the woman lean into her husband, and Macy almost felt sorry for her. But as she and Stone walked through the marble-floored foyer, she pushed her sympathy aside. The couple's relationship was not as picture-perfect as it appeared. Photographs and news interviews in the media painted false portraits of happiness and bliss all the time.

Esme and her husband told a different story.

Disturbing thoughts congregated in her mind as she slid into Stone's police car.

"I think they're lying," Stone said as he veered onto the main highway leading back toward town.

"Yes," Macy agreed. "The question is to what extent." Different scenarios played through her mind. "If Walkman slept with my mother and his wife found out, she could have been angry with my mother. Or under the duress of her grief, she could have forgiven him, and they reconciled."

"We have to determine if that lump cash payout came from them," Stone said, his jaw clenched. "But I don't think we have enough for a judge to issue a warrant or to subpoena their financials."

"Or to obtain a sample of his DNA." Macy twisted her mouth in thought. She knew a guy at the Bureau who could do a little hacking into the financials. But obtaining a DNA sample without Walkman's permission would be even trickier.

Her mind began to sort through all they knew. "We can't forget that the dead man in the wall at my house was a hit man. As an attorney, Prentice Walkman would have had access to contacts or criminals who connected him to Hubert."

"Good point," Stone said.

Macy nodded. "He could have hired Hubert to kill my

mother so she couldn't expose his dirty little secret." Her lungs strained for air.

That dirty little secret was her.

STONE CLENCHED THE steering wheel. The Walkmans' house was beautiful, the house ornate, the couple inside a portrait of marital bliss, devotion and longevity.

But he sensed something was off. That Mrs. Walkman had intentionally made the comment about Macy's mother to rile her. Or to imply that Macy might be unstable herself.

Had she known about her husband's philandering and turned a blind eye for the sake of their marriage and his career? Had he slept with women other than Lynn Stark?

Then the more disturbing question, one he knew was haunting Macy. Was he Macy's father?

"About the DNA," Stone said. "Walkman was in the military years ago. The armed forces maintains a DNA reference specimen collection in an automated database to assist in identifying human remains."

"You're right." Macy pulled her phone from her pocket, punched in a number and called her FBI boss. "I know this is dancing the line, but I need your help." She explained her theory about Walkman and that she wanted his DNA compared to her own." Tension stretched for a moment while she listened to his response. "Okay, thanks;"

"He's going to do it?" Stone asked, impressed as she ended the call.

"As a favor to me," Macy said.

A smile twitched at Stone's mouth at her comment, but the seriousness of the situation quickly forced it away.

They needed proof against Walkman. Making accusations without evidence could ruin his career. And if they were wrong, it would compromise both of their jobs.

But if they were right and Walkman had hired Hubert to kill Lynn Stark, then Macy's father might be a killer.

NIGHT HAD FALLEN by the time Macy and Stone arrived back in Briar Ridge. The sun had faded, a slight breeze stirring the humid air as rain clouds moved across the sky, rumbling with the promise of a summer storm.

Stone drove to his cabin, and Macy shivered as they went inside. She kept replaying the possibility that Walkman was her father. Was he capable of having someone murder her mother?

If he was, he was a monster…

Macy set her laptop up and so did Stone, then he set out the dinners they'd picked up on the pine table.

"I have a PI named Delwood I work with sometimes," she told Stone. "Let me call him. He might be able to help."

Stone nodded, and she stepped onto the back deck and called him. He had expert hacking skills. They might not be able to use what he found in court if he crossed the line, but she could use it as a lead to find the truth or pressure the Walkmans to talk. "It's Agent Stark. I need you to do something for me and to keep it confidential."

"Only way I work," Delwood said.

Macy chuckled. If he didn't, he'd go to jail. She didn't like stepping into the gray areas, but sometimes it was the fastest way to get things done. "I need whatever you can find financial-wise on Prentice Walkman," Macy said.

"What?" Delwood rarely reacted. "You mean *the* Prentice Walkman running for senate?"

"Yes," Macy said. "I'm interested in going back about twenty-seven, twenty-eight years ago. Look for any large cash withdrawals or payouts, especially to women."

A tense second passed. "Exactly what are you looking for?"

Macy chewed the inside of her cheek. "I think he had an affair, maybe more than one, and may have paid the women to keep quiet." She hesitated. "Also look for any connection, a payout, to a hit man named Voight Hubert. He served time in prison."

Delwood whistled. "You out to get this guy or just ruin his campaign?"

"I don't give a damn about his campaign, although that's why I called you. This has to be handled with discretion. I don't want to malign his character if he is who he claims to be." Although she already knew different. "Understand?"

"Understood. This case must be important."

More important than he knew. Her life depended on uncovering the truth. "It is," Macy said with a shudder as she remembered the fire at her mother's house.

She thanked him, then hung up and went to join Stone. He was on the phone.

"All right, I understand." He hung up and raked a hand through his hair. "I tried to get a warrant, but the judge refused."

Macy nodded. "I'm not surprised. Walkman is high profile."

Macy clenched her hands by her side and sank into the chair. Soon she would know if Prentice Walkman was her father.

All the more reason to dig deep and find out if he was also a killer.

Chapter Twenty-One

Stone scarfed down the pot roast dinner special while he dug through records in search of the attorney who'd represented Hubert years ago. Meanwhile, Macy ate chicken potpie and looked for articles about Prentice Walkman and his wife.

It took a while, but he finally found the information he was seeking. Hubert was represented by a public defender named Willie Robard. The prosecutor was a man named Damon Huntington. There was no mention of Prentice Walkman as his attorney. Although with his law contacts and access to databases, Walkman could have easily accessed Hubert's list of priors and met with him in private. With his job, he would also know not to leave a paper trail.

Next, he searched for cases Walkman had represented dating back twenty-seven years. Like many attorneys, he'd started out as a public defender. But he'd obviously been young and ambitious and quickly moved to a law firm called Bartles & Cohen. A search in public records at the courthouse in the county gave him a list of cases he'd represented that went to court. Again, Hubert was not among them.

On a hunch, though, he decided to call Bubba Yates, Hubert's former prison cellmate. The man didn't answer, so Stone left a message asking him to return his call.

Macy looked up from her laptop. "So far, I haven't found anything except praise for Walkman's skills as a litigator." She rubbed her forehead. "He married his college sweetheart who was a paralegal for a while, then she stayed home with their son when he was born." Sympathy flashed in her eyes. "There's a story here about the accident. So sad."

Stone nodded. To lose a child would be the worst kind of horrible.

Could a grieving mother possibly understand her husband turning to another woman for comfort? Or would she see that as the ultimate betrayal?

"Walkman worked a couple of high-profile cases involving gangs about ten years ago. I couldn't find any articles dating back twenty-five, twenty-seven years ago. He was young, so those cases were probably small and not newsworthy."

Stone's phone buzzed. "Sheriff Lawson."

"It's Bubba Yates."

"Yes, thank you for returning my call. I had another question for you." Stone drummed his fingers on the table. "What was the name of the attorney who represented you when your case went to trial?"

Yates sighed. "His name was Walkman. He's big now, saw him on the news running for senate."

Stone's stomach clenched as he hung up. "Macy," he said. "I just found the connection between Walkman and Hubert."

"WHAT IS IT?" Macy asked.

"Walkman worked as a public defender when he first started practicing law. Although he didn't represent Hubert, he did represent Hubert's cellmate Bubba Yates."

Macy's heart stuttered. "Then he could have met him or known about him through Yates."

"Exactly. Yates was quick to tell us how mean Hubert was. He probably would have told his attorney, too."

Macy nodded, her earlier headache returning. Her eyes were gritty from studying the computer files, her head spinning with her encounter with the Walkmans.

The entire time she'd sat in his living room, she'd studied the man, searching for some sign that he was her father, that she had his nose or mouth or jawline or some tiny feature. That he'd known and kept it secret. That he would have tried to hurt her mother.

That he hadn't just lied to her face.

But he was cool as a cucumber under pressure. That quality alone made for a good litigator and politician.

It also meant he'd want to protect that reputation.

She scrolled through photos of Walkman from the media. He was a handsome-looking man. Neat and well groomed. A charming smile. Narrow face. A slight cleft in his chin. Eyes that twinkled when he smiled.

Again she searched for herself in his face and those eyes, but saw no resemblance.

She went back years in her search and finally found a photo of him when he was a public defender. He was young, midtwenties. She could easily see why her mother might have been tempted to sleep with him.

The article about his son's death made her chest squeeze. The couple stood huddled together, the wife's head buried against his chest as she sobbed at the funeral. Walkman's own expression looked tortured.

Had her mother felt so sorry for him that she'd ignored the fact that he was married and crawled in his bed to comfort him?

The next few weeks, there were more articles and photographs. The couple had started a charity in their son's name and held a fundraiser. In those photos, though, the couple's grief seemed to have grown even more intense, the stage of grief playing out. Shock, denial, anger, anguish.

No longer was Mrs. Walkman leaning into her husband. In fact, they stood a foot apart on stage as they addressed the guests.

Another candid shot showed Walkman smiling down at one of the servers. Something about his eyes suggested he knew her. Maybe intimately.

Macy stood and stretched. If he had had multiple affairs, how had his wife not known?

She might have forgiven one, but more than one? How did a woman live with that kind of betrayal?

STONE COULDN'T IMAGINE how Macy was feeling, but at least tonight he knew she was safe. She walked over to the fireplace and seemed to be studying the river rocks on his mantel.

"I need to talk to the Walkmans again," Macy said as she picked up a stone and ran her finger over the slick surface.

"Of course." He walked up behind her and rubbed her arms. "But not tonight. It's storming. You need to rest."

She shivered as thunder boomed outside, then gave a little nod and set the rock back on the mantel. "You collect river rocks?"

He rolled his shoulders, emotions hitting him. "My mom loved them. She named me Stone after the smooth river rocks she found when we went camping. She used to paint messages on them and leave them around town."

Macy turned to him with an odd look in her eyes. "Oh my God, Stone. I used to collect those. The messages she wrote on them inspired me to have hope."

Stone's throat clogged with emotions. Macy had never met his mother, but somehow knowing she had collected his mother's rocks touched him deeply. "She was special," he murmured.

"She was." Macy looked away, then rubbed her arms as if to ward off a chill. Stone took out the bottle of whiskey he kept in the cabinet and poured them both a small tumbler. Macy stared at it for a moment, then accepted the glass and sipped.

He tossed back the shot, savoring the warm burn of alcohol as it slid down his throat. His gaze met hers, and temptation rolled through him. Macy was tough and strong and even more beautiful because of it. He wanted to alleviate all her worries.

Macy turned her glass up and finished the whiskey, then ran a hand through her hair. "I'm tired. I think you're right. I need to get some rest."

Concern for Macy made him want to reach for her. But before he could, she grabbed her phone and disappeared into the bedroom. Stone wanted to go after her and hold her, but he sensed she needed time to process what was going on, so he let her go.

He poured himself another shot, then went to the sliding glass doors and looked out at the storm as it raged through the sky. Lightning zigzagged across the treetops, thunder rumbling as the rain began to pour and beat at the house.

He scanned the yard for an intruder, then checked the locks on the sliders and the front door. Then he set his alarm.

If Walkman was guilty and had hired Hubert years ago, he might be panicked now that they'd questioned him. Who was to say that he might not hire someone else to come after Macy?

MACY JUMPED AS the storm thundered outside. Lightning illuminated the mountain peaks, and she rushed to the window and looked out. The jagged lines of the trees resembled monsters clawing at her, just as they had when she was a child.

Fear seized her, making it hard to breathe, and she quickly closed the curtains, then crawled beneath the covers and pulled them up over her head. The rain pummeling the roof sounded like nails hammering tin and sent a shiver through her.

She pressed her fist to her mouth to stifle a sob and closed her eyes, but the storm transported her back in time. She was five again, hiding in the dark, terrified of the thunder and lightning.

Finally, it quieted enough for her to fall asleep, but sometime later thunder startled her awake. Then she heard the voices.

A woman...her mother screaming. Something being thrown. Furniture overturned. Another woman's voice? No...a man's. Deep, sinister. Footsteps.

Another scream. Her mother crying...

She slipped from bed, tiptoed to the door and peeked through the opening. It was so dark she could barely see. A shadow...a man. Lightning shot across the hallway, then a shadow moved. Her mother was screaming and kicking again. The man hit her and she flew across the room and smacked the wall.

Cold terror gripped Macy, and she couldn't move.

"No!" her mother screamed. She tried to get up, but the man turned and punched her again, then he stalked toward Macy's room.

"Run, Macy! Run!" her mother cried.

Macy finally made her legs move and ran back toward her bed. She crawled underneath it, trembling as she hid her face in her hands. She heard the door screech open. Peered between her fingers and saw the man's shoes... coming closer.

Then her mother screamed again and lunged at the man.

"Macy!"

Stone's voice dragged her from the memory, and she heard him walking toward her. Slowly, she lowered the covers to make certain it was him.

The bed dipped as he sat down beside her, and his fingers gently brushed her cheek. "Are you okay? I heard you screaming."

She hadn't realized she'd screamed out loud. He wiped her tears with his finger, and she had to swallow twice to make her voice work. "Nightmare."

His dark gaze raked over her. "Want to talk about it?"

She sat up and pushed her tangled hair from her face. "It was about that night. I... The man was in my house. I think it was Hubert."

He breathed out. "You saw him?"

"Not his face, but a man. My mother was screaming, and he was coming toward my room, but she tried to stop him."

"He was coming into your room?" he asked gruffly.

Macy nodded, a shudder ripping through her. "My mother yelled at me to run, but there was nowhere to go, so I hid under the bed."

Stone muttered a curse. "He came to kill your mother and he was going to take you."

"Or kill me," Macy said in a strangled voice.

STONE CLENCHED HIS jaw so tight he thought it would break. Dammit. Would Walkman have ordered his own daughter to be murdered?

Anger hardened his tone. "If Walkman is responsible for all of this, he's going to pay."

Macy clutched his hand. Another boom of thunder roared, and she startled, her breath gushing out. He couldn't resist. He pulled her into his arms and rubbed her back. She pressed her head against his chest and clung to him, trembling in his arms.

"It's all right," he murmured. "You're safe tonight." And he'd keep her that way if she'd let him.

He held her for what seemed like forever, stroking her hair and back. Her breathing grew more steady, then she lifted her head and looked into his eyes. Their gazes locked, heat sizzling between them. Desire bolted through him, and he lifted his fingers and brushed her cheek again.

She licked her lips and cupped his face between her hands. "Thank you for being here, Stone."

His heart pounded. He told himself to walk away, but Macy pulled his face toward her and pressed her mouth to his, and he lost his will and kissed her. One taste and he wanted more. She moved her lips against his in a sensual rhythm that tied his belly in knots, and he deepened the kiss. Need and desire blazed through him, but he forced himself to pause and looked into her eyes.

"I don't want to take advantage of you," he murmured.

A smile sparkled in her eyes, the most beautiful thing he'd ever seen. Then she traced her finger over his lips, and his body hardened. He sucked her finger into his mouth, and she drew him to her again.

Their lips melded together, tongues dancing, and he wrapped his arms around her. She leaned into him, then tugged at the top button of his shirt. His breath stalled as she unfastened the buttons, and she pressed a kiss to his chest.

He lowered his head and nibbled at her neck, tugging at the strap to her tank top. Another kiss and another, then they tore at each other's clothes. His shirt hit the floor along with his jeans, and he lifted her tank top over her head, exposing her generous breasts.

He paused to study her smooth skin and cupped her breasts in his hands. Her breathing grew more erratic, and she raked her hand across his chest and slid it lower to stroke his hard length.

"Macy?" he whispered. "Are you sure?"

She flipped him to his back, then climbed above him and straddled him. Her long hair brushed his chest as she kissed him again, and he pushed at her pajama shorts, stripping her naked and cupping her butt in his hands.

She groaned and removed his boxers, then they deepened the kiss, and she impaled herself on him. He groaned and gripped her hips, their breathing mingling as the tension built and she rode him into oblivion.

Chapter Twenty-Two

The next morning when Stone rolled over, he studied Macy's sleeping form. For once, she seemed actually at peace.

They'd made love again in the night, then she'd curled in his arms. She was sleeping so soundly he decided not to wake her, but he slipped from bed, showered and brewed a pot of coffee. He called his brother, and the phone rang and rang but Mickey didn't answer, so he scribbled Macy a note that he had a quick errand to run.

Stay put and have some coffee and breakfast, he wrote. *I'll be back in half an hour.*

He set out a mug, pulled some cinnamon rolls from the pantry and put them on a plate for her, grabbed his keys.

He hated to leave Macy alone, but he was worried sick about his brother. And he needed to get his head on straight about Macy.

He was supposed to be finding the person who wanted her dead, not falling in love with her.

The thought made him jerk to a halt, and he glanced back at the closed bedroom door. *Was* he in love with Macy?

The thought sobered him. He needed some distance. As soon as they solved this case, Macy would leave Briar Ridge.

And he could never leave, not with Mickey here.

He grabbed his holster and weapon, set the house alarm, then stepped outside. Instincts on alert, he surveyed his property as he walked to his car to make sure no one was lurking around or had followed them.

No one knew Macy was here, he reminded himself. She would be fine until he returned.

Still, his nerves were on edge as he drove toward Mickey's. A light sprinkling of rain began and a thin fog had developed, blurring the trees as he rounded the curvy mountain road. He wound toward town, then veered onto the turn to Mickey's, scanning the streets as he went in case of trouble. Two more days until the Fourth of July parade.

When he reached Mickey's, he hurried up to the door and knocked. Tapping his foot, he waited a couple of minutes, then shouted through the door as he pounded on it. "Mickey, open up!"

He glanced at the window. It was dark inside, but then again, Mickey rarely turned on a light.

"Mickey!" He jiggled the door and was just about to pull out his key when he heard footsteps shuffling inside. Finally, the door opened.

"What is it now?" Mickey growled.

Stone shifted. "You didn't answer the phone when I called."

"I'm busy." Mickey tunneled his fingers through his shaggy hair. He wore a T-shirt and jeans, and he hadn't shaved in days.

"Busy doing what?" Stone asked.

Mickey gripped the door edge to keep Stone from entering. "I've got company," he muttered. "Now go back to your life and let me live mine."

Stone gritted his teeth. "Why are you so pissed at me?"

"Because you treat me like a kid," Mickey said. "Now

I really do have company. Go home." He shut the door in Stone's face.

Stone clenched his hands into fists and backed away from the door. He wondered who was in Mickey's place. He sure hadn't wanted Stone to come inside.

Because he didn't want him to know who was in there? If not, why?

MACY WOKE UP to find the bed empty. She could still feel the warm imprint of Stone's body on the pillow and smell his masculine aftershave. Last night had been...incredible. The storm had upset her and triggered her memories, but Stone had helped her forget.

At least for a little while.

But today was a new day. Back to reality.

She couldn't shake the feeling that Mrs. Walkman had known about her husband's affair...or affairs.

Her phone buzzed. Delwood.

"Hey, Macy, I may have found something."

"What is it?"

"The Walkmans had a separate account under the name Maids, Inc. I found several large withdrawals in cash ranging from twenty-five thousand to seventy-five thou."

Seventy thousand was what her mother had received to pay off her house when Macy was one. Instead of Mr. Walkman bribing her mother and the other women he slept with to keep them quiet, Mrs. Walkman might have been the one to pay them.

"Can you tell who opened the account?"

"Mr. Walkman," Delwood said. "Does that help?"

"Yes. Let me know if you find anything else." She hung up and paced over to the window and looked out into the woods. Although the sun was fighting to break through the trees, a light rain drizzled down, a reminder of the night her mother threw her outside.

The night everything changed.

Prentice Walkman might not admit the truth, but somehow she had to reach his wife. Find out if she knew about the payments. Maybe if she talked to her alone…

She quickly dragged on clothes, then hurried to the kitchen. Stone had left a note with coffee so she poured a mug and nibbled on one of the cinnamon rolls. He still hadn't returned, and she was too antsy to sleep. He'd driven his squad car, so she made a snap decision to borrow his pick-up truck to retrieve her car.

Deciding Mrs. Walkman might open up more if she had a woman-to-woman conversation with her, she called and asked her to meet her at a coffee shop named the Brew Pot. The woman reluctantly agreed, and Macy gave her the address.

Maybe without her husband's presence, she'd convince the woman to talk.

LYNN STARK PACED the woods behind the house. She wanted so badly to tell Macy the truth. Tell her everything. But she would never believe her. No one would.

She was a nobody with depression issues. Taking medication for bipolar disorder would not work in her favor. Everyone would say she was crazy.

And she had gone crazy a while back.

Seeing Macy back at the house had done something to her, though. Watching the house where she'd raised her daughter lit on fire…hovering in the shadows while sirens screeched…that sheriff running in and carrying Macy out…

If Macy kept digging, she would find the truth. Then she'd send her to jail. She couldn't be locked up in a damn cage. She'd die in there.

She had to stop Macy.

She patted the gun in her pocket, then pulled the burner phone she'd bought from her pocket and made a call.

THE RAIN SLOWED Macy's drive, but she got her car, and made her way to the Brew Pot. Stone probably wouldn't be pleased that she'd gone without him, but she could take care of herself.

She planned her strategy as she drove, but when she pulled into the Brew Pot's parking lot, she saw Mrs. Walkman rushing from inside the coffee shop to her car. She looked all around her as if she thought someone was watching her, her eyes panicked as she jumped into her sedan and sped off. Rainwater spewed from the back of her car, and her tires squealed as she cut the steering wheel too fast.

The woman was obviously in a hurry to leave. Why? She'd agreed to the meeting. Where was she going?

Macy followed her, careful to stay a car length behind so the woman wouldn't see her. After several miles, Mrs. Walkman veered off the main highway onto a winding road that led toward some mountain cabins. The area was remote, the woods swallowing her as she maneuvered the narrow road.

Occasionally they passed another car, and twice Macy slowed and allowed a car in front of her to keep Mrs. Walkman from spotting her. They passed several cabins set half a mile apart, then she turned onto a graveled road that wound up a hill.

Macy swerved into a drive and waited a few minutes, then pulled back and started up the road again, which led to a driveway and a cabin set on the hill surrounded by oaks and pines.

She parked on the side of the road beneath a cluster of trees, cut the lights, then slid from the truck. As quietly as she could, she climbed the hill, taking cover between the trees as she went. A few hundred feet and she spotted

Mrs. Walkman's sedan parked in front of a large rustic-looking cabin surrounded by trees. Flowers grew in beds along the front, and a wraparound porch ran the length and sides of the house.

Macy froze, remaining still as her gaze scanned the yard for signs of the woman. Inside, she saw a light flip on, and then a shadow appeared in the window. Holding her breath, Macy moved closer, carefully staying beneath the overhang of the tree branches as she inched to the side of the house and crept up on the porch. She had practice in treading quietly and was relieved the structure was newer and the flooring didn't creak.

A noise sounded from the inside, then she heard voices. Mrs. Walkman's. Then another woman's.

Macy went still again, then inched her head up to see through the window.

Shock stole her breath. The other woman was her mother. And she was aiming a gun at Mrs. Walkman.

STONE WAS NOT only worried about Mickey, but angry as hell. Growing up, they'd been so close. Like most boys, they'd tumbled and wrestled in the grass, hiked and fished with their father, and played sports. Stone's had been football, whereas Mickey played baseball. He was also the artistic one and once had dreams of writing music and starting a band.

All those dreams seemed to have died when he became impaired. Although for a short time, he'd rallied and worked for that video game company, creating sound effects and background music. But Stone knew Mickey's heart wasn't in the work.

His heart wasn't in anything anymore.

Frustrated, he drove back to his house, the wet roads and drizzling rain making the asphalt slippery and the visibility foggy. He passed a fender bender, but his deputy was already on the scene handling things, so he hurried on.

By the time he reached his house, he was anxious to see Macy. But when he turned up his drive, he noticed his pickup truck was gone.

A frisson of alarm shot through him. He swung the squad car into Park, then hit the ground running. As soon as he went inside, he knew Macy wasn't there. A hollow emptiness rang through the house as he called her name. An emptiness that made him miss her already.

Still, he raced through the house, shouting her name. Her luggage was still in the guest room. The tangled sheets taunted him with a reminder of the night they'd shared together.

He hoped it wouldn't be the last.

Inhaling a deep breath, he noted her weapon was gone and there was no sign of foul play. He raced back to the kitchen and found the note he'd written to her. Below his scribbled message, she'd written her own.

Gone to meet Mrs. Walkman at the Brew Pot for a woman-to-woman chat.

She left the name of the coffee shop for him. Thank God.

He snatched his phone and pressed her number. The phone rang once, then went straight to voicemail. "Call me, Macy. I'll meet you at the Brew Pot."

Furious that she'd left instead of staying safely at his home, he hurried back outside to his squad car. His tires squealed, water and gravel spewing as he sped away. He called Macy several more times as he drove, each minute that passed intensifying his anxiety.

Dammit, she shouldn't have gone off alone. Why hadn't she waited on him?

Because he'd crossed the line and slept with her?

Didn't she trust him by now?

The rain continued to fall as he wound around the mountain. By the time he reached the coffee shop, every muscle in his body screamed with worry. When he swerved into the parking lot, he didn't see his pickup truck. She might have swung by and gotten her own car but it wasn't there either and neither was Mrs. Walkman's.

He checked the tracker on Macy's phone and confirmed she was not at the coffee shop. The GPS coordinates were for a place in the mountains a few miles away.

He flipped on his siren, then sped from the parking lot. Dammit, where was she going? Was she alone or with Mrs. Walkman?

Fear clawed at him. If she knew they were close to unraveling the truth, Macy might be walking into a trap.

MACY STARED IN shock at her mother. She looked wild-eyed, her muddy brown hair a tangled mess around her pale face, the gun bobbing up and down in her trembling hand.

Dear God, she was going to kill Mrs. Walkman.

Macy inched to the door, eased it open, then pulled her service weapon and gripped it at the ready as she crept inside.

The women were screaming at each other, so she activated the recorder on her phone.

"You screwed my husband, you little whore," Mrs. Walkman shouted. "And now your bastard child is trying to ruin my life and Prentice's."

The gun wavered as Macy's mother cried, "I didn't seduce your husband. He pressured me into having sex."

"We were grieving for our son, and you took advantage," Mrs. Walkman shouted. "First you met him at those empty cabins you cleaned. I guess you thought I was a fool and didn't know but I followed him." Her angry breath heaved out. "Then you came here, to my own family's place, like it was some little hideaway of your own." She slid her hand in her pocket and pulled out a .38. "Then you had the audacity to get pregnant. I know you were going to trap my husband into leaving me so he could shack up with you and that illegitimate baby."

Tears streamed down Macy's mother's face. "No, I wasn't. I wanted to get away from him. He was the one who chased after me."

"You're lying!" Mrs. Walkman screamed.

"I wasn't the first one," Macy's mother said. "And I probably wasn't the last."

"You should have left us alone like I warned you to," Mrs. Walkman said in a shrill tone.

"You're insane," Lynn said. "You gaslighted me. You took Macy from the park that day. I went crazy looking for her, and all the time you had her."

Macy struggled to recall the incident. Tidbits of the memory returned in quick flashes. A woman, getting in her car to see a puppy, them going for a drive. Then the woman pushing her out of the car in front of her house. Her mother screaming and crying hysterically, slamming her fist on the car.

"That was a warning," Mrs. Walkman snarled. "But you didn't listen."

Her mother paced across the room, waving the gun wildly. "So you sent that man to my house. He broke in and tried to kill me. And he was going to kill my daughter, too."

Macy gasped. Had Mrs. Walkman hired the hit man?

She didn't know what to believe. Knowing she needed to defuse the situation, though, she stepped from the shadows of the doorway. Her mother jerked her head up, crazed eyes widening in shock.

Mrs. Walkman swung toward her, the gun bobbing up and down. "You...you're ruining everything!"

Macy lifted her hand in defiance. "It's true, isn't it? I

remember the man fighting with my mother in the hall. He knocked her down, then came into my room and was going to take me, but then…" She turned to her mother. "You tackled him."

Her mother's face crumpled, her voice a raw whisper. "I grabbed the kitchen knife. I had to protect you, Macy."

"He tried to get the knife, but you stabbed him over and over and over," Macy said, the image of the blood spattering haunting her.

"I'm sorry, Macy…" she cried. "I had to save you. But then… I got scared that no one would believe me." She gestured to Mrs. Walkman. "Prentice was an attorney. He had connections. I thought he sent the man and if I'd called the police, he would have lied and then I would have gone to prison, and you would have ended up in the system."

Tears blurred Macy's vision. "But you threw me out in the rain."

"I had to get you out of the house. I didn't want you seeing all that blood," Lynn cried. "And I had to get rid of the body."

"So you put him in the wall," Macy said. And then her mother had had a psychotic break. "I thought you didn't love me," Macy said. "That you wanted to get rid of me."

A sob escaped Lynn. "No, but I…was traumatized after that. Every time I closed my eyes, I saw that man trying to take you, saw all that blood. It was gurgling from his throat and running all over the place. Then his body jerked and his eyes went blank and…" She aimed the gun at Mrs. Walkman's chest. "You lost your son, but you were going to have my daughter killed. How could any mother do that?"

"Don't expect me to feel sorry for you," Mrs. Walkman snarled. "Prentice promised to take care of you once and for all. He thought money would do it, but I knew you'd just keep coming back for more. I had to be the one to get rid of you." Fury filled Mrs. Walkman's face as she whipped the gun up and fired at Lynn.

Macy lunged toward her to grab the gun, but her mother fell to the floor, blood gushing from her stomach. Then Mrs. Walkman turned the gun on Macy.

But Macy fired her own weapon and the bullet pierced the woman in the chest. The impact flung her backward against the wall, blood spurting, then she sank to the floor, body convulsing.

Chapter Twenty-Three

Stone heard the gunshots, pulled his weapon and stormed into the cabin. Mrs. Walkman was lying on the floor, eyes staring wide open in shock, blood dribbling from her mouth. Macy was kneeling beside her mother, blood soaking her hands and clothing.

Fear pounded inside him. "Macy?"

She angled her head toward him, and he realized her mother was shot and Macy was trying to stop the bleeding with her hands.

"Call 911!" she yelled.

He rushed to Mrs. Walkman, kicked her gun away and checked for a pulse. But it was too late. She was dead.

Stowing his gun in his holster, he pulled his phone and called for an ambulance. Then he hurried over to Macy and her mother.

"Are you hit?" he asked Macy.

She shook her head no.

"What happened?" Stone asked.

"She was trying to protect me like she did years ago," Macy said. "I remember Hubert breaking in. Mrs. Walkman hired him to kill us both." A tear trickled down her cheek. "I got it all on tape."

Stone swallowed back the horror, then squeezed her arm, ran to the kitchen and grabbed a handful of kitchen towels from a drawer. He carried them back to her to use as blood stoppers, then called a crime scene unit to process the house.

The next hour was pure chaos as the ambulance arrived. Lynn was going to make it but needed surgery to remove the bullet from her stomach.

"I'm going to arrest Walkman," Stone said. "Even if his wife ordered the hit, he was an accomplice."

Macy nodded, thanked him, then climbed into the ambulance with her mother. His heart ached for her and for the years they'd lost. She'd grown up thinking her mother didn't love her.

Instead, her mother had loved her so much she'd killed to protect her.

But her father... Now she knew his name. That he hadn't wanted her.

That his wife had tried to kill her and her mother.

How could she live with that?

Two hours later, Macy kissed her mother's cheek and went to meet Stone in the waiting room for an update. She had a feeling the shock would set in at some point, but for now she was grateful her mother had survived surgery and that she was going to be all right. At least physically.

She still had to deal with the emotional trauma, but during the ambulance ride, her mother promised she'd return to the inpatient program and do whatever it took to get better.

Macy believed her. Even the psychiatrist she'd spoken with while her mother underwent surgery seemed hopeful that now that Lynn had faced and confronted the past, she might be able to recover and move on.

Was it possible that she could have a relationship with her mother now? That the two of them could be friends, even?

Stone strode into the waiting room, his big body tense.

Gretta Wright rushed in behind him, took a look at Macy, whose clothes were still stained in blood, and gaped at her.

"Oh my God," she muttered.

"Do not put your camera on Macy," Stone hissed.

Gretta shook her head. "No, I won't. But I want an exclusive. I heard that you arrested Prentice Walkman and that his wife is dead."

Macy gritted her teeth. "Tomorrow we'll do a press conference and go over everything. But not tonight."

For once, Gretta didn't argue. She accepted the deal and turned and left.

Stone walked over to her, his look of concern touching a place deep inside her, stirring more emotions. "How are you holding up?"

"Okay." Although she wasn't okay and they both knew it.

But she would be. She was tough. Resilient. She had friends, Kate and Brynn. Her mother had loved her.

And Stone was here.

But she couldn't voice those feelings right now. "The doctors gave my mom a good prognosis. She's agreed to go back to the psychiatric facility for treatment."

"That's good news," he agreed.

Macy's stomach twisted with worry. "She did kill Hubert and hide him in the wall," Macy said. "Do you plan to charge her?"

Stone's gaze met hers. "She obviously killed him in self-defense. Her real crime was covering it up."

"Because she was afraid," Macy said. "She was protecting me."

Stone brushed a strand of hair from her cheek. "I understand that. And I think a judge will, too."

Macy wanted to kiss him. But she was a bloody mess, and Kate and Brynn rushed in, looking frantic as they hurried to her.

"I'll need to confront Prentice Walkman," she told Stone.

Stone nodded. "Not yet. He's already lawyered up. Tonight just clean up and rest." He offered Kate and Brynn an encouraging smile as they approached. "And be with your friends."

She gave a little nod, although she wanted to ask him to stay with her. To make love to her again.

But Macy didn't ask for things. And soon she would need to leave. No need to think that Stone had been doing anything the night before except comforting her because he was such a caring man.

She needed to pack in the morning. She could come back and visit her mother when she wanted. But her life wasn't here anymore.

Chapter Twenty-Four

One week later

Macy packed her suitcase with mixed emotions and dragged her bag to the car. She'd come to Briar Ridge for a class reunion and to sell her mother's house. She'd thought she'd leave it all behind.

But that was harder than she thought. Especially now that she understood more about her mother's issues and that she had risked her life to protect her. She had her answers.

She'd even confronted Prentice, who was hiding behind his attorneys. Gretta had led the press in an attack on him and revealed that her mother had been victimized.

Stone pulled up in front of the inn and climbed out, his big sexy body sending her heart fluttering and her emotions all over the place.

"Hi," he said as he walked toward her. "Are you ready to leave?"

Was she? She bit her lip. "I'm packed," she said.

"What's happening with your mother's house?"

"I hired a service to clear the debris left from the fire and whatever was left inside, then demolish what was left. The real estate agent assured me the land would sell better once the ruins of the house were clear." And she'd sleep better once it was gone. "How's Mickey?"

Stone had finally confided about his brother's drinking problem, and she admired his dedication to helping him. She also understood why he'd never leave Briar Ridge.

"He's actually doing better. He came to see me yesterday and told me he's joined AA. He's also been writing and plans to start singing at Blues & Brews. Music always was his passion."

"That's great," Macy said, and meant it. "I remember him playing in a band in high school."

A smile flickered in Stone's eyes. "It was his dream. I'm glad he's coming back to it now."

They stood for a tension-filled moment. She wanted to say more. To tell him how much he meant to her. That part of her didn't want to leave.

But her father hadn't wanted her. What if Stone didn't, either?

"Good luck, Macy," he said in a gruff voice.

"You, too." She stood on tiptoe and kissed his cheek, then he wrapped his arms around her and hugged her tight.

"If you ever need anything…"

"Thanks." She pressed her hand against his cheek, then kissed him again and slid into the car. A muscle ticked in his jaw as he watched her close the door and start the engine.

Macy forced herself not to look back as she drove away. But memories of the night she'd spent in Stone's arms taunted her as she stopped for gas. She reached inside her purse for her wallet, but her palm brushed over something hard and slick.

She closed her fingers around it and pulled it out, then realized it was a river rock. She smiled as she ran her fingers over it, remembering Stone sharing that his mother left messages on the rocks to leave around town. She narrowed her eyes and read the words he'd written—*Remember me, Macy.*

A myriad of emotions swirled inside her, and she grabbed her credit card, inserted it and filled her gas tank. But as she started the engine, she turned in the opposite direction. Ten minutes later, she found herself at the river, walking along the riverbank, picking up stones and putting them in her pocket. She'd run from Briar Ridge to escape her past. But coming home, facing it and being in Stone's arms was helping her heal.

She rushed back to her car. What the hell was she doing? Her two best friends, her mother and the man she loved were in Briar Ridge.

The storms had passed, and the skies were clear, fluffy white clouds floating across the sky. Summer wildflowers sprang up on the mountainside.

Stone's pickup and squad car were parked in his drive when she arrived. She got out, then walked up to the cabin. But when she knocked, there was no answer.

Suddenly nervous, she peeked through the glass front door and saw him standing outside on the back deck, looking out over the river.

Nerves bunched in her stomach. What if he didn't feel the same way she did?

She started to turn and leave but silently chastised herself. She'd left Briar Ridge out of fear. She'd faced the worst coming back. She couldn't run again.

She confronted dangerous criminals all the time.

She had to have the courage to face the man she loved.

Inhaling a deep breath, she opened the door and entered, then walked to the sliding glass doors, which were ajar. Stone turned to look at her, his eyes sparking with surprise. Then worry.

"Did something happen?" he asked gruffly.

"Yes," she whispered. "I couldn't leave. Everything I love is here."

She slipped the river stone in his hand. His brows

arched, then a smile curved his mouth as he read the message of love she'd written.

"I love you, too, Macy," he whispered. He opened his arms and she went into them, then his mouth closed over hers and Macy knew she had finally found the home she'd been looking for all her life.

A home in Stone's loving arms.

* * * * *

CAVANAUGH JUSTICE: SERIAL AFFAIR

MARIE FERRARELLA

This Book Is Lovingly Dedicated

To The Most Important

People In the World to Me:

My Family:

Charlie, Jessica, Nicholas,

Melany, Logan

And my brothers,

Michael and Mark

Without You There Is Nothing

Prologue

At first, Liberty didn't even realize that the murders were connected. It was a matter of not seeing the forest for the trees—until she suddenly began comparing notes.

Calhoun, Arizona, wasn't exactly a big town. The population numbered less than a thousand even during the times when it was "booming," and the town wasn't thought to be booming for a while now. However, what Calhoun had always been was a nice, peaceful, law-abiding town right from the very beginning.

Or at least that was what Liberty had believed until she'd begun to compare notes and notice things that had escaped her attention before.

For the first tumultuous eighteen years of her life, the young woman who was to become Detective Liberty Lawrence had lived an altogether different, nomadic life.

Abandoned almost from the moment she was born, Liberty had never had a place she could call home

and was, quite frankly, on the path to self-destruc-
tion—until Florence Bishop had come into her life.

Florence had been a forty-five-year-old head nurse
working in the ER when Liberty had been brought
in looking as if she had beaten and abused to within
an inch of her life. The tough-talking sixteen-year-
old orphan had rejected any and all pity. All she'd
wanted to do was to leave the site of her humiliation
and possibly find a way to retaliate against her newest foster mother who had done this to her.

Despite Liberty's attempts to push her away, Florence had seen something in the angry young orphan
and immediately opened her heart to her.

Even though Liberty had fought her at every turn,
Florence decided to take her in as a foster mother,
consequently providing the rebellious teenager with
the only real home she had ever known.

It wasn't an instant alliance and definitely not all
sunshine and roses. It had taken Liberty a while before she let even *some* of her barriers down. Although
she never said the words out loud, Liberty was eventually very grateful to the sharp-featured nurse for
taking her into her home and for making sure that
she went to school even as she rebelled against any
show of authority.

There was no doubt about it in Liberty's mind.
Florence brought out the best in her; a "best" Liberty
hadn't even been aware of having until Florence had
taken her in hand.

It was because of Florence's efforts that Liberty

had graduated high school and then gone on to get a college degree. And it was because of Florence, Liberty finally told the woman during what turned out to be their last visit, that she actually *had* a life.

Things at that point had looked as if they were finally on the right track.

And then tragedy struck.

Less than three weeks later, Florence's body had been found lying in the alley behind the hospital where she worked. The nurse had been strangled.

Liberty had been beyond devastated.

By that time Liberty had worked her way up to being the small police department's only other detective, and she was determined to find Florence's killer. At the time of the murder, she had absolutely no experience in murder cases—Calhoun wasn't exactly a place that had any sort of a body count. Despite that, Liberty threw herself into working the case every chance she could for the next few months. Come hell or high water, she was determined to find her foster mother's killer.

It was during this time she discovered that Florence was not the killer's first victim.

Or his second.

The more Liberty looked into the cases, studying similar ones in the southwest area, the more she discovered. She found that this was not just an ordinary killer. This was a serial killer. A serial killer with, it eventually turned out, a high body count.

In total, there were thirty victims spread out across

small towns in Arizona, New Mexico and Nevada. The cases all had a few things in common. The victims were all nurses over the age of twenty-five and under the age of fifty. They each had also all been strangled with piano wire.

Becoming almost obsessed with finding the killer, Liberty investigated as much as she possibly could while still doing her regular day-to-day job at the police station.

And now the latest victim had just turned up in Aurora, California.

That meant that the killer was getting bolder because, looking up information about the most recent place that a killing had taken place, she found that Aurora had a much bigger police force than any of the other towns where the killer had struck.

Was the killer getting more brazen, or was there another reason for this sudden switch in venue?

The more research she did, the more confident Liberty became that she could get someone interested in the fact that all of these murders had been the work of a serial killer.

Her own chief, Elliott Atwater, had just expressed relief that the killer no longer appeared to be roaming their streets, but had evidently moved on. Atwater confessed he hoped that life could get back to normal.

But for Liberty, life would never get back to even *close* to normal until she could finally achieve closure. And closure would only come once the killer was captured and stopped.

The only way that was going to happen, Liberty decided, was if she took some time off and followed this latest trail to the killer's most recent killing site: Aurora, California.

Making up her mind, Liberty walked into Atwater's small office and announced, "I'm going to take my vacation now, Chief."

The chief looked up from his morning coffee. He didn't look surprised. "It's that serial case of yours, isn't it?"

Liberty saw no reason to pretend otherwise. He had always been good to her, if somewhat too lax in his methods for her taste.

"It is," she replied.

Atwater paused to examine his records. "Well, since you're not that big on taking vacations, you've got a total of three weeks amassed." Because she was the youngest on his force, he apparently felt it behooved him to warn her. "But if you wind up taking any longer," the chief told her, "you might not have a job to come back to."

Being a detective was very important to Liberty. It finally felt as if she fit in somewhere. But finding Florence's killer was worth every sacrifice. She owed the woman a huge debt she would never be able to even begin to repay.

"I understand, sir," she told the chief. "And I'm willing to take my chances."

Elliot Atwater merely shook his head. He didn't want the young woman taking chances, although he

knew she would. He had come to learn that Liberty
was exceptionally stubborn once she set her mind to
something.

"Stay safe, Liberty," the chief ordered her. "I don't
want to lose my best detective."

Her mind was already making plans for her trip to
Aurora and she was only half listening. "Don't worry,
Chief, you won't. I fully intend to remain safe," Liberty promised the older man, her partial mentor, with
feeling.

The chief almost believed her.

Chapter One

The anger was finally beginning to fade.

But then, it usually did right after one of his eruptions. And this flare-up had really felt like a major one. So much so that it felt as if it would never pass.

But, eventually, it did.

Exhaling a long breath, he glanced at his watch to see how long it had taken this time. He never managed to keep track while it was going on—predominantly because he couldn't.

The anger and rage that had shot through him, causing such damage as it vibrated within him, left him on the very brink of oblivion until it was all finally over with.

The last time it had happened, it had taken over twelve hours for him to emerge and come up for "air" again.

Someday he knew he probably wouldn't emerge. But "someday" wasn't now, and that was all he was concerned about.

Now.

All he could remember when one of these eruptions hit was an overwhelming wave of white heat.

And anger.

Lots and lots of anger.

When it was finally over, he would always find himself standing in an entirely different place than before.

And she was dead.

Again.

The problem was she never stayed dead. Oh, she tried to fool him. She would take on different voices, different features, different hairstyles and color, but it was *always* her.

Always.

She couldn't begin to really fool him.

She had *never* been able to fool him. Evil had a certain kind of look about it, and no matter what, it always came through. Sometimes it just took longer, but it couldn't remain hidden indefinitely.

She couldn't remain hidden indefinitely.

This time, he left the body where it had fallen. Hidden in the weeds.

It was time to get back to his life again and finally put Sarah behind him where she belonged.

Until she emerged again the next time.

"Hey, Cam, there's someone out here to see you," Campbell Cavanaugh's partner, Brandon Choi, called out as he crossed the squad room floor to reach Campbell's desk.

Brandon found he had to put his hand against his partner's chest to keep the man from shooting out of the room like a launched missile.

Detective Campbell Cavanaugh was a man who was obviously on a mission.

The next minute, he said as much. "Do me a favor," Cam requested. "I'm planning on getting a head start on Christmas shopping this year. *You* see this guy for me."

Brandon frowned, momentarily sidetracked. "Christmas shopping? Forgive me if I'm wrong, but isn't this just the beginning of December? You don't usually get rolling until the second week of December is over. And, besides, I thought you and that lady friend of yours broke up and became history a while back ago. Is there someone new in your life you haven't told me about?" Brandon studied the man whose ability to attract women without any effort had made him envious, despite the fact that Choi was happily married himself.

Campbell shrugged off the question. "It never hurts to be prepared," he told his partner. "Besides, I do have other people to buy gifts for," he pointed out. "The people in my family could populate a small town as it is. I learned my lesson last year when I wound up forgetting Jacqui, my own sister. This year I'm bringing a checklist so nobody gets left out."

"Well, look at you being all conscientious and everything," Choi marveled with a laugh. "Personally,

I don't know how you manage to keep track of your family. Hell knows I couldn't."

He wanted to get going. "So you'll talk to this guy, whoever he is?" Campbell asked as he started to walk out of the room.

"Well, number one, I would, but Susan might get *really* jealous," he said, referring to his wife of less than two years. "And number two, this isn't a guy," Choi added.

Campbell raised an eyebrow, his interest clearly piqued. "Oh?"

"Yeah," his partner replied, grinning. "Definitely 'oh.'"

Despite Campbell's reputation as an appreciator of lovely-looking women—a street that ran both ways— the homicide detective was not the type to be easily fooled or led astray, no matter how beautiful the woman promised to be. Beauty alone was not enough to sustain Campbell's interest—but it certainly was enough to capture it for a short while.

Campbell looked at his partner suspiciously. Something didn't seem quite right about this. "Okay, what's the catch?"

"No catch, partner. The woman is here on business," Choi informed him.

But Campbell wasn't buying it. Something was up—or maybe he had just been on the force too long and had grown too suspicious.

"What sort of business?" He wanted to know.

Choi merely smiled again at his partner in response. "Tell you what, why don't you ask her?"

"Because I'm asking you," Campbell pointed out. His green eyes met his partner's. "I'd rather not have any surprises."

Choi's wide grin seemed to almost say, *Yes, you do.* His smile grew even wider. "Sorry, partner, can't help you there."

All thoughts of getting a jumpstart on his holiday shopping—he was a sucker for Christmas, always had been—was pushed into the background. This person who had come looking to talk to him had captured his attention—but not to the exclusion of everything else.

"Try," Campbell stressed, his eyes pinning his partner in place.

"Okay, but you're taking all the fun out of this," Choi told him more seriously, "She's a detective out of Calhoun, Arizona—"

"Where?" Campbell asked. To his recollection, he had never heard of Calhoun, Arizona.

"Calhoun," Choi repeated. "From what I gather, it's more or less a hole-in-the-wall in Arizona."

"Okay." Campbell nodded, accepting that for now. "And why is she here?"

"It seems that case you caught the other day when I went in to fix my broken tooth…" Brandon began to explain.

"Okay, what about it?" Campbell pressed.

"Well, according to the detective, your case bears a

lot of similarities to one of hers," Choi told him. "The upshot is that she would like to talk to you about it."

"If that's the case, why were you grinning?" Campbell asked. He still wasn't fully convinced that this wasn't some sort of a prank on Choi's part, or that he wasn't dealing with misinformation. Otherwise, why would a detective from a tiny town in Arizona come all the way out here, looking to talk to him?

"Maybe she's just passionate about her work. You'd have to see her to understand," Choi explained then added, "Trust me on this."

Now his curiosity was definitely aroused. Campbell sat back down at his desk.

"Okay," Campbell told the other man, "why don't you bring her in?"

His partner nodded, obviously pleased. "I'll be right back," Choi promised.

Campbell barely had time to contemplate his partner's strange behavior before Brandon Choi returned. And, as promised, he wasn't alone. In front of him, he was ushering a very shapely young blonde into the room.

So this, Campbell thought, had to be the detective from Calhoun, Arizona. He was instantly interested and totally captivated.

"Sorry about the tight spaces," Choi said to the blond detective, apparently intrigued by her hair in one thick braid down her back. Belatedly, he waved his hand at the disarrayed room. "Our squad room really needed to get a facelift and the powers that be decided to do it just before Christmas—and also before, according to them, the rates are supposed to go up. Be careful not to walk into anything," he warned, appearing ready to catch her if that proved necessary. "You'll either get paint smeared on your clothes or wind up tripping."

"Thank you, Detective Choi," the attractive young woman said, "but I learned how to walk a long time ago."

From the look on Choi's face, Campbell decided he had no idea what to expect. The visitor was either going to be the type to bring a cold shiver racing up and down his spine—or a very warm one.

After listening to her speak, it seemed as if it was definitely going to be the latter.

"Mystery solved," Campbell murmured to himself as he belatedly got to his feet.

Liberty was certain that she heard the other detective say something and she eyed the tall, broad-shouldered, dark-haired man.

"Excuse me?" she asked. "What did you just say about mysteries?"

She really is a knockout, he caught himself thinking. Coming to, Campbell found his tongue. "That I liked solving them," he answered after a beat.

Liberty looked at him a little curiously, not quite sure what to make of him, then finally said, "Nice to know," although she thought it a rather odd comment for the detective to make.

"I'm Detective Campbell Cavanaugh," Cam said

by way of introduction, putting his hand out to the visiting detective. "I take it that you've already met my partner, Detective Brandon Choi." He nodded at the man standing next to her.

"Yes, I did," the blonde confirmed.

Not exactly a great conversationalist, Campbell mused when nothing more followed that sentence.

"And you are?" he prodded, waiting for the woman to tell him her name.

"Detective Liberty Lawrence," she answered.

Campbell caught himself smiling at the name. "Very lyrical."

The young woman shrugged carelessly. "I suppose," she murmured.

She was still standing, Campbell realized. He strove to make her feel a little more comfortable, as well as hoping to get her to relax. He sincerely doubted that he could make her feel *less* comfortable even if he tried.

"Why don't you sit down?" Campbell finally invited, gesturing toward the chair that was facing his desk.

The detective from Arizona looked at the chair he pointed to as if she weren't all that comfortable about sitting in it. They exchanged glances in silence before she finally gave in and did as the detective suggested.

Liberty sat on the very edge of the chair, looking as if she was ready to spring to her feet at any second.

Campbell looked at Choi, whose expression was definitely not illuminating. Campbell took the lead, finally saying, "My partner here tells me that you have a case that's similar to ours."

"Not 'similar' to yours," Liberty corrected him. "*Exactly* like yours. As a matter of fact," she continued, "at last count, I discovered that there were thirty murder victims altogether, including the one you just found, all exactly like yours."

"You discovered all the bodies?" Cam asked. It was obvious that he didn't believe this detective from the little Arizona hole-in-the-wall town.

"No, I didn't find them," she informed Campbell, a trace of annoyance in her voice because he was obviously being condescending. "I just counted them. Other detectives found the bodies. A lot of other detectives," she emphasized. "But no one connected the cases until I started putting things together and seeing the similarities. The murders were all obviously committed by the same serial killer."

The woman was coming on a little strong for his tastes, Campbell thought. Detectives this obsessed usually missed a lot of things just to make their theories fit the crime they were looking into.

"Are you sure about that?" Campbell asked the woman, studying her.

There was not a second's hesitation on her part. "Absolutely," Liberty answered.

"So, Detective Liberty—" Campbell began but got no further.

"It's Detective Lawrence," she corrected the detective then reluctantly told the man, "or you can call me Liberty if that makes you feel more comfortable talking to me."

The look on her face fairly dared him to resort to using her first name.

Which was why he did.

"All right, *Liberty*," Campbell began gamely, "what makes you think those thirty bodies you've collected—"

"Cases I reviewed," Liberty said, correcting him once again.

"'Reviewed,'" Campbell amended with a nod of his head. "Just what makes you think this is all the work of the same killer?" he asked.

Obviously she was going to have to lead this horse to water, Liberty thought. But this was extremely important to her—not to mention the latest victim—and she wanted a chance to see the evidence as soon as possible.

"Number one," Liberty enumerated, "all the victims were nurses between the ages of twenty-five and fifty. Number two, every one of them was strangled using piano wire. And, number three, all the bodies were discarded in the alley somewhere close to the hospital where they worked—if not directly *by* the hospital where they worked. The killer was obviously recreating something," she concluded.

Campbell thought for a moment then said, "Certainly looks that way." His tone was less distant than it had been a moment ago. He raised liquid green eyes—eyes that mirrored the eyes of most of the men in his family—to Liberty's face. Inclining his head, he told the detective, "I apologize."

The apology took her aback. She wasn't accustomed to someone apologizing to her. Usually, when she turned out to be right—and she often was—whoever had disagreed with her just backed off and the matter was dropped.

It was always far better just to back away.

But Liberty wasn't after accolades—she never was. What she wanted to do was to right a wrong. In this case, the wrong required bringing the killer to justice—once she was able to find the killer.

The next piece of the puzzle as far as she was concerned. But this detective had just completely thrown her with his apology.

"I don't understand," Liberty said, still confused. "Just what are you apologizing for?"

"For sounding as if I was discounting what you were saying," Campbell confessed quite honestly. "It sounded as if you were filling in empty spaces, making the evidence fit your pattern of the crime. But apparently it turns out that you were right. In this case, the pieces of the puzzle are exactly as simple as they seem."

She nodded her head. "We just need to find how all these people came in contact with the killer. And why these particular women and not other women."

"Simple questions," Campbell agreed. "But not such simple answers. Why are you so caught up in this?" He wanted to know.

"I don't like murder," she said evasively, not about to explain to him about Florence. For one thing, dealing with the investigation was a conflict of interest since one of the victims was someone she cared about. Someone she was determined to avenge. She didn't want to just hand this detective any ammunition to use against her.

"Most homicide detectives don't," Campbell said, commenting on the fact that she'd said she hated murderers. "But that still doesn't explain why you followed this trail of breadcrumbs to another state."

Liberty's eyebrows drew together. She didn't care for being challenged—or interrogated. "I had no idea I had to submit an essay written in triplicate."

"You don't," he told her mildly. "Where's your partner?"

"I don't have a partner," she told him.

"Something happen to him—or her?" Cam asked. Or was it a case of her being too difficult to work with? he wondered.

"Yes. Availability. Calhoun is a very small town. I'm the only detective they have at the moment. The other one retired and wasn't replaced. It's not as if we have a lot of murders to follow up on. Now, if you're satisfied, I want to ask you a few questions before I leave or you get called away."

Cam nodded as he leaned back in his chair, never taking his eyes away from hers. She had the lightest blue eyes he had ever seen.

"Go ahead," he urged. "Ask away."

Chapter Two

"Actually," Campbell interjected, "before we get started, I've got some questions of my own for you."

She knew what he was going to ask. "I'm doing this on my own time. I took all of my accrued vacation so I could do some independent investigation into the various victims. Anything else you want to ask me?"

That sounded pretty ambitious from where he was sitting, not to mention that she sounded rather defensive. But if he was going to get involved in this, he needed things to be crystal clear.

"You said there were thirty victims in all that you knew of," he said.

"Yes?" Liberty asked guardedly.

"Would you happen to have a list of those names?" Campbell asked.

For the first time since she had met him, she found herself smiling. He'd thought he was going to corner her—but he wasn't.

"Funny you should ask," she told him. The next moment, Liberty took out a folded piece of paper from her purse. Opening it up, she held the paper out for his benefit.

What Campbell noticed first was the *way* the names were written. The woman's handwriting was exemplary. He didn't come across that too often these days.

Looking up at her, Campbell made a calculated guess. "Parochial school?"

"Foster system," she answered crisply. Seeing the surprised look on his face, she decided to explain. "There's not all that much you can do by way of entertaining yourself when you're in the system. Me, I practiced my handwriting because it was something that wasn't done anymore and it didn't cost anything, just paper and a pen."

Because she had momentarily gotten excited about finally getting somewhere with the case and had admitted way too much to this good-looking stranger, Liberty immediately withdrew.

"Now, if we're through playing Twenty Questions about my life, I'd like to get back to focusing on these cases. Has the autopsy on your victim been done yet?"

"As a matter of fact, she's probably almost finishing up by now—or at least, it's on her schedule," Campbell told the visiting detective. "You really seem eager." He couldn't help noticing. "Let me guess. This is your first murder case, isn't it?"

She wasn't about to fall into that trap again. "Something like that," she told him vaguely.

"'Something like that'?" he repeated, puzzled by

her terminology. "It either is or it isn't." When he paused, the detective from Arizona didn't add anything, so he decided to prod. "Okay, which is it?"

"Why is that so important to you?"

"Just trying to get an idea of who I'm working with," he answered.

"Okay. Then you first," she said, turning the tables on the glib detective.

"All right," he told her good-naturedly. "I'm the fifth-born kid in a seven-sibling family and, before you ask, yes, we're all cops. As are most of my cousins," he added. It was a fact he took for granted, but he reminded himself that there were still people who didn't know that.

"Just how many cousins do you have?"

His beaming smile seemed to radiate from every part of him. Had she just stumbled onto an inside joke? She couldn't tell. "You remember that small town you mentioned that you came from?"

Her guard was instantly up. "What about it?"

He noticed the expression on her face but, for now, he let it go. "Well, those cousins I just mentioned? They could have easily populated it."

"You're exaggerating, right?" she asked warily.

He merely smiled at her. "Just ask anyone here about the Cavanaughs," he told her. "You'll find out if I'm exaggerating or not."

For the time being, Liberty gave him the benefit of the doubt. "That big, huh?"

Campbell's smile simply grew wider. He had to admit that the glimmer in her eyes just got to him.

"That big," he told her without any fanfare and then changed the subject. "Look, I think the ME who's currently on duty is my cousin-in-law Kristin. If she's finished with the autopsy, I could call in a favor."

These Cavanaughs were everywhere, weren't they? she silently marveled. "What kind of a favor?"

"I could ask her to speed up writing the preliminary draft of the report so she could get it into my— *our* hands," the detective corrected.

Okay, this was almost too much to absorb, Liberty reasoned. Was this family actually *everywhere*? "Let me get this straight," Liberty enunciated slowly. "You're telling me that you're related to the ME, too?"

"To one of them, yes."

"Oh, just one of them?" Liberty asked sarcastically, not sure if she actually believed this detective or not. What he was telling her didn't seem possible.

"Don't be a wise guy," Campbell told her, cutting through whatever rhetoric was about to follow. "I'm offering you a chance to get in on this while it appears to still be in the works," he pointed out. After all, she was the one who'd approached him, not the other way around. "If it is what you're telling me it is, it sounds like, once the news gets out, all hell is going to break loose and you might have trouble getting close to it. Now, are you interested or not?" he asked her even though he had more than a hunch that he knew full well what her answer was going to be.

Liberty frowned. She didn't like coming off as being so needy, but this did involve Florence and she owed the woman more than she could ever possibly say. Consequently, Liberty was forced to make an admission she would have never made otherwise. Certainly not willingly.

"Oh, I'm interested," she told the detective then emphasized, "Definitely interested."

And if for some reason it turned out that this detective was playing her, Liberty thought, she made a silent promise that she would find a way to make him pay for it.

Big-time.

"Then let's go," Cam was saying as he stood from his desk.

"Right now?" she asked, hoping he wasn't trying to lead her on just to "change" his mind at the very last minute.

"No time like the present," he told her pleasantly. "Unless you've decided to change your mind."

"Not me," she told him firmly. Gathering her things together, she slipped them back into her purse. "Just where is this morgue? I'll get my car and follow you."

"No need for that," he answered.

"I'd rather go in my own car," she said firmly, cutting in. That way, she felt she would have control over where she was going. Control meant a great deal to

Liberty. It had ever since she'd been old enough to understand what that entailed.

Campbell inclined his head as he led the way out of the squad room. "Have it your way," he told her. "But it might be kind of tough getting your car into the elevator."

Liberty stopped walking and stared at the detective. "Come again?"

If possible, his smile grew even larger. "The morgue is located in the basement," he told her. "We moved it into the police station a while back to make accessing the morgue more efficient. It eliminates traveling back and forth between destinations in order to view the body and to talk to the medical examiner. This way, everything's all in one place."

Why did she get this feeling that this sexy detective was gloating, or talking down to her?

"You have a point," Liberty conceded.

"You sound surprised," he noted, overlooking her frosty tone as he pressed for the elevator.

She supposed that maybe the man was trying his best to be helpful. "Actually," she admitted, "I am. I don't usually associate efficiency with a big-city police department."

For a second, she'd lost him. "You mean Aurora?" he asked.

"Yes, I mean Aurora," she answered. Maybe she'd been too quick to offer praise, she thought. "What did you think I meant?"

He shrugged. "I guess I still think of Aurora the way most of the old-timers do."

"Old-timers?" she questioned. He couldn't be referring to himself. "You're what? In your twenties?"

"It's not a matter of age," Campbell clarified. "It's a state of mind passed on from my parents. From a lot of parents who came out here to live, back in the day." He could see that she wasn't following him, so he explained further. "Aurora was initially a small town that just kept taking baby steps and growing. It never really stopped growing, but be that as it may, it still retained that small town feel to it."

Campbell considered his words. "I guess that's what makes it so unique and keeps the people here hanging around," he told her.

The elevator car arrived at their floor and opened its doors. Campbell waited for this visiting detective to get on before following her in. When he finally got on, he pressed for the basement.

"You sound like a former tour guide," Liberty commented.

"No," Campbell told her. "I'm just a citizen who loves his hometown." He let his answer sink in before he added, "That's why I decided to join the police department."

She filled in the blanks. "Because you like being in a position of authority?"

"No," he told her. "Because I like preserving the peace and making sure that the people who live here are safe."

That sounded far too noble, she thought. And then she looked at him. The detective was perfectly serious. "You mean that, don't you?" she asked Campbell as the elevator came to a stop.

While he was used to questioning things as a detective, the way he viewed things as a person was an entirely different matter.

"I wouldn't say it if I didn't," Campbell said simply. He gestured to the open elevator doors. "I believe this is our stop."

Stepping out of the elevator, Liberty looked down the long hallway. She was surprised to find that it was brightly lit. Her own precinct believed in saving on electricity.

Campbell saw the look on her face and offered a guess. "Were you expecting to find a darkened dungeon?"

"Calhoun doesn't have an official morgue. We have to use the county morgue that's located in Madison."

"Going on a field trip to view the body of the deceased can't be a fun excursion," Campbell commented as he led the way to the offices used by the medical examiner.

Liberty couldn't help thinking back. Not to when she'd had to view the nurse who had been the killer's latest victim, but to when she'd had to go to identify her foster mother's body.

For just one harrowing moment, she felt a cold chill down her spine, alternating with a flash of overwhelming heat. The sensation effectively paralyzed

Liberty until she was finally able to draw air back into her lungs.

She realized that they had stopped walking and that the too-handsome-for-his-own-good detective was watching her. There was concern in his eyes. "Are you all right?"

"I'm fine," Liberty answered him all too quickly.

"You don't look fine," he said. "You want to sit down or have something to drink? Water? The computer lab's right over this way." He pointed toward another door. "I'm sure they won't mind if you stop to—"

"I said I'm fine," she told him more sharply. She shrugged. "I just get a little claustrophobic when I'm underground."

He nodded as if he believed her, making her feel worse. "Why don't you go back upstairs and wait in the squad room?" Cam suggested. "I can get the report and bring it to you when it's ready."

"That's all right," she told him dismissively. "It passed."

He looked at her more closely. It was obvious that he didn't believe her. "You sure?"

"I said it passed," Liberty said curtly.

He stood there looking at a woman who was trying his patience. "Has anyone ever told you that you make it difficult to be nice to you?" Campbell asked.

Liberty tossed her head. "It's been mentioned," she answered. The moment she did, she regretted snapping at the detective. "I'm sorry. But I am over it," she added when she saw that he was waiting for something further.

"It?" he questioned, trying to get to the bottom of what was really bothering her rather than just accept some made-up excuse. He was a Cavanaugh and Cavanaughs liked to get to the bottom of things. Not out of some morbid curiosity, but because it made them see things more clearly.

At least, that was the excuse he used, he thought, and it did have validity.

A thought occurred to him. "Were you the one who found the body?" he asked her.

Liberty avoided his eyes. It wasn't something that she wanted to get into, especially not with a stranger. "Not exactly."

"Then what 'exactly'?" Campbell asked.

She shrugged. "Viewing the body just reminded me of something," she said evasively.

"Can I ask what?" Campbell inquired in a lowered voice.

"You can ask," Liberty responded.

Campbell studied her. He had faced enough stubborn family members to be very familiar with the look that was currently on her face. "But you're not going to tell me, are you?"

A partial smile broke through. "You catch on fast, Cavanaugh."

"I have to," he admitted. "There's a lot of competition in my family." He knew he wasn't going to get anything out of her on the subject, at least not today.

"Well," he told her, "I'm here if you decide you need a sympathetic shoulder to lean on."

"I'll keep that in mind," she said crisply, doing her best to bury his offer the moment it was tendered.

"You do that," he told her.

There was more going on here than just a simple detective trying to cut her teeth on her first murder case, he thought. This case meant something to the woman and he intended to find out just what it was.

But he could also see that he wasn't about to get anything out of her by pressuring her or bombarding her with questions at this point. This would take finesse—and patience.

If the woman wound up hanging around that long.

As he came to the door that opened into the medical examiner's offices, he paused with his hand on the doorknob.

"Something wrong?" Liberty asked him when he made no move to go in.

"Just making sure you're up to this," Campbell told her. "First times are hard."

"This isn't my first time," Liberty informed him.

He smiled at her, sending shockwaves all through her system. "Just making sure."

She resented his inference. She didn't like being a lightning rod for someone's concern. It made her feel fragile, and those days were permanently behind her.

Or they were supposed to be.

"Don't you have a sister or a cousin to take care of instead of me?" she asked, trying to redirect the detective's attention to someone or at least some*thing* other than her.

"Not at the moment," Campbell answered.

Turning the doorknob, he opened the door then gestured inside. "All right, let's go," he said.

To Liberty, it sounded almost like a battle cry.

Chapter Three

Dr. Kristin Alberghetti Cavanaugh had just untied her face mask, lowering it. It still hung at half mast around her neck, its blue color matching the scrubs she wore whenever she performed an autopsy. She had met Malloy, the man she was destined to marry, while performing wholesale autopsies on bodies uncovered beneath an out-of-the-way cacti nursery.

Kristin maintained that if all those unexpected bodies hadn't caught her off guard, then nothing ever would.

But Kristin had to admit that she was shaken up this time. She had just discovered, after having conducted the autopsy, that the body she'd just worked on was one of the many, according to the woman she had just met, that had been left by a prolific serial killer. That had rattled her to the core.

Kristin nodded at her husband's cousin, but her attention was drawn to the young woman he had brought into the morgue with him.

"Hi. I hear that our latest murder victim brought

you in all the way from Arizona," Kristin said, smiling at Liberty.

"Calhoun, Arizona," Campbell specified, knowing that Kristin liked details whenever possible.

Hearing the name, Kristin shook her head. "Sorry, I'm not familiar with that name," the medical examiner apologized.

"Don't worry about it. Not many people are," Liberty told her. Her eyes were drawn to the body on the table. "Is that the victim?" she asked. Without thinking, she had automatically lowered her voice out of respect for the deceased.

"It is," Campbell confirmed. And then, to lighten the mood, the detective quipped, "They frown on the lab assistants taking naps on the tables when it's slow."

"Don't pay any attention to Cam," Kristin told the woman from Arizona. "Yes, to confirm what Campbell just said, that is the latest victim." She watched as the blonde who had come in with Campbell slowly approached the table, circled it, looking at the body from all angles and studying the woman. There was a very strange expression on the detective's face. "Did you know her?" Kristin asked.

"No, not her," Liberty answered, only half paying attention to what the medical examiner had just asked her.

"But you knew one of the killer's victims, didn't you?" Campbell guessed, going with his gut reaction.

The detective's words sank in belatedly and Liberty's eyes darted to his face when she realized what he was saying. She inadvertently stiffened just a little.

"Why would you say that?" she asked defensively.

"Call it 'copley intuition.'" Campbell told her in all seriousness.

"'Copley'?" Kristin repeated with a laugh. "Well, that's a new one on me," she confessed.

"Calling it intuition sounds a lot better than a 'gut' feeling," Campbell told the two women.

"Maybe," Kristin agreed. "But 'copley'?" The medical examiner shook her head, showing how she felt about the strange term. "I really don't know about that. Is that even a word?"

The corners of Campbell's mouth curved. "I'll work on it," he promised glibly. "So," he said, addressing the ME more seriously, "is this victim similar to the others?"

"According to the reports I reviewed earlier, right down to the grade of piano wire the killer used," Kristin answered. It was obvious by the way the medical examiner spoke that she had divorced herself from the actual deed being investigated. Otherwise, she would have had difficulty remaining removed as she performed these autopsies.

Liberty studied the deceased more closely. "Was death immediate?"

The detective from Arizona might have seemed removed, Campbell thought, but something in how she asked about the deceased told him that this was personal to the investigator.

"If you're asking me if she suffered," Kristin said, "I don't think she did. There are no defensive wounds on the victim, indicating that the killer caught her by surprise. And then the piano wire did the rest."

"That's a relief," Liberty murmured then added, "That she didn't suffer. It means that the killer wasn't doing this in order to watch the victim suffer and plead with him for her life."

"Campbell mentioned that you said the victims were similar," Kristin told Liberty, interested in gathering as much information about the case as possible for her notes.

Liberty nodded. "All the victims so far have been nurses," she told the doctor. "And they were between the ages of twenty-five and fifty."

"No other similarities?" Kristin asked. "Hair color, eye color, weight?" She ticked off each item, watching Liberty's face as she mentioned it.

Liberty thought, doing a quick mental review of the victims she had compiled. She shook her head. "Nothing else except for the piano wire—and they were all Caucasian."

Kristin glanced at Campbell then asked the visiting detective, "Why do you think the killer would use piano wire?"

"My guess is that it probably has something to do with the original murder victim," Campbell answered, keeping one eye on Liberty to see if she agreed or had something contradictory to add. "Maybe the first person he killed this way was his mother or some other female relative who happened to be a nurse who also either taught music on the side or forced the killer to practice the piano as a boy. You'd be surprised what idiosyncrasies—"

"You said that *all* the victims were nurses?" Kristin asked. She found herself being drawn into particulars of this case.

"So far, they have been," Liberty verified.

"Maybe they also taught music. Say, on the side?" Campbell suggested, searching for a way to connect the two things.

"Good question," Liberty responded. "I don't know, but that will definitely be one of the questions I intend to ask."

"Are you planning on tracking down the victims' families and interviewing them?" Campbell asked. Considering that there were thirty victims, it sounded like a very ambitious undertaking to him. She was going to need help.

"If I can find them," Liberty acknowledged. "If I can't, then I'll try to find anyone who knew the victim and talk to them to get some kind of insight."

This was beginning to sound more like an obsession than just a case. "How long did you say you plan on taking off?" Campbell asked.

"Three weeks." Liberty had a hunch that she knew what he had to be thinking. "But if I feel like I'm getting somewhere, I can try to get an extension," she added.

"Out of sheer curiosity, how many people do you

have working with you?" he asked. "I know you mentioned that you were the only detective in Calhoun,
but do you have any assistance, or police officers
helping you go through these cases?"

She hated being put on the spot or admitting that
there wasn't anyone to turn as she worked this investigation.

"It's not about the number of people I have," Liberty replied.

It wasn't hard to read between the lines, Campbell
thought. "So it's just you," he guessed.

Liberty raised her chin. "Sometimes it just takes
one person," she said defensively.

The detective smiled at her. "In a perfect world,
maybe. But then, in a perfect world, these kinds of
things don't happen," he concluded philosophically.

Was he goading her, or was he just having fun at
her expense? Either way, she didn't take kindly to it.
"Is there a point to this?" she asked him.

"Well, the key point is that this investigation you're
proposing to spearhead would go a lot faster if you
had help."

She certainly couldn't argue with that, even though
she would have wanted to, especially since she felt as
if this detective was deliberately pressing her buttons
to get a reaction out of her.

"I'll put an ad to that effect in the local paper when
I get home," Liberty told him.

"No need to do that," Campbell said. He made it
sound as if he had some sort of a solution to her situation.

"Oh? Well, I'm open to any suggestions," she said glibly then added, "*Decent* suggestions." The look in her eyes challenged him. "All right, so what's *your* idea?"

He smiled, sensing that she wouldn't like this, but then, if she was all alone in this, she really didn't have much choice, did she?

"Well, I've got some time coming to me," Campbell told her.

Liberty frowned, totally forgetting about the medical examiner in the room for the moment. "And what good does that do me?"

She also didn't care for the amused smile that curved the detective's lips—never mind just *how* appealing that smile made him look.

"Not much for adding two and two together, are you?" Campbell asked her.

Kristin cleared her throat, temporarily drawing their attention away from one another. "Not that it isn't fascinating watching the two of you spar, but I do have work to get to. I can have a rough draft of this report in your hands within an hour or so. Until then, maybe you can take this outside?" she suggested brightly, looking from one to the other.

"Sorry, Kris," Campbell apologized, giving her cheek a quick, affectionate kiss. "I'll be on my best behavior when I come back to get the report," he promised with a wink.

As he began to leave, he realized that the woman he had brought in with him still hadn't made a move to follow him. She had remained standing next to the medical examiner.

"Um, Arizona?" he said, waiting to get her attention so that she would leave with him.

Instead, Liberty looked almost sheepishly at Kristin. Maybe she did need to apologize. "I'm sorry, Doctor. I don't usually allow myself to get carried away like this. It's just that you were right," she admitted. "This *is* a very special case for me. And not just because of this latest case—" she nodded at the body on the table "—or the one that I caught in Calhoun, even though murder in Calhoun is a very rare occurrence. We don't exactly have murderers in town, much less serial killers."

Kristin nodded. "I understand perfectly."

This was where she walked away, Liberty silently reminded herself. She had smoothed out the feathers that she had ruffled—or at the very least, the feathers appeared to be smoothed out.

Despite that, Liberty continued to stand where she was. She needed these people's cooperation and it appeared that the detective was willing to pitch in even after she had become so prickly. The very thing that had her being so closemouthed when she was around the chief and his people back in Calhoun now had her willing to open herself up to this detective and the medical examiner.

She really didn't have a choice in the matter.

"Actually," Liberty began, her eyes sweeping over

the medical examiner and then over toward Campbell, "you don't."

Kristin appeared to be at a loss as to whether or not to press Liberty for any further details, but Campbell had no such misgivings. "All right, then why don't you explain it to us?"

Liberty pressed her lips together, carefully weighing her words. "It's personal," she finally responded to Campbell.

"Are you talking about the case or the explanation?" Campbell asked.

Liberty took in a deep breath before answering, telling him, "Both."

That was still rather ambiguous as far as Campbell was concerned. "Why don't you tell us about one or the other to start with?"

She might as well give him some of the background, Liberty decided, even though part of her really wished she hadn't started out on this path to begin with. But she had, and she did owe him for being willing to help.

"I didn't tell anyone in Calhoun that the case was personal for me because, as a rule, I wouldn't be allowed to investigate a case that was personal, even though it actually is part of a larger case involving a serial killer."

"No argument so far," Campbell told her, nodding his head. He could feel Kristin looking at him, which stopped him. "What?"

"You know perfectly well *what*," the medical examiner told him, then looked at Liberty and began to explain what was actually behind her comment. "There have been more than a few members in the family who have either looked the other way or hoped the authorities in charge would wind up looking the other way when they, the members, took up an investigation that was close to them.

"Cavanaughs," she continued, "you'll find out, aren't exactly married to the rules when those rules manage to get in the way of their solving a crime."

Liberty flashed a smile at the medical examiner, surprised that the doctor was willing to admit that to her.

"Well, that's good to know," the visiting detective acknowledged.

Campbell decided to dive in.

"You were saying before Kristin interjected her sidebar?" he asked, waiting for Liberty to continue and to hopefully give him the answer to the question he had asked when she'd first come to him with this case.

"I said that the case was personal," she repeated, still attempting to find the right words to explain her dilemma.

"Yes, I got that part," Campbell assured her.

His eyes met hers and this time, he wasn't struck by how very blue they were. He was struck by the sadness he saw there.

"Was the person who was killed by this serial killer someone in your family?" Kristin asked.

"I don't have a family," Liberty answered automatically. "I never did." Even after all this time, the words still tasted bitter on her tongue.

And then she pressed her lips together, pushing on. "But Florence was the closest person I ever had to a family and I owe it to her to find the worthless excuse for a human being who did this to her."

"Florence," Campbell repeated. "That was one of the names on that list you showed me."

It wasn't a guess.

Despite herself, Liberty was impressed. "There were thirty names on that list."

"He's blessed with one of those memories," Kristin told her.

"You mean photographic?" Liberty asked. "That must come in handy in your line of work."

"Not exactly photographic," Campbell corrected. "But it's the next best thing. I remember things. I just have to see it written once or hear it said, and it's pretty much sealed in."

"I guess I'd better watch what I say around you, then," Liberty said half seriously.

"Only if you decide to lie, because then it'll trip you up. Otherwise," Campbell said with a grin, "you have nothing to worry about."

"What I just said about this being personal…" she began.

Campbell could guess where she was going with this. "Sorry, I wasn't listening."

Kristin smiled. "That's his way of saying don't

worry. But you two really have to make yourself scarce now—unless you don't want this report."

"We're gone, Kris," Campbell assured her, opening the door.

Liberty preceded him out. She was more than eager to hold the report in her hand.

Chapter Four

"I take it that you've already notified Cynthia Ellery's next of kin?" Liberty asked as they walked out of the medical examiner's office.

"Actually, we've just managed to locate the victim's next of kin late yesterday," Campbell told her. "Her sister, Judith, was away on vacation. When we reached her, she said she would be getting back into town today."

A very cold chill ran up and down Liberty's spine. "Does she know what she's coming back to?" Liberty couldn't help asking. The situation brought back so many of her own memories of when she'd found out about her foster mother's murder.

"She guessed before I could tell her," Campbell admitted.

The answer surprised Liberty. "She *guessed* that her sister was dead? Doesn't that strike you as being a little odd?" she asked Campbell. "If someone called me about my sister, my first guess wouldn't be that you were calling because she was dead."

Something just wasn't making sense to Liberty.

Could the woman's sister have had anything to do with Cynthia's murder?

"When I identified myself as being part of the police department, she immediately thought I was calling to notify her that something had happened to Cynthia, like a car accident," Campbell said.

Liberty rolled that explanation over in her mind. "Well, I suppose that does make more sense," she responded.

Campbell nodded. "I had to tell her why I was calling."

Liberty recalled that she had had so many questions of her own once the shock of her foster mother's death had had time to register.

The elevator arrived and they got on. "But you are going to follow up, on your phone call, right?" she asked the detective. "You're not just going to leave it at just a phone notification."

"Sounds like you already know the answer to that one," Campbell replied.

"Let's just say I was hoping that you wouldn't disappoint me." She turned her face up to his. "Would it be all right if I tagged along? And no, I don't know the answer to that question, but I'm hoping that you won't say no."

Liberty couldn't read the expression that passed over Campbell's face and, for a moment, she found herself suspended in limbo, her mind scrambling to come up with a way to convince the detective, if he did turn her down, that she would be an asset if she were allowed to come along.

Campbell took pity on her and put her out of her misery. "First of all, it would be rather cruel of me to tell you that you couldn't come along when I talk to the victim's relative after you came all this way to inform me that there were more victims. Second, I would be lying if I said that I couldn't use the backup. These notifications can become very uncomfortable and get rather sticky. Having a woman come along might make the victim's sister feel marginally better. So yes, you can definitely come along."

Liberty had to admit that she was surprised, as well as relieved, that it wound up being so easy.

"Thank you. Frankly, I was bracing myself for a fight," she admitted.

"Well, I'm glad I could disappoint you," he said with a laugh. "Unless, of course, you're the type who thrives on confrontations and arguments."

"No, not usually," she told him as the elevator came to a stop on the first floor. "But if you're wondering, I don't run away from them, either."

Campbell laughed, his smile managing to set up residency in her chest despite Liberty's best efforts to block her reaction to this man. He had a smile that somehow managed to undulate through her entire system.

"Can't say that surprises me," he told her. Campbell began to make his way to the building's front exit.

"So, unless you've decided that you have something else to turn your attention to—"

"Not at this very moment," she told him a bit too emphatically.

"Then let's go pay Cynthia Ellery's sister a visit," he said, secretly grateful he wouldn't be facing the ordeal alone. It wasn't that he shirked his responsibilities or would even put them off, but he had always felt that there was emotional safety in numbers. "All right. I'll drive."

Liberty had no problem with that and wondered if he was expecting her to argue with him over the arrangement. "It's your town and you know your way around,"

"It's my *city*," he corrected. "But yes, I do. My car's parked right over here in the rear lot." Campbell pointed it out for her benefit, leading the way to a brand-new, fully loaded silver sedan.

Liberty let out a low, appreciative whistle. The car was a fine-looking piece of machinery.

"I guess they must pay detectives really well in Aurora," she commented.

For a split second, Campbell didn't know what she was referring to and then he realized why she had said what she had. He wasn't all that into cars.

"Oh, you mean the car," he proclaimed. "The department just replaced my old car. They had to," he confessed. "I was really very partial to my previous vehicle until the driver of the car I was pursuing decided to make a sudden U-turn and tried to flatten it so that I wouldn't wind up taking him in."

She could vividly picture that confrontation. "Were you hurt?" Liberty asked.

A quick scan of the man showed her that he didn't seem to have a scratch on him. Was he lucky, or was he just putting her on?

"Actually, I wasn't. But the car really was," he said sadly. "I managed to jump out of the car and get out of the way just in time—except for this." He pointed to a thin, long scratch along his neck.

"Oh, ouch," Liberty said, sucking in a breath. She hadn't seen the mark before because it was on the side that she hadn't been facing—until he had just pointed it out.

Campbell laughed under his breath. "That wasn't exactly quite the word I used at the time, but yes, 'ouch,'" he agreed.

"And you said that your car was totaled?" Liberty asked him.

The memory of that incident was still very vivid to him. "Yes, it was."

"I guess you're lucky that nothing worse happened."

That wasn't exactly the way he viewed it. "Well, I consider losing a car pretty bad," he told her.

She looked at his vehicle skeptically. Maybe driving it bothered him. A little like a bad memory he couldn't get rid of.

"Would you like me to drive?" Liberty offered. "My vehicle isn't nearly as pretty, but it is reliable."

He wasn't sure why she was making the offer. "The accident wasn't my fault."

"I never said it was." She told him the first thing that came to mind. "I just thought you might like a break and I could drive."

"As you pointed out, this is my city and I know where I'm going," he told her. He had no idea where she could have gotten the idea that he might want a break from driving.

"You could give me directions," she said. Her lips curved ever so slightly. "I'm sure you're very good at telling people where to go."

"Why, Arizona, did you just make a joke?" Campbell asked with a laugh.

"No, just an observation," she answered. "And why do you keep calling me Arizona?" Liberty asked. After all, he did know her name.

"That's where you're from, isn't it?" he asked, starting up the car after she had buckled up. "And you have to admit that it sounds better than calling you Calhoun," he added with a grin.

"Why would you have to call me any of that? Did you forget my name?" she asked, assuming that was the only reason he had for falling back on calling her by the state she had initially come from.

"Well, you don't much look like a 'Lawrence,'" he said.

Her brow furrowed as she tried to make sense out

of what he was saying. "But I look like an 'Arizona' to you?"

"Yes." When she looked at him quizzically, he explained. "It's the smell of wind in your hair. Makes me think of Arizona," he said, adding, "I visited there once. Tucson, specifically. Ever been?"

"Not that I recall," Liberty answered evasively. Actually, she had been to Tucson. She had been to several cities in Arizona, none of which she really cared to remember. That was back during the time when she'd found herself being passed from one foster home to another, fitting in nowhere and longing to be old enough to be on her own. Tucson was one of the places she'd run away from in her effort to be independent because she'd felt that no one had earned the right to take control of her life.

Not until Florence had come along and taken her in hand.

Liberty banished the memory out of her thoughts for the time being. Being nostalgic wasn't going to find Florence's killer or bring him to justice, she reminded herself.

Campbell noticed that the detective had lapsed into silence and couldn't help wondering if something he had said had struck a nerve.

IT DIDN'T TAKE long for Campbell to bring them to their destination. He pulled up in front of a tidy, one-story home and parked by the curb.

"You ready?" he asked Liberty.

She sighed, looking at the small house and thinking of the person who lived there. Nothing was ever going to be the same once they talked with her.

"Is anyone ever ready to shatter someone else's world?" Liberty asked.

Maybe this was a bad idea, Campbell thought. "She's already been informed about her sister's death. And you don't have to come if it makes you uncomfortable."

"Yes, I do," Liberty insisted. It was her duty. "And my comfort has nothing to do with it."

He studied her face, unable to make up his mind about this woman. "Are you always so difficult to deal with?"

"'Difficult'?" Liberty repeated in genuine surprise. "And here I thought I was being easygoing."

Campbell shook his head.

"Think again," he told her, but Liberty noted that there was an amused smile on his face.

Getting out, Campbell circled around to the front passenger side and opened the door for her before she had the chance to.

Liberty continued to sit where she was, staring at him as Campbell held the door for her. "What are you doing?"

"I thought that was rather obvious. I'm holding the door open for you. Hasn't anyone ever held open the door for you, Arizona?" he asked.

As far as she knew, she was the very picture of independence. "Why would they want to?" Liberty questioned.

His eyes met hers. "You know, before you go back

to that little town of yours, Arizona, you and I are going to have to have a long talk."

"Yeah, we'll see," Liberty said without committing to anything. She got out of the vehicle.

Campbell noticed the way she was looking around as they went up the front walkway. It made him think of a wistful kid, which had him wondering about the woman who was accompanying him. If she remained in Aurora for those three weeks she had mentioned, he promised himself that he would get her to talk about how she had arrived at this point in her life—and what she had experienced prior to that. Maybe that would be construed as meddling, but he was a Cavanaugh. Good or bad, it was a family trait.

He had a feeling that she had gone through a lot of experiences, good and bad, that had made her the woman she had become.

Maybe he was wrong, Campbell thought—but he had a sneaking suspicion that he wasn't.

Liberty had just assumed that the detective with her was rather laidback, but then she saw him squaring his shoulders just a fraction of a second before he rang the doorbell.

Maybe he wasn't as blasé as he was attempting to portray.

It made her feel better about the man. He was genuine.

When no one came to the door, Campbell rang the bell again.

"Maybe you got the time wrong," Liberty suggested. "Or Cynthia's sister decided she wasn't up to talking to the police just yet."

Campbell frowned. "The longer she puts it off, the worse it's going to get for her." He knew that for a fact.

He was about to ring the bell a third time when the front door finally swung open. The woman in the doorway was a startling sight to see.

Judith Ellery's face was all puffy and swollen, like someone who had been crying for the better part of the day, which she obviously had.

The victim's sister looked almost bewildered when she eyed the couple standing on her front doorstep.

To set the woman's mind at ease, Campbell immediately took out his wallet and badge.

"I'm Detective Campbell Cavanaugh," he told the grieving woman, introducing himself. "I believe we spoke earlier on the phone." He put his identification away and nodded toward Liberty. "This is Detective Lawrence. She's from Arizona, and is consulting with me on this case." Glancing past the woman's shoulder, he could see that she was alone. "We would like to ask you some questions, if it's all right with you?"

"All right with me?" the woman echoed almost incomprehensibly. "Nothing is ever going to be all right again," she lamented as she tried to hold back a fresh wave of sobs.

Judith Ellery held up her hand to stop the detective from saying anything further until she could get herself under control again.

"Can I get you some water to drink?" Liberty asked, taking the lead and surprising Campbell.

The victim's sister pressed her lips together, shook her head and then swallowed before taking in a deep breath.

"No, that's all right," Judith told the two detectives standing in her doorway. "Just give me a minute," she requested, still struggling to regain control over herself.

"Take all the time you need," Campbell told her kindly.

Fresh tears were sliding down the woman's shallow cheeks, taking the very same path they already had previously.

Judith's voice was shaky as she spoke. "I warned her, you know. I told Cynthia that if she wasn't careful, something bad would happen to her. But she just laughed at me, told me she was a 'big girl' and that if she could take care of all those patients who came into the ER, she could certainly take care of herself in the outside world."

Tear-filled eyes looked from one detective to the other. "But she couldn't, could she?" Judith asked, her emotion-filled voice cracking.

"What did she mean by that?" Campbell asked. "'Take care of herself in the outside world'?" He wanted to know, repeating the words the victim's sister had just used.

"She was talking about those stupid dating sites," Judith angrily snapped. "You know, those anonymous ones where you make arrangements to meet up with men who could be Jack the Ripper for all you knew." Judith began to sob again. "I warned her this could happen. I *warned* her. But she wouldn't listen to me. She always acted as if she knew better than me."

Judith looked at the detectives with tear-swollen eyes. "But she didn't, did she? Damn it, why couldn't I make her listen?" she sobbed.

Chapter Five

So, the victim was in contact with a dating service. It was definitely an avenue to explore, Liberty silently decided.

She made a mental note to look into whether any of the other serial killer's victims had availed themselves of dating sites. At least it was a place where she could start.

"Would you happen to know any of the names of the men your sister met with?" Campbell asked the woman before Liberty had a chance to do the same. "Or maybe the name of the site she used?"

At the very least, they could try to get the necessary information from the dating site, as long as they explained the situation and promised to keep the investigation a secret, Campbell thought. Granted, it was a long shot, but it just might work.

However, Judith shook her head. "I really don't know any of that," she confessed. "Cynthia knew I didn't approve of her using sites like that, so she didn't talk about it with me. She might have mentioned something about it to some of her friends at the hospital. From what I gathered, they all thought the same way she did. Except they're still alive."

Judith pressed her lips together as she paused for a moment. Tears were getting the better of her again. She let out a deep, emotional breath. "I told her there was nothing wrong with meeting men the old-fashioned way, but she wouldn't listen to me. And now she's gone." Judith's voice broke again.

"'The old-fashioned way,'" Campbell repeated. "And that was…?" His voice trailed off as he waited for the victim's sister to complete the sentence.

"Through her place of work, and church," Judith answered. She wiped away her tears. "I met my late husband that way. He was a teller at the same bank that I was. But Cynthia said she didn't want to have her choices limited like that." More tears began to stream down the woman's face. "And now she has no choices at all," Judith sobbed and then covered her face with her hands. "Oh, lord, I wish she had listened to me. Cynthia would still be alive now if she had." Judith sounded as if her heart was literally breaking.

Liberty exchanged glances with the detective at her side. They couldn't just leave the woman in this condition.

Putting her arm around Judith's shoulders to comfort the distraught woman, Liberty asked, "Is there anyone we can call for you? Maybe a friend? Or another relative?"

Judith waved away the question. "I have someone I can call," she finally answered, her voice throbbing with emotion. "I'll be all right," she assured the two detectives with her.

"Well, if it's all the same to you," Campbell told the woman, "we'll wait until they get here. We wouldn't feel right leaving you alone like this." The statement was apparently directed toward Liberty, since the victim's sister had her head down, struggling to get control over her emotions.

Detective Cavanaugh's stock went up considerably in Liberty's estimation and she nodded her agreement with his statement.

Meanwhile, Judith deferred Campbell's offer, saying, "You don't have to." But the pitiful smile she offered both of them said far more than her words.

THE DETECTIVES WOUND up staying with the victim's sister until her friend showed up—which turned out to be within the hour. When the woman, Angie, came on the scene, Campbell quickly explained the situation to her in its entirety. Judith's friend vacillated between shock and sympathy.

Campbell left both women with his business card and told them not to hesitate calling him if they remembered anything pertinent, even the smallest thing.

"Think it's someone that Cynthia met on a dating site?" Liberty asked Campbell as they left the victim sister's house.

Campbell shrugged. "It's as good a possibility as any, I guess. At least it's a place to start. Starting a murder investigation is a lot like being confronted with a thousand-piece puzzle. You dump out all the pieces on the floor—wondering how in the hell all the pieces are going to fit together—and then you realize that at least five of those pieces were left out of the box.

"But you can't let that get to you," he told her as they got into his car. "You just keep working the pieces until they finally somehow all fit together."

"Is that how you view the investigation?" she asked Cam. "I've got to say, that description is kind of daunting."

"If it were easy, there would be a lot more investigators to go around instead of dropping out," Campbell told her. "What do you say we go to the hospital and see if we can find some of Cynthia's friends? Maybe at least one of them knows what dating site she used."

Liberty nodded. "I was just going to suggest that," she told Campbell.

"Great minds think alike," Campbell said, flashing her a smile.

Liberty looked at him with suspicion. "Are you making fun of me?"

He glanced at her as he turned the corner. Why would she even think that?

"No, I'm not," Campbell told Liberty. "That was supposed to be a compliment. You know, you're going to have to learn how to tell the difference. For one thing, not everything is meant to be an insult or taken to be fighting words."

He was right, she thought. She was too quick to take offense. She would have to tone that down.

"Sorry," she murmured.

"Don't be sorry," he told her. He didn't want her apologies, he wanted to be able to work with her. "Just learn how to relax a little."

"Right. Relax," she mocked. "While investigating a serial killer."

She was definitely making fun of him now. But Campbell decided to take it in stride. He told her what his uncle, the chief of detectives, had told him when he'd first came to work on the police force.

"If you don't find some humor, however small or inane, to hang on to, in the long run, you're going to wind up losing your sense of humanity."

"What is that, something from a fortune cookie?" Liberty asked him.

"No, from Chief of Detectives Brian Cavanaugh," Campbell answered mildly.

Color shot into her cheeks. She had certainly put her foot into it that time, she thought. "I didn't mean to insult anyone…" she began.

Campbell's smile was meant to reassure her. "You didn't. The Chief of D's has a very thick hide—and a very decent sense of humor," he added with a wink just as he pulled into the Aurora Memorial Hospital's front parking lot.

Cynthia Ellery had been an ER nurse for the last

five years, so the ER on the first floor was their first stop.

"I guess they've all heard the news by now," Liberty commented, looking around at the staff populating the general area.

It was obvious that the murder of one of their own had deeply affected a great many of the nurses and orderlies, as well as the doctors who were currently on duty during this shift.

Asking around, Campbell and Liberty had no trouble locating people who not only knew the late victim, but had nothing but kind words to say about Cynthia Ellery.

But as far as knowing anything personal about the nurse that might help them in the investigation, that unfortunately turned out to be an entirely different story.

The detectives kept coming up against dead ends time after time.

"Well, I knew she was single, but that's about it. She was a great nurse, though. And she was always willing to fill in in a pinch no matter how long a shift she had put in," the head nurse on the floor told them.

"I didn't even know she was looking to get fixed up," another nurse told them when they questioned her about her association with Cynthia.

"If I'd known, I would have introduced her to my cousin, Joe. He's not exactly a catch, but he's a good man with a big heart," yet another nurse volunteered.

Over and over again, they heard the same responses to their questions. Everyone knew Cynthia, but no one really seemed to *know* her.

In the end, although it took some doing, they did find a nurse who'd known that Cynthia was looking for a match on a dating site ironically named *Finding the Right One*.

"Would you happen to know if she used her real name when she signed up?"

"Oh, I know she did," the nurse, Abby, told them. "I can't say if the guy she went out with did. She saw him several times, though. Always at a restaurant. Cynthia was a hopeless romantic, but she wasn't stupid."

Liberty crossed her fingers. "Would you happen to know which restaurants she went to in order to meet this guy?"

"I know that she went to the Blue Hawaiian, but as far as the other restaurants she went to—" The woman lifted her shoulders in a hapless shrug then let them fall again. "I'm sorry. If she told me, I don't remember. We're usually very busy here in the ER."

"Don't worry about it," Campbell told her. "Anything you can tell us, anything at all, will be helpful."

The nurse shook her head, embarrassed. "I'm drawing a blank," she confessed. "It's like my brain froze."

"Well, if it happens to unfreeze," Campbell said, giving her his card, "please give me a call."

"Well, we didn't exactly strike out," Campbell told Liberty, sensing that she might need a little bit of a pep talk to bolster her confidence after they walked away. "We've got the name of a dating site plus a restaurant. Maybe someone at the restaurant might remember seeing her—and with whom."

It was obvious that their next stop was going to be the Blue Hawaiian restaurant.

But in the end, before they left the hospital, it was an orderly who supplied them with at least some of the answers.

The orderly, Luis Montenegro, a short, thin man who had a habit of blending into the background, overheard them talking as they were about to leave the ER.

"Are you two investigating what happened to Cynthia Ellery?" he asked, placing himself in front of the two detectives.

Campbell glanced in Liberty's direction. It was obvious that he was very pleased, not to mention hopeful, that this man would be able to finally supply them with a few answers.

"You knew her?" Campbell asked the orderly.

Luis nodded, his thick, salt-and-pepper hair not moving an inch. "Ever since she came to work in the emergency room. From the very first day, Cynthia was a really nice lady. With all her experience, she never acted as if she was above anyone. She held her temper even when some moron got in her face. Just took it all in stride," he recalled, getting a wistful, faraway look on his thin, chiseled features. "Me, I would have really told them off, but she was always cool about it." And then his face darkened with barely suppressed anger as he asked, "Do you know who did this to her?"

"That's what we're trying to find out," Liberty told the orderly. "Anything you can tell us about that dating site she was using would be really helpful."

"Just that she kept setting herself up with losers." He shook his head. "One guy more disappointing than the next."

A number of possibilities ran through Liberty's mind as she slanted a look in the orderly's direction. "And you know this for a fact?" she asked.

"I don't know about 'fact,' but I know that's what she said," the orderly told them. Then, seeing that the detectives appeared skeptical, Luis told them, "We were friends. She would tell me things she wouldn't share with the others because she was afraid she might look foolish to them."

"But she wasn't afraid she would look foolish to you?" Campbell questioned.

"No. Like I said, we were friends," Luis told the man questioning him. "Besides, she knew I wasn't about to hit on her, so she felt comfortable talking about her 'matches' with me." He looked from one detective to the other to see if they understood what he was telling them.

"Would you happen to know any of these so-called dates' names?" Campbell asked.

"I know all of them," the orderly confidently replied. He wasn't bragging, Campbell realized. The man was merely stating a simple fact.

"Could you write them down for us?" he asked.

"Sure," he told Campbell. "All I need a piece of paper and a pen."

"Coming up," Liberty said, opening her small shoulder bag and taking out the requested tools.

Taking them in hand, Luis began writing as if the fresh information would disappear if it weren't quickly preserved.

In all, there were five names. Five candidates who might or might not have been guilty of murder.

"Would you happen to know if these were aliases or their real names?" Campbell asked.

"That, I really couldn't say," he answered honestly.

At least they had something to continue investigating, Campbell thought. Folding the piece of paper, he tucked it into his pocket. "Thanks for this," he said to the orderly.

"Just find whoever did this to her," Luis told the detectives.

"We fully intend to," Liberty promised sincerely.

Leaving the hospital, Campbell looked at Liberty. "Are you hungry?"

She stared at him, startled, as they approached his vehicle. Was he saying what she thought he was saying? "You can actually eat?" she asked him.

They were dealing with homicides and multiple murders. Her own stomach felt as if was in turmoil and Liberty doubted that she could keep anything down, much less a whole meal.

"Whether I can or can't isn't the question here. I *should*," he told her with emphasis. "You've got to keep up your strength when investigating a murder— or *murders*," he clarified, since this wasn't just about Cynthia Ellery's murder, but about thirty victims altogether... *If not more*, he couldn't help thinking.

"So in the middle of all this, we're taking a break," she said, trying to wrap her head around it.

He could tell from her tone of voice what she thought of the idea.

"No, not a 'break,' we're refueling," Campbell reworded. "Just enough to keep us going."

She sighed. She wasn't up to arguing. "Well, you're the senior investigator, so I guess I can't argue with you."

His smile seemed to bloom all over his face. "But you want to, don't you?"

"I believe this is where I'm supposed to plead the fifth," she responded.

Campbell laughed. "You're learning, Arizona," he told her. "You're learning."

HE DROVE OVER to a take-out place he favored, a Chinese restaurant that had been family owned and operated for the last thirty-five years. It served Cantonese-style food, and had expanded to include Mandarin in the last couple of years.

"Do you have a certain prescribed amount I'm

supposed to consume?" Liberty asked as they walked inside the restaurant.

The atmosphere was warm and welcoming.

For his part, Campbell was still getting a kick out of her as he followed the hostess to a table. "Now you're making me sound as if I'm anally retentive," he commented, waiting for the sexy looking detective from Arizona to take a seat. "Is that what you actually think?"

"I think you're the type to make your kids eat whether they want to or not," she told him.

"Well, luckily for them, I don't have any," he quipped.

"No children?" she asked.

"No, and no marriage, either," Campbell replied.

"You could still have children," she pointed out.

"Touché." He laughed. "But no to either, if you're asking. And, if you really don't want to eat, no one is going to make you. Although I do strongly recommend it."

She glanced at him. "You're making it sound as if I had a choice." Her eyes met his as she picked up the menu on the table before her. "But I don't, do I?"

"You're the detective," he told her. "What do you think?"

"I think I'd better find something on the menu that I will be able to keep down," Liberty said, opening the menu up.

His eyes smiled at her. "Good guess," Campbell told her with approval.

Chapter Six

The server, who was the owner's grandson, brought over their orders and placed them before them. Campbell waited until the young man withdrew before he asked Liberty, "Are you sure that's all you want?"

He eyed her order: a cup of wonton soup and a couple of egg rolls. In his opinion, that wasn't enough to keep an anemic pigeon alive.

"I ordered this mostly to satisfy you," Liberty told him. "And to get me from point A to point B." She saw the skeptical look on the detective's face. "I told you, I'm not really hungry."

"Obviously," he noted. "But as I pointed out, it's not about hunger. If it was, then this could officially be thought of as a date rather than just a working late lunch."

She could feel her back going up. Why was he saying that? "Why don't we just skip the label, eat the meal and go?"

Campbell smiled at the way she summarized this entire venture. "Are you that anxious to get somewhere with this case?"

There was no point in attempting to deny how much she wanted to find answers. "And that, I'm assuming, is what makes you such a great detective," Liberty quipped.

"Oh, I'm just in it for the fascinating company," he told her.

She looked at him. Did he mean that as a slam against her? she wondered. Not that she didn't have it coming. "Well, I'm sorry you didn't luck out."

His smile went directly into her stomach, causing minor tidal waves within it. She needed to get a grip.

"I'm not complaining," he told her.

All things considered, the detective appeared to have a more than decent temperament, she decided. Taking herself in hand, Liberty shifted the focus of their conversation.

"What do you think our chances are of getting that dating site Cynthia used to open its doors to us?" she queried.

"Honestly?" Campbell asked.

When she nodded, he answered. "Small to none. We might have better luck if we go to that last restaurant Cynthia went to and look at their surveillance tapes. We might be able to see if we can get a license plate number off our victim's date's car. That way, we might be able to verify his name. Once we have that, and locate him, then we can bring him in for questioning."

This had been a slow, tedious process, but at least it was beginning to take form, she thought. For the first time in a long time, she began to feel hopeful that, eventually, she would be able to see this to its proper, well-deserved end.

Nodding, Liberty told him, "That definitely sounds good to me."

"But it's also going to take time," he pointed out, wanting her to be aware of that fact. Out of the blue, he asked, "Where are you staying?"

That was a detail she hadn't arranged yet. She had been obsessed with the big picture, not the details that made up the minutia.

"I haven't thought that far ahead," Liberty confessed. "But this looks like a big city. I figured you had to have motels here, right?"

"We do," Campbell conceded. "But even that runs into money, Arizona."

Liberty frowned at what he was saying. "I didn't exactly anticipate staying in one for free."

"I have a way around that."

She didn't follow him at first and then the radar suddenly went off in her head. She was not about to stay at his place.

"Thank you, but no thank you," Liberty told him, turning down the offer.

He looked at her in surprise, especially given the tone she'd used. "Come again?"

All right, she would put it into words that he would understand. "I'm not about to stay with you, Detective Cavanaugh."

He bit his lower lip, suppressing a laugh. "Well,

tempting though that might seem—for you," he added with a grin, "I was going to suggest that you stay with one of my sisters. You have your choice between Jacqui or Blythe. If either one of them doesn't work out for you, I also have several single female cousins you could stay with."

Liberty stared at him. Granted she didn't have any relatives of her own and never had, but she doubted what he was proposing was considered standard practice amid families.

"Are you in the habit of offering up your sisters' or cousins' living quarters to perfect strangers?" she asked.

"I'd hardly call you perfect, Arizona," he said, his mouth curving. "And you're not exactly a stranger. We've been together for the better part of the day."

"Well, be that as it may, I am a stranger to them and I'm sure that they wouldn't be all that thrilled having to put me up."

"Maybe not thrilled," Campbell allowed, "but certainly happy to. We're a big, open family. It's a given."

However, Liberty still had misgivings. "Somehow, I doubt it. We'll talk about this once we meet with the company running the dating site. If we don't get anywhere with them, or the restaurant where Cynthia went on her last date, *then* we'll see what my next move is."

Campbell nodded. "I'll hold you to that," he promised with a smile. "In the meantime, can I get you anything else before we go?"

She shook her head. "No, I'm stuffed."

Compared to what she had consumed, he had had a serving of soup, lobster Cantonese and a fortune cookie, and he still felt as if he could have eaten more. But then he had always had a big appetite.

"Well, you should know," he told her. He raised his hand to get the waiter's attention, signaling that he was ready for the check.

The server, who by his familiar manner obviously knew Campbell, was quick to bring over the bill.

She waited until the man had left before asking, "How much is my share?"

Campbell took out several bills and placed them inside the folder. "Don't worry about it. It's taken care of."

Liberty drew herself up. "That's very nice of you," she said in a reserved manner, "but I like paying my own way."

"And I appreciate that," Campbell told her patiently, "but your part of the bill came to next to nothing and I really think I can handle that."

"But—"

Campbell looked at her. "Arizona, if we're going to continue working together, you are going to have to learn how to be gracious about accepting a gesture every now and then. Now, I'm paying for this meal. You can pick up the next one. Okay?"

She wasn't happy about it, but she couldn't argue with him about everything. Like it or not, she needed him. Arguing with the man was not the right way to cement a decent working relationship.

"Okay," she responded grudgingly. Then, after a beat, added, "Thank you," as if it really pained her to utter the words.

It was hard for Campbell not to laugh, but somehow he managed to refrain.

"You're welcome, Arizona," he replied.

"By the way, that was a pretty big tip you left on the table," she commented as they left the small restaurant.

"Well, they work hard running the restaurant," he told her, "and I like the family. They've been through some pretty tough times and weathered their share of ups and downs running that place." He held open the passenger door for her. "It's my way of ensuring that my favorite restaurant sticks around a while longer."

"Why?" she asked, her curiosity aroused. "Do you think they're going to go out of business?"

"I don't think so. But I've learned to take absolutely nothing for granted these days," Campbell said.

"I know how that is." She voiced the sentiment almost to herself.

As a kid, she'd never known if the bed she went to sleep in would be the one she would be allowed to wake up in the following morning. Or if, for some reason or another, somewhere in the middle of the night she would be forced to play musical homes and be whisked off to another foster home.

"Something you'd like to share?" Campbell asked her, curious.

The sound of his voice brought Liberty back around to the present.

"No," she told him. "I would not."

He nodded, seeing the sad, almost grim expression on her face and thinking he had stumbled across some place he shouldn't be. He could feel his curiosity being aroused. That was the problem with being a detective. So many mysteries, so little time.

"Duly noted," he told her as he waited for her to buckle up.

THE PLACE THAT ran the Finding the Right One website was located not too far away.

As Campbell had predicted, the people in charge of the dating site were not forthcoming with the information they needed. While they were very sympathetic about the circumstances and the reason for the request, Miles Perkins, the man in charge of managing the website, told them, "I'm afraid that my hands are tied. I can't release that information."

"You do realize that the person who availed herself of your site is now dead, right?" Liberty asked curtly.

"Yes, I realize that," Perkins told her, the soul of benevolence, "but it still doesn't allow me to release the names of the men she met on the site. I have an obligation to maintain their privacy."

Liberty was struggling very hard to hold on to

her temper. "What about your obligation to Cynthia Ellery?"

The expression on the manager's face was pained as well as very sympathetic. "What happened to her is tragic," he admitted, "but it could all just be circumstantial."

Her eyes narrowed until they almost looked as if they were shooting lightning bolts. "Murder is not circumstantial, Mr. Perkins. It's a very ugly occurrence," Liberty argued.

Perkins shook his head. "I'm afraid you're going to have to talk to our lawyers," he told the two detectives. "I am very sorry."

He almost sounded sincere, but that didn't help the situation any. "Sorry is not enough to keep the next young woman from dying," Campbell informed the manager.

Perkins appeared shocked. "Wait, there have been others?"

"Thirty in all—that we know of," Campbell deliberately qualified.

"And it's one of the men she met on my dating site?" the manager questioned, vacillating between being appalled and defensive.

"That's what we're trying to ascertain," Campbell answered.

The short, personable website manager looked like a man torn between two paths, neither one of them satisfactory.

"Well," Perkins finally said, making up his mind,

"until you have proof positive that one of these people was responsible, I'm afraid I can't help you."

"And we can't get our hands on 'proof positive' until you release the information we need to trace this path to its logical conclusion," Liberty insisted.

Perkins seemed distressed but, in the end, was forced to stick to his guns. "I'm afraid I can't help you."

"Can't or won't?" Liberty asked.

The manager's eyes met hers. "Can't," Perkins repeated.

"We'll be back," Campbell promised the website manager.

Liberty did not look as if she was ready to retreat just yet. "Campbell," she protested.

But he put his arm around her shoulders and directed her toward the door. "We don't have a leg to stand on," he reminded Liberty, then told her, "We'll be back when we do."

She had no recourse but to leave with Campbell. "So we're just going to retreat?" she questioned, clearly not happy about the way this was going.

"For now, yes. I'm part of the police department. It's my job to enforce the law, Arizona, not break it whenever the mood hits me."

The expression on her face did not absolve him. "What about your job to get justice for Cynthia and all the other victims who suffered at the hands of this sick, sadistic killer?"

"Number one, getting bogged down in red tape

isn't going to do Cynthia—or the others—any good. And, number two, our time can be better spent finding our way around all this."

He tried again. "Look, Arizona, I want you to get something straight. I am on your side. I am on the victims' side. Wasting time arguing and getting nowhere with a narcissistic website manager is not going to accomplish anything. Now let's see if we can find someone at the restaurant who can be more accommodating than this jerk was. With luck, we'll get access to the surveillance tapes of the area with Cynthia's last date with 'Mr. Possible Right,'" Campbell said.

Liberty took a deep breath. She had no choice but to go along with Campbell's assessment. "Are you always this annoyingly calm and levelheaded?" she asked grudgingly.

"Always," he replied with a grin. "My dad thought it was my best feature."

She looked at him pointedly. "Well, your father was wrong."

"I'll let him know the next time I see him. Although I wouldn't hold my breath if I were you," he said, driving his vehicle to the Blue Hawaiian, which was due south.

"Oh, and why's that?" she asked, expecting to hear some sort of a flip answer from the detective.

He answered her without any fanfare. "My dad died five years ago."

His answer rendered her temporarily speechless. The casual way he just glossed over his father's death took her totally by surprise. Liberty glanced at the detective to see if he was just pulling her leg.

But one look at Campbell's profile told her he wasn't. He was serious.

"I'm very sorry for your loss," she told him. The words always struck her as being horribly empty, but there was nothing else she could say that even began to get the message across, so she fell back on the familiar, if inadequate, saying.

"Yeah," Campbell responded. "Me, too. But if there is a heaven, then he's finally with Mom," he told Liberty, "which was the only place he ever wanted to be."

"Well, then I suppose that's comforting," she said, although Campbell wasn't all that sure she meant it.

All he could do was let her know how he felt about the situation. "Yes," Campbell answered. "It really is. It's actually the mental image I like to hang on to, Arizona." He came to a stop at a red light and glanced in Liberty's direction. "Let's see if we can find someone at the restaurant who's more helpful than the manager of that dating site."

"Amen to that," Liberty murmured.

The light turned green, and he took off.

Liberty sat back and tried to think positive thoughts, even if it wasn't in her nature.

Chapter Seven

The Blue Hawaiian restaurant's parking lot was fairly packed, especially given that it wasn't a Friday or Saturday night, Liberty thought as she scanned the general area.

"Is it always like this?" she asked Campbell.

He shrugged in response. "To be truthful, I wouldn't know. But I've heard that this is a pretty popular place to take a date. Especially, if you're trying to impress her."

"You don't bring your dates here?" Liberty asked, trying to sound as if she was just making conversation and not trying to pry into his personal life. "It looks like a pretty nice place."

"I'm sure that it is, but I'm more of a spur-of-the-moment kind of guy," he confessed. "Going to a place like this takes making reservations ahead of time. In my line of work, long-term plans have a way of not working out for one reason or another." Campbell shrugged philosophically. "Maybe I'll give this place a try some day."

Because the lot turned out to be so crowded,

Campbell was forced to park in one of the spaces reserved for trucks making deliveries. He made sure
that he left the vehicle's flashing lights on the roof.

Liberty frowned just a little. "That should enhance
the mood," she commented as they walked away from
the police car and went into the restaurant.

Campbell thought of the vehicle and where it was
positioned. "I just put the lights on the roof to let whoever's in charge tonight know that this vehicle is here
on official police business. Otherwise, we might come
out and find that it's been towed away."

That didn't strike her as likely. "Did that ever happen to you?" she asked as she walked in front of him
toward the reservation desk.

"Not to me personally, but it did happen to my sister, Jacqui." The grin on his face widened as he recalled the incident. "I had no idea that she knew such
colorful language."

Liberty laughed. She had never had her vehicle
towed away, but she could certainly identify with
that feeling of frustration the detective's sister must
have experienced.

It took Liberty a moment for her eyes to adjust to
the subdued lighting throughout the restaurant.

"Do they keep the lights low like this to promote
romance or to make sure that the customer doesn't
see that the meal's been undercooked—or burned?"
the visiting detective guessed.

"Probably a little of both," Campbell speculated.
He made his way up to the desk.

An incredibly dapper and trim reservation manager glanced up and saw them approaching. It looked as if the smile he offered pained him to form. His small, brown eyes swept over them rather critically. "Do you have a reservation?" he asked coolly.

Campbell had dealt with people like this before, men impressed with what they took to be their own self-importance.

"I'm afraid not, Mr. Davis," Campbell said, reading the man's name tag as he placed his badge and police ID face-up on the desk and waited for that to register with the man.

"Oh, how can I help you, Officer… Cavanaugh, is it?" the manager asked, raising his eyes to the detective's face.

"That's *Detective* Cavanaugh," Campbell corrected with no emotion. "And you can direct us to where you keep your surveillance tapes. But first, were you here three days ago after 6:00 p.m.?" he asked the pompous little man.

It seemed to Liberty that Davis appeared to withdraw into himself, as if bracing, even though he didn't appear to know for what.

"I was," Davis finally replied crisply. His eyes darted back and forth between the duo at his desk. He was obviously waiting for more.

Campbell held up Cynthia's picture for him. "Does this woman look familiar to you?" he asked.

The manager squinted as he looked at image. "Possibly," he answered vaguely. "I see a lot of people here. The Hawaiian is a very popular restaurant," he proudly informed the couple before him. And then his rather high forehead suddenly wrinkled. "Why are you looking for her? Did she do something?"

"Yes," Liberty answered, losing her patience with Davis, whom she felt was playing games with them. "She died."

Her statement horrified the overly fastidious little man at the reservation desk. His small dark eyes seemed to grow to almost twice their size.

"How?" Even as he asked, the answer seemed to hit him. "Oh, wait, is she that woman they had on the news?"

Unaware of what Davis might have been exposed to, Campbell answered, "Most likely."

Davis looked as if his mouth had suddenly gone completely dry.

"And you think the killer brought her here before he—?" Davis couldn't get himself to finish the question. The mere suggestion of what he was thinking seemed to stick in his throat.

"We don't know," Campbell answered. "That's why we'd like to view your surveillance tapes from that night. I'm assuming that you have several cameras going at all times, monitoring your restaurant both inside and out."

The reservation manager's face paled by several shades. For just a moment, he looked as if his knees would buckle.

Mopping his brow, he said, "Yes, yes, we do. You

actually thought this monster brought her here first before he…?" Davis stopped, unable to complete the question.

"Like Detective Cavanaugh said, we don't know what to think yet," Liberty told the reservation manager. "We're investigating all the possibilities. That's why we'd like to be able to see your surveillance tapes."

The manager looked at Liberty as if he hadn't even realized that she was asking him a question until just this very moment.

He shook his head as if to clear it. "I'm sorry," he said, realizing that she wasn't there with the detective as his companion but in some official capacity. "And you are?"

Getting really annoyed with you, fella, Liberty thought.

As if reading her mind, Campbell stepped in, ready to divert any possible problem before it could form. "This is Detective Lawrence," he said by way of an introduction. "She's a consultant from Arizona here to help us out with this case. There have been several women killed there by this man."

Davis turned even paler than he already had. It didn't take much for him to put two and two together. "You mean we're dealing with a…a serial killer?" The man was clearly traumatized.

"That appears to be the case," Campbell replied. "But we really don't know that for a fact yet. We can tell you more once we view the tapes," he repeated, pinning Davis with a probing look. He wanted to move this along as quickly as he could. "So, if you would take us to where you house your surveillance monitors, we'll be out of your way."

"But I can't leave you with them," Davis protested. By the expression on his face, doing so would clearly be a violation of protocol, as far as he was concerned.

"Then stay in the room with us. Do whatever you have to do as long as we get to review the tapes," Campbell said, trying to curb his impatience.

In the end, the reservation manager called over one of his assistants. He had the young woman take the two detectives over to where the security tape equipment was housed.

The assistant, Polly Howard, appeared to be new at her job—but exceptionally eager to help. "Are you two *really* detectives with the police department?" she asked.

"Yes, we're really with the police department," Campbell replied.

"Mr. Davis looks really spooked," she confided, lowering her voice. "Did he do something? I mean, other than point out how everyone who works for him is just always falling short of his standards?" Polly asked in an even lower voice.

Campbell had no intentions of being sucked into any sort of a discussion regarding the reservation manager. "How about you show us where those surveillance tapes are? And then we can take it from there."

Instead of becoming embarrassed and backing away from the subject, the young woman happily continued talking and speculating.

Polly led them into a small room. There appeared to be only one working monitor set up within the room to enable viewing the surveillance tapes.

Pointing to the monitor, Polly hovered on the sidelines. She didn't look as if she wanted to leave.

"Is there anything else I can do?" she asked.

The restaurant grew noisier and the increased noise was beginning to invade their space.

"You can shut the door on your way out," Liberty told her in all seriousness.

The assistant looked to Campbell for instructions, turning her doe-like eyes in his direction. "Is that what you want, Detective?" she asked Campbell almost breathlessly.

"Yes," he confirmed. "We can take it from here," Campbell assured her.

Disappointed, even Polly's hair appeared to fall slightly. "I'll be right outside if you need me," she said.

"Good to know," he acknowledged.

Davis's assistant was already forgotten by the time Campbell started to insert the tape labeled two days ago.

Liberty looked at him. "You know how to work these things?" she asked, eyeing Campbell skeptically.

He gestured at the surveillance monitor. "How hard can it be?"

"So, no," Liberty concluded. Moving closer to the space where Campbell was standing, she put out her hand and said, "Give it to me."

It was his turn to doubt her. "*You* know how to work this equipment?" he asked, waiting for her to reply to his question.

She took exception to his tone. "I'm from Calhoun, not Sleepy Hollow. You'd be surprised at the kind of technology we have in that little town," she assured him. "Now let me work."

Campbell inclined his head and then saluted. "Yes, ma'am."

"And hold the sarcasm," she said.

He grinned at her. "Consider it held."

Liberty decided she would be better off if she simply ignored the tall, handsome detective and just focused on the video tapes.

Since there was only one monitor for viewing, it proved to be rather slow going. They wound up spelling each other to make sure they wouldn't miss anything and also to keep their eyes from crossing, thanks to too much close viewing.

But finally they were finished.

"I think I might just wind up giving up watching TV for a while," Liberty told Campbell, shutting her eyes and rubbing the bridge of her nose. "The worst part of it is, after all that, we only got a partial license plate number *and* it looks like her date wound up leaving the restaurant without her." She frowned. "What that means is anyone's guess."

"That doesn't mean that they didn't get together later on the next day," he pointed out.

"The day she died," Liberty emphasized.

Campbell's eyes meet hers. "Exactly."

Liberty dragged her hand through her hair. "So how do we find him? We only have that partial license plate and a less than stellar video of his face."

Campbell thought over what she had just said. "That might be enough."

She didn't see how, but she was willing to be convinced. "Keep talking," Liberty said, eager to grab at anything.

"I have this cousin who works in the CSI lab," Campbell told her. "She works miracles with and without the computer."

"Miracles, huh?" Liberty asked. "What kind of miracles?"

He merely smiled at the visiting detective. "You'll see. First thing we need to do is make a copy of this tape. And then I'll take this to Valri tomorrow."

"Tomorrow?" Liberty repeated, clearly disappointed. She was shifting from foot to foot. "Why not today?"

He was surprised that she had to ask. "Because it is almost tomorrow and, as good as Valri is, sometimes she needs to get at least a few minutes of sleep before she's ready to go again. Now let's see if we can find that assistant so we can tell her that we're through here for now, but that we're going to need a copy of this portion of the tape."

"If it's that late, maybe Polly already went home?" Liberty told him.

As it turned out, Polly hadn't gone anywhere. The moment Campbell opened the door, the faithful little assistant came all but bounding into the room.

"Can I help you?" she asked eagerly, her question directed to Campbell.

"Yes," Campbell said, taking the surveillance tape from Liberty and handing it to the young woman. "We need a copy of this tape."

"Just one copy?" Polly asked. She almost sounded disappointed.

"Just the one," Campbell confirmed. "We'd really appreciate it," he added for good measure.

"Is the killer on this?" the assistant asked, her voice dropping even lower, as if the killer might overhear her.

"That's where the investigating part comes in," Campbell told her with a wink.

Polly's eyes were all but shining with anticipation. "Sure, sure, I get it. But if you find out, will you tell me?"

"If we find out, *you'll* find out," Liberty assured the young woman.

The assistant all but skipped out of the room to make the requested copy.

"Why did you tell her that?" Campbell asked. They both knew they couldn't release that kind of information to the public.

"To get her moving," Liberty told him. "She looked as if she thought she was suddenly part of a murder mystery. There's no harm in fueling her imagination. Who knows, maybe in a strange way, it'll keep her safe."

"The killer preys on nurses, remember?" That meant that this little assistant was safe, Campbell thought.

"I know, but there might be some other killer out there who doesn't make that distinction," Liberty pointed out. "Doesn't hurt to keep a young innocent like that on her toes," she told Campbell.

"You're right," he agreed. "It doesn't."

The assistant returned within ten minutes. She was holding up a fresh copy of the surveillance tape she had just made.

"Here you go," Polly announced. "That tape you requested." She handed it to Campbell. "Now, you'll remember to keep your promise, won't you?"

Liberty could see that he was drawing a blank. "About telling her the minute we find out if the man on the tape is our killer," she said, refreshing Campbell's memory. "Of course Detective Cavanaugh will let you know. If it wasn't for you, he wouldn't have a tape to help him make that comparison, would you, Detective Cavanaugh?"

"I definitely wouldn't," he said, already on his way

to the door. "Thanks for all your help and take care of yourself."

Polly sent them—mainly Campbell—on their way with a dreamy sigh.

Chapter Eight

Liberty knew what Campbell was up to and she was not about to allow him to do it.

"It's after eleven, Cavanaugh," she pointed out as they drove away from the restaurant.

"Well, I guess that answers my question if you can tell time or not, Arizona," he quipped.

She gave him an icy stare. "Very funny. You know what I'm getting at."

"Probably," Campbell replied. "But just for fun, enlighten me."

She found herself fighting the urge to strangle the man. "I am not about to allow you to wake up one of your sisters—or one of your cousins—so that I can have a place to crash. Just take me back to the police station so I can get my car and then point me toward the nearest hotel or motel. I'll take care of the rest from there."

He just shook his head. "Sorry, but I can't have you wandering around Aurora at this time of night."

"But I'm a police detective," she noted, flabbergasted at the objection he had just raised.

Campbell added an addendum. "Yes, but in a strange city."

She was just too tired to argue coherently with him. "All right, you must have beds in the squad room where your detectives can crash when they're working through the night." She sighed, leaning back against her seat. "Take me there."

"I have an alternative," Campbell said.

Alerted, she shot him another annoyed look. "I'm not sure I want to hear it."

He ignored her protest. "I'll take you back to my place," Campbell offered. "I've got a spare bedroom. You can crash there."

"No," she said flatly, wondering what it took to get through to this pigheaded, stubborn man.

"You have nothing to worry about," he assured her. "I'll even take a pledge of celibacy if that makes you feel better."

She doubted if the man knew the meaning of the word *celibacy*. He just didn't look like the type. However, she was willing to be entertained.

"That would almost be worth it," Liberty said with a laugh.

Almost, she thought, *but not quite.*

Campbell glanced in her direction. "Why?" he asked. "Would you try to entice me?"

The grin he flashed her managed to get under her skin.

"I make it a point never to play with fire," she informed him coolly.

"You're telling me that you're not even a little bit intrigued?" Campbell asked. His eyes were back on the road, but she could have sworn she felt them studying her.

"Not so much as an iota," she replied.

If this were another time and another place, maybe she might have been a little intrigued, she conceded silently. But right now she was focused on doing whatever it took to solve this case and absolutely *nothing* else mattered.

"Okay," he told her. "This is what's going to happen. I will bring you to the police station so you can collect your car. But then, in the interest of getting an early start, I'd appreciate it if you just follow me to my place." Before she could protest, he quickly added, "I promise you'll be safer than if you were staying in a convent." To add weight to his statement, he even crossed his heart.

Did he really think she was that naive? "I'm not sure about that."

"Oh?"

"I looked you up on social media," she told the detective. "According to that, you have quite a reputation."

"Not that I'm not flattered that you took the time to do that," Campbell told her, "but you're also bright enough to know that things are greatly exaggerated on social media."

"Maybe," she allowed, "but I live by the saying that I would rather be safe than sorry. And right now, the most important thing in the world to me—the *only* thing—is finding this serial killer and getting him off the street."

Campbell could definitely understand that. Yet he could also sense that there was more to it than that. "And if we find him, will you tell me why you are so obsessed with getting *this* man?"

She stared at his profile, astonished. "Why would you even ask that? Catching the bad guy and making him pay for all those killings he committed doesn't seem like enough to you?"

"Oh, it definitely would be," he answered. "Nevertheless, I get the sense there's something more going on here, and I'm the type who can't sleep well until I have all the answers."

She laughed dryly in response to his words. "Something tells me, Detective Cavanaugh, that you don't sleep much."

He shrugged just as he pulled into the station parking area. "I get enough."

There were a minimum number of vehicles parked in the lot. Campbell pulled his car up beside hers, then engaged the hand brake and turned off the engine.

"So, what'll it be?" he asked, turning to face Liberty. "Did I manage to talk you into following me to my apartment?" Even in the sparse lighting, he could see the reluctant look on the visiting detective's face. "There is one more alternative."

"Another alternative," she repeated, amused despite herself. "Okay, I'm listening."

"I could take you over to my uncle Andrew and his wife Rose's house. They're the unofficial patriarchs of the family. You'd have no reason to complain about being put up at their house."

"It's late. They're probably asleep. I'm not about to wake up older people," she said, enumerating just some of her reasons.

Campbell laughed. "I won't tell them you said that. Look, they're patriarchs of what amounts to a police dynasty. That means that they wake up for emergencies. It's a given. And calling them 'older' will *not* endear you to them no matter how understanding they are."

"I am still not going to be responsible for disturbing them," she informed him in a tone that said she was not about to change her mind.

Campbell shook his head as he blew out a breath. "You really are a hard person to negotiate with, Arizona."

"I wasn't aware that we were 'negotiating,'" she retorted.

"*That* might be part of the problem," Campbell told her. "All right," he said, his negotiations, not to mention his patience, reaching their final stretch. "What's it going to be? I've given you a choice of picking one of my sisters, one of my cousins, or the family patriarch—or me."

"You forgot about going to a hotel," Liberty reminded him.

"No, I didn't forget. That was never a viable option as far as I was concerned. Now pick," he urged.

Liberty frowned. "You realize that this whole thing is rigged, right?"

He looked at her innocently. "I have no idea what you're talking about, Arizona."

"Uh-huh," she answered, rolling her eyes. This was getting her nowhere and she had a feeling the detective wasn't about to give up until she agreed to one of his options. Tired of going around in circles, she said, "All right, we'll go to your place."

"Glad to hear that you've come around," Campbell told her.

Come around, my foot, she thought. But she was in no mood to continue the back-and-forth on the subject. Frowning at him, she said, "You should be aware of the fact that I sleep with my gun."

He gave no indication of being surprised or caught off guard. "Duly noted. I hope the two of you are very happy together. Now are you ready to go?"

She supposed she had no choice. And, at bottom, she did believe that she would be safe. Ultimately, she believed that the detective wouldn't try anything. She'd take him at his word that he was honestly just taking her to his apartment so that she could get some rest.

But if for some reason she had miscalculated, Cavanaugh would be the one to pay the price, she assured herself.

"All right," Liberty said out loud as she got out

of his vehicle and got into hers. "Lead the way to your place."

He was sorely tempted to say something snappy, but refrained. Instead he merely said, "It's close by. You won't regret this."

"I already do," she answered. She waved at his car. "Lead the way to your apartment before I decide to go to sleep right here."

"Can't have that," Campbell told her. "My place is three miles from here. Can you make it?" he asked, thinking how tired she'd just said she was feeling.

Her smile was slightly lopsided. "Can I make it? In my sleep."

"That's what I'm afraid of," he joked. "I'm still going to go slow."

"Why?" she asked suspiciously. Wasn't the whole point to get there quickly?

"So I can keep an eye on you in my rearview mirror," he told her.

Liberty's mind did a double-take. "I don't know whether to be touched by this display of thoughtfulness on your part, or insulted because you think I'm incapable of going from point A to point B."

"Go with touched," he counseled with a grin. "It's simpler that way. Now, if there's nothing else, let's get a move on."

"Well, now that you've mentioned it..." Liberty began, ready to rethink the whole idea of crashing at his apartment.

"Good, let's go," he declared, pretending he hadn't

heard her attempt to extend the argument. Starting his car, he glanced up into his rearview mirror.

Campbell mentally crossed his fingers as he pulled out of his spot. He released a sigh of relief when he saw her start up her own vehicle.

Liberty followed him from the parking lot and into the street.

So far, so good, he thought.

Even so, Campbell kept checking for Liberty's car in his rearview mirror the entire short distance from the police station to his garden apartment: Sunflower Creek Apartments.

He pulled into his carport and got out in time to indicate to Liberty that she should find a spot in guest parking. Because of the hour, there were only a few spots left.

Campbell walked over to the area and waited until she parked her car.

"I'm flattered," she said as she exited her vehicle and popped open her trunk. She took out the overnight bag she had packed. He started to take it from her but Liberty held on to the straps. "I can carry it," she informed him. "You're already going the whole nine yards, escorting me to your apartment and to a spot in guest parking. Or do you want to carry my bag because you're thinking I'm going to bolt at the last minute?"

"I wasn't thinking about you bolting. But it is dark," he pointed out. "You might not find your way to the right apartment. I've seen residents go stumbling around at night, looking for their own door. Of course, they'd had a few too many at the time," he added with what Liberty could only view as a wicked grin.

"When would I have had the time to imbibe?" she couldn't help asking.

"Good point," he agreed. "But it is dark and you don't know your way. Why don't you just say 'thanks' and let it go at that?"

By now they had reached the bottom of the stairway that led up to his second-floor apartment. Gritting her teeth, Liberty forced out the words. "Thank you."

His hand on the railing, Campbell pretended to grasp it to steady himself while putting his other hand to his chest. "I'm overwhelmed," he declared.

She turned to look at him and issue one final warning.

"If you're on the level, thank you. But if you have any ideas…" Her voice trailed off, leaving the warning unspoken.

"I'm a police detective. I *always* have ideas," Campbell told her. "But I promise not any of them pertain to you."

Which, at this point, Campbell thought, *is a lie.* Since she'd walked into his squad room, several ideas had sprung up in his mind and formed around her.

But he was smart enough to know that breathing even one word of that to this extremely sexy Arizona detective would spell the end of their working relationship, not to mention any other potential relationship that even had a prayer of happening anywhere in the near or even foreseeable future.

His two-bedroom apartment was not only located on the second floor, it also overlooked a rather large communal pool.

All in all, the first word that came to Liberty's mind was *peaceful*.

When he unlocked his apartment door for her, it was also, considering the fact that a bachelor lived there, incredibly neat, Liberty thought.

"Was the maid just here?" she asked, looking around at the immediate area before she set down the small, overnight bag she had brought in.

Campbell looked at her curiously. "What maid?" he asked.

"Yours, I'm assuming," she answered.

He still wasn't clear on what she was referring to. "Why would you think I have a maid?"

"Well, because—" Liberty gestured around the living room. When he still didn't say anything, she filled in the blanks for him. "It's so neat. You either have a maid or you—" It suddenly hit her. "Your girlfriend did this." He hadn't said anything about having a live-in girlfriend, but what other explanation could there be? There weren't even any dishes in the sink.

"Nope, no girlfriend," he said. "I would have mentioned one before inviting you over," Campbell assured her.

She was at a loss as she looked around again. "Then how—"

"There is another explanation," Campbell told her.

"And that is?" she asked, curious.

"I was raised by a mother who insisted that we all carry our own weight. We took turns doing the chores, which included, among other things, cleaning up after ourselves as well as anyone else in the family who needed overseeing at the time. To answer your question once and for all, I am not involved with anyone at the moment, so there won't be anyone turning up either in the apartment or on my doorstep at any point. Now, if you're ready to move on to something more immediate, let me show you to your room so that you can sack out and get some rest—unless there's something else?" he asked, looking at her.

Liberty had to admit that he had answered everything, and she was out of things to ask. "No, you've answered everything sufficiently."

"Good. Your room is this way." Before she could reach for it, he picked up her overnight bag. "And I have no intention of wrestling you for this overnight case," he informed her as he walked toward the back of the apartment without looking in her direction. "So just deal with it."

For once, she didn't offer a protest.

Campbell smiled to himself as he led the way to the spare bedroom.

One battle down, a thousand to go.

Chapter Nine

Liberty had to admit that she was more than a little impressed. The double bed in the spare bedroom not only had clean sheets, but when she pulled back the covers, they looked to be crisp as well.

"There are fresh towels in there," Campbell pointed out, indicating the small adjacent bathroom. "You have your own bathroom so you don't have to worry about sharing one. And if you need anything else," he went on," just let me know. I'm right down the hall." He nodded toward his own bedroom. "Otherwise, I'll see you in the morning, Arizona."

And with that, since she hadn't said anything, he was gone.

Despite the fact that Campbell had brought in her overnight case and left it on the floor beside the bed, she decided to sleep in her clothes—just in case. It was a habit she'd developed during all those "first nights" she had spent in so many different bedrooms. A habit born out of the fact that if anything went wrong—the way it had in one of the foster homes she had gone to—she was ready to run if she had to.

Because of that incident—her foster parents' teen-
aged son who'd felt anyone in his house was there
for his own personal pleasure—it always took her a
while to trust someone.

By the time Florence had taken her in and become
her foster mother, trusting someone had been a luxury
Liberty felt she couldn't afford. Consequently, it had
taken her a long time to be won over. But Florence
had never given up. The nurse had kept at her until
her walls finally came down.

Stretching out on the bed, Liberty sighed. The bed
turned out to be exceedingly comfortable, but she
still couldn't relax.

You would think that after all the different beds
she had slept in, falling asleep wouldn't be a problem.
She should have the ability to fall asleep at the drop
of a hat, especially in one that was this comfortable.

But she couldn't.

Liberty was just too tense. And the good-looking
detective had next to nothing to do with it. A very
large part of her was afraid that this investigation was
going to turn out to be just another wild-goose chase
that would lead her nowhere.

"Knock it off, Lib," she lectured herself. "What did
Florence always say? Negative thoughts lead to negative energy and that'll get you absolutely nowhere.
You're going to find the dirtbag who killed all those
women even if it takes you forever."

Clinging to that thought as if it were the proverbial
life preserver, Liberty finally managed to fall asleep.

WHEN LIBERTY VENTURED out of the guest bedroom nearly seven hours later, she found that Campbell was already up and in the kitchen, puttering around by the stove.

Cooking.

Something else she didn't think was typical of the male of the species. At least, not any male she was acquainted with.

The scent of rich, freshly brewed coffee caught her attention and drew her in.

Campbell looked up and over his shoulder just as she entered the kitchen. Walking away from the stove, he smiled a greeting at her. "Hi, did you sleep well?"

She didn't want to admit that she'd had trouble sleeping in a new bed, so she merely shrugged and said, "I slept."

"But not well," Campbell guessed, reading between the lines.

She supposed it wasn't that unusual a trait, so she admitted, "It always takes me time to adjust to a new bed."

Campbell took the information in stride. "I guess I'm lucky that way. I can fall asleep hanging from a hook in the closet."

Liberty laughed at the image that created in her head. "I'd like to see that sometime."

The homicide detective smiled at her. "I'll keep that in mind. Would you like some breakfast?" He indicated the frying pan on the stove.

She stared at Campbell. The question came automatically, even if she could see what was happening for herself. "You cook?"

"I cook." He would have thought that would have been self-evident because of his question. "Is that a yes then?"

"I like living dangerously," Liberty wisecracked. "So, yes."

He offered her a choice. "Scrambled? Poached? Sunny-side up?"

"Whatever is easiest," Liberty answered, then felt obligated to add, "And, for the record, I'm very impressed."

His eyes met hers. "Well then, let's hope I keep impressing you."

Liberty had no answer why those simple words would send such a warm shiver shimmying up and down her spine, but they did.

Big-time.

"Well, to make that happen," she told him, "all you have to do is help me track down this SOB."

Campbell grinned as he turned to the stove to finish making breakfast. "Don't ask for much, do you?"

"I didn't say it would be easy," she reminded the detective.

"No," he agreed as he placed a plate of scrambled eggs, toast and bacon right in front of her. "You did not. But it's a challenge I'd be more than happy to try to meet," he told her.

And, for once, she felt he was being serious. She had no reason to doubt him.

"VALRI, I'VE BEEN singing your praises to this visiting detective from Calhoun, Arizona," Campbell announced to his cousin as they walked into the computer lab a little more than an hour later.

Valri Cavanaugh Brody looked up from her computer. But rather than make eye contact with her cousin or the woman who had walked in with him, the much-touted wizard of the computer lab turned her eyes up to the ceiling.

"I don't remember hearing any predictions about snow today," she said.

Liberty looked quizzically at Campbell. Before he could say anything, Valri went on to say, "So why am I on the receiving end of such a snow job?"

"No snow job," Campbell denied. "Everyone knows you are a wizard when it comes to finding answers on the computer even if looks as if there just aren't any to be found."

Valri eyed him with a knowing expression. "Very flattering, Cam, but you still have to go to the end of the line. There are just so many hours in the day and just so much of me to go around."

"That's a shame," Campbell told her placatingly. He then went on to make the introductions as if Valri hadn't said anything. "Arizona, meet my cousin, Valri Cavanaugh Brody. Valri, this is—"

"Detective Liberty Lawrence," Liberty said, taking half a step forward and putting her hand out to the blonde sitting at the very impressive computer monitor. She wasn't about to have the woman thinking that her name was Arizona.

"She—now *we*," Campbell told his cousin, "are on the trail of a serial killer. His victims total thirty women, possibly more. Show her the list, Arizona."

Liberty obliged, taking the folded sheet out of the messenger bag hanging from her shoulder.

Valri took the paper and looked at it. "You're sure this is all because of one person?" she asked.

Liberty nodded. "Oh, I'm sure," she answered. "This is all over the course of four years." And then she went into some particulars. "He has a very unique signature. He only preys on nurses between the ages of twenty-five and fifty. He strangles them using piano wire."

Valri took in the information. "That does sound unique. Anything else?"

Liberty nodded. "Until recently, he had confined his 'spree' to Arizona, except for a couple of killings he did in between in Nevada and one in New Mexico. But now he's spread his 'net' to include Southern California. The last victim we have was trying to meet men via a dating service. Thanks to information from one of her friends, we have a partial license plate number and a partial image of the last man she met through the site.

"It just might be a coincidence, but right now, that guy's our only lead," Liberty told Valri.

"We're planning on interviewing the family members of the last few victims, who were from California," Campbell added, "but we thought that anything you could add to our very sparse collection of information would be gratefully appreciated."

Valri glanced at her cousin. "I take it you're assuming that you're no longer at the end of the line?"

He couldn't read her expression, so Campbell made his plea. "Valri, the guy's a serial killer and it's only a matter of time before he's going to get itchy and kill again. If the past is any indication, it will be soon."

Valri sighed and looked toward the door leading into the office. "I knew I should have asked Uncle Brian to put a lock on my door. A lock," she added, looking at Campbell and feeling as if this argument had already been lost, "that you wouldn't be able to pick."

He knew better than to celebrate a victory. "Why, Valri, you wound me."

"Don't tempt me," his cousin warned, already trying to figure out how to squeeze this in with the rest of her mountain of work.

Rather than Campbell saying something flip in response, it was Liberty who spoke up.

"Thank you," she said to Valri. "I know this isn't your usual protocol, but it does mean a great deal to me."

Valri looked at the other woman, picking up something in her tone. "You make it sound personal."

Liberty was about to shrug off Valri's assumption but then wrestled with her better judgment. Maybe if she told her, Valri wouldn't be so undecided about finding the time to help.

"It is," Liberty admitted quietly. "He killed my foster mother."

Both Valri and Campbell were momentarily stunned.

Valri recovered first. "I am very sorry for your loss, Liberty. I realize that those words don't even begin to cover it, but at least it does give me a reason to bump the case up to the head of the line—at least for a little while," she qualified.

The wattage of the smile Campbell flashed at his cousin was nearly blinding.

"Thanks, Val. You're the best," he declared. "And you really should have an assistant helping you."

"I do," she told him. That was the odd thing about this. The more assistants she had, the bigger the workload became. "I have three of them," she told Campbell. "However, that doesn't begin to put a dent in the workload." She looked over at her desk and shook her head. The piles were overflowing.

"You know, for one of the safest cities in the country, you wouldn't think there would be this many caseloads, but there are… Okay, go," Valri ordered, waving them away. "I have work to do—and so do you. Keep me abreast of anything you find out," she instructed her cousin.

"Count on it," Campbell promised.

He headed for the door. Opening it, he waited for Liberty. The latter walked through the doorway without looking in his direction.

They walked in silence to the elevator. When it arrived, they got into the empty car and Campbell pressed for the first floor. When the doors closed, he finally broke the silence.

"So that's why."

Liberty looked at him as if she had forgotten he was with her. "Excuse me?"

"I said so that's why this case is so important to you," Campbell said, extrapolating on his initial reaction.

She shouldn't have said anything, Liberty upbraided herself. But she had really wanted Valri to look into the case for them—now and not when it came up in the queue. The more help she got with this, Liberty thought, the better.

"Every case is important," she informed Campbell coolly.

He wasn't about to argue with that, but he knew what she was trying to do. She was trying to cover up the truth. "Don't give me platitudes, Arizona. Now, are you referring to that woman you mentioned earlier? Florence?" he specified.

"That doesn't matter," Liberty told him, attempting to try to shrug it off.

"Yes, it does," he told her firmly. "It matters to you and it matters to this case. Now, are you going to tell me if I'm right, or am I going to have to look up every one of those women in the list and pull up all the details from the various news stories until I find out if Florence was the person responsible for you taking up this quest?"

The elevator door opened and they both got out. Liberty looked at the detective. She could tell that Campbell wasn't about to let up until she gave him the answer he was looking for.

Resigned, Liberty said, "I'd rather not go into it on the first floor of the police station."

"Fair enough." As long as she answered his question, he wasn't choosey about where she did it. "Pick the place."

She thought for a second. "You have a local diner around here?"

"No, but we have coffee shops," he told her. "I'll take you to the closest one."

She nodded. Going to a coffee shop would buy her some time to collect herself, Liberty thought. She didn't want to just blurt out details at random. Florence had been a private person and she knew the woman wouldn't appreciate having her life dissected by strangers, although she also knew that if this case had a prayer of getting solved, anonymity was going to have to be surrendered, at least in part.

Liberty discovered that she didn't have as much time as she thought. The coffee shop Campbell took her to turned out to be located a block and a half away from the police station.

THE COFFEE SHOP wasn't crowded, but it wasn't exactly empty, either. But then, given its location, it never really was.

"What'll you have?" Campbell asked Liberty as he parked in the lot in front of the shop.

"Doesn't matter," she answered. "Just something to hold on to when I talk."

He thought that was an odd way to put it. "This isn't an interrogation," he told her. "Just one partner filling in another."

"We're partners now?" she questioned. Did he think she was stupid? She wasn't about to be put at ease so quickly.

Or fooled, either.

"Yeah, we're partners," Campbell answered.

"And when did this happen?" she asked. "I was just the 'visiting detective from Arizona' a little while ago."

"Sometime during our visit to Valri." When she'd had told his cousin why the case was so important to her, Campbell had found himself feeling her pain. "The point is we're partners and we'll continue to be partners until we either put this to bed, or you get sick of being out here and take off for your home ground."

Liberty looked at him. "Got an answer for everything, don't you?" she asked.

Campbell detected a bit of admiration beneath the sarcasm in her voice.

"I give it my best shot," he told her. "And I've got an entire family in law enforcement to draw on, so that makes me more or less prepared for anything. What'll you have, Arizona?" he asked, nodding toward the coffee counter.

"Coffee."

"There're a lot of different kinds to choose from," he said, waving his hand at the menu board.

"Just coffee," Liberty repeated.

"Okay, coffee it is," Campbell obliged. Turning to the person behind the counter, he ordered, "Two coffees, please."

The squeaky-clean server smiled obligingly. "Very good, sir. And the name, please?" he asked, taking out a magic marker.

"Cavanaugh," Campbell answered.

The server sighed. "Yeah, like that's unique," he murmured under his breath, writing the last name on each of the two containers.

"I take it your whole family comes here?" Liberty asked.

"Other than Murphy's, this is their favorite watering hole," Campbell said, stepping to the side to wait for the coffees.

"Murphy's?" she asked, unfamiliar with the name. "What's that?"

"It's a cop bar owned and run by a retired cop. We can go there sometime," he offered.

At this point, she wasn't ready to commit to anything, "We'll see," she answered vaguely and then added, "If we wind up having something to celebrate."

Chapter Ten

Instead of taking the two containers from the clerk behind the counter and going outside, Campbell brought the containers over to a small table for two on the side of the coffee shop. Indicating that Liberty take a seat, he did the same.

After a moment, Liberty lowered herself into the chair.

"Take your time," Campbell counseled. "Talk whenever you feel you're up to it." Mentally, he was prepared to wait her out.

Liberty frowned slightly, staring into the coffee container. The overhead light shimmered on the dark surface.

Ever so slowly, she began to open up.

"Her name was Florence," she told him, then added simply, "And she's the reason I'm not in prison."

Whatever Campbell was expecting to hear, it certainly wasn't that. He wanted to say something but wasn't about to interrupt her, or she might stop talking again.

"That was the general consensus of what my future held," Liberty said, "given the path I was on. But Florence kept insisting I was better than that. She told me that she had faith in me." A fond expression played on her face. "I fought her all the way. But, ultimately, because of her, I graduated high school then went on to college. After that, I went on to the police academy.

"Florence never got married or had any kids, so I guess I was her whole family and she was mine," Liberty said, talking to a spot on the wall right above Campbell's head. It seemed easier that way for her. She let out a long breath. "Florence was a force to be reckoned with and so full of life, I just couldn't believe she would ever die. Until she did," she added quietly.

"What happened?" Campbell coaxed when she stopped talking.

The memory rose in her mind's eye like a terrible specter. "I was working at the Calhoun police station at the time, when my sergeant took me aside and said they had found Florence's body behind a dumpster in an alley. She was still in her nurse's uniform." Liberty's voice broke.

His heart went out to her. Campbell put a comforting hand over hers. She was clearly suffering. "You don't have to say any more."

But now that she had started, Liberty was determined to face her demons and get this all out. "She had been strangled with a piano wire. It didn't make any sense to me at the time. There didn't seem to be a connection because she neither taught nor played piano. And I know she wasn't putting herself out on any dating sites."

"Maybe she was just looking for companionship," Campbell suggested.

Liberty shook her head. "She was a big believer in 'if it was meant to be, it would happen.' The only conclusion I could come to was that her killer had to either be a patient at the hospital, or maybe a former patient."

"I take it you stayed close," Campbell surmised.

"Yes," she answered emphatically.

"Did she ever mention anyone she had a problem with, or that she was afraid of?" Campbell asked her.

Liberty shook her head. He wasn't asking her anything she hadn't asked herself a hundred times before. "The only thing I can think of is displacement."

"Displacement?" Campbell questioned, not sure what she meant.

Liberty nodded. "The way I see it is that the killer is obviously trying to kill someone from his past. You had to know Florence. She was like a stern mother figure. Always trying to help, but always keeping a steady hand over things." Her smile faded as she released a shaky breath. "At the time, I was too broken up to think straight—and I had no idea that the guy was a serial killer. I thought Florence being killed was an isolated incident that just didn't make any sense to me."

"But now we have more pieces to work with,"

Campbell reminded her. "Or we will once we start interviewing victims' families."

In an odd way, Liberty found comfort in his words, as well as in finally being able to talk about Florence.

She looked at the man sitting opposite her, waiting for him to say something that would make her regret sharing this with him. But he didn't.

Instead, Campbell told her, "We'll find this guy, Arizona. It might take a while, but sooner or later, he'd going to slip up and then he'll wind up paying for all the lives he ended so prematurely."

She was surprised that the detective was making this promise to her. "Isn't it supposed to be against your training to make promises like that? You know, ones you have no way of knowing if you can keep?"

He didn't look fazed about being taken to task. "Maybe that's what it says in some official hand-book," Campbell admitted, "but in my family, the only reason *any* of us go into law enforcement is so that we can protect and serve—and we honestly believe that. The day we stop feeling that way is the day we hand in our shields and go into something else." He looked at her coffee container. She had managed to drain it without realizing it. "Ready to go?" he asked, nodding at the empty container.

Liberty wasn't aware that she'd had any of her coffee, much less finished it. With a smile, she crumpled the container, ready to throw it out. "I guess I am," she replied.

As they rose from the table, he let her lead the way out. He had one more question to ask her.

"How are you coping with your loss now?" Campbell asked.

She was surprised that he would ask, and touched as well. "I'll let you know once we catch this bastard," she told him.

He completely understood.

THEY WENT BACK to Campbell's squad room at the police station. Commandeering a bulletin board and placing it in a conference room, he tacked up each and every one of the victims' names and left a space just beneath the names for any pertinent details they'd gather during the investigation. The slightest thing just might wind up affecting the individual case.

Peering at the board gave Liberty a hollow feeling. "That looks pretty daunting," she commented, staring at the empty spaces.

"It's just a board that hasn't been filled up yet," Campbell assured her. "It's only a matter of time until it takes shape."

She looked at him, beginning to feel that she had never met anyone quite like Campbell. "Is everyone in your family this optimistic?" she wanted to know.

"It's a prerequisite for being in the family," he deadpanned. "It's also in our DNA," he confided. "Okay, let's get Choi in here and we'll each take ten names to look up. Once we put the background information together, we'll question however many family members we find. Or in absence of that, any of the victims' friends we can find."

"Are you sure this is all okay with your boss?" Liberty was acutely grateful that this was being looked into, given the initial case had not belonged to this police department. "I wouldn't want to get you into any sort of trouble on my account."

This was certainly a far cry from the gung-ho detective who had come storming into his squad room yesterday, demanding cooperation, Campbell couldn't help thinking.

"Think of it as a joint project. Lieutenant Trask doesn't like serial killers any more than the rest of us do," Campbell told her. "But don't worry, this investigation has already been sanctioned by the powers that be."

"By God?" she asked whimsically as she continued labeling folders with the names of the victims.

"In a manner of speaking, I guess you could say yes," he answered. Then, to be perfectly clear, he clarified, "It's the Chief of D's."

"You ran this past the chief of detectives?" she asked, surprised.

When had he had the opportunity to do that? She had only brought the case to him yesterday and he hadn't appeared to be that taken by her request to begin with. The detective, she couldn't help thinking, was full of surprises.

"Well, not personally," Campbell admitted as he wrote down a few notes to himself as he prepared to get his partner to delve into the victims.

She didn't understand. How did the Chief of D's become involved? "Then—"

"Let's just say that nothing stays secret in the police department. News around here travels *very* fast." He summed it up for her because she was still looking at him quizzically. "The minute you walked in and stated the reason for your visit to Aurora, theories began to spring up."

"Wow," was all she could say. Liberty shook her head, stunned. "And I thought news traveled fast in a small town."

Tickled, Campbell laughed. "A small town's got *nothing* on us," he assured her. "We're close-knit and closemouthed when we have to be—and *only* when we have to be. The rest of the time…" His voice trailed off. "I'm going to go get Choi. You pick the names of the people you want to work up from that list you brought with you, and Choi and I will take the others," Campbell told Liberty as he left the room.

SHE HAD A good feeling about this. For the first time in a very long time, Liberty was actually feeling hopeful.

Although she didn't realize it, she was smiling when Campbell came back into the conference room. Choi was right behind him.

"You're smiling," Campbell noted. "You find something?"

"Yes," she answered. Before he could ask her what she had found, she told him. "Hope."

He understood immediately and was happy that she had found something positive to hang on to. He had always been a firm believer that everyone needed to have hope in their lives, especially at the lowest moments.

"Good," Campbell said, pulling out one of the chairs and dropping into it. "Let's work with that."

Although they divided the names among themselves, the task didn't get any easier. Finding the necessary information was a challenge, even in this age of endless access.

Some of the victims had very little information noted on any data bank. Those names were put to the side, earmarked for more extensive searches later. In the meantime, Campbell, Liberty and Choi compiled what information they could and noted it beneath the names of the victims on the bulletin board.

BY FIVE O'CLOCK, the list of people to contact for nineteen of the victims had in some cases grown extensively. The other eleven victims would necessitate more in-depth research.

"I don't know about you guys," Choi said, scrubbing his hands over his face and stifling a yawn, although not all too successfully. "But I'm going to call it a night." He glanced at the list he had printed out next to his computer. "All in all, I think we did some pretty good work." Campbell's partner glanced in Liberty's direction. "What about you?" he asked the visiting detective.

"Well, it's a start," she said with a nod. And then, abruptly, Liberty realized that she probably had sounded ungrateful about all the effort that had gone into this afternoon's work. "But it's a good one," she added, flashing Choi a smile.

"Don't mind her," Campbell told his partner. "She's happier than she sounds. Arizona tends to get really caught up in things to the point that she's wearing blinders when it comes to anything else."

"I said it was a good start," Liberty pointed out.

"And we all know you mean that," Campbell told her.

To Liberty, it still sounded as if Campbell was just humoring her, attempting to placate her. But then, maybe she was rather tired. She felt like her nerves had been stretched almost beyond their maximum endurance.

"You know," Campbell said, putting down the pen he had been using to make notes to himself, "I think this would be a good place for a break."

Preoccupied, Liberty absently asked, "For the hour?" In her head, she was already making plans on what she wanted to look into after dinner.

"No." Campbell corrected her misunderstanding. "For the night."

"That's definitely my cue to leave," Choi said, rising. And then the homicide detective looked at the two people at the table. "The kids don't like watching Mommy and Daddy fight."

"Nobody's fighting, Choi," Campbell told his partner patiently.

"Right." The detective glanced from his partner to the visiting detective. "Give it a few minutes," Choi replied under his breath. "I'll see you two in the morning. Me, I've got a less than happy wife to appease."

Liberty was not about to just walk away. Maybe they could order in and continue working. She tried to get him to focus on that agenda by asking Campbell as cheerfully as possible, "When would you like to get back to work?"

"Tomorrow morning." There was no arguing with the tone he used.

Undaunted, Liberty decided to give it one last shot. She looked at him, her eyes all but silently pleading with him. "Then that's it?"

There was a large, old-fashioned clock hanging on the rear wall of the conference room. Campbell jerked his thumb at it for emphasis. "I'd hardly call an almost ten-hour day 'it.' All in all, we've all worked pretty hard today."

She did what she could to harness the sudden, final blast of energy she felt threatening to run amok within her. Taking a deep breath, she collected herself. "You're right. I would have never expected to get this far on my own. And I know I have you to thank for that. If I seem to sound as if I'm being ungrateful, I'm definitely not. It's just that I've never gotten this far before and I don't want to stop because part of me is afraid that it'll somehow all disappear by morning."

He was looking at her as if she were crazy, so Liberty tried to explain. "You know, like Cinderella, fleeing from the ball at midnight just before the horses turned back into mice and the coach turned back into a pumpkin right under her."

"Nobody's turning into mice or pumpkins, Arizona." He gestured toward the monitors. "All this will keep until morning. However, you might turn into mush if you keep pushing yourself this way. So, in the interest of keeping you from self-destructing, I'm going to make you eat dinner."

"You're not planning on cooking again, are you?" she asked. After the full day he had put in, that made her feel more than a little guilty. And she definitely wasn't up to making an attempt herself.

"Nope, not me," he told her.

"Are we getting takeout? Or going to a restaurant?" she asked when he didn't say yes to her takeout question.

"We are going to Chez Andrew," Campbell told her whimsically.

"Is that the name of a restaurant?" Liberty asked. It wasn't a name she was familiar with, but then, she reminded herself, there were a lot of those around.

"No. That's the name of one of my uncles," he told her. "The family patriarch, as a matter of fact."

She stared at him wide-eyed. "You're making the poor man cook for us?"

Campbell laughed. He was going to have to remember this story to tell Andrew. "One does not 'make' Uncle Andrew cook. One cannot 'stop' the man from cooking. One can only get out of his way when he gets started whipping up meals. My uncle, the former chief of police, by the way, can call together a family gathering at the drop of a spatula. He uses food as a form of bribery to get the family together," he confided with a very large grin. "And when I told him about your investigation, he expressed a desire to meet you. For him, that involves making you dinner."

"He doesn't have to make me anything," Liberty stressed.

"Would you actually deny the man the pleasure of serving you one of his meals?" Campbell asked.

She stared at Campbell. "You're serious?" she asked. Liberty was having a great deal of trouble wrapping her mind around the very idea of a man actually *wanting* to prepare a meal for a perfect stranger prior to meeting her.

"Yes, I'm serious," he told her. "Nobody kids about Uncle Andrew's meals. When he retired from the force to take care of his kids, he took up cooking as a way of easing his tension. In very short order, it became his passion."

But something else Campbell had said had caught her attention. "Why did he have to take care of his kids?"

"That is a long story. One I'm sure he'd love to tell you over dinner—" Campbell glanced up at the clock on the wall "—which should be ready any min-ute now. So I suggest we get going."

Dumbfounded again, Liberty could only stare at Campbell as he led her away.

Chapter Eleven

The moment the front door of the recently renovated two-story house opened, Liberty was enveloped by warm, delicious, tempting smells. Smells that triggered the thought that this was what family was all about.

It was like walking into a Norman Rockwell painting. The sight made her think of all those stories she used to weave in her head whenever she would pretend that she was someone else and not the orphan in secondhand clothing going from one home to another.

When she was very young, Liberty used to think that the people who ran child services were trying to lose her, hoping someone would just misplace her. It was only by accident that she wound up living with Florence. The nurse had turned out to be the best thing that ever happened to her.

Along with the wonderful aroma that swirled around her, Liberty found herself looking at a silver-haired, muscular man who brought the phrase "larger than life" to mind. She would have judged him to be in his late sixties and fitter looking than a lot of men she encountered who were much younger.

The man knew how to take care of himself, she thought.

"You must be Liberty," Andrew Cavanaugh greeted her in a deep, warm voice that, like the aroma permeating throughout his home, all but engulfed her.

"I must be," Liberty replied even as she silently upbraided herself for uttering such a lame response.

"Well, come in, come in," Andrew said, urging her as well as his nephew into his house. "I hope that you're hungry."

"She hasn't eaten much the whole day, Uncle Andrew, so I'd say that was a pretty safe bet," Campbell said, walking in behind her.

Andrew nodded knowingly. "I know what that's like. You get so caught up in your work, you forget to eat, or even drink anything. But you can only do that for so long."

At that moment, a very attractive older woman with silver streaks in her mostly blond hair came out to join them. She flashed a sunny smile at both visitors.

"You're right on time," she told them. "Andrew's pot roast is ready to serve. I have no idea how he does that," she confided. "The man just cooks rings around me. But then, he always has. I found that disconcerting when we were first married," she told them, then added with a wide smile, "But now I love it."

Andrew easily slipped his arm around the woman's

waist. "Liberty, allow me to introduce you to the love of my life, my wife, Rose." He turned toward Rose, pressing a kiss to her temple. "Darling, this is the young detective from Arizona that Brian was telling us about. Liberty Lawrence."

Andrew's words caught Liberty off guard. "The chief of detectives told you about me?" she asked. Maybe he was referring to another Brian.

"I just refer to him as my little brother," Andrew said with a chuckle. "But yes, for all intents and purposes, he is the Chief of D's."

Liberty looked at the former police chief uncertainly. "But I don't remember meeting him," she protested.

"You didn't," Andrew told her. "At least, not face to face, to my knowledge. But Brian has a way of taking in things quickly. Even if he's just passing by. And he always makes sure he gets filled in on details that are important to him. Between you and me—" Andrew leaned in a little closer "—I think he reads minds."

Rose looked over her shoulder into the family room. "Dinner's on the table, Andrew," his wife prompted.

"Yes, and it's getting cold as I speak," he guessed. "Yes, I know." He turned on his heel and led the way to the next room. "Please, follow me to the family room. I thought we'd eat there. It's cozier."

That was the word for it, Liberty thought, getting

her first glance into the room as she walked behind the former police chief.

And then she stopped dead in her tracks. There, in the middle of the room, stood a giant twelve-foot tree, almost completely decorated.

"You have your Christmas tree up," she noted in surprise.

"Yes, it goes up the first of December," Brian told her proudly. "The way I see it, with all the time it takes to put up the decorations, we might as well enjoy it for the entire Christmas season."

For a few seconds, Liberty felt like the kid she had never been, not until the day she'd come to live with Florence.

"It's very impressive," she finally told her host and hostess.

"You like it?" Andrew asked, pleased. "Feel free to come over any time while you're in Aurora. Our door's always open to anyone working with members of the family," he told her. "You can even help out with the decorating. As you can see—" he gestured toward the tree "—it's not done yet."

"He means that, you know," Campbell said. "Both about the decorating and about just coming over."

"Of course I mean it," Andrew said. "I was taught never to say anything I didn't mean." He glanced at his wife. "Right, Rose?"

"I can definitely attest to that," Rose told Liberty with a nod.

Andrew smiled at his wife. "All right, everyone,

dig in. Please," he urged, gesturing at the pot roast with its array of four different vegetables surrounding it. "And later, when we're finished, if you want to hang a few ornaments, you can take your pick," he told Liberty.

"We haven't quite finished decorating the tree. With all the members of the family involved, it's a never-ending process," Rose told their guest as she sat at the table. "So feel free to pitch in later."

"I don't think you'll have to twist her arm, Aunt Rose," Campbell said. He had caught the wistful expression on Liberty's face.

"I've just never seen a tree that big," Liberty confessed. "Just how big is it?"

"It's a twelve-footer," Andrew told her.

Rose smiled. "Andrew believes in doing things in a big way." She looked over at her husband. "Hence the large family."

"You can't blame that all on me," Andrew protested. "My father, Seamus, and his late brother, Murdoch, were responsible for starting that," he explained. "My father had four sons. Murdoch had three sons as well as a daughter."

"And they all went forth and multiplied," Campbell quipped.

"Say, why don't I have a family gathering?" Andrew suggested, saying it as if the idea had just occurred to him for the first time rather than with a fair amount of regularity. "That way, you can meet most of the family and we can also finish decorating Rose's tree."

"He calls it that because the first time he bought the giant tree," Campbell told Liberty, "it was to celebrate the year he found Aunt Rose."

"You mean when they got married?" Liberty asked, not completely following what Campbell was telling her.

"No, Campbell means when Andrew finally found me." Rose saw the perplexed look on Liberty's face. "Long story," she said. "And you didn't come here for that. You came for some of Andrew's cooking and to talk about the case that brought you here."

"That's my girl," Andrew said affectionately. "Always cutting to the heart of the matter." He looked at the two people at his table. "Why don't we eat, then we can discuss the case you two are working? And I'll help in any way I can," he promised, although to his way of thinking, that went without saying.

Campbell smiled at the family patriarch. "Sounds like a good deal to me," he said and then amended as he glanced toward Liberty. "To us." After all, she had been the one to bring his attention to the fact that the cases appeared to be connected.

IN THE END, Liberty left the Cavanaugh house full and she also left with a great deal of confidence that with enough patience and help, she would be able to track down the vicious serial killer.

Andrew Cavanaugh was more than partially responsible for that feeling once she heard the full story behind what he had meant by his "finding Rose."

Apparently, the couple had had an argument and, atypically, Rose had driven off in a huff. That one angry incident had been the cause behind eleven years of grief. In her anger, Rose hadn't paid attention to where she was going. It was raining hard, and Rose wound up driving off the road and into the lake.

The car had been found the next day, but no matter how much they'd looked, no one had found any sign of her body. Eventually they'd given up and everyone advised the then police chief to move on.

But Andrew had stubbornly refused.

In the years that followed, Andrew had never given up hope that his wife was out there somewhere, alive. After a while, he'd taken early retirement to take care of and raise his five children. Every so often, he would get a lead and did his best to follow it up, but always to no avail.

It wasn't until his youngest, Rayne, following up on a case north of Aurora, had stopped at a diner that life had suddenly taken a turn for the better. Rayne could have sworn that the waitress who'd served her looked like an older version of her mother's photograph. When she'd come home and told Andrew about it, he'd lost no time in checking the story out.

The waitress had turned out to be his wife, except she hadn't known it. Because of the nature of the accident she had suffered—her car going off the road into the lake—she'd sustained amnesia. She'd had no memory of what had happened to her before she'd crawled out of the lake.

A good Samaritan had found her and taken her to a hospital. She'd built her life up from there.

Andrew had managed to convince her to come back with him to Aurora. He'd patiently tried to re-introduce her to her old life. But it wasn't until an in-cident with a faulty shower head that sprayed her in the face with a torrent of water that Rose's whole life had suddenly come flashing back to her.

The upshot of that was, Andrew told her, if you believe in something, you don't have the right to give up until you finally manage to make it happen.

Liberty left, totally impressed.

"No offense, Campbell, but I think I love your uncle," she told the detective on the way home.

"None taken," Campbell assured her with a laugh. "Most everyone I know feels that way about him to some degree. Uncle Andrew is pretty damn terrific. Nobody else I know would have been able to continue searching for his wife after all that time. And the best part is that it finally paid off."

"Yes," she agreed quietly. "It did." The story had filled her with excitement as well as energy. "There's no chance of us going back to the police station to-night, is there?"

"Tomorrow," Campbell told her. "We haven't got-ten enough in to be able to determine the guy's iden-tity, so there's no point in running back there tonight, Arizona. Uncle Andrew would be the first one to tell you to get your rest so you can get a fresh start in the morning. Maybe by then, Valri will have gotten somewhere with the surveillance tape that we left for her to review."

She sighed. He was right. "So, back to your place?" she asked, staring out the passenger window, watching the lights go by.

"Don't worry. I don't collect rent until the third week in," he said dryly. Then, in case she thought he was being serious, Campbell told her, "I'm just kidding, Arizona. You're welcome to stay as long as you'd like. And, like I said the other day, if my place doesn't suit you, there are a lot of people in my family who would willingly take you in."

Hard as it was for her to fathom, she was beginning to believe that, even though she had never come across people like his family before.

"Kind of the Cavanaugh version of musical beds, eh?" she asked.

Campbell laughed. "I suppose that's one way of looking at it. Another way to look at it is that we're a big law enforcement family and we always take care of our own."

"But I'm not part of your family," Liberty pointed out.

"It's all in how you look at it. There's 'family,'" Campbell told her, "and then there's *family*. In spirit," he underscored. "You qualify for the latter."

"Well—" She stifled a yawn. "You're lucky because I'm too tired to argue," Liberty admitted. "So, okay."

Campbell smiled, amused. "Knew I'd wind up wearing you down."

"Campbell?" Liberty said as he pulled into the carport.

"Yes?" he asked, getting out and coming around to her side in time to open the door for her. He watched, fascinated, as this ball of fire got out in what, for her, was slow motion. She had to be very tired.

"I really had a nice time tonight," she told him. "Thanks for taking me to meet your uncle and aunt."

"I had very little to do with it," he told her, locking the vehicle and then carefully steering her toward his second-floor apartment. "Uncle Andrew insisted on meeting you. I guess hearing about your determination to find that serial killer struck a chord for him."

For whatever reason, she was glad she'd gotten to hear the chief's story.

"That was a pretty inspiring love story when you get right down to it," Liberty said. "In all that time, your uncle never gave up hope of finding his wife alive. Anyone else would have moved on."

They were inside his apartment by then and she turned to Campbell as he closed the front door. "Thank you," she said.

And then, she surprised them both by punctuating the two words with a deep, heartfelt kiss.

It just happened without warning, astonishing both of them. One moment she was thanking him for the evening, for the story, for *everything*. The next moment, she was kissing him. It was hard to say who was more surprised.

Or who enjoyed it more.

She jolted, stepping back as if suddenly realizing what was happening. And that it shouldn't be.

"I'm sorry," she apologized, stunned at what she had just done. The words rang hollow in her ears. "I didn't mean to do that."

"I was kind of hoping that you did." She looked like a deer unexpectedly caught in the headlights, and Campbell found himself searching to put her at ease. "Don't worry," he told her, "I'm not about to follow up on what just happened." Although, he would have liked nothing better than to do just that. He could still taste her on his lips. "I realize that you're tired and not thinking clearly, and I'm not the kind of guy to push himself on a woman."

She still eyed him uncertainly.

"Even if I were so inclined, I've got sisters and cousins—and a few brothers—who would skin me alive if I even so much as *tried* to follow up on that," he said. "And, if you're the slightest bit concerned, you've got that lock on the *inside* of the bedroom door that I know you've already tested out. See you first thing in the morning, Arizona," he told her, turning away and heading toward his own bedroom.

As he walked away, Campbell pressed his lips together. He could *still* taste her.

A warm, tempting feeling shifted through him. For just a second, Campbell allowed his mind to drift.

But then he deliberately blocked any further thoughts about the woman from his mind. There was nothing to be gained by going that route. She was here trying to find a serial killer who had taken the life of someone important to her. He couldn't allow his own feelings to get in the way of that.

Later, when this was over—*if* it was ever going to be over—there was time enough to pursue this other avenue to its most likely end.

But until then, he had to keep his mind focused on the prize—which was *not* the sexy visiting detective down the hall.

At least, he thought, it wasn't the prize *yet*.

Chapter Twelve

Despite hardly being able to keep her eyes open, Liberty didn't really sleep well that night.

The entire time, every time she did fall asleep, she kept having recurring dreams about Campbell.

Not only that, but she had dreams about her foster mother as well. Throughout, the dreams were interspersed with moments that highlighted the very short contact of her lips on his.

In addition, even in her dreams, Liberty was acutely aware of the fact that she had been the one to initiate the kiss and not the other way around.

Consequently, when morning finally came, she felt as if she was more exhausted than when she had initially gone to bed.

She really hoped that if Campbell noticed that she looked less than bright-eyed and bushy-tailed, despite her artful application of makeup, he would have the good grace not to mention that fact.

Moreover, she hoped that his silence would extend to his *not* saying anything about that misstep of hers last night.

That was the only way she could think to refer to her having given in to an impulse and kissed him, although, in the absolute sense, she really didn't think of what she had done as a misstep but more of an accident.

The more she relived it, the more right it seemed—although there was no way she would ever admit that to Campbell.

Bracing herself, Liberty walked into his kitchen, prepared to see Campbell at the stove, making breakfast just like yesterday. However, it appeared that breakfast was on hold.

Campbell was on the phone, obviously talking to someone he knew. He seemed exceedingly serious. She mentally crossed her fingers and hoped that this was about the case and not about something else.

"All right, I'll be right there," Campbell said into his cell phone just before he terminated the call.

Liberty waited until he put his phone away before she made her presence known to him.

Clearing her throat, she prompted, "You caught a case that's taking you away."

Campbell turned around to face her. If he was surprised to see her standing there, he didn't show it. "Not 'away' in the sense that you mean," he answered. "Catching this serial killer just became a top priority. He just killed another nurse. Some homeless guy just found her body in a dumpster while foraging for his breakfast. According to the medical examiner on the scene, the poor guy threw up what little food he had in his stomach," Campbell said sympathetically as he thought to turn off the burner beneath his frying pan.

Breakfast forgotten, Liberty was eager to get going. She crossed the kitchen to the tiny foyer and picked up the purse she had put there.

"Okay, let's go!" she urged.

Campbell glanced at the frying pan. "Don't you want anything for breakfast?" he asked.

Doubling back, she picked up the two slices of toast he had placed on the plate sitting at her place setting on the table.

"Got it," Liberty declared. "Now let's go," she repeated. And then she thought that maybe he wanted to have breakfast himself. "Or, you can meet me at the squad room when you're done."

"Hold your horses, Arizona," he called out. "I'm coming with you. Just wait for me to pack up a few things," Campbell told her.

"I don't want to interrupt your breakfast," she protested, one hand already on the doorknob, twisting it open.

She made him think of a racehorse pawing on the ground at the starting gate.

"I already ate," he told her. "This is for you." He nodded at the contents of the pan. "I made this western omelet for you and I'll be damned if it's going to be left behind." Campbell emptied the pan and wrapped the contents in foil. "You can nibble on it while we work."

Liberty had been slightly hungry when she'd come

down, but the minute Campbell had told her that yet another body had been found, that completely nullified her appetite. Still, she had to admit that she was touched by his thoughtfulness. Moreover, she definitely didn't want to insult him.

"Thanks." She took the foil-wrapped offering from him as she flashed a smile at Campbell. "Does the victim fit the profile?" she queried as she followed the detective out the door.

Locking the door, he headed for the carport. "Yes. She was a nurse and about thirty-five, which puts her in the right age bracket. And the killer used the same weapon. Piano wire," he told her. "But there was a difference this time."

He had her complete attention. "Oh? What was the difference?"

"The victim wasn't wearing scrubs," he told her as he pulled out of the complex. "She was dressed up, as if she was going out for the evening."

Liberty's heart skipped a beat. They were getting closer, she could *feel* it. "You think she found him on a dating site," she asked Campbell. "Like the last victim?" It sounded as if the killer was upping his game.

"I don't know. That's for her friends or family to tell us," Campbell suggested.

Since she had first begun exploring this connection, there was one question Liberty had shied away from asking or even thinking about. But she had never been the type to stick her head in the sand, either, even though she really didn't want to think about this possibility because of her foster mother.

Liberty knew it had to be faced sooner or later. "Was she violated?" she asked Campbell.

"They obviously hadn't done a thorough autopsy yet, but in his initial exam, the medical examiner didn't find anything to suggest that the victim had been raped," Campbell told her.

While she was grateful the victims might have been spared that ultimate degradation, in a way, that also cut down on the possibility the killer might have slipped up. If he didn't violate his victims, then that was one less way he would have left behind some of his DNA, she thought. DNA that could ultimately lead to making an identification.

"It's been less than a week between the two murders," Campbell pointed out. "That means that the killer is escalating." He took a left turn at the end of the block as he headed for the crime scene. "That also means that somewhere along the line, he's going to get sloppy. And when he does," he said, sparing Liberty a significant glance, "that's when we'll get him, Arizona. We'll get the SOB."

Liberty nodded, almost too afraid to hope. But then, hope was all she had.

They arrived at the scene of the latest murder. The area at the rear of the restaurant had been roped off. Foot traffic at that hour of the morning was rare and the people who were out walking stayed clear of it. The idea that an actual murder had taken place so

close to their own homes genuinely upset and un-
settled them, although there were a couple of strag-
glers milling around, craning their necks to catch a
glimpse of the body.

But the victim had already been placed in a body
bag and loaded onto a gurney, so there wasn't much
to see, Liberty thought, looking around as Campbell
pulled his car up in the restaurant's parking lot.

The homeless man who had found the body was
sitting on the steps of the ambulance that had been
called in. A paramedic was checking him out. The
homeless man was exceedingly pale, the shock of dis-
covering the body imprinted on his face.

Making his way over to the man, Campbell said to
the paramedic, "Give us a few minutes."

"I can give you the rest of the day—he checks out
okay," he said, putting away the instruments he had
used on the homeless man. "By the way, he says his
name is Jake 'Smith' and I think that ghostly white
is his natural color."

At that moment, Jake made eye contact with Liberty and she smiled at him.

In a way, Liberty felt a kinship with the homeless
man. In her own way, she reasoned, she had been
homeless, too, and she had definitely felt that same
emptiness he had to be experiencing right now.

As Campbell introduced himself to Jake, preparing to ask him what he might have noticed when he
stumbled across the dead nurse, Liberty dug into her
purse. She took out two twenties and handed it to the

homeless man. Jake looked up at her as if she were some sort of angel sent his way in answer to a prayer.

"Get yourself something to eat," she told him. "That must have been a terrible shock for you this morning."

Jake nodded his head as he shivered in agreement. "I'll say," he mumbled in response.

"When you found the body," Campbell gently prompted, "did you happen to see anything or anyone in the general area?"

Jake shook his head. "Just her," he answered, the words coming out in a single breath. "She had this wire around her neck, it was pulled really tight. She wasn't expecting it," Jake added after a beat, shivering at the memory.

"How do you know that?" Campbell asked.

"By the look on her face," Jake answered. And then he shook his head. "It was awful. That look is going to haunt me for the rest of my life," he told them, shivering again.

"And you're sure you didn't see anyone milling about?" Campbell persisted.

Jake shook his head again. "Nobody to see," he told the two people listening to his story. "I always wait until there's nobody around before I go through the dumpster behind a restaurant. Having me foraging through what a place like that throws away isn't exactly good for their image."

"Understood." They were done for now, Campbell thought. He reached into his pocket and took out a card. Making sure it was the right one, he offered the card to Jake.

"This is the name of a homeless shelter in the area. You'll be able to get a hot meal there and a clean bed for the night, or however long you want to stay. They can also help you find a job if you want one," he told Jake, watching the homeless man's face to see if that caught his attention.

Jake stared at the card in his hand for a long moment and then pocketed it before handing Liberty back the money she had given him.

Surprised, she looked at him quizzically.

"If I'm gonna go to the mission, I guess I should give this back to you," Jake told her almost shyly.

Liberty shook her head, pushing his hand away. "You keep that," she told Jake. "You never know when you might need it."

For the second time since he had met her a few short minutes ago, Jake looked totally astonished. For a moment, he didn't look as if he knew what to say. And then, stumbling over his own tongue, he managed to thank her. Profusely.

Meanwhile, Campbell was scanning the area for one of the patrol officers he knew was on the premises.

"Hey, Rafferty, do me a favor and drive Jake here over to the homeless shelter on Winfred. Tell them he needs a place to stay for a few days. If they need any further explanation, have them call me."

"That was very nice of you," Liberty commented to Campbell as the officer took Jake to his vehicle.

"I could say the same thing about you and that money you gave him. Most people give a couple of bucks, if they give anything at all," Campbell told her.

"There's not much you can buy for a couple of bucks these days," Liberty said. "Referring him to a homeless shelter that can connect him to a hot meal, as well as a possible job, is the far more hopeful way to go."

Campbell wasn't about to make too much of that just yet and he said as much to her. "You can lead a man to water, but you can't make him drink."

She glanced over to where the officer was putting Jake into his vehicle. "Oh, I have this feeling that Jake is going to be more than happy to drink that water," Liberty told him. And then, rolling the comment over in her head, she laughed. "I guess that some of your optimism is finally rubbing off on me."

"Nice to know," he told her. "Let's find out if Choi managed to get the restaurant owner to come in."

Campbell circled around the building, making his way to the restaurant's front door. He continued with his narrative for Liberty's benefit.

"Choi gave the man a choice of coming in early to talk to us, or going down to the precinct." He looked in through the glass door to see how the situation had gone. There was a heavy-set man inside, looking less than happy as he talked to Campbell's partner. "Looks like the owner decided that coming in was the easier choice," he told Liberty.

"The guy's not overly thrilled about either choice, but this was the better way to go," Choi told his partner as he pushed open the front door to admit Campbell and Liberty. He guessed at the topic under discussion. "As a matter of fact, brace yourself."

"Why?" Liberty asked.

"Because the owner is clearly a wreck," Choi confided.

"My guess is he's probably afraid that this is going to affect his business adversely," Campbell said. "After all, he does own the restaurant, right?"

"Right," Choi agreed then added, "Well, it's certainly not exactly good for business." And then realizing how that must have sounded to Liberty because of her connection to one of the serial killer's victims, Choi flushed. "Sorry, no offense intended," he told her.

She appreciated the apology and knew that Choi's comment hadn't really meant anything. "None taken, Detective."

Coming into the heart of the restaurant, they saw the distraught owner. Alan Baker looked as if he was going to go all to pieces any moment now. His deep brown eyes appeared as if they were about to fall right out of his head as he glanced from one detective to the next and then back again.

When he spoke, Baker sounded as if he was on the

verge of hysteria. "How could this have happened?" he demanded, his voice all but cracking.

"That's what we're attempting to find out, sir," Campbell said to the man who appeared to be envisioning financial disaster waiting to leap out and grab him by the throat.

Campbell's response didn't seem to placate the owner. "This is a high-end restaurant in one of the safest cities in the entire country," Baker all but wailed. His unspoken question was clear. Why had something like his happened here?

"We know that, sir," Campbell told the owner patiently. "If we could get a look at your surveillance tapes from last night, specifically from the camera that's facing the alley where your dumpster is located, we might be able to clear up at least some of that mystery for all of us."

"I can take you to the room where the monitors are all kept," Baker told the police detectives, still looking distressed. "But I really don't know the first thing about extracting any information off those tapes." Realizing how that had to have sounded, he quickly explained why. "There're just too many details involved in running a restaurant this size. I leave these minor details to my security guard while I tackle the bigger things."

Campbell wasn't about to attempt to stroke the man's ego and make him feel better about the way he handled things. "And where is your security guard?"

Baker looked at the front door, as if willing the

guard to materialize. He didn't. "He doesn't come in until we open up," Baker explained after a beat. "I could try calling him, but he's usually hard to reach. The calls go to his voicemail. He does good work when he's here."

"Try calling him anyway," Campbell instructed.

"That's okay," Liberty told Campbell, speaking up. "Don't bother. I know how to load the tapes and cue them up," she told the other two detectives. She had already done that at the first crime scene the other day. This should be no different. "Just take me to the surveillance room."

Both Campbell and Choi appeared pleased. However, for the first time, the owner looked rather doubtful. "Well, I don't know..."

"Look," Choi said, finally adding his two cents to the discussion. "It's either let Detective Lawrence here view the tapes, or we bundle the tapes *and* you up and take both of you to the precinct. Your choice, Mr. Baker," he said, looking at the owner pointedly.

It didn't take Baker long to make up his mind. "They're kept right in here," the owner said, leading the way to the back room.

"Need any help?" Campbell offered, looking at Liberty once they got to the room. There were several monitors lined up, one next to the other. All in all, it looked like a rather daunting undertaking.

"I've got this," Liberty assured him. "Why don't you and Choi see if Baker or any of his staff has any information they're not aware of knowing."

That, Liberty mused, turned out to be the case more often than anyone would have thought possible.

"What?" Choi asked, looking at Liberty, clearly bewildered.

"I know what she means," Campbell told his partner.

Choi shrugged. "That makes one of us," he murmured, following his partner out of the small, cramped room.

Liberty hardly heard him. She was already busy reviewing the tapes.

Chapter Thirteen

As Liberty sat, carefully reviewing all the surveillance videos from not only the alley, but also from within the actual restaurant, Campbell and Choi were busy questioning the restaurant workers. That included all the servers as well as the kitchen staff, all of whom the owner had been told to call in.

They'd all come in, some looking rather leery and nervous because the story about the strangling victim discovered behind their restaurant had already hit the news.

Questioning the staff ultimately led nowhere. To a worker, no one had seen anything that appeared to be the least bit suspicious. But then Campbell really hadn't thought they would have, otherwise someone might have come forward by now.

Still, he thought, there was always that outside chance, so he'd been bound to give it a try.

Finished questioning the last staff member, Campbell and Choi left the owner's office where they had been conducting the interrogations.

"Let's hope Arizona was more successful than we were," Campbell said to his partner.

"Well, I really doubt that there was any way she could have been less successful," Choi remarked, following Campbell down the hallway.

Knocking on the security room door, Campbell popped his head in. He fully expected to find Liberty frowning and murmuring under her breath—or, depending on her level of frustration, vocally threatening to drop kick one of the monitors.

"Anything?" he asked her, trying not to pin too much hope into his tone.

"Something," she responded.

That caught Campbell's attention, as well as surprised him. "You're kidding. Really?" Campbell came into the room, closely followed by his partner. It was a tight squeeze, but Campbell hardly noticed. He was focused on the monitor Liberty was looking at. "What?" he asked. "What did you find?"

Glancing at Choi to see if his partner saw anything, the latter merely shook his head and shrugged.

Liberty rewound the tape and then cued it to the portion that had caught her attention.

"Does this guy look familiar to you?" she asked, pointing out a dark-haired man walking away from the alley.

Campbell leaned over her, taking a closer look at the monitor. She did her best not to respond to the body heat she felt passing between them, but because of the intimacy her search managed to create, it wasn't easy.

Due to the camera angle, there was only a partial view of the area. Campbell shook his head. "No, should he?" he asked Liberty.

"I could swear he resembles that guy we saw pulling out of the parking lot in that previous murder you caught." To jog Campbell's memory, she said, "You know that clip containing that partial license plate that is currently with Valri," she told him. "All I know is that it looks like the same guy to me."

She turned to look at Campbell's face to see if the detective agreed.

"The blurry guy with no name," Choi suddenly recalled, making the connection.

Liberty flashed the other detective a smile. "One and the same," she acknowledged, pleased that Choi had picked up on it as well. "And there's something else," she told the two detectives. Rewinding the tape again, she paused a number frames before the shot she had just shown them, then hit Play.

"Notice anything?" she asked both men, looking from Campbell to Choi.

The partners watched the tape again. When neither detective responded to her question with an answer, she rewound the tape a third time.

This time Campbell was the first to notice it. How had he missed seeing it? he couldn't help wondering. "Someone—or *something*—moved the surveillance camera a little to the left."

"Bingo," Liberty declared. "Give that man a cigar. Whoever did it—my guess is that's it our serial killer—made sure he remained out of camera range while he repositioned the camera in order to dump the body without being seen."

"You want to get the forensic team out here to check the camera for any possible prints they might find?" Choi asked his partner.

"Probably a waste of time," Campbell told him. "If the guy's smart enough to reposition the camera, he's smart enough not to leave behind any prints for us to find. But it still wouldn't hurt to have them go over everything—just in case." He paused briefly. "In the meantime, we need to get a copy of that tape and have Valri follow up on it as well. Maybe if she compares this one with the one from the other restaurant, she can get some decent facial recognition—even if we don't have a name yet."

Liberty nodded. "Which of you gentlemen wants to ask the owner if we can borrow the tape?" she asked the detectives. "Since I'm the one who did the viewing? By the way, remind me to stop and get some eye drops on the way back to the station," she told Campbell. "I feel like my eyes are tread-worn—and dry enough to probably catch fire."

"Now there's something I wouldn't want to see," Campbell commented. He nodded toward the video machine. "Pop the tape and bring it with us."

She did as he requested then handed the cassette to Campbell. "But you do the asking as per our agreement."

"I don't recall any agreement. Do you recall any agreement, Choi?" he asked his partner innocently.

It was obvious by the latter's expression that he didn't care for being caught in the middle of this, but since his loyalty was with Campbell, he said, "Nope, I don't."

"That's okay, I recall for all three of us," Liberty informed the other two detectives cheerfully. She placed her hands on Campbell's back and tactfully pushed the man out of the tiny room. "All right, let's get moving, Cavanaugh."

A wry smile curved Campbell's mouth. "I'm beginning to understand why that tiny town of yours had no objections sending you out here and away from them, Arizona. They probably felt that they all needed the break."

"Just keep moving, Cavanaugh," Liberty instructed.

"You know, you two should insist on a cover charge for the show," Choi told them, looking amused as he shook his head.

"WE COME BEARING GIFTS, Valri," Campbell said as he and Liberty walked into the computer lab less than an hour later. Choi had temporarily left them to follow up, while Campbell and Liberty went to see Valri, on another lead they'd managed to uncover.

The two detectives were both hoping she had made some sort of progress with the tape they had left with her. In addition, they wanted to bring this newest one to her.

Valri sighed patiently at Campbell's reference to bearing gifts. "Why am I not surprised?" she said, looking up at her visitors.

"Because you're every bit as smart as you are beautiful," Campbell told her.

Valri made a long-suffering noise under her breath as she gave him an eye roll. "You're spreading it a bit thick, Cam."

"Ah, but I mean every word of it," Campbell told his cousin cheerfully. "Okay, cutting to the chase, have you gotten anywhere with facial recognition yet?"

"Unfortunately, no. I did manage to enhance the guy's likeness, but even so, I can't seem to find a match, which means either he has no record at all, or this guy is a master of disguises."

"Which way are you leaning?" Liberty asked the woman she already regarded as a computer wizard.

"Well, it is possible that he has no record," Valri said. "A lot of serial killers do elude being caught for an inordinate amount of time."

"But none of them had you on their 'trail,' so to speak," Campbell pointed out.

Valri rolled her eyes again. "Go back into your corner, Cam. I'll let you know if I find anything to actually go on."

Campbell nodded. "Fair enough," he told his cousin then turned toward Liberty. "I believe that we've just been given our cue to leave. Valri doesn't like having any witnesses around when she works her magic."

"If I could work magic," Valri informed the detective, "I'd find a way to turn you into another cousin."

"Another cousin?" Campbell said with an amused laugh. "Oh, face it, Val, you know we all drive you crazy to some degree or another. I've heard you say so more than once."

"Some accomplish that more than others," was the only comment Valri would allow herself to commit to, giving Campbell a telltale look. "Just remember, Cam, the longer I talk to you, the less time I have to focus on this." She waved her hand at her computer screen, which currently contained the likeness of the man driving away from the restaurant where Campbell's last victim had been discovered.

"We're already gone," Campbell told her. He looked over his shoulder at the detective from Arizona. The latter hadn't made a move to follow him out. "Aren't we, Arizona?" he prodded.

"Sure, whatever you say," Liberty responded, coming to.

He waited until they were out in the hallway. "Okay, what's on your mind?" he asked as they walked back to the elevator.

"What makes you think I have something on my mind?" Liberty asked.

"That's easy enough. You sound preoccupied," he told her. "Why? What gives?"

She pressed her lips together, thinking. "I'm just wondering why no bells went off."

She had lost him. "Any particular bells you're talking about?"

"From the looks of it, our serial killer was apparently on at least two dating sites."

"Okay?" he responded, waiting for her to make a point. He still didn't see why something like that would "ring bells."

"Well, don't you think it's rather off for our guy to be out on two dating sites to begin with. Wouldn't a low profile be more in keeping with his character?" she asked Campbell.

Campbell shrugged. "Maybe he was awkward and needed help," Campbell guessed. "I wouldn't know myself. But that was probably the story he told to get his victims to lower their guard. Also, reviewing the information on the dating site is a great way for him to hone in on nurses, since they seem to be his victim of choice."

"You have a point. Most likely, too, they took one look at our mystery man and probably felt as if they had hit the proverbial jackpot," Liberty commented grimly.

"Some jackpot," Campbell said.

"Hey, you're going in the wrong direction, Arizona," he called out to Liberty when she suddenly did a one-eighty and headed back to Valri's computer lab.

"No, I'm not." She tossed the words over her shoulder. "I've got an idea."

"Care to share?" he asked, quickening his gait as he followed her back to his cousin's lab.

"Sure," she answered. "You're welcome to come along."

Campbell blew out a breath. "I'm beginning to understand why you never had a partner. It wasn't that the town was so small, it was because no one would put up working with you."

"No comment," she responded "innocently."

By then, Liberty had reached the computer lab and, after a quick knock on the door, she went in.

Valri looked up. If she was surprised to see them, she hid it well.

"Twice in one day. Any reason why I'm so lucky today, Cam?"

"Ask her." He jerked his thumb in Liberty's direction. "She's the one who suddenly decided to make a beeline back to your office."

Liberty jumped in with an explanation. "Can you enhance that guy's photograph and print a copy for us to show around?"

"Sure. That's the easy part," Valri told her cousin's counterpart. "Give me a minute," she requested, hitting a few keys to get the photograph just right before printing a copy. Satisfied with the image on her computer, Valri hit Print. A faint noise was heard coming from another part of the lab, then ceased.

"I'll get it," Valri told them, getting up. Moving quickly, she retrieved the photograph and returned, holding it in her hand. "Will this do for your purposes?" she asked, raising the photograph in front of the Arizona detective.

"Perfect," Liberty told her. She lifted her eyes to Valri's. "Do you think I could possibly have a few more copies?"

"You can have as many as you want. I can even make up a few wallet-sized ones. Starting a scrap-book?" she asked glibly.

"No, handing them out to however many detectives your cousin can get to, to try to track this guy down," Liberty answered.

"Okay, let's make it twenty—five—copies to start," Valri said. "Does that work for you?" she asked, looking at Campbell.

Campbell spread his hands, disavowing any opin-ion when it came to this. "Hey, apparently I'm just along for the ride. You two work it out," he told Valri good-naturedly.

"So, twenty-five copies to start okay with you?" Valri double-checked with Liberty before she finally typed in the number.

"Twenty-five will be just fine, Valri," Liberty agreed. "Besides, I can always come back here and ask the legendary wizard for more if the need arises, right?"

Valri smiled in response then regarded her cousin, who was standing off to the side. "I like her, Cam," she told him.

"Of course you do," he said dryly. "So, are we ready to go?" he asked Liberty. "Or is there something else you want to ask the wizard to give you before we leave?"

"I can think of one thing," she said, then immediately banished the thought from her mind. "But no, I think we're good for now." She took the pile of photographs that Valri handed her. "This'll help a lot," she assured the other woman.

"Whatever you need," Valri told her in all honesty. "I'm here to help."

"Hey, why don't you ever say that to me?" Campbell asked his cousin, pretending to be offended.

"You're family," Valri told him. "I don't have to be nice to you. Besides, you're used to abusing the privilege of being related to me. While she, on the other hand," Valri said, nodding at Liberty, "knows when not to cross the line and is nothing but polite when asking for something."

Campbell frowned. "You've known her for—what, a whole three days? Not even."

"Ah, but I'm a quick judge of character, not to mention a very good one," Valri pointed out.

"I think I need to get going," Campbell said, "before I'm tempted to commit whatever the proper term is for dressing down a cousin."

"If you find out, be sure to let me know, Cam," Valri called out after him as he and Liberty left the computer lab.

"Count on it," he promised just before he closed the door behind him.

Chapter Fourteen

"Just why did you want so many copies of this guy's picture, Arizona?" Campbell asked the woman beside him as they walked down the hallway back to the elevator. "We don't even know for sure if he actually *is* the serial killer."

"Let's just say that I've got this gut feeling," Liberty answered.

Campbell laughed under his breath.

"What's so funny?" she asked.

"In my family, we're the ones who talk about having 'gut feelings,'" he told her.

Liberty nodded. "Well, maybe when it's your family, you do. But Florence was as close to family as I had," she told him. "As for the pictures, the worst thing that can happen is that the guy in the photo turns out *not* to be the guy we're after and we toss the photos. And if he *does* turn out to be our serial killer, then we'll have enough photos to blanket the entire area and everyone will be alerted to what he looks like," she told Campbell. "I find that people remember things more clearly if they have a photo to hang on to rather than just depend on their memories. And this way, if they happen to cross paths with this Romeo down the line, all they have to do is whip out the photo to make sure."

"I suppose that does have some merit," Campbell agreed.

Her mouth curved. She was surprised that he didn't want to argue with her about it. When they had initially met, he had struck her as someone who was willing to argue about *everything*.

She was gratified that he wasn't.

"Thank you for that," she told Campbell. "I know how much that had to cost you."

"Didn't cost me a thing," he told her in all innocence. "I'm open to anything. I just don't agree with everything I hear."

As they stood waiting for the elevator, Liberty spared him a glance. She had worked with visiting detectives in her hometown who acted as if they were the last word when it came to working theories. And they treated her as if she was just one step removed from a hayseed.

It was nice to discover he wasn't like that.

When she came right down to it, she had to admit that she liked their association. If nothing else, this was the first time she had entertained a measure of hope about finally being able to close in on the serial killer.

Liberty smiled at him. "Nice of you to admit that."

"This job is hard enough without posturing and

bringing in egos." They got off the elevator. "What do you say we take those photos and run them past Cynthia's sister and her coworkers? Maybe it actually will jar someone's memory the way you hoped."

If only, Liberty thought. Out loud she told him, "Fingers crossed," as they went to the front entrance.

THEY WENT TO the victim's place of work at the hospital first. Several of Cynthia's coworkers thought that they had noticed the man in the photograph somewhere on the premises, but on closer examination, they weren't really sure.

One of the nurses, Penelope Dixon, all but drooled over the photograph, apparently forgetting who the man in the photograph was supposed to represent.

"He really was a gorgeous guy," Penelope recalled. "I was tempted to sign up on that dating site myself— except I'm sure that my husband wouldn't be understanding about it." Penelope sighed wistfully. "But that is one delicious specimen of manhood."

And then, realizing what she had just said—and possibly about whom—she flushed, attempting to negate her words to Campbell. "At least Cynthia knew a little bit of joy before that terrible thing happened to her."

"Tell me, did you ever wonder why someone as good-looking as this man appears to be needed to use a dating site before finding someone to go out with?" Campbell asked the nurse. He exchanged glances with Liberty and gave her a nod.

That was his way of giving her credit, Liberty thought, which meant that he really did buy into the theory she had advanced to him.

Another one of the day nurses who had worked with Cynthia, Sally Hopkins, added her two cents. "I just thought that Cynthia was the luckiest woman on the face of the earth—until that homicide detective came to inform us that she had been murdered." The nurse stared at the photo in her hand and frowned. "Is this the guy who did it?" Sally asked.

"We don't know yet," Campbell replied. "But he is a person of interest and we're trying to locate him in order to bring him in for questioning. Since capturing his partial likeness on camera, he seems to have disappeared from the face of the earth."

Sally looked at the photo again and released a heartfelt sigh. "Unless he's the killer, some woman might have snapped him up and taken him to her lair, unable to believe her good fortune."

"As for 'good fortune,' we'll reserve judgment on that," Liberty told the nurse. She flipped the photograph over for the woman's benefit. "Detective Cavanaugh's number and my number are on the back of the photo. If you or any of your friends happen to see this man, do not approach him. Please, just give Detective Cavanaugh or me a call."

"Absolutely," Sally replied. She glanced down at the photograph. "I can keep this, right?" the nurse asked hopefully.

"Right," Campbell told her, sincerely hoping Liberty was correct about her "gut" feeling. They needed to close in on this killer before any other victims fell prey to this man's charms, the way these women apparently had.

THEY DISTRIBUTED SEVERAL more photographs but, realistically, didn't think that they'd really managed to "jar" anyone's memory.

Their next stop was to go visit the victim's sister.

. Liberty almost felt guilty because the woman looked so hopeful when she'd first seen them on her doorstep.

"Did you get him?" Judith cried.

"Not yet," Campbell told her. "But we haven't stopped working on it."

Liberty held up the photograph for.the woman to view. "Do you, by any chance, recognize this man?"

Staring at the photograph, Judith turned completely pale. "Is he the one who killed Cynthia?" she asked, her voice sounding almost hollow and tinny.

"As I said, we don't know yet, but there *is* a slight possibility." And then Liberty had an idea. "Would it be possible for you to go through your sister's things for us?"

"I suppose," the woman replied warily. "What am I looking for?" she asked. "And I'm going to have to brace myself first. I have come to terms with never seeing her again."

She knew how that was, Liberty thought.

"It just occurred to us that there might be a chance

that your sister could have made a copy of her date's picture from the actual dating app or site," Campbell suggested. Then he prompted, "You know, to show you once you got back from your vacation."

Cynthia's sister didn't seem to understand. "We were never in competition for men," she protested.

"I wasn't suggesting that there was a competition," Campbell told her. "Maybe she just wanted to share his picture with you, if things went well, because she was happy. And if this guy really does turn out to be the serial killer, he might have been camera shy—with apparently good reason, so she had to be clever about getting his picture to show you."

"And if she did make a copy off the website, then we'll have his bio—or his made-up bio," Liberty amended for the woman's benefit.

"The point is, we'll have a place to start," Campbell told the woman.

Judith set her mouth grimly. "I'll look through Cynthia's things," she promised. "Maybe I will find something," she said, looking at both detectives.

"It's a long shot," Campbell agreed, doing his best to be encouraging. "But you never know."

Liberty watched the woman pull back her shoulders, as if she were literally bracing herself for the ordeal.

"This might take some time," she warned the detectives.

"Because of the emotional cost?" Campbell suggested.

"No, because my sister was a semi-hoarder. Nothing overwhelming," she quickly assured them, not wanting to cast any sort of shadow on her sister. "She just never was able to get rid of any papers she thought were important in her life."

"Like the information about a potential date she pulled off the internet site?" Liberty asked hopefully.

The woman's eyes temporarily lit up. "Yes, like that."

"How do you do it?" Liberty asked Campbell once they were back in his car and driving to their next destination.

They had left Cynthia's sister to deal with the emotional task of sorting through what appeared to be ten years of papers, possibly more.

"I'm going to need more details, Arizona. How do I do what?" he asked. He hit a long stretch of road with sparse traffic, so he allowed himself a quick glance in Liberty's direction.

She took a deep breath, searching for patience as she answered. "How do you keep from screaming after going around in circles?"

"I'll let you in on a secret," he told her with a wink. He jerked his thumb at the seat behind him. "That's why I carry a pillow around."

He was kidding. There was no pillow behind him. Liberty felt herself responding to him. There was something incredibly sexy about the detective's wink. She was fairly certain that if the serial killer had a wink like that, he could undulate incredible waves through his victims.

She couldn't help thinking that all those women, hungry for affection, would easily be susceptible to a wink or attention coming from a smooth, good-looking operator with his own agenda.

So now they had the "how," what they needed was the "why." As in, why was this man killing women and why was he so selective with his victims, targeting only nurses?

Campbell glanced at her again. She had gotten very quiet and that wasn't natural for her, at least not the detective he had gotten to know in the last few days. Something was up.

"Where are you?" Campbell asked.

Clearing his throat, he repeated his question.

Liberty blinked, suddenly aware that he was talking to her.

"Did you say something?" she asked Campbell.

"Yes," he said patiently. "I asked you where you were."

"Lost in a quagmire," she told him.

He frowned at what he felt was a flippant answer. "You need to clear that up for me, Arizona," he told her. "I speak English, I'm fluent in Spanish, and I can manage a little bit of French. I am *not* fluent in gibberish. Sorry."

"I was just thinking that I can't understand how someone who could be so intelligent—like a nurse—could just lose all her common sense and go running off like that with someone they really didn't know." Campbell thought he detected a break in her voice as she told him, "Those women's mistake was that they trusted the dating site to live up to its claim they looked into the profiles of all the people appearing on their site."

"There's such a thing as being too trusting," Campbell noted.

"There's also such a thing as being lonely and really hoping against hope that for once in their hardworking life, they had lucked out. You know, like 'other people have happy endings, why not me?' That kind of thing," Liberty pointed out. "It's a terrible thing to be lonely."

He definitely heard something in her voice. He didn't want to pry, but he also didn't want to just back away from the subject she had broached.

"You almost sound as if you're speaking from experience," he told her.

"No," Liberty answered a bit too flatly, dismissing Campbell's suggestion. "But I have a very good imagination and my sympathy gene is alive and well." Then, because he was being concerned and deserved an explanation, she said, "I was looking through my foster mother's things."

That caught his attention. "Are you going to tell me that you discovered your foster mother went on a dating site after all?"

"I honestly don't know," Liberty admitted. "I suppose it might have been a possibility." Staring straight ahead, a sad expression slipped over Liberty's face. "I know she felt she led a good, decent life and wound up accomplishing things, especially in her line of work. She was a great nurse and a fantastic foster mother, but I also know that it wasn't enough to fill the void in her life."

"She talked about that void with you?" Campbell asked, surprised.

She grew silent for a moment then told him, "No, not really. I found her diary almost six months after she had been murdered. The reason I did was because her landlady called me in to clear out her things and get rid of anything I didn't want to keep." A fond smile curved her mouth. "She kept Florence's apartment for as long as she could, but the building owner was putting pressure on Mrs. McGinty to clean up the place and finally get it ready for someone else to rent."

It had been painful, going through all those memories, but she'd managed to force herself to just keep going until it was all packed up.

Campbell didn't understand something. "Isn't it kind of hard to rent out a place where someone was murdered?" he asked.

"But she wasn't killed there," Liberty pointed out. "She was killed while living in the apartment building. There is a difference," she said. "Anyway, I wasn't about to give the landlady a hard time when she was being so nice. I just headed out, packed up Florence's things and never looked back. I did wind up reacquainting myself with what a fantastic, wonderful woman she had been. I mean, I always knew she was a good woman, but she had this huge capacity for caring. I didn't realize at the time how amazing she truly was."

Campbell didn't realize the noise he heard was Liberty quietly crying until he looked at her. At a loss for words, he pulled over to the side of the road and put the gear in Park.

Doing what she could to pull herself together, she scrubbed her hands over her cheeks, getting rid of her telltale tears.

"Why are we stopping?" She wanted to know.

"To give you time to pull yourself together," he told her simply.

Liberty had trouble dealing with his being so thoughtful. "I'm together," she protested, her voice hitching.

"Okay, then to give me a chance to pull myself together," he said cryptically. "Correct me if I'm wrong, but I don't think you ever gave yourself the time to properly grieve."

"There's time enough for grieving when we catch the SOB who did this to her and to all those other women," she said a bit too fiercely.

But he let the vehicle idle. "We're not going anywhere until you get this out of your system."

Her eyes narrowed. "I don't need to get this 'out of my system.'"

"Okay, then *I* need you to get it out of your system.

Look, I know how devastated I'd feel in your place. Humor me, Liberty," he told her.

She blinked. "You just called me Liberty," she said in surprise. "Not Arizona."

Campbell shrugged. "Occasionally, I slip," he admitted. "This isn't a nickname moment."

She tried very hard to ignore him, to shrug away his kindness, but she found she just wasn't able to. So when he slipped his arm around her shoulders and drew her closer to him, she struggled to push him away. But then, the next moment, something just broke within her. That was when the tears began to flow in earnest.

"Look what you've done to me," she sobbed.

"Sorry, didn't mean to be understanding, Arizona," he told her.

So, it was back to Arizona, was it? She had to admit that part of her was more comfortable that way. If she was "Arizona," she wasn't being her, which meant she wasn't being vulnerable. She didn't like showing weakness this way.

"Well, you're not forgiven," she informed him.

Then, as he began to give her space, she locked her arms around Campbell and gave in to all the feelings that had suddenly welled up inside her. She just began crying.

Campbell said nothing. He only held her to him and stroked her hair, trying to help her transfer the affection she had felt for Florence to something she was able to handle: the woman's memory.

It helped somewhat.

Chapter Fifteen

Slowly, Liberty felt herself coming around. And on the heels of that came a wave of almost oppressive shame and embarrassment.

Pushing her hair aside and avoiding Campbell's eyes, she did her best to try to pull herself together for the second time that day.

"Sorry, I didn't mean to have such a meltdown," she apologized. Pressing her lips together and venturing a look at Campbell's face, she said, "I know you probably won't believe me, but I don't usually go all to pieces like this."

He gave her a quizzical look. "Why wouldn't I believe you?"

"Because I could just be lying in order to save my pride," Liberty answered.

Campbell shook his head. "Nah, you're not the type."

"How would you know?" she questioned. After all, he didn't really know her.

"Call it instinct," Campbell answered simply. "I thought I made that clear in the beginning." He grinned at her. "We Cavanaughs are great believers in gut instincts."

"You do realize that you make it impossible to argue with you," she said, blowing out an exasperated breath.

"Good," he replied, his eyes shining. "That was my plan all along."

Liberty wasn't about to take him to task about that. It just sounded too easygoing and nice.

"So where are we off to now?" she asked him, changing the subject.

"To a little town north of here. Gainesville," he informed her.

"Why Gainesville?" she asked. "What's in Gainesville?" He hadn't said anything about it to her earlier.

"Well, thanks to you, I did a little digging and came across a case just like the ones we were looking into. The name didn't make your original list—the one you brought with you—but the victim was murdered with the exact same MO."

When did all this happen? They had been together almost constantly since she had arrived. "And when did you do this so-called digging?" Liberty asked.

"Last night, after you went to bed, or at least into the guest room." He glanced in her direction. Each time he did, he became aware of just how compelling and striking a woman she really was. But he didn't want to make her uncomfortable, so he said, "By the looks of you this morning, you didn't get all that much sleep."

"Flatterer," she quipped dryly, relieved that they were back to bantering and trading barbs. "From the sound of it, you didn't get all that much sleep yourself, either. Why don't you look it?" she asked. The man actually looked rested. That didn't seem fair.

They were on another empty stretch of road and he looked at her for what seemed like a lingering moment. "Because I have the ability to push on like a machine when I need to."

A warm shiver slithered down her back. Why did that sound like a promise to her?

Get a grip, Libby, she lectured herself. *Your recent crying jag must have scrambled your brain.*

"Okay, 'Mr. Machine,'" she said out loud. "How did this 'killing' escape my attention?" She needed to know. "I went through all the reports on strangulation murders that took place in the last four years where the victims were nurses." And then a thought hit her and her eyes widened. "Don't tell me he's gone and broadened his victim base." That would bring them back to square one, she realized, trying not to let that thought bring her down.

Campbell had a different theory about that. "No, but given the timeline, this might be victim zero."

Why would he even think that? Campbell had totally piqued her interest. "Okay, I'm listening. What makes you say that?"

"Well, the exact time that this particular victim— a part-time nurse, by the way—was murdered was a little difficult to pinpoint."

"Why?" Liberty asked. "Was the medical examiner new at the job?" That would have been the simplest explanation, she thought.

"No, the body was buried in the woods. No one found her until after she had been missing for four years," Campbell told her, remembering what he had read. "And then her body was discovered strictly by accident. A construction crew was digging in a newly cleared area to pour the foundation for a building. Ironically enough, the building was intended to be the new police station."

"Business slow?" Liberty quipped. "They had to go digging something up to investigate?"

"Oh, good," Campbell quipped. "You have your sense of humor back."

Liberty was aware of what she had to have sounded like. "Right, if you like your sense of humor on the macabre side."

He looked at her, just relieved that she had managed to lighten up from the way she had been earlier. "Right now, I'll take my humor any way I can get it. We'll work on sides later."

WITHIN ANOTHER THIRTY MINUTES, Campbell had driven to what appeared to be the edge of town.

Liberty scanned the area, rather surprised by what she saw. The town was the size of an elongated postage stamp. "I didn't think you had towns like this in California. This place is smaller than Calhoun."

"That shouldn't surprise you," he said. "Are you

kidding? We have everything in California. You don't have the exclusive rights to tiny towns, Arizona. That is probably part of the reason why this particular murder went unnoticed for as long as it did. I think the residents around here were too stunned to believe that this sort of thing happened in their own town and that there was a monster like this who walked among them."

Liberty agreed completely. "It not an easy thing to come to terms with."

"Let's go talk to Gainesville's police chief and see what he can say to enlighten us about the situation," Campbell told her as he pulled his vehicle up in front of a small, two-story building that called itself the current police station.

"Doesn't look as if they can fit many police officers in here," Campbell commented.

Then he looked in Liberty's direction as they approached the station. Mindful of the fact that she had come from a police station that numbered among its force one chief of police, one detective—her—and two officers, he found himself apologizing, "I'm sorry, was that insensitive?"

"No," she answered. "That's actually rather accurate." Liberty headed toward the station's entrance. "Now let's see if that gut of yours is as fantastic as you claim it is."

Campbell grinned and winked at her. "You're making me blush."

"Oh, right, like that's even remotely possible," she said with a dismissive laugh.

Liberty sincerely doubted if Campbell had *ever* had the ability to blush, not even when he was a kid. But what he did have—and she sincerely appreciated—was the ability to make her feel better. For that—although she wasn't about to tell him—she truly blessed Campbell.

They found the police chief sitting at his desk inside what appeared to be a slightly enlarged cubical of an office. The chief, a giant of a man, was too large for his desk.

Chief Alexander Jenkins III looked up as they walked in and, from his expression, didn't seem surprised to see them. Rising to his feet, he shook first Liberty's hand and then Campbell's.

Liberty caught herself thinking that the man's hands were like big paws, but exceptionally gentle.

"You called ahead?" Liberty asked the detective beside her as he returned the chief's handshake.

"I know my manners. Besides, you can't take a chance on just dropping in without notice. The chief might be out of town on business," he told Liberty between near immobile lips.

Or away cutting down his Christmas tree for the holiday, she thought, which seemed to her to be the more likely scenario.

"Chief Jenkins," Campbell said. "We spoke on the phone earlier this morning. I'm Detective Campbell

Cavanaugh from Aurora and this is Detective Liberty
Lawrence from Calhoun, Arizona."

The chief flashed them a wide, welcoming smile.
"You people south of us certainly have lyrical names,"
he observed. Then, with a good-natured shrug, Jenkins told them, "You can call me Al, if you want. My
given name is a mouthful," he admitted. The chief
gestured to the two chairs standing in front of his
desk. "Take a seat. What can I help you with? When
we spoke earlier, you said you were working on a serial killer case."

"We are. You said you recently discovered the
body of a woman who had gone missing a few years
earlier," Campbell prompted.

The chief nodded. "Sarah Hanesworth," he said,
supplying them with the victim's name. "We only
managed to identify her through her nephew's identification. What do you want to know?"

"Everything," Liberty answered. Without realizing it, she had moved to the edge of her seat. "Did
the woman live here?"

"Yes," the chief answered. "The victim moved here
a couple of years before she went missing."

"If you don't mind my asking, who reported her
missing?" Campbell asked.

"Well, at first no one. That struck me as kind of
sad," he confided. "To make no impression on anyone's life so that they don't even realize you're not
there anymore. But then the clinic where the victim
had worked said she hadn't shown up to work, which

struck her boss as rather strange, because she seemed like a conscientious person.

"Since she hadn't been there at the clinic for very long, they considered the fact that maybe she had just taken off to find a better paying position. Then her nephew reported her missing a month later. Said he hadn't heard from her and that he was worried something might have happened to her."

Liberty perked up at the added detail, like a dog spotting a new bone. "And where was he up to this point?" she asked the chief.

"According to the nephew, he was out of town on business. As a matter of fact, to hear him tell it, his business kept him on the road quite a lot. When he swung by, he had only intended on making a quick stop to check in on his aunt, but then her neighbors and the people who worked with her at the clinic said they hadn't seen her, so he got worried and came to me."

The words the chief had used to describe the situation stuck in her mind. "You met him, right?"

"Right."

"Does this nephew strike you as the type who worried?" she asked the chief.

The man's brow furrowed as he tried to understand her question. "Excuse me?"

"Well, you said he was her nephew, and I'm just saying that from my experience, nephews don't generally worry about relatives who they're just occasionally in touch with." For no particular reason, she was experiencing that strange gut feeling again. Something didn't feel right—or maybe it was just her imagination. "Would you have a picture of this concerned nephew?" Liberty asked.

"What are you thinking?" Campbell asked her, interested.

She could only shrug and admit, "I don't know yet."

"Fair enough," Campbell said agreeably. "I'm sure there must be a picture of the guy somewhere. Since he's on the road so much, at the very least, he's got to have a driver's license."

"Hanesworth," Liberty said, repeating the family's last name. "Can't be that hard to locate."

But the chief shot her down by shaking his head. "Her nephew had a different last name than she did."

"Why am I not surprised?" Liberty murmured.

"All right, then what *is* this nephew's last name?" Campbell asked.

"Give me a second," the chief requested as he began to flip through the papers inside the report. "It's here in the report," Jenkins said. "He was the one who identified the victim's body." Finding what he was looking for, he skimmed down the page—and then frowned. "Well, that doesn't ring a bell."

That didn't sound good, Liberty thought. "What doesn't?"

"The nephew's name." He looked up from the report. "I'm sure that's not what he told me, or what I thought I wrote in the report." And then he shrugged.

"But I guess it must have been. It's right here." The chief tapped the page where he had found the information. "I guess I must have had a memory lapse."

Campbell was still chewing on the manner. "You said that this nephew was out on the road a lot."

"Yes?" the chief asked.

Campbell was playing a hunch. For the moment, what he was considering provided one possible explanation. "What does he do that takes him on the road? Is he a salesman?" the detective asked.

"No, he said that he services and updates those new computers. Tried to talk me into one, but I wouldn't have any part of it," he admitted rather proudly.

"Fixes them? Programs them? Or...?" Campbell questioned, letting his voice trail off and leaving it for the chief to provide a suitable answer.

"I'm afraid your guess is as good as mine," Jenkins confessed. "You do know that this is officially a cold case, right?"

"Doesn't mean it can't heat up," Campbell told him. "And as for what Sarah Hanesworth's nephew does for a living, my guess is that it gives him the ability to alter whatever was originally input on a computer."

The light bulb went off over the chief's head. "Like his name?" the chief asked.

"Like his name," Campbell agreed.

"Wow," the chief murmured, clearly floored by the theory.

"That would be my word for it," Liberty agreed.

"You said the victim and her nephew moved here a couple of years before she went missing?"

"That's right." The chief waited for another question to follow.

He didn't have long to wait.

"Would you happen to know where they originally came from?" she asked.

"Well, his file appears to be rather creatively worked on," the chief said with more than a note of skepticism in his voice.

"All right, what about hers?" Campbell asked. "She had to have filled out an employment form or something to that effect when she initially applied for her job."

Campbell had a feeling that they were being too optimistic in their projection. "Little towns like this have a tendency—at times—to resist change, to cling to the old way things were done rather than go with the innovative."

In which case, he thought, the sort of information they were looking to gain access to might not be available.

But the chief proudly shook his head. "Well, not me. I enjoy progress and everything that it might bring with it."

"Then hopefully, there are other people in town who think the same way you do and we'll be able to find a rather decent picture of Sarah's nephew to work with," Liberty said.

She wanted the photograph so badly, she could almost taste it.

"Then I guess I'd best get started on that." Getting up and heading to the doorway, the chief called out, "Hey, Abe. I've got an assignment for you. And bring your glasses." He glanced over his shoulder at the two detectives behind him. "He's always leaving them on his desk. Insists that he doesn't need them," the chief confided, lowering his voice, "but between you and me, he really does."

The officer who responded to the chief's summons looked utterly unenthusiastic as he ambled into the office. "Can't this keep?" he asked. "I was just about to take off, Chief."

"If you don't mind, I'd like you to delay that take-off, Abe," the chief requested, his tone leaving no space for an argument. "I've got a little hunting assignment for you."

The young police officer's face lit up at the mere mention of the word *hunting*.

"Sir? What do you want me to go hunting for?" he asked eagerly. It was obvious that he enjoyed hunting.

"I want you to find a photograph of Sarah Hanesworth's nephew. You know, the guy who came in to identify her after they found her buried where they were planning on pouring the foundation for the new police building—the one they currently have on hold," the chief added for Campbell and Liberty's benefit.

"Oh." Abe's face fell at least half a foot. His disappointed was almost palatable.

Chapter Sixteen

Frowning, the chief watched his police officer dejectedly lumber out of the room to an adjacent area.

"As you can see by Abe's face, I'm not sure just how long it's going to take to locate a picture of this guy you're asking about. We're a small town, but we're not *that* small. Ideally, we should have it at our fingertips but, well…" The chief's voice trailed off as he rubbed the fingertips of his right hand together, signifying that what they were looking for might have very well just slipped through the cracks.

"So, the way I see it," he continued, addressing the two visiting police detectives, "you have one of two ways to go. You can either drive back down to Aurora and return tomorrow, or we've got a couple of nice family hotels where you can rent rooms for the night. I can personally vouch that the food is good and the bedding is clean at least in one of them. I've had to stay there on one occasion."

The chief had aroused Campbell's curiosity. "If you don't mind my asking, why would you have to stay in a hotel in a town where you live?"

"I don't mind. That was the unfortunate result of having one of my kids leave the front door open and a skunk deciding to wander in. Our dog, Scout, took offense and started to raise a storm, defending us. Needless to say, he didn't fare very well." The chief shook his head as he recalled the incident. "The poor guy stank up the whole house. The upshot was that we wound up going to the hotel while our place was aired out."

Liberty knew that most hotels didn't welcome pets, especially not ones that smelled like a skunk. Concerned about what had happened to the poor pet, she asked, "Where did the dog stay?"

Obviously getting her drift, the chief smiled as he answered her. "We have a very understanding vet who boarded Scout for us. Doc Adams worked hard and finally managed to get that awful smell to dissipate.

"Anyway," he said, resuming his story, "those are your choices. Aurora or one of the local hotels. So what'll it be?"

Campbell glanced in Liberty's direction and said, "We'll go back to Aurora. It's not *that* far and I sleep better in my own bed," he confessed.

The nature of his response surprised her, but Liberty decided to make no comment.

"Thanks for all your help, Chief," Campbell went on. "We'll get out of your hair now and, if everything goes well, we'll be back to see you in the morning."

The chief nodded, glancing in his officer's direction. "Hopefully, Abe over there can make heads or tails out of all the paperwork he's wading through," the chief said as he walked his two visitors to the front door of the police station.

Liberty merely smiled at the man as they parted company but said nothing. Instead, she waited until she and Campbell were back in the latter's vehicle and were driving toward Aurora before she asked, "Why did you say that?"

The question, coming completely out of the blue the way it did, totally threw him. He had no idea what she was referring to.

"Say what?" Campbell asked.

It was dark now and since he was in an unfamiliar area, he decided it wouldn't hurt to have a little extra insurance. He hit the GPS navigating system, pressing Home to help guide him on the unfamiliar road.

He knew damn well what she was talking about, Liberty thought. "That you have trouble sleeping in anything but your own bed. Weren't you the one who told me that you could fall asleep hanging on a hook in the closet? What you said to the chief about not being able to sleep in a strange bed was for my benefit, wasn't it?"

"I have no idea what you're talking about," Campbell told her innocently.

Okay, she thought. She'd play along and spell it out for him. "You didn't want me having to admit that I have trouble sleeping in strange places. You probably thought admitting to something personal like that would make me uncomfortable," she guessed.

Liberty shifted in her seat and stared at his profile. "You really are gallant, aren't you?"

She was torn between thinking that he was too good to be true and thinking that, for some reason, Campbell was just playing her due to some hidden agenda of his own design.

Instead of giving her a teasing answer the way she would have expected, Campbell told her, "I was always taught never to make anyone uncomfortable if I could possibly help it—unless, of course, they were the scum of the earth." He glanced at her as he flashed his thousand-watt smile in her direction. "And you, Arizona, definitely do not qualify for that description."

He fell silent for a moment, as if thinking, before looking back at the road. "Look, it's going to be at least another half hour, if not more, before we get back home, so if you want to sack out and take a cat-nap, I'm okay with that."

He was saying that he absolved her of her obligation of staying awake and keeping him company with mindless conversation. Well, she could hold up her end as well as he could.

"I don't take catnaps or any other sort of furry animal naps. I'm fine," Liberty informed him in no uncertain terms.

The way she saw it, since he had to stay awake, the least she could do was remain awake with him and provide moral support—or take over driving altogether—if for some reason the mighty "superhero" began to suddenly fade on her.

Campbell shrugged at her protest. "Have it your way, Arizona. I was just trying to be thoughtful."

She made what sounded like a dismissive sound under her breath. "Don't overdo it."

Because the road had straightened somewhat, he felt he could risk sparing her another, longer glance.

"Wow, it's like trying to walk a tightrope with you," he marveled. "One wrong step and it's all over." He shook his head at what that seemed to convey. "You might want to rethink that approach."

Liberty felt a stab of guilt. Did she really come across as being that difficult? she couldn't help wondering. She certainly hadn't meant to.

She was about to attempt to make some sort of an apology to Campbell when he suddenly changed the subject on her. She had a feeling he was doing it to spare her again.

"So tell me about this gut feeling you have concerning the case we're working." He asked her, "What's up with that?"

She didn't want to make it seem as if she were making a big deal out of it. Having been the object of ridicule more than once, for more reasons than one, she had become very careful about not setting herself up.

"I could be all wrong," she prefaced, wanting him to be aware that *she* was aware of that.

"That's already been taken into consideration,"

Campbell told her. "But I saw that expression on your face when those wheels in your head started turning, Arizona." That in turn coaxed another memory to the foreground and he laughed. "If I didn't know any better, I'd say that you almost qualify to be an honorary Cavanaugh. I've seen that same look on my brothers' faces, not to mention on the faces of a number of other relatives."

Campbell was staring straight ahead at an almost hypnotic road as he navigated them toward home. He was trying his best to distract himself. "Tell me what you're thinking—without the disclaimers," he warned, aware now of how she tended to work.

She was still a little hesitant to share this outright. "Well, it might be just a coincidence—"

"But?" he asked when her voice stopped. "And remember, I said no disclaimers."

"Right," Liberty nodded as she forged ahead. "Don't you think that it's rather odd that first this computer-expert nephew *doesn't* worry when he can't get in touch with his aunt—the aunt who brought him with her when she moved. And then he files a missing person's report after waiting more than a month after this woman who supposedly raised him and put a roof over his head had disappeared?"

He thought of possible explanations and the most common one came to mind.

"Well, a lot of pseudo-adult kids and their parents, especially substitute parents, don't stay close or even see eye to eye. There could even be a period of es-

trangement before things eventually smooth themselves out."

"Is your family like that?" she asked.

"Actually," he admitted, "I guess you could say
that my family is the exception to the rule. And as
for this MIA nephew, maybe he was just busy and
assumed everything was fine with his aunt. That's
another way to go."

"Maybe." Liberty seemed to almost chew on the
word before it finally emerged.

Campbell spared her another look. The road had
become better lit in this latest section so he didn't feel
he was flirting with a possible accident if he looked
away for a split second.

"But your gut tells you no," he guessed from the
tone of her voice.

Liberty sighed, feeling as if she were opening herself up for possible ridicule. But he did ask. "My gut
has a mind of its own."

Rather than laugh at her, he seemed almost de-
lighted. "Oh, Uncle Brian is going to love you."
Campbell guaranteed.

She'd heard him mention the name before.

"Which one is he again?" she asked.

There were just too many names to remember that
weren't case-related. She had no trouble remembering
all the names of the thirty—now thirty-two—serial
killer victims, but when it came to the large volume
of her temporary partner's family members, she had
to admit it was somewhat confusing.

"He's the Chief of D's," Campbell patiently reminded her.

"Right," Liberty responded, sounding for all the world as if she was humoring him.

"Do you guys wear name tags, you know, when you get together or do you just avoid using any proper names at all to avoid calling someone by the wrong one?" she asked him.

"That generally doesn't happen," he told her. "Newcomers to the family ranks make mistakes at times, but no one minds. We're aware of how overwhelming the ranks might be at first sight." And then he smiled broadly. "And you'll get to find out yourself soon enough."

That put her instantly on the alert. "What do you mean by that?"

"Well, if I know Uncle Andrew, and I do—" he emphasized with a grin "—he's about due to have one of his 'family gatherings' and your being here has provided him with the perfect excuse to throw one—not to mention that it's almost Christmas and that's when he has his biggest blowout. This year Uncle Andrew probably feels that he has double the excuse to have one of those big gatherings."

This didn't sound real to Liberty, especially considering her emotionally impoverished background. It was something she wouldn't have even dreamed about.

"You're kidding, right?" she asked Campbell.

He congratulated himself on maintaining a straight

face as he told her, "Parties are very serious business to Uncle Andrew."

She was having trouble wrapping her head around that. It was hard to believe that these people were actually real. And yet, that same gut that had her attempting to unscramble the clues to finding this serial killer told her that the Cavanaughs were all very real.

The words just slipped out before she could think to censor herself. "I would have given my eyeteeth to have been placed with a family like yours when I was growing up," she said wistfully.

Liberty pressed her lips together as she shut her eyes. *Terrific, you've probably just scared the man.*

And then she heard him say, "Well, it's never too late to rectify things." Campbell sounded almost too serious.

Liberty felt her cheeks redden and blessed the darkness that hid that from Campbell.

She resorted to humor in an attempt to distract the detective from her discomfort over opening herself up to this extent.

"Right," she wisecracked, "your family's going to adopt me."

Rather than laugh at the idea, or say anything flippant that would result in putting the whole thing to bed, Campbell told her, "Why don't we just take this thing one step at a time, Arizona, and see where it winds up going?"

Stunned, she just looked at him for a long moment. "You are the strangest man," she marveled.

"I've been called more flattering things in my time, but I'll accept it," he told Liberty.

Feeling somewhat awkward, she focused on her surroundings and was relieved to see some signs that were beginning to look somewhat familiar to her.

Looks like we're home, Toto, she thought, watching the road. "I think we just crossed into the city limits," she said to Campbell.

He laughed, knowing full well what she was really saying. "And just in time, too, right?"

Liberty didn't attempt to deny it. "You said it, I didn't."

"Just putting your thoughts into words," he told her. Within minutes, he was pulling into the residential area where his garden apartment was located. And then into his carport.

"No," she corrected him, referring to his previous explanation. "You're putting words *into* my mouth and I am very capable of speaking for myself."

Amen to that, Campbell mused silently. "No argument there."

Getting out, Campbell circled around the back of his vehicle and went to open the door on her side. But Liberty had already opened it.

He put his hand out to help guide her, then withdrew it when she gained her feet. This one, he thought, was independent to a fault.

"All right, what shall we argue about now?" Campbell asked her as he led the way to the stairway to his second-floor apartment.

Liberty didn't understand why he would say that. "What makes you think that we're going to argue?" she asked.

To her way of thinking, they had just spent a long, exhausting, but very productive day, and that fact went a very long way to making her happy, not argumentative.

His eyes met hers. "History repeating itself," he answered.

"Well, think again," she told him, waiting for him to open the door.

The key slid out of his hand, falling to the cheerful but slightly dusty doormat that welcomed everyone to a Happy Home.

Campbell made the mistake of bending to retrieve the key at the very same moment that Liberty did the very same thing.

The result was predictable: they bumped heads and stumbled backward.

His hand flying to his forehead, Campbell reached out to grab Liberty's hand with the other in an attempt to steady her. He barely succeeded.

"We couldn't have played that any better than if we were following the actual script for a skit," he said.

Liberty winced as she attempted to right herself as she rose to her feet.

"Except, in a skit," she told him, "I have a feeling that my head wouldn't feel like it just played the part of a cracked egg." Belatedly, she looked at Campbell, concerned. "Does yours hurt?"

"Not so much." He grinned. "But if I was a kid and this happened, this would be the part that I would ask you to kiss the boo-boo."

She blinked, staring at him. "I'm sorry?"

"Nothing to be sorry about," he assured her. "You were just trying to be polite and pick up my keys. What happened was an accident. I absolve you," Campbell told her lightly.

"Still, that doesn't negate the hurt you sustained when we crashed into one another."

He paused to smile at her. "Having you around negates the hurt."

Liberty stared at him, confused. "What is that supposed to even mean?"

"Anything you want it to." With that, he unlocked his front door. Holding the door open, he let her enter first.

When she did, she took exactly three steps and stopped dead.

The apartment had *not* looked like this when they had left this morning. "Um, Cavanaugh, don't look now, but I think someone broke into your place and decorated it." When she turned around to look at him, she was surprised to see that he *wasn't* surprised.

And with good reason.

"That would probably be the work of one of my sisters. Maybe both. Jacqui and Blythe are both off this week and they knew I was busy working on this case with you."

She was doing her best to understand the logic. "So they broke in and decorated?"

He laughed at her question. "Pretty much."

Well, she reasoned, *they probably have the resources for it.* "You were all probably born with silver spoons in your mouths."

"No," he denied, "but with a strong work ethic and an even stronger sense of family. Now this talk is tabled for the night. You need to get to bed."

His unexpected declaration had her heart beginning to hammer.

Hard.

Why did those incredibly simple words sound like an invitation to her?

And why in the world did she desperately want it to be?

Chapter Seventeen

Looking back, what happened in the moments after that almost seemed as if it was just all a blur. Liberty really wasn't sure exactly how any of it transpired, only that, deep down, she was incredibly happy that it had.

Maybe it was even spurred on by the possibility that they were finally getting somewhere with this soul-sucking case that had all but pushed her over the brink.

Or maybe what ultimately transpired just happened because she was tired and, as such, was far from being able to think clearly.

Although, when she reflected on it later, a better explanation was that Campbell's kind, understanding manner had opened something within her that made her capable of *feeling* something beyond a sense of duty for the very first time in her life.

Not to mention the fact that what she was experiencing had somehow taken down the protective barriers she had always *always* kept up around her heart.

For whatever the reason, whatever the cause, all

Liberty really knew was that one moment Campbell was leaving her at the guest room door, telling her to get some well-earned rest, and the very next moment, she was calling out his name.

Campbell turned from the doorway and looked at her.

"Did you want something?"

He asked the question so quietly, Liberty could barely hear him. Quite honestly, she almost *felt* him say the words rather than heard him say them.

She whispered her response in the same tone.

"Yes."

The single word seemed to come on its own accord, propelled by an inner desire that—again—she had been totally unaware of feeling but that had somehow bloomed, full-bodied, within her, taking up every inch of space she had to offer.

What it came down to was a matter of their souls communicating without an actual exchange of words.

The look in her eyes when she raised them to his face was what ultimately pulled Campbell in.

Moreover, it was that very same look within her expressive eyes that had him putting his arms around Liberty and pulling her to him.

Campbell had always been a great believer in the fact that there were times when actions really did speak louder than words. And this, he thought, was obviously that time for him.

His eyes holding hers captive, Campbell leaned forward and let his lips silently do his talking for him.

He kissed her with such force, such emotion, the very act almost completely undid her.

Liberty not only found herself responding to his kiss, but hungering for more. She didn't even remember putting her arms around his neck, they were just suddenly there. It was as much to hold herself steady as to press her body against his.

There were no words to express how much she enjoyed that.

His warmth filled her.

Stirred her.

Made her head feel as if it were spinning almost dangerously out of control.

Liberty's arms tightened around the back of his neck and the pressure of her mouth increased. And as it did, the very act ignited them both.

It was as if this one single action—kissing her with total abandonment—opened the door to all the rest, giving him permission to do what his soul was begging him to do: worship her with his hands, with his mouth, with the fingertips that were lovingly caressing all the tempting, supple curves she had to offer.

Because of how dedicated he had inadvertently become to the career path he had chosen, Campbell was fairly certain the simple happiness that could be found within the life other members of his family had been fortunate enough to all but stumble across would wind up eluding him.

Not for any concrete, hard and fast reason he could actually point to or cite, but because there were only so many hours in the day and his hours were taken up by his work.

And then this woman had all but dropped into his life from out of practically nowhere.

It was almost as if it was fate. This woman with her doe eyes and her utterly overwhelming vulnerability had him suddenly feeling things he had only enviously heard about from other family members.

Like feeling the desire to protect her, to make her happiness one of his main priorities.

This was what it meant to be more than just mildly attracted to a woman, Campbell thought.

He felt his excitement building. He couldn't wait to discover what else this interlude would reveal to him about this woman and this wondrous experience he found himself on the brink of.

The passion was all but exploding within him, but Campbell forced himself to move slowly, like a man working his way across a very thin tightrope stretched across a raging river.

He didn't want to rush this first experience between them, no matter how very urgent his own needs felt.

Most of all, Campbell didn't want to take a chance on frightening Liberty off—just in case she misunderstood his intentions.

In truth, there was nothing holding him back—except a lifetime of common sense and his own family values to serve as a yardstick.

But good intentions or not, restraining himself certainly wasn't easy.

Not when he really wanted to rip away her clothes, and especially not when he felt her hands slipping in under his shirt, loosening the belt buckle on his trousers and then almost seductively tugging the material away from his hips.

He saw the desire and need growing in her eyes, mirroring that same desire and need echoing in his soul, Campbell realized, his breath catching in his throat.

"If I didn't know any better, I'd say you were looking to have your way with me," Campbell breathed, pressing a small network of light kisses along her face and down her neck.

"Then you'd be right," she answered in a voice so very low it all but rippled along his skin to register.

The fact that Campbell's breathing was audible and growing more so had the totally unexpected side benefit of turning Liberty on to an overwhelming degree. The very sound of his breathing caused her heart to hammer so wildly, she was certain it was just about to break through her chest.

And it seemed even more inclined to do so as she felt his hands touching her—slowly—in all the important, very sensitive places.

Touching her.

Possessing her.

Making her permanently and indelibly his as he undressed her.

Liberty would have died before ever letting him suspect this, but she had gone past the point of no return.

If she had been able to think about it, Liberty really couldn't remember the last time she had been intimate with a man—or the last time she had even wanted to be.

But this...this was something else again. Something so intense, it brought her reaction to an entirely new level. She felt as if she were running toward a goal. A goal that involved submerging herself in unending waves of ecstasy as she lay beneath him on the bed.

Rather than finding himself satiated, with every passing moment, every passing warm, hot kiss, Campbell just wanted more.

More of this wondrous sensation.

More of her.

And unless she suddenly decided to abruptly put a stop to things, he intended to continue with this incredible journey until they were both just spent puffs of smoke.

Liberty had turned out to be an endless source of wonder for him and he was dying to find out if this experience would ultimately live up to all his expectations.

Because it certainly felt that way.

When Campbell realized that he couldn't hold out any longer, he slowly and completely anointed her with his mouth and tongue one last time.

And then he slid his primed and ready body up along hers.

One look into her eyes told him that Liberty was more than ready for him. Kissing her deeply and thereby intensifying the union that was to be, he gently entered her.

Holding her, pressing his body against hers, Campbell began to move.

At first he moved slowly, then with mounting intensity, going faster and faster until they were both caught up in this heated carnal marathon, breathlessly racing to the very pinnacle of the mountain and that delicious, final, mind-blowing explosive moment.

When it happened, enveloping and ensnaring them both in an incredibly gratifying euphoria, Campbell and Liberty fell back against the bed. They were desperately trying to catch their breath and to remember exactly where they were within this wild, mazelike new place they had just stumbled across and discovered.

Like victims of a mass hypnosis, their brains felt completely disoriented.

"Are you all right?" Campbell asked the woman lying in the crook of his arm when he finally felt he could speak without having his voice just disappear.

"I'm not sure," Liberty admitted. "What just happened here?"

His smile was soft and just a little stunned. "I think we just might have crossed over to another world, Arizona." His arm tucked around her, he drew Liberty a shade closer to his side. "You are really a revelation, you know. I had a feeling that you had a more smoldering side beneath all that civilized calm, but *this* was way beyond anything I could have possibly imagined."

"Good imagined?" she asked almost shyly even though she was desperately attempting to project an air of nonchalance.

"'Good' doesn't even begin to describe it," Campbell told her honestly. "As a matter of fact, I don't think a word has been invented to begin to describe the magnitude of what just occurred here in this small, heretofore peaceful bedroom."

"Peaceful, right." She laughed at his description. "Like before this evening, you were living the life of a monk."

"Not a monk exactly," Campbell allowed, pressing a kiss to her forehead. "But definitely not at that escalated level I found myself visiting with you just minutes earlier," he told her.

Before she could stop, she heard herself telling him, "I really wish I could believe you."

He crooked his finger beneath her chin and brought her head up so that she could meet his eyes.

"You can," he told her in all seriousness.

Damn it, but she found herself believing him. She knew that would be a mistake of the first order. But she believed him because she really *wanted* to believe him.

That would be a super mistake, Liberty reminded

herself. One she was too smart to allow herself to make. For one thing, it would negate all the residual, wonderful benefits of what had just gone down between them.

This was not about laying the groundwork for the future, this was just an exquisite interlude she had had the very excellent good fortune to have experienced.

That should be enough.

Liberty tried to deflect the effect his words had on her. But it wasn't easy.

"I guess that's what makes you such a good detective," she told him. "You have this way about you that gets people to believe what you're telling them. It's a rare gift."

He surprised her by not arguing the point but by agreeing with her. "It is." He nodded, slowly stroking her skin in small, sensual circles. "And I do have it. But you're not 'people,'" he told her.

She didn't understand where he was going with this. "I'm not?"

"You're not. You, Arizona, are in a category all by yourself," he told her.

She sighed, flattered in her own way although not yet ready to be taken in by what he was saying. She was also too tired to argue with him about this, so she let it stand.

"Okay, I give up," Liberty told him. "Have it your way."

His eyes shone. "Thanks. With your permission, I fully intend to."

Liberty could have sworn that she was officially being put on notice, but then, she thought, that wasn't really such a bad thing, was it?

She shifted her body into his. "I guess, then, we had better get started before it gets to be 'tomorrow,'" she told him.

He was already nibbling on her lips. "That...is...an...excel...lent...idea."

Before she could lace her arms around his neck and curl up against the man who had woken all these new and deliciously tantalizing feelings within her body, the cell phone Campbell had in the pocket of his trousers began to ring.

"Leave it. It's probably a nuisance call," she guessed. But even as she said it, she knew neither one of them would be able to just ignore it. Not picking up wasn't acceptable.

"Probably," he agreed, reaching for the cell, which was now a resident of the bedroom floor. "But just in case, we did hand out both our numbers today. Maybe someone remembered something."

"Or wants to sell us on a new medical breakthrough," Liberty said, which was more likely the case.

Finding the phone, he got back into bed as he pressed in his password. "*You* are enough of a medical breakthrough for me," Campbell assured her. "Cavanaugh here," he said into his cell.

It took listening to the person on the other end say several words before Campbell realized that the chief from up north was calling him. The name coming in on his screen had gotten somehow garbled.

"Well, it took him half the night, but he did it," the chief almost crowed. "Abe found the information on that dead woman's nephew."

Liberty watched the detective suddenly sit up very straight, as if good posture made the news all the more important. "We'll be right up there," Campbell promised.

"I'll be waiting for you at the police station," she could hear the chief's voice promise.

Liberty was already throwing off the sheets on her side of the bed.

Chapter Eighteen

Campbell quickly hurried into the clothes that had been discarded on the floor earlier when he and Liberty had made love.

"That was the chief," he told Liberty.

"I gathered that much," she answered as she hustled into her own clothing.

Apparently the pullover top she had worn earlier had somehow managed to find its way into a knot. Muttering under her breath, she did her best to undo it so she could just pull it on.

As he finished getting dressed, Campbell continued to talk and fill her in. "That officer working for him managed to find that woman's nephew."

She wondered how sleepy Campbell thought she was that she would have missed that. "Yes, I gathered that, too," she told him as she zipped up her jeans.

Her shoes had somehow found their way across the room, although she couldn't remember kicking them off. Liberty grabbed them up and made her way back to the bed to slip the shoes on.

Finished, Campbell turned to look at her. He was

surprised to find that Liberty was already dressed as well.

"Look, I can take it from here," he told her. The statement managed to surprise her. "You don't have to come if you're exhausted."

Liberty blinked. She couldn't have been more stunned than if Campbell had just declared that he really thought that the world was flat.

"Hold on. Back up," she ordered, raising her hand like a traffic cop. "I'm not any more exhausted than you are—and besides, we're going to be driving there. I'm not going to be flapping my wings and flying there," she pointed out. "So unless there's another reason you don't want me coming along—and it had better be a damn good one—I'm coming."

Campbell raised his hands high in exaggerated surrender. He should have known she would react that way. "I'm just trying to be thoughtful, Arizona," he told her.

She allowed herself brief contact and brushed her hand against his cheek. "You took care of that little detail earlier," she said very seriously. "Okay, let's go," she declared, heading for the door.

Following her, Campbell felt obligated to tell her, "You know, you do look like an unmade bed." He punctuated his statement with a laugh.

"Maybe," she allowed. "But I *am* ready."

Within minutes, they were back in Campbell's vehicle and on the road heading toward the town they had left behind them less than four hours ago.

A lifetime ago, Liberty couldn't help thinking, given what had happened between them since they had left Gainesville.

"When he called, did the chief say anything else about this nephew?" she asked.

"Only that there might have been a slight glitch in the file," Campbell told her, choosing his words very carefully.

"What sort of a glitch?" she asked suspiciously, attempting to brace herself for who knew what.

"Turns out the nephew isn't a traveling IT guy after all," Campbell told her.

That managed to catch her by surprise. "Then what is he?"

Campbell slanted a glance in her direction, confident that this would undoubtedly knock her for a loop. "Well, according to what was just uncovered, the nephew just might be an FBI informant."

She blinked, certain that she had misheard him or her brain was playing tricks on her, stealing her ability to concentrate. Maybe Campbell was right. Maybe she was too tired to come along on this trip.

Still she asked, "Say what?"

"An FBI informant," Campbell repeated, enunciating the words very slowly.

Liberty felt her jaw drop. She was about to tell him that was someone's idea of a macabre joke, or an absurd fabrication, when the direct opposite hit her and she considered the idea.

"You know, that just might make sense," she said.

Her face became animated as she straightened. She could see that he was about to discount the theory. She started talking quickly. "Think about it. He's tracking nurses, professional women. He has to come across as someone in their league. Working with the FBI puts him in that rarefied capacity. *And* if he just happened to have enough computer tech savvy to be able to hack into those dating sites, maybe he's looking for a certain type, which would require him unearthing some pertinent background information." She was all but tripping over her own tongue to get this all out. "Well, he's got that covered, too."

Liberty glanced at the speedometer on the dashboard. "Can you drive this thing any faster?"

"Not safely," Campbell pointed out. Because the road they were on was empty, they were already exceeding the allowable speed limit. To go any faster would really be pushing it. "Besides, what's the hurry? It's not like we're going to catch this guy leisurely sauntering through town."

"I know that," she answered impatiently, "but once we have his file and the additional information, we'll be one step closer to bringing this guy down."

Campbell made no comment but he grinned broadly in her direction.

"What's so funny?" she asked. It was dark, but she could detect his smile by the curve of his cheek. He had a nice smile, but she didn't want it being at her expense.

"There really *is* an optimist inside you," Campbell happily declared.

"You ought to know," she told him, thinking of the wonderful interlude they had just spent together. "You put her there."

That brought an even heartier laugh from him. "You can thank me for that once we're back in bed again."

She thought of everything that stretched ahead of them before they could get back. "That might not happen for a long time."

"Maybe not," he agreed, nodding. "But it is something for us to hold on to."

Lord help her, but he did make her feel special. Or at the very least, Liberty thought, that they had some sort of a small future ahead. Nothing major—she wasn't expecting to be lucky enough for what had happened between them to turn into a permanent thing. But from the sound of things, it might survive the weekend—and maybe a tiny bit beyond that point.

Don't do it, Lib. Don't count those chickens before the hen even gets to lay those eggs. Remember the Merriweathers, she cautioned herself.

The Merriweathers had been the closest thing to a perfect family she had encountered in her young life, and they had seemed interested in taking her in. The key word here being *seemed.* In the end, they had gone with a blond-haired, blue-eyed girl named Mandy who looked as if she had been created expressly with the Merriweathers in mind. It was almost as if she'd been literally *designed* to fit into their Christmas photographs.

And Liberty...well, she had been too skinny, her hair too straggly looking.

At that point, Liberty had completely given up any and all hope of finding a family to belong to and just decided to go her own way—until Florence had unexpectedly come into her life.

The thought of Florence had Liberty freshly resolving to find this so-called nephew—or whatever he was—and pump him to within an inch of his life. If the creep turned out to be the serial killer, she'd know it, she promised herself. And if he turned out *not* to be the killer, she was certain that she would know that, too.

Campbell glanced at her. Liberty had become far quieter than he was accustomed to her being.

"Everything okay?" he asked.

"No, but I have every faith that it's going to be," Liberty told him with what seemed like unshakable conviction.

He knew that she had nothing else to base it on except for a feeling. But, hell, he was a Cavanaugh, so that "gut" feeling was definitely good enough for him.

DAWN WAS BEGINNING to just stir the brilliant colors on the horizon when they finally pulled into town.

There was no sign of traffic—or life, for that matter—in the streets. Gainesville was one of those towns that made her think of the phrase "rolled up the sidewalks at night." This town certainly had rolled up theirs, but now, here and there, there were signs of people waking up.

"There's a light in the police station," she pointed out eagerly.

"I see it," he answered, dispensing with the urge to comment that at least they didn't do their work in the dark.

"Sorry," she apologized, knowing she was allowing her enthusiasm to get the best of her. "I didn't mean to suggest that you didn't."

"That's okay, I forgive you," he told her with a wink. "Let's go see what the chief has to show us."

Campbell was aware that Chief Jenkins could have forwarded the information he had acquired, but knew it would be better received if Liberty could actually hold the file in her hands. That way, she would also be able to ask the chief any pertinent questions.

Getting out of the vehicle, they walked into the station.

They found the chief in, but he had his arms crossed in front of him on his desk and was resting his head on the semicircle they had formed. The man had obviously spent the night in the office combing through all the information they had asked for.

"Nice to know that there are dedicated men even out here in the sticks," Campbell said to Liberty in a hushed voice.

"Hey, watch it with that 'sticks' comment. As for me, I wouldn't expect anything else from the law officers working in a small town," Liberty told him in all seriousness.

She abruptly stopped speaking as she saw the chief stirring. The man emitted a little moan as he moved his stiff shoulders.

"I can hear you, you know. I wasn't sleeping," the chief told her. "I was just resting my eyes."

Campbell was not about to argue with the man. "As well you should be, given that you've been working around the clock to help us find that woman's nephew, not to mention getting us that much closer to the serial killer we're looking to bring down."

The chief flashed him a smile, knowing full well that the detective was padding the scenario. "You've got a good way of putting things," he told Campbell. "You ever get tired of working in Aurora, I can always find a place for you here."

Rather than politely turn him down, or tell the chief about the huge network of family members working in the city he was from, Campbell politely thanked the chief for his offer. "Thanks. I'll be sure to keep that in mind." Out of the corner of his eye, he could see that Liberty was all but biting her tongue not to interrupt and ask a whole barrage of questions.

"So," he began, doing his best to keep this all as low-key as possible, "just what did your police officer find?"

"Well, from all indications, this nephew is either a very busy, very clever guy who works with computers as well as that secret life that's been hinted at in the records—or the man really knows how to lie—big-time." The chief looked at the two people in his office. "The final verdict is up in the air. Anyone want to hazard a guess?" the chief asked.

"Maybe it's a little bit of both. Or he's exaggerating so much just to put us off," Liberty told the two men.

"Come again?" Campbell asked.

"Think about it. He laid it on so thickly in this file because it's true, but he was trying to throw off whoever was reading the file by making it sound as if it couldn't possibly be true, that he couldn't be ac-complishing as much as he claimed he did, juggling two lives. And thereby making that so-called double life of his that much easier to lead.

"You know, it's more of a case of 'now you see him, now you don't.' Except in this case, you don't know exactly who it is you're seeing," she concluded, looking from one man to the other to see if they agreed with her.

The two men looked a little puzzled for a moment, and then Campbell nodded at her. "You know, in a strange, lopsided way of thinking, that actually makes some sort if sense."

"Of course it does," Liberty answered. It was ac-tually very simple. There was one main thought at the root of all this.

"Serial killers think they're smarter than everyone else, and that, sooner or later, leads to their down-fall. We just have to hope that it's sooner than later. Now is this his real name, or is he using an alias?"

She wanted to know, pointing to a line in the folder. "Better yet, give me any names that you have on file for this guy."

She turned hopefully toward Campbell. "Can Valri do a deep dive into all the available records to see just how much information there is available on this so-called 'broken up' nephew who keeps pulling these disappearing acts?"

"Valri?" the chief questioned, looking from Liberty to the detective with her.

Liberty had gotten so caught up in the file, she had almost forgotten that the chief was there. "Valri Cavanaugh is one of his cousins," she explained, nodding at Campbell.

"Valri is a total computer wizard. If it can be found on the internet, or even somewhere on the dark web, Valri is the one who can find it."

"Can she now?" the chief asked, impressed. "She sounds like a really good person to know, especially since our own officer, Abe, doubles as a computer tech, but his computer skills leave something to be desired," the chief told them.

Liberty felt a little guilty, flaunting Valri's abilities in front of the chief. "I have to tell you that she's pretty pressed for time from morning to night. Most of the time, she gets things done but only by working an inordinate amount of hours," she said, quoting what Campbell had told her. "The poor woman hardly has a private life outside the office."

"Well, other than this guy—" the chief nodded at

the file on the desk "—we don't really have anything that would even begin to interest your computer wizard. No need to worry," he assured them. "I won't be calling her. Here." He pushed the file toward them. "Take the file with you. I already had Abe make a copy for our office. Hold on to this as long as you need. If it actually winds up helping you catch the guy and he turns out to be the serial killer, then more power to you. Just be sure to let me know."

"Count on it," Campbell and Liberty said almost in unison.

Chapter Nineteen

It was back.

That same feeling was back.

He could feel it slowly taking over, moving through his body like an all-consuming snake, chewing away at him until there was nothing left but that feeling.

Demanding to be fed.

After the last time, he had honestly thought that he was done with it. That he had reached the very apex of this all-but-draining need to make Sarah pay for what she had done to him. That he had finally conquered her.

But he had been wrong.

That overwhelming need was back. Back and filling up spaces inside him at an incredible, breathtaking speed.

He knew what he had to do.

And soon.

"WHERE DID YOU get all this information?" Valri asked, skimming through the various notes in the file Liberty and Campbell had brought in for her to look over and review.

"It seems that Benjamin Wallace—our alleged serial killer's real name—had a juvenile record that had somehow slipped his attention. Lucky for us, it managed to fall through the cracks. It never even crossed his mind when he was busy creating his alter ego," Campbell told his cousin.

It was, he thought, like stumbling across a gold mine.

Valri continued searching through all the data. There was a lot to work with.

"Alter ego," she repeated. "You make him sound like a superhero."

"Well, we know that he's far from that," Campbell guaranteed. "If even half the things attributed to him are true, the guy's the devil incarnate," her cousin told her. He indicated the file. "We've brought you all the extraneous information we were able to gather up from that police chief's office. There's even a set of fingerprints on file, not to mention a rather decent mug shot of the guy when they arrested him for some teenage infraction."

It seemed to Valri they had everything they needed to build their case. "And just what is it that you would like from me?" she asked the two detectives.

"Well, in short, can you put all the pieces together and track down this guy's current whereabouts? He seems to be missing," Liberty told the computer tech.

"You mean you want me to close my eyes, wave

my hand and presto chango, tell you that he's hiding in the library?" Valri asked whimsically, sarcastic humor curving her mouth.

Campbell saw that his cousin was having fun at their expense, and this was way too important for that. "Something a little more sophisticated than that, Val," Campbell told his cousin.

Liberty broke it down to its simplest components. "What we're really trying to find out is if his likeness appears on any of the current dating sites."

"Dating sites," Valri repeated. It felt as if they had come full circle in their pursuit of this killer. "Do you have *any* idea how many of those things there are out there?" Valri asked them.

"Probably tons," Liberty guessed. If that wasn't the case, they wouldn't have come to Valri in the first place, but she refrained from pointing that out. "Maybe you could narrow it down to ones that focus on strictly professionals. He is preying on nurses, so he needs to focus on an array that would give him his choice. Plus, he likes showing off how smart he is and how exciting a life he leads, working for the FBI—or at least telling these women that's what he does," Liberty qualified. Finished for now, she held her breath then looked at Valri hopefully. "Does that give you anything to work with?"

"As a matter of fact, it does," the other woman replied. It gave her a lot of possibilities to work with. "But, despite anything Cam here—" she nodded toward her cousin "—might have told you, I do not arrive at answers faster than the speed of light. Pin-pointing this guy's location is going to take time—if it's even possible," she reminded Liberty. She wanted the woman to be aware of all the drawbacks.

Liberty tried not to look disappointed. Time was the one luxury they didn't have. By all indications, the serial killer had escalated his agenda in the last couple of weeks. Where once he had killed a victim every month or so, in the last two weeks he had killed three women. Whatever was causing him to kill these women, the urge had suddenly, somehow increased, and he was apparently switching tracks.

Campbell squeezed his cousin's shoulder to silently encourage her. He had long ago made peace with the fact that theirs was a touchy-feely kind of family who actually benefited from that silent contact.

"Do what you can," he told Valri.

"I always do," his cousin replied. She looked at Liberty rather than at Campbell when she promised, "And I'll notify you the second I find something for you to go on. In the meantime, try to focus on something else. Better yet, unwind."

Right, Liberty thought. Like that had even a re-mote chance of happening right now. But in any event, both she and Campbell thanked Valri for her time and for any help that she could give them in their investigation, and then they left.

"I don't know about you," Liberty said to Campbell as they once more headed down the hallway toward the elevator, "but I'm going to start poring through the various dating sites, starting with the one that Cynthia Ellery was on."

"What makes you think you'll find Wallace under his name?" Campbell asked her.

"I probably won't," she told him, "so I'm just going to go through all the photos of dark-haired, good-looking men presenting themselves as law enforcement agents. Or men claiming to work for the CIA, DEA, or any one of those alphabet agencies."

Campbell looked at her when they reached the elevator. "You think he's good-looking?"

"That's the only thing that he's got going for him. Not good-looking like present company, of course," she told Campbell with a teasing grin as they got on the elevator, "but the man definitely isn't going to stop any clocks—unless, of course, you're basing that on what his soul is capable of."

Campbell inclined his head, giving her the point. "Nice save."

"It's the truth," Liberty replied simply. They were on their way up to the homicide department. "Do you know if there's a free computer in your squad room or conference area?" She was dying to get started in her search of the dating service.

"Yeah, Ed Raffinelli's on medical leave for a week," Campbell recalled, "so his desk is free."

"Sorry to hear that," she said then realized she needed to clarify what she meant. "That he needed to go on medical leave, but not that there's an empty desk for me to use."

Campbell nodded. "His desk's one row away from mine—in case you need anything."

Liberty merely smiled at the information. "I think I'll be able to find you without having to resort to a tracking dog," she told him. And then she grew serious. "Your superior won't mind having me in his office like this?"

Campbell shook his head. "What the lieutenant cares about, first and foremost, is having this case solved and closed. If you can help in any way with that, then you're golden."

"I THINK I'M going blind," was Liberty's response several hours later when Campbell asked her how she was doing. "I had no idea that there were so many people out there looking to have someone in their lives. It's kind of sad, really," she told him. Of course, she had never been in a position to need someone to complete her—until she had encountered Campbell, she realized. Now she totally understood where those other women were coming from.

"Any luck finding our killer?" Campbell asked.

She looked at the profiles she had printed up. "A few possible candidates, but nothing for sure," she said. "The photos they've posted aren't the best. That is, they are, but they don't look as if they're current."

She looked worn out, he thought. He definitely knew what that was like. "I just finished that report I'd said I would turn in. Since that's out of the way, why don't I join you in going through that dating site you have open, and whatever other site you can think of." Saying that, he thought of something else. "Tell you what, why don't I ask Choi to join us as well. We should be able to pull up a few possible likely suspects between us. Fresh eyes might help."

"Anything you can do to keep me from going cross-eyed will be greatly appreciated," she told him with feeling.

"Can't have you walking into walls now, Arizona. What sort of host would that make me?" he asked with a straight face.

"One who wants to keep his own eyesight," she answered. "The really funny part is that finding this man's so-called 'bio' amid all these various entries is supposedly the easy part. Catching him before he kills again is going to be the really tricky part," she concluded.

"If this guy actually does turn out to be the serial killer," Choi pointed out, joining them when Campbell waved him over. "When you come right down to it, we still haven't pinned that part down yet."

She was well aware of that. She was also very aware of this gut feeling that hadn't abated since they'd found the last buried body. "I'm willing to bet that he's the one."

"And you know this how?" Choi asked, curious if he had missed something.

"Just a gut feeling," she answered, meeting his eyes head-on. She wasn't embarrassed by her convictions. Somehow, it didn't feel as "out there" as it once might have, especially when Choi didn't just laugh at her reasoning.

Instead, the detective looked at his partner and grinned. "Hey, Cam, she's perfect for you. She's got the same kind of sideways thinking as you do," the detective laughed.

Instead of getting annoyed, Campbell merely brushed off his partner's comment by saying, "Haven't you heard great minds think alike?"

"Know what I think? I think you've been dipping into the spiked eggnog a little too much," his partner commented.

"Okay," Liberty declared, "back to work."

LESS THAN TWENTY-FOUR hours later, thanks to a really concentrated effort on all three of the detectives' parts, they managed to find four different dating websites that boasted photos as well as profiles of four different men. All of whom bore a very striking resemblance to the man the Gainesville police chief's version of a computer tech had tracked down for them.

As expected, each of the men had different names but only slightly different descriptions, backgrounds and careers. But the one thing that remained the same was that each man expressed an interest in finding a woman involved in the medical field. The dating profiles never specified a nurse, but it wasn't all that hard to realize that was what these four different men were all looking for: a woman who was a nurse.

"Okay," Liberty announced, leaning back and studying all four men—whose photos in her mind were all just slightly different retouches of one and the same guy. "Now I need to come up with a profile that 'Jason Anderson,' 'Jimmy Allen,' 'Jordan Arroyo' and 'Jerry Abernathy' would all be attracted to," she said, wondering if there was any significance in the fact that all the men's initials were J.A.

"I think, with a little bit of makeup wizardry as well as appropriating a new hairstyle, I can get myself to resemble the last couple of victims," she said, more to herself than to either one of the men in the room.

"Okay," Campbell said, not wanting to oppose her, although everything within him was against any of this happening. "I realize you have to bait this trap, but you're not really thinking of turning up on these so-called dates are you?" he asked Liberty.

She looked at him in surprise. Was he kidding? "Well, of course I am. How else are we going to be able to get this guy?"

"By having someone else pretend to be a nurse on the dating site," Campbell said.

That was when it really hit her. Campbell was trying to prevent her from getting the goods on her foster mother's killer. This was the only straightforward way she knew how to accomplish that. "Are we going to have a problem, Cavanaugh?"

"No, no problem, Arizona," he told her, setting his jaw. "Not as long as you listen to me."

Liberty tried another approach, looking at it from his viewpoint. "Look, Campbell, I appreciate your concern, I really do, but nobody—and I mean *nobody*—is closer to this than I am or can do a better job getting the goods on this guy than I can. I have been living and breathing this case for a while now—and it's been eating away at my gut from the moment Florence became a casualty. I *have* to do this," she insisted.

"Why? Because no one else can do it the way you can?" Campbell asked with an underlying mocking tone in his voice.

Liberty raised her chin, looked him unblinkingly straight in the eye and never hesitated in her answer. "Yes."

Choi spoke up then, doing his best to break the tension and lighten the moment. "Look, man, we're all going to be out there, watching her back. This guy's not going to get a chance to hurt so much as a single hair on her head."

Cavanaugh scowled at the imagery. "It's not her hair I'm worried about."

To Liberty's recollection, no one had ever worried about her before. Oh, once she had entrenched herself within the law enforcement structure in Calhoun, she did feel that she wasn't just out there alone as she did her job, but she had never felt like she was being looked after, like someone with a guardian angel looking over her shoulder. She smiled at Campbell and nodded.

"Duly noted and appreciated," Liberty told him and then, with all the conviction she could muster, said, "Okay, gentlemen, now let's see if we can get this SOB so that he never, *ever* hurts a hair on anyone else's head ever again."

She said the words with such feeling that as worried as he was that she was risking her life, Campbell couldn't find it in his heart to try to talk her out of it.

What he did do was resolve to keep her safe at all costs. It was the only way he could see out of this complicated situation.

"Write up your profile and Choi and I will look it over before you post it."

She had thought about going a more direct route. "I just thought I might contact him on the website," she told Campbell. More than anything, she wanted to get this over with as quickly as possible.

"No," Campbell said, vetoing the idea. "Only as a last resort. Otherwise, you might wind up spooking him. He's lasted this long because he's got some pretty keen survival instincts."

"He's right, you know," Choi told her, backing his partner up.

"Yes, I know," Liberty said grudgingly. "That doesn't make it any easier to go along with."

"We could always get someone else to play the part of the nurse," Campbell told her.

She gave the detectives less than a sunny look. "I'm writing it, I'm writing it," she informed them, her fingers flying over the computer keys as she composed her profile.

Campbell only wished that he could feel triumphant over this newest development—but he didn't.

Chapter Twenty

How did people do it?

Liberty couldn't help wondering that as she shifted in her seat at the restaurant. This was her fourth so-called "date" garnered from almost as many websites in four days.

She was doing it because she was on a mission. But if it wasn't because she was trying to zero in on this sick, cold-blooded killer and bring him down—if she were in this strictly to find someone to share at least part of her life with—she would have definitely felt ready to throw in the towel and call it quits.

Permanently.

How could regular people possibly put themselves through this grueling process? Even playing the part, Liberty was damn tired of putting herself out there, doing her best to look eager and interested every time the door to the trendy restaurant opened and a new customer walked inside.

She had never considered herself an outgoing person, but for the purposes of making this look genuine and, more importantly, to make it work, Liberty had

had to transform herself. That meant she had made herself seem like the last word in eagerness when it came to meeting this potential new "candidate" for her attention and, supposedly, her affection.

The truth was, she wouldn't have been caught dead going through all these contortions just to have someone in her life. She had always felt that if it was going to happen, it would happen.

This isn't for you. This is for Florence. Not to mention all those poor women who lost their lives because they had gone looking for love in, as it turns out, all the wrong places.

She blew out a breath, feeling exceptionally uncomfortable as well as impatient.

Scanning the semi-filled establishment, she could see Campbell appearing to share a dinner with a young woman he had earlier introduced to her as his sister, Jacqui. They were talking about something and he looked incredibly serious.

His partner, Choi, was sitting at another table with a female detective who had been recruited for this at the last minute. His previous "date" from the other night had had a family emergency to deal with. There was also another pair of detectives posing as a couple at another nearby table.

These were her reinforcements, Liberty thought. She knew she should feel comforted by their presence.

But when the restaurant door opened and her so-called newest "date" walked in, Liberty felt as if she was very much on her own. Taking a deep breath, she forced a smile to her lips as she watched her date— this time he had called himself Joseph Abbott—scan the immediate area, looking for her.

She knew the moment the man saw her. He smiled broadly.

Depending on her point of view regarding the situation, Liberty had a good feeling/bad feeling about this.

It was him.

She didn't know why she was so certain, but she was. Maybe it was the way he smiled when he saw her. Or the fact that his eyes, even as they took in every inch of her, seemed flat as they washed over her. Flat enough to send a chill down her spine as he made his way toward her.

"Barbara Ellen?" he asked in a deep, baritone voice when he reached her table.

Liberty nodded, responding to the alias she had used on the profile. "Joseph Abbott?" Liberty asked, trying her best to sound pleased to meet him. The man was even better looking in person than she had initially thought he was when she had looked at the photo in his profile. He resembled the others she had gone through on the various dating sites—and yet there was something different about him.

"Guilty as charged," he told her, flashing a bright smile as he slid into the booth and took the seat opposite her. "Am I late?" he questioned, referring to the fact that she had apparently been there for a while.

"No, I'm early," she told him. "I came straight from the hospital because I was afraid I was going to be late. I'm afraid I didn't have time to change." She glanced down at her nurse's uniform. "I hope you don't mind."

"Mind?" he echoed incredulously. "No. As a matter of fact, I have a confession to make." He leaned in a little, as if actually sharing a secret with her. "I've always had a weakness for a woman in a nurse's uniform."

Something in Liberty's stomach tightened just then. She really hoped that nothing in her expression gave her away and tipped him off.

"First time I've ever heard that," Liberty told the man sitting across from her. She found it difficult to contain herself.

The smile on his lips unnerved her. And then he opened his menu. "Have you ordered anything yet?" he asked her.

"No, I thought it would be better if I waited for you," she replied.

"To see if I'd show up?" her "date" asked her knowingly.

So, he was going to play this with a bit of honesty, was he? That freed her up to do the same, she decided. "Well, frankly, yes," she answered.

He almost sounded interested as to her reasons. "Been burned on this route before?"

She weighed her options then admitted, "Once or twice."

"Well," he said magnanimously, "you can put that all behind you." When he spoke, he made it seem as if she was the only one in the room. "If this goes as well as I think it will, you won't have to endure going on those dreaded 'first dates' anymore."

Her eyes met his. She tempered her response with just enough caution. "That sounds promising."

The smiled that claimed every corner of Joseph's mouth seemed almost genuine—until she looked into his flat eyes again. They seemed almost positively reptilian.

"You have no idea," Joseph assured her with just the proper amount of enthusiasm. He nodded toward the menu lying next to her. "Order anything you want. The sky's the limit," he told her loftily, adding, "I want you to look back on this night and feel that *this* was the beginning of the very best part of your life."

Rather than appear to get carried away, she said, "That sounds promising, but I try to keep my expectations low."

"Bad experiences?" Joseph asked with what almost sounded like genuine concern in his voice.

But again, his eyes gave him away, she thought. A concerned person just wouldn't look like that, she told herself.

Still, she murmured, "Something like that," in response to his question.

"Well, I'll do my best to wipe that all away for you," he promised. "Would you like a drink?" Joseph asked as he saw their server approach their table with a basket of warm bread.

"No, thank you. I like keeping a clear head," she said, turning down his offer.

He didn't seem bothered by her refusal. Instead, he nodded. "Very smart of you," he told her then smiled. "I find levelheaded women a definite turn-on."

She knew that the comment was calculated to put her at ease and make her smile. Even so, Liberty could feel herself growing progressively tense.

"I guess that gives us something in common," Liberty acknowledged.

"Good," Joseph declared. "Now let's see what else we have in common," he proposed. Then, out of what seemed like left field, he asked, "What made you want to become a nurse?"

All she had to do was channel Florence and she had her answers, Liberty thought. "I guess I always liked helping people."

"Noble," he commented, nodding his head in approval. The smile on his lips said otherwise.

Heaven help her, it made her skin crawl.

"Not everyone feels that way."

Something in his tone alerted her. "Why, did you have a bad experience with a nurse?"

For a split second, she saw his face darken when she asked that.

She had hit a nerve, Liberty thought, hoping that the others listening in on this exchange had taken note of the way he had paused. She fought the temptation to look in Campbell's direction, but she knew better than to give in to that.

And then Joseph resolved that dilemma for her by saying, "Let's talk about something more pleasant."

He flashed her a bright smile that from where she was sitting seemed to her to be just the tiniest bit stilted and forced.

"I'm certainly all for that," Liberty told the man she was now certain was Benjamin Wallace. "Life's too short to waste with unpleasantries."

FOR THE NEXT forty-five minutes, Liberty found herself caught up in an exchange of some rather aimless banter. Along with the somewhat mind-numbing conversation, she found herself consuming some far tastier offering of lobster bisque.

When the dinner was finished, Liberty's date suggested, "Why don't we go somewhere to top this off?" he said. "I know somewhere that serves great espresso and makes their own out-of-this-world cheesecake. Are you interested?"

Not in the slightest, she answered him silently. But there was no way to prove she was right about this man just going on her gut feeling. No matter how strong it felt to her, she knew she was going to need more than that.

"Sure," she said gamely. "Where did you have in mind?" She hoped the others listening in on her wire were picking this up.

"This little hole-in-the-wall I know of on the outskirts of town. I just stumbled across it," he told her proudly. "My job working with the FBI takes me to all sorts of out-of-the-way places," he told her, raising his hand to get the server's attention. He wanted to pay the bill and get going.

A sense of urgency was pushing him.

"That really sounds fascinating," she all but gushed. The words almost caused her to choke.

She could see that Joseph really absorbed her enthusiasm. "You have no idea," he told her almost smugly.

"WHAT'S SHE DOING?" Campbell asked his sister, immediately going on the alert. From where he sat, the man sitting across from Liberty was looking at her like a cat eying a mouse he had picked out for dinner.

"Her job, Cam," Jacqui told him pointedly. "Like it or not, her job."

Campbell frowned, never taking his eyes off the man they suspected of being the serial killer. He didn't like any of this. "We didn't review this part," he all but growled at his sister.

"Maybe she thought it was time to up the stakes a little. Face it, Cam, right now all we have is that the guy bought her dinner. From where we're sitting, that's not exactly an actionable offense," she pointed out. "You can't arrest him for that."

Campbell shot her a look. "Don't talk to me like I'm an idiot."

"Then don't act like one," Jacqui said with a wide smile.

Campbell was on the alert again. "They're leaving," he needlessly told his sister.

She could guess what was going through his head and she felt for him. That didn't change the situation. "She's wired, big brother. We're not going to lose her," she assured him.

He wasn't convinced of that. "I like covering my bets," Campbell told her. "And that *never* involves being too confident," he said with feeling.

"There're six of us," Jacqui calmly reminded her older brother, "not counting Liberty, who struck me as being very competent the one time I met her."

He didn't care what his sister felt, he wasn't about to take any chances. "You know that old saying that anything that can go wrong will go wrong?" he asked Jacqui.

On his feet, Campbell left a twenty and a five on the table to cover their two coffees and desserts, and a little more. He was not about to waste any time waiting for the server to write up their bill.

Making eye contact with Choi, Campbell nodded. His partner and date and the other couple all followed Campbell and his sister out of the restaurant, then circled around to the rear parking lot.

When they got there, they saw that Liberty's car was still parked where she had left it near the rear exit. Liberty, however, even though she had just walked out with her date, was nowhere in sight.

Neither was her date.

Campbell stood there, scanning the area from one

end to the other, searching for some sign of either one of them.

There wasn't any.

"Where the hell is she?" Campbell demanded angrily, his nerves getting the better of him. He could feel his heart all but seizing up in his chest.

Liberty wasn't anywhere around, he thought, his breaths growing shorter and more pronounced with each second that went by.

They looked all around the immediate area. It was Choi who zeroed in on it.

"Cavanaugh, look," he said, calling attention to the object on the ground next to her vehicle's rear right tire.

Campbell was instantly on his knees, picking it up. "It's her phone," he said numbly. Liberty never went anywhere without her phone. He had thought more than once that she was all but glued to it.

This was definitely not good.

"Now what?" Choi asked.

Campbell had always felt that he was equal to any emergency that came up, any unforeseen development, but he had never been personally involved the way he found himself being now.

It was as if his brain had just stopped functioning and he couldn't think.

"I don't know," Campbell answered, his mind going in a hundred different directions at once, searching for a solution and trying to think of what he could do to prevent an irreversible disaster from happening. "Give me a minute to think."

"Well, while you're thinking, I'm calling Valri," Jacqui declared, taking out her cell phone.

THE THROBBING IN Liberty's brain was slowly beginning to subside.

Blinking in the darkness, she tried to make out her surroundings. The lack of any fresh air and the crammed position her body was in told her that somehow, her date must have shoved her into a trunk.

But not *her* trunk.

Attempting to clear her aching head, Liberty tried to piece things together. She recalled walking with Joseph to his car. He had told her that he'd wanted her to see it so that she could more easily follow him to the restaurant he had told her about. The one with the so-called world's best espresso.

Liberty remembered noticing that one of his rear tires had looked just a little flat. He couldn't see it and had said as much, so she'd pointed to it, although she didn't get all that close to it. Even so, Joseph had somehow used the time to pop open his trunk and, rather than take out his spare tire, he'd shoved her inside instead.

It had all happened so fast, she hadn't had time to fight back. Mainly because, before she'd known what he was doing, he had hit the back of her head, knocking her out and, she now assumed, pushed her into the trunk.

Everything had gone black by then. For how long, she had no idea, but she had a feeling that it couldn't have been all that long.

It was hard for her to focus.

Not because of the dark, but because of the throbbing headache that refused to abate or clear up.

She couldn't help wondering if this was what Florence had felt in the final moments of her life. Confused, disoriented, afraid—and horribly violated. Not physically violated. But, as a person, her space had definitely been violated.

Liberty was certain he was preparing to get rid of her the way he had the others. Well, she did not intend to go easily.

She didn't intend to go at all, really, when she came right down to it. She resolved to make this animal pay for every single life he had taken during his hideous spree.

Growing accustomed to the dark, Liberty tried to find something within the trunk she could use as a weapon.

Anything at all.

She focused on what felt like a tire iron tucked into one side of the trunk's interior. Shifting awkwardly, Liberty managed to wrap her fingers around the filthy piece of metal and tugged.

It took her several tries to loosen the tire iron in the space where it had been secured for who knew how long.

Liberty scraped her knuckles in the process and

she could feel them bleeding, but finally, she got the tire iron free. It was something she could use to defend herself.

She was not about to go quietly, she vowed, and if this killer thought that, he was in for one hell of a surprise.

Her breath caught in her throat as she felt the car slowing down and then stopping.

Her hand wrapped around the tire iron, Liberty braced herself for what she knew was going to have to be the fight of her life.

Chapter Twenty-One

The moment the trunk lid popped open and Liberty saw Wallace's face leaning in directly over hers, Liberty knew she only had one chance to save herself.

Without even thinking about it, Liberty swung the tire iron she was holding at his head as hard as she could.

She made contact with Wallace's face, specifically his cheekbone, and she managed to smash it. Liberty could hear the bone crack at the same time that Wallace let out a blood-curdling scream of pain and outrage.

Liberty immediately vaulted out of the trunk, simultaneously shoving the man back and away from her with both hands.

She pushed him as hard as she could.

Stunned and caught completely off guard, her would-be assailant stumbled backward, but he still somehow managed to catch himself quickly enough.

"Why you little bitch!" Wallace shrieked angrily at her.

As Liberty started to run away from him, he

grabbed her by her hair and held on tightly as he jerked her back. Handfuls of hair were yanked out.

Tears of pain sprang to her eyes and slid down her cheeks. It didn't stop her. She put up one hell of a fight, screaming at the top of her lungs, calling for help.

This wasn't the middle of the night. *Somebody* had to hear her, she desperately reasoned.

Determined to fight him off, Liberty recalled every single defensive move she had ever learned and used. Not just the ones she'd been taught when she'd joined the police force, but ones she had made a point of learning way back when she was being passed from one foster home to another. She'd wanted to be prepared in case someone wanted to get too handsy with her—the way that one kid, the son of the woman who had taken her in, had attempted. She'd lasted at that house for exactly one night, but what she was proudest of was the fact that she hadn't allowed Stephen to touch her.

Liberty had almost managed to get away from Wallace when she suddenly felt her ankle being grabbed. She went down hard as Wallace pulled her, flailing, to him.

Desperate, repulsed and incensed, she twisted around onto her back and kicked Wallace as hard as she could in his manhood with her other leg. That elicited another shriek of pain, followed by a barrage of ugly curses from him.

"You're really going to pay for this," he promised

viciously, scrambling to his feet. He chased after her. "Big-time!"

He was going to have to catch her first, Liberty vowed, sprinting from him as fast as she could go. The temperature had dropped and it was cold out, but she was sweating profusely as she raced to get away from the enraged killer.

Because she was unfamiliar with the area, Liberty found herself running blindly down one street.

It turned out to be a dead end.

Wallace was right behind her and quickly managed to close off her avenue of escape. Her back was literally against the wall.

He leered at her, his triumphant air unmistakable. "Looks like your luck ran out. And I promise that you're not going to go easy. You lost that option," he told her with terrifying relish. "I am *really* going to enjoy making you pay, Sarah," he promised the woman who wasn't there.

His eyes all but gleamed with anticipation.

Liberty cast about for something to throw him off balance. She needed to taunt him with the name of the woman it was apparent that he'd been trying to kill over and over again.

"What, a weakling like you?" she laughed, watching his face darken in rage. "You're not man enough. You've *never* been man enough." She began to throw words at him that she was creating on the spur of the moment. "I couldn't beat it into you or discipline you enough to make that happen, although, lord knows I tried. You're just a useless husk of a man." She spat the declarations. "You always have been."

Wallace shrieked, almost blind with fury as he lunged at Liberty.

She ducked down out of the way at the last moment, doubling up her fist and sinking a hard right into the center of his gut.

She had caught him off guard, but she hadn't managed to stop him.

Spitting blood, her assailant wrapped his hands around her throat, murder blazing in his eyes as he began to squeeze.

Hard.

In one quick movement, he had somehow wrapped piano wire around her throat and then begun tightening it more and more.

"I get the last laugh, Sarah!" he crowed happily as well as ominously.

"Think again!" Campbell shouted, bursting into the alley. His gun was aimed dead center at the serial killer's head.

Surprised, the killer didn't release his hold on Liberty. Instead, Wallace shouted almost maniacally, "Don't you understand? She deserves to die! Why won't she stay dead?" he cried.

It was obvious the man intended to carry out what he felt was his mission. Campbell didn't waste any more words on the killer. Instead, he quickly got off two shots, one into each of the man's calves.

Wallace screamed obscenities as he went down, his grip instantly loosening on Liberty's neck.

"'Cuff him!" Campbell yelled back at Choi as he quickly grabbed Liberty's sinking body and pulled her to him. "You're okay, Liberty. You're safe. He's not going to hurt anyone ever again," he promised her as he scooped her up in his arms. "It's over, baby. It's over," he told her over and over again in a calm, soothing voice.

Liberty could barely focus and taking air into her lungs was a huge effort. But she finally managed to get the words out in what sounded like a whisper. "What took you so long?"

Campbell laughed then, irony mingling with a huge wave of relief in his chest. He pressed a kiss to her forehead.

"Traffic," he answered and then called over his shoulder to his sister, "Call two ambulances, Jacqui. One for Arizona and one for this worthless piece of scum." Campbell nodded at the screaming criminal lying on the ground, clutching his wounds and rolling in pain.

"I...don't...need...an...ambulance," Liberty protested weakly. She tried to tug on his arm, but her hand fell without being able to make contact.

"Don't argue with me, Arizona. You're getting checked out," he told the woman in his arms.

"Put...me...down," Liberty ordered him weakly.

"I will. When the ambulance gets here." Looking down at her face, Campbell found he was talking to an unconscious woman.

CONSCIOUSNESS RETURNED SLOWLY.

When Liberty could finally open her eyes and was able to make out her surroundings, she saw Campbell's face looking far more worried than she would have ever thought he was capable of.

When she could finally speak, her voice sounded as if it was coming from deep inside an echo chamber. "If you're not careful, those wrinkles on your forehead will set in permanently."

Campbell bolted upright. At first, he thought he was just imagining things. He had willed Liberty to speak a dozen times in the last ten hours. At this point, he was afraid to believe his ears.

Moving closer, he clutched her hand and brought it closer to him. Impulsively, he pressed a kiss to her knuckles.

"You're awake," he cried, almost unable to believe it.

"Either that, or we're both having the same dream," she told him then winced. It felt as if the interior of her throat had been scraped with a flaming knife. "I don't think my throat would be hurting like this if I were dreaming," she told him, putting her hand against it to contain the pain.

He felt for her. "No, it wouldn't," he answered. Then he said seriously, "I'm sorry we didn't get there in time. When I think of what could have happened…" His throat all but closed up as the terrible possibilities of what *could* have happened crowded his brain.

Liberty didn't want him dwelling on that. There was no point, and it would only make him suffer. Instead, she focused her thoughts on the positive side.

"How *did* you even find me?" She wanted to know. "That sick bastard took my phone. When I came to in the trunk, I couldn't find it and I *knew* he had to have thrown it. I was certain I was doomed."

Campbell didn't want to tell her that he'd had his own gut feeling about how things could turn out on this mission. Instead he just said, "I like being prepared for all contingencies. That's why in addition to the wire you were wearing, I planted a tracker on you when you went on that first 'date' you arranged on that dating site," he told her.

Liberty didn't understand. "Why didn't you tell me you did that?"

"Simple. Because I didn't want to hear you tell me about how you thought I worried too much or overthought things," he told her.

She was not about to take him to task about that. The pluses of his actions definitely outweighed any possible minuses.

"I'm just glad you did. I don't know how much longer I could have held that monster off," she confessed. "I could literally feel my time running out."

He kissed her forehead, grateful beyond words. "You did better than anyone I know, Arizona," he told her honestly.

"Well, I'm glad for both our sakes that I could surprise you," she said. Sitting up, Liberty told him,

"Now bring me my clothes so I can get out of here. Hospitals make me nervous."

"You can't just leave," he reminded her. "You need to be signed out."

"Then if you care anything at all about me, make it happen, Campbell. I *need* to get out of here so I can focus on the next part," she stressed.

"Next part?" Campbell questioned. "What next part?"

"Getting that bastard to trial so he can be made to pay for what he did," she told Campbell with fierce conviction.

For a moment, he was worried that what she meant by "the next part" was that she was planning on going back to Arizona. Not only wasn't he ready to let her go, he was planning on doing his very best to keep her here. Permanently.

"We'll do it together," he promised her. "But as for now, I'll go get that doctor and *if* he says you can go," Campbell stressed, "I'll take you home."

"No 'if,' Cavanaugh," she told him firmly. "You're taking me home."

Campbell surprised her by meeting her words with a grin. "Oh, yeah, they're definitely going to love you," he said with conviction.

She had no idea what he was talking about. "Excuse me?"

"The family," Campbell explained. And then he backtracked a little. "Uncle Andrew said that the minute you're well enough to be released and up to it, he wants to have that family gathering he mentioned. This way, you can meet everyone and enjoy a genuine Cavanaugh-style family Christmas."

"But it's not Christmas…" she protested. Then she suddenly looked at him in surprise. "Is it?" she asked, clearly startled.

Just how long had she been out? Was it possible that it hadn't just been a short interval but one that involved the last couple of weeks? She tried to think but she had no way of gauging the time lapse.

"No," Campbell immediately assured her. "It's not Christmas."

"Just how long was I out?" she said.

Campbell was still wearing the same clothes he'd had on when he had brought her to the hospital, but that wasn't really a true gauge of how long she had been there. He might not have gone home to change clothes at any point, choosing to remain at her side.

He seemed like the type, Liberty thought.

She waited for him to give her an answer.

Campbell glanced at his watch. "You've been here ten hours. Long enough to be checked over for any stray bullet wounds and to sleep, not long enough to miss Christmas," he told Liberty. "Now, can I go get that doctor to check you over one last time before he signs you out?"

He expected her to immediately jump at the chance. Instead, Liberty surprised him by saying, "In a minute."

"Okay," he replied, stretching the word out and

waiting for her to jump in with an explanation or at least a reason why she was asking him to delay getting the doctor for the moment.

"Campbell?" Liberty said his name hesitantly.

He drew closer to her, looking down into her face. "Yes?" he asked encouragingly, waiting.

"Would you mind just holding me for a minute?" She made the request almost shyly.

This was a side of Liberty that he was definitely not used to or prepared for. He felt as if he were walking a very delicate line playing it light and taking this seriously.

"Well, it'll be hard," he admitted, "but I think I can manage for a little while." Campbell sat on the edge of her bed and gathered Liberty into his arms.

The moment he did, he could feel the tight control she always maintained over herself coming dangerously close to breaking.

And then it did.

The tension of the last four days, not to mention finally coming face to face with the man who had killed so many, who had taken away the life of the only woman Liberty had ever admired, the man who had nearly succeeded in killing *her*—had finally gotten to her.

Campbell knew she had resolved to move heaven and earth to make sure that the man they had caught would be convicted for every single one of those crimes he had committed.

While Liberty was looking forward to the fight,

a small part of her felt almost daunted by what lay ahead. She was genuinely afraid in the center of her soul that, somehow, some enterprising defense lawyer would manage to get the worthless piece of scum off on a technicality, and the very possibility frightened the hell out of her.

Liberty sat there in her bed, so many emotons undulating through her. And then Campbell took her back into his arms again.

Maybe it was foolish to think this way. After all, she was first and foremost a realist. But there was something about being in Campbell's arms this way that made her feel totally safe.

She knew she was being irrational, but she didn't really care. All she wanted was to experience the end result of having Campbell hold her. She would deal with the rest of it later.

Much later, but not now.

Chapter Twenty-Two

Two hours later, after she had been given a clean bill of health by the discharging physician on ER duty and warned to take things easy for a few days, Liberty was lying curled up beside Campbell. It completely amazed her how a place she hadn't even known about less than a month ago now felt like it was her safe haven in more ways than one.

Especially when she was lying in the shelter of Campbell's arms.

They had made love—against his better judgment. Before they'd begun, Campbell had reminded her of the doctor's orders about taking it easy. "Making love," he'd pointed out, "doesn't really come under the heading of 'taking it easy.'"

But she had told him to let her worry about that and swore that making love with him would do her far more good than harm—unless he didn't want to, she'd qualified at the end.

Since Liberty had worded it that way, Campbell had had no choice but to give in to her, as well as to himself. But he was careful to go slow, which in turn had a beauty all its own.

Now, in the aftermath of the euphoria that wrapped itself around them, Campbell held Liberty to him and softly asked, "Can I get you anything?"

"You already have," Liberty replied, smiling at him. Then, because she could see that he didn't understand her meaning, she whispered, "You."

He kissed her, soundly and with a great deal of affection, not to mention an accompanying huge feeling of relief because nothing had happened to her—and it could have.

Because it wasn't in his nature for Campbell to keep things to himself, he told her, "I don't *ever* want to feel the way I felt today when I thought that I might have lost you."

"What did you feel?" she asked, not to be coy but because she needed to know and trusted him to give her an honest answer. Maybe that made her naive since, up until now, it had never been in her nature to be like this. But this man had made nothing short of a huge difference in her life. And even though she felt that she was being unwise to be so blindly trusting, heaven help her, she was.

"I have never been so scared in my whole life," he admitted sincerely. "It was like I had a part of myself cut out using a jagged piece of glass."

She winced at the vivid description. "That sounds painful."

"Believe me, it was," he told her. "It felt like nothing short of an eternity until I was able to finally find you." Overcome with emotion, Campbell kissed her again. "You know what I'd like to do?"

She shook her head in response.

"I'd like to put you inside a glass case. But since that's not possible," Campbell went on, "what would you say to marrying me?"

She stared at him, completely stunned. He had just sprung that on her out of the blue without warning.

"You're kidding, right?" Liberty finally asked.

For once, he didn't laugh. "I've never been more serious in my whole life. And," he added before she could say anything in response, "you can ask anyone in the family when you meet them at the party. They'll tell you that I have *never* come close to proposing to anyone."

Liberty laughed softly at that. "Like they wouldn't lie for you."

"Actually, they wouldn't," he replied in all seriousness. "Lying isn't in our DNA. Even for a family member."

"Wow," she marveled, drawing back a little to study his face. "You said all that with a straight face."

Campbell ran his fingertip across her lower lip. "Because I *am* serious," he told her. And then he took her off the hook for now. "You don't have to give me an answer right away. I just want you to think about it." he told her. "Just keep in mind that saying yes would make a *really* great Christmas present for me. You wouldn't have to brave all those crowded stores with their wall-to-wall holiday shoppers," he pointed out as a final selling feature.

Liberty grinned at him. Sometime the man just astounded her, she thought. "You've got it all figured out, don't you?"

Campbell inclined his head. "I do try," he told her.

For now, she focused on something else he had just said. "So you're still taking me to this family gathering of yours?"

"Hey, why wouldn't I? Besides, it's really out of my hands," he conceded. "If I don't show up at the party with you, there's going to be a bounty put on both our heads."

"Well, we wouldn't want that," she said, struggling to keep a straight face.

"Nope, we certainly wouldn't," Campbell agreed.

Just as he drew her back into his arms, his cell phone began to ring. Pausing for a moment to consider his options, Campbell waved his hand at the cell and said something he had never said before.

"I'll just let it go to voicemail."

The next moment, Liberty's cell phone began to ring as well. She sighed. So much for ignoring the call. "I think we need to answer this," she told him, about to pick up her phone.

He frowned, putting his hand on hers. "Let me pick up mine," he volunteered.

Unlocking his phone, Campbell warned the caller, "This had better be good."

"That depends on which side of this thing you're

on," the female voice on the other end on the call informed him.

It was Jacqui. If she was calling him at this time of night, he knew it had to be important. He resigned himself to hearing her out.

"It's Jacqui," he told Liberty, glancing in her direction.

"Is Liberty there, too?" his sister questioned. "Good. She's going to want to hear this."

Campbell wasn't sure how to take this. "Hear what?"

"Apparently our serial killer suspect hanged himself in his jail cell tonight shortly after being officially processed," Jacqui informed her brother.

Campbell bolted upright in the bed. "How?"

Startled, anticipating the worst, Liberty asked, "What happened?"

But Jacqui was in the middle of answering his question. Placing the call on speakerphone, Campbell held out his cell phone for Liberty to hear as well.

"Seems that someone at the jail slipped the guy a sheet," Jacqui answered. "Apparently he supposedly made a noose and hanged himself with it." It was obvious that Jacqui had her doubts.

Stunned, Liberty asked in disbelief, "Then he's dead?"

"Deader than a doornail," Jacqui answered. "I'll call you two with more details as I get them," she promised.

Liberty was already throwing off the sheet she had

wrapped around her and put her feet on the ground. "Never mind," she said, raising her voice for Jacqui to hear. "We're going there."

Momentarily distracted by what he viewed as Liberty's exquisite body, Campbell had trouble drawing his eyes away from her.

"We are?" he asked.

"We definitely are," Liberty said with conviction. "I want to be able to identify that scum's body and make sure he's dead and not just somehow faking it." It seemed like faking it would be an impossible endeavor, but if it could be done, she knew this maniac could do it.

"You heard the lady," Campbell said into his phone. "We're coming to the morgue."

"I'll meet you there," his sister promised just before the connection went dead.

Chapter Twenty-Three

Now that it was just the two of them, Campbell had his doubts about taking Liberty with him to the morgue. "Are you absolutely sure you want to go?" he asked Liberty.

She didn't hesitate. "Absolutely. Think of me as a villager," she told him. When Campbell looked at her, confused, she explained, "I need to see proof that the vampire's dead."

He viewed her comment skeptically. "You're not going to ask to see his head mounted on a pike, are you?"

"Don't give me any ideas," Liberty countered as she threw her clothes on quickly.

"You're getting to be really good at that," he said, nodding at her jeans and jersey.

"A girl always needs to build up her skills," Liberty asserted cryptically.

"Personally, I like watching you shed your clothes better," he told her as they left his apartment and headed toward his car.

"One thing at a time, Cavanaugh. One thing at a

time," she told him as she got into the vehicle on the passenger side. "Who do you think smuggled in that sheet to that SOB?" she asked, buckling up.

Campbell started up his car and pulled out of the carport. "Any one of a number of people who wanted revenge for a loved one would be my guess."

She rolled the idea over in her mind. "A better revenge would be to see him convicted in a trial."

There was one problem with that, Campbell considered as he drove out of the residential complex. "Yes, but that's leaving things up to chance. Things *can* go wrong in a trial. Hell, he might even be set free. What happened tonight is a far more permanent solution."

His comment caused her to pause for a moment, thinking. "I guess you have a point," she allowed.

Campbell's eyes crinkled as he grinned at her. "I'm a Cavanaugh. I always have a point." And then he looked at her doubtfully again, concerned. "Are you *sure* you're up to this?"

"Even if you have to carry me piggyback on your shoulders," Liberty affirmed.

"Now there's an interesting image," Campbell responded.

BECAUSE OF THE time of night, the roads were all but empty. But it still felt as if getting there took forever to Liberty. She could feel herself almost squirming inside.

It wasn't hard for Campbell to pick up on her tension and impatience. "Almost there."

"There's someone at the morgue now?" she asked him, trying to picture the same situation back in Calhoun. To accommodate them, the medical examiner would have had to come in from a neighboring town.

"There's *always* someone at the morgue," Campbell told her. "Even if it's just a part-time assistant. Don't worry, the place won't be locked up," he said, anticipating what she was thinking. "You'll get to identify the body before sunrise."

"I'm not worried," she told him. "Worse comes to worst, I'll just camp out on the morgue's doorstep until I get to make the identification."

Campbell merely shook his head. She was one incredible, determined woman.

"Well, luckily that won't be necessary because I happen to know someone who has some pull even if the morgue *was* locked."

He was humoring her, and she realized that she probably came across as being too obsessed with this case, she thought as they got out of the car. But one way or another, she needed it to be over. The only way that was going to happen was if she got to view the killer's remains so that she could close this awful chapter once and for all.

"Knew I kept you around for a reason," she quipped with a grin.

"You better have kept me around for more of a reason than that," he informed her, a whimsical smile playing on his lips.

She paused on the top step right before the police station's entrance. Turning to him, she cupped Campbell's cheek with her hand. "Maybe for a couple of reasons."

Because they were totally alone for the moment, Campbell stole a quick kiss. "You're turning my head."

"Just as I intended," she answered.

Liberty was bantering to help relieve the vast amount of tension thrumming through her veins. This was the culmination of what had felt like an interminable quest for her, the hunt for her foster mother's killer, which until recently had felt endless.

Campbell took her arm and guided her into the building even though he knew she didn't need any help. He just did it to let her know, silently, that she wasn't there alone and that he was here for her.

The entrance right before the elevator wasn't as brightly lit as it was during the daytime. But there were still enough lights on to banish the darkness.

They rode down to the basement in silence.

Once again he stopped her just before the entrance to the morgue. When she looked up at him, he asked her for a third time, "Are you *sure* you want to do this? Seeing him this way could haunt you," he warned.

"Not seeing him this way would be worse," she

told him. Her mind made up, Liberty pushed open the door and went inside.

The on-call medical examiner appeared half asleep but immediately came to.

"You here to see our latest resident?" the ME asked.

"That's what we're here for," Campbell confirmed. "Would you mind?"

"Not at all. Always glad to close the book on a serial killer," the doctor told them with unmistakable relish. "I heard that this one chalked up quite a body count," he said as he went to one of the drawers that provided a temporary resting place for any of the bodies that were viewed here.

The ME pulled the drawer open. "Here you go," he announced. "Take your time. I don't have anywhere else to be."

Liberty hardly heard the doctor. She had all but slipped into a trance as she stared at the ghostly pale face of the man who had, at last count, created such havoc throughout three different states. One body would have been one too many. Thirty-three or more was completely out of bounds.

But at least now, it was over.

Campbell slipped his hand on her shoulder and gave it a quick, heartening squeeze. "It's finally over," he whispered to her, as if reading her mind.

Her words emerged on a sigh as she stared at the face that had loomed, threateningly, over hers. "Yes, it finally is."

Chapter Twenty-Four

Liberty thought she knew what to expect when she walked into the former chief of police's house, especially since she had been there for dinner less than three weeks ago. At that time, she had even seen the twelve-foot Christmas tree that, even partially decorated, had taken her breath away.

Or at least, she had assumed that the tree was fully decorated. But when she walked into the chief's house with the unbelievably incredible scents of Christmas Eve dinner wafting in the air all around her, Liberty was nothing short of totally overwhelmed.

And then, without her even realizing it, tears had risen in her eyes.

As had always been his custom, Andrew greeted his visitors at the door. He was about to bestow a warm hug as he told Liberty hello when he stopped short because he saw the tears in her eyes.

Without a word, a handkerchief materialized in his hand, and he silently offered it to her. "But you haven't even tried my Christmas Eve dinner," he pretended to protest. "There's no reason for you to cry yet."

"I'm not reacting to the tempting aromas—which, by the way, smell heavenly," she told him. "I'm reacting to the Christmas tree."

"You don't like it?" Callie, Andrew's oldest daughter asked, disappointed as she came forward to join Liberty and Campbell as well as a few of the other relatives milling about in that area.

"Like it?" Liberty echoed incredulously. "I adore it," she said with enthusiasm. "If *any* version of that tree had ever been part of my childhood, I would have felt as if I had died and gone to heaven." She knew she probably wasn't making any sense to Andrew's family, behaving this way. "I'm sorry," Liberty apologized, at a loss as to what to say as she wiped at her tears. "I'm not usually like this."

Andrew waved away her apology. "Don't give it another thought," he told her, giving her hand a quick, encouraging squeeze. "I find it comforting to find out that underneath that tough exterior is a soft young woman who blends in so well with the rest of us." He then turned toward his nephew. "Campbell, why don't you show Liberty the Christmas decoration that Rose picked out for her to hang on the tree?"

That caught Liberty by surprise. "You have a decoration for *me* to hang?" she asked in disbelief.

"Rose has a great knack for finding just the right decoration for a particular family member. It's a tradition," Andrew told her with a wink.

Liberty was about to protest that she *wasn't* a family member—she hadn't given Campbell an answer—then decided that, just for today, she could pretend that she was. What harm would it do?

"I'd like that," she told the couple with a broad smile.

The next thing she knew, Andrew's wife was handing her a small Christmas ornament box along with an accompanying hook so that she could hang the decoration on the tree.

Liberty felt both nervous and excited as she opened the box, even though she told herself that she was being foolish feeling this way. For heaven's sake, she was a grown woman who had outgrown her need for Christmas and the decorations that went with the particular holiday years ago.

But logic still didn't seem to abate the excitement she felt bubbling up inside of her as she opened the small box.

Her breath caught in her throat when she saw the ornament: a sweet-faced little teddy bear. Liberty found herself blinking back a fresh onslaught of tears. The only thing she had ever wanted as a child was a teddy bear like the one her first foster mother's little girl had had. To her, it had represented a symbol of acceptance.

One she had never felt destined to receive.

"How did you know?" Liberty finally asked, her voice sounding breathless. She had never told anyone about the teddy bear, she thought, mystified. This had to be a coincidence—didn't it?

Andrew's smile told her differently. "Let's just say that I like honing my investigative skills every once in a while," he said with a conspiratorial wink, leaving the explanation at that.

"C'mon, you need to hang it on the tree in order for the ceremony to be official," Campbell urged, taking Liberty by the hand and drawing her over to the Christmas tree. The tree looked completely overloaded at this point.

That was the way she saw it. "There's no room for this," Liberty protested, indicating the decoration in her hand.

"Oh, come on," Campbell said with a laugh then assured her, "There's *always* room for one more." He went on to tell her, "You just have to look hard."

"Get Liberty a ladder," Andrew called out to one of his sons. Then, turning toward Liberty, he explained the procedure. "We always leave the bottom of the tree for the kids to decorate."

"The kids we don't want climbing up on the tree yet," Rose told her.

All in all, like everything else that involved the Cavanaughs, Liberty noted, hanging the decoration—which she had fallen in love with—turned out to be a true family affair. She climbed up on the ladder that had been provided and, after doing a bit of searching, finally found a spot on the tree where she was able to hang her decoration.

"Watch your step," Campbell cautioned as she started to come down.

"I have no intentions of falling," Liberty informed him just a second before her foot slipped on one of the rungs as she descended.

Anticipating a possible fall, Campbell wrapped his hands around her hips to keep her steady as he helped her.

"And *that* is the proper way to come down a ladder," he told her.

Rather than take offense, Liberty caught herself laughing. "Being here with your family is just a continuing education," she couldn't help commenting with a smile.

Her words were met with approval from several different sources. She could feel her insides warming. After all those years of being on the outside looking in, Liberty felt an unmistakable sense of homecoming.

And for however long it would last, she intended to cherish it.

"ALL RIGHT EVERYONE, dinner is severed," Andrew announced several hours after an enjoyable exchange of conversations had taken place.

"Already?" Liberty questioned in surprise.

"What do you mean 'already'?" Campbell questioned. "We've been here for five hours. If Uncle Andrew hadn't put out all those platters of snacks and treats, we would have probably started chewing on one another hours ago." Leaning into her, he confided, "This has always been a very hungry crowd."

Because, as usual, Andrew had invited all the many family members, not to mention family friends, there were several very large tables set up throughout the area, all within shouting distance of one another.

DINNER, AS LIBERTY had expected, turned out to be a very relaxed, very genial affair that once again made her feel that this was the kind of family she had been missing and looking for all of her life.

"Had enough?" Campbell asked, pushing away his own empty plate and leaning back in his chair.

"One more bite and I'm liable to explode," she confessed. Looking at her plate—which wasn't empty—she shook her head. "It's hard to believe I was ever hungry."

He smiled warmly at her. It wasn't over yet. "Well, you've got fifteen minutes for dinner to settle in," Campbell told her.

Liberty looked at him suspiciously. "And then what?"

"And then there's the opening of the presents," he told her as if it were a specific event.

She couldn't be included in that, Liberty thought. She had already gotten her gift—an official Christmas ornament for the family tree. And besides, she thought self-consciously, she hadn't thought there would be any gifts exchanged. She hadn't brought anything with her other than a bottle of wine for the host and hostess.

Thinking it best to state that up front, she protested, "I didn't bring anything."

Campbell wasn't having any of it. "Doesn't matter," he told her. "There're still things under the tree with your name on them."

"You're kidding," she cried, convinced he had to be pulling her leg.

"Well, I know of at least one thing," he told her. "You can't hang back, Liberty," he said as he took her hand and began drawing her into the room with the Christmas tree. "It's against the rules."

She was still convinced that Campbell was just teasing her. There were so many of these family members here, she couldn't possibly have a gift waiting for her as well.

But she also knew it wouldn't be polite to fight him on this so she went along with it for form's sake. Besides, she thought that it would be fun taking part in a family tradition, even if it wasn't her family or even her tradition.

Being a spectator here for the proceedings was good enough for her.

Liberty listened patiently as the cards on the gifts were read aloud and each present was handed to the proper recipient. She enjoyed the whole ceremony and didn't even realize it at first when her name was said out loud.

"That's you," she heard Rose say to her in a stage whisper.

Liberty blinked, surprised. "There has to be some mistake."

"No, no mistake, dear. It says it right here." Rose pointed to the card for emphasis. "Liberty Lawrence. That's you, right?" Rose asked with a bright, warm smile.

"Yes, but—" Liberty protested, still certain there had to be some mistake.

"Not buts, dear," Rose told her. "Your name, you open it," the woman said simply, holding out the box to her.

Liberty felt utterly self-conscious, but she felt bound to do as her hostess suggested.

With the most careful of movements, Liberty tore the wrapping paper away from the box. Opening it, she found there was another gift-wrapped box inside.

And then another box inside that one.

Until, four boxes later, Liberty had worked her way down to a very small black-velvet box.

Holding her breath, Liberty opened that one as well.

Her breath caught in her throat as silence enveloped the room and the lights on the Christmas tree were caught and imprisoned by the heart-shaped diamond ring inside the box.

Stunned, Liberty immediately looked up at Campbell even as she felt the inside of her mouth grow dry.

"You were serious. The other day, when you proposed, you were serious," she cried, momentarily forgetting that she was saying those words in front of most of his family.

"My dear, by now you should have figured out that Cavanaughs do not fling about proposals like chicken feed in front of chickens," Brian's wife, Lila, told Liberty. And then, in an effort to afford Campbell and Liberty a measure of privacy, Lila announced to the others, "Coffee is being served on the patio. Let's go, people."

Within moments, Liberty found herself alone with Campbell.

"Did you think I was kidding?" he asked her at that point.

Momentarily speechless, Liberty nodded. "I didn't think I would get so lucky twice in one lifetime—to survive a serial killer and to have you actually propose to me—and mean it," she added, feeling as if she was in a trance.

"Oh, Arizona, you have so much to learn," Campbell told her, "and I'm really going to look forward to teaching you—provided you say yes, of course," he qualified.

For the first time in his life, Campbell felt nervous.

But he found he had no reason to be. He saw his answer in her eyes.

"Of course yes," Liberty cried and threw her arms around his neck just before she kissed him—unmindful of the fact that his entire family was looking on from the patio.

Had she noticed, she would have taken it as a sign of things to come—and been incredibly thrilled. Because along with the love of a good man, she finally had the family she had always wanted from the very beginning.

* * * * *

COMING SOON!

We really hope you enjoyed reading this book.
If you're looking for more romance, be sure to
head to the shops when new books are
available on

Thursday 12th May

To see which titles are coming soon, please visit
millsandboon.co.uk/nextmonth

LET'S TALK
Romance

For exclusive extracts, competitions
and special offers, find us online:

 facebook.com/millsandboon

@MillsandBoon

@MillsandBoonUK

Get in touch on 01413 063232

For all the latest titles coming soon, visit
millsandboon.co.uk/nextmonth

JOIN US ON SOCIAL MEDIA!

Stay up to date with our latest releases, author news and gossip, special offers and discounts, and all the behind-the-scenes action from Mills & Boon...

 millsandboon

 millsandboonuk

 millsandboon

MILLS & BOON
Desire

Indulge in secrets and scandal, intense drama and plenty of sizzling hot action with powerful and passionate heroes who have it all: wealth, status, good looks…everything but the right woman.

MILLS & BOON
MEDICAL
Pulse-Racing Passion

Set your pulse racing with dedicated, delectable doctors in the high-pressure world of medicine, where emotions run high and passion, comfort and love are the best medicine.

MILLS & BOON
True Love
Romance from the Heart

Celebrate true love with tender stories of heartfelt romance, from the rush of falling in love to the joy a new baby can bring, and a focus on the emotional heart of a relationship.